Pack Up Your Troubles

Anne Bennett was born in a back-to-back house in the Horsefair district of Birmingham. The daughter of Roman Catholic, Irish immigrants, she grew up in a tight-knit community where she was taught to be proud of her heritage. She considers herself to be an Irish Brummie and feels therefore that she has a foot in both cultures. She has four children and five grandchildren. For many years she taught in schools to the north of Birmingham. An accident put paid to her teaching career and, after moving to North Wales, Anne turned to the other great love of her life and began to write seriously. In 2006, after 16 years in a wheelchair, she miraculously regained her ability to walk.

To find out more about Anne and her books, visit her on Facebook, Twitter and her website:

www.annebennett.co.uk
www.facebook.com/AnneBennettAuthor
@annebennett20

Pack Up Your Troubles

ANNE BENNETT

HARPER

This novel is entirely a work of fiction.
The names, characters and incidents portrayed in it are
the work of the author's imagination. Any resemblance to
actual persons, living or dead, events or localities is
entirely coincidental.

Harper
An imprint of HarperCollins*Publishers*
The News Building
1 London Bridge Street
London SE1 9GF
www.harpercollins.co.uk

This edition published by HarperCollins*Publishers* 2016

4

Copyright © Anne Bennett 2000

First published in 2000 by HEADLINE BOOK PUBLISHING

Anne Bennett asserts the moral right to
be identified as the author of this work

A catalogue record for this book
is available from the British Library

ISBN: 978-0-00-754780-7

Printed and bound in Great Britain by
Clays Ltd, St Ives plc

MIX
Paper from
responsible sources
FSC
www.fsc.org   FSC™ C007454

FSC is a non-profit international organization established
to promote the responsible management of the world's forests.
Products carrying the FSC label are independently certified
to assure consumers that they come from forests that are managed
to meet the social, economic and ecological needs
of present and future generations.

Find out more about HarperCollins and the environment at
www.harpercollins.co.uk/green

ACKNOWLEDGEMENTS

I am very glad this book is having a second airing because of all the books I originally wrote for my previous publisher, it is this book that has been asked about more than any other. Unfortunately, I've never been able to help anyone obtain a copy until now, for it was first published in the year 2000 and was out of print for some time. With this new edition, I have the chance to bring the acknowledgements up to date.

I am immensely grateful to Maggie Hanson at Birmingham Library's Social Science Department, who helped a lot with local history and maps etc. Roy Yeats was then the Harbour Master at Dún Laoghaire and he used his dinner hour to find out the names of the mail boats crossing the Irish Sea at that time. He even found out what they looked like; how many funnels, how much it cost for breakfast on board and so on and even described the pink curtains covering the portholes in the canteen.

My children, and now my grandchildren too, give me immense joy and show me what life is all about and I am always grateful for their support, and sometimes they can be so helpful too. My late mom-in-law, Nancy, was a wonderful lady who I loved very much and she used to work in a draper's shop before she was married. She knew the price of every article they sold to the last farthing. I half-filled an exercise book with notes one time when she was visiting and I got her talking of times past, so the prices of the clothes I speak of in the latter part of the book are real.

So many people are helpful to me, I find – like my youngest daughter, Tamsin, who came up with the title of this book when I hadn't a clue, and my long-suffering husband, who puts up with us all so well.

However, the ones I really write the books for are you, my lovely, loyal readers. For if you weren't out there buying books or loading them on to e-readers or borrowing them from the library, then there would be no point in any of it, so thanks a million to you all.

I am dedicating this book to Denis
for the immense help and unfailing support
he has given me over the years.
Thank you.

ONE

Maeve Brannigan couldn't believe she was actually leaving the little farm in Donegal where she'd lived all of her eighteen years. It had been worth the cajoling and pleading, her mother's tears and her father's bad humour that had made him moody and snappy with them all. She'd survived it all, as well as the old biddies in the parish, who'd prophesied that no good would come of it, and did she think she ought to go when, after all, she was such a grand help to her mother, for wasn't the woman herself always saying so?

Maeve had been brought up to have manners and it had only been that innate politeness that had stopped her screaming abuse at the interfering old gossips. Did they think she didn't know all that? She was the eldest of seven and even when Maeve had begun work in the grocery store in the town when she was fourteen, there had always been a list of chores for her at home.

Well, now it was the turn of Kate and Rosemarie, who at eleven and twelve years of age were well able for it. Maeve was sick of being at everyone's beck and call; fed up with the isolated farm, and of the suffocating small town where everyone knew everything about you and yours. Her total social life revolved around church activities, and the weekly dance, held only in the summer months, where she met boys she'd known for years, as familiar to her as her brothers and just as exciting. Few of them had any ambition and were content to live in Ballyglen all their lives, and expected the wives they would eventually take to be satisfied with that situation too.

Maeve decided it wasn't for her. But she wasn't to go to Dublin, or 'God forbid' London, a desperate place altogether, her parents claimed, and where she knew not a soul. No, she was to go to Birmingham where Maeve's mother, Annie, whose maiden name had been O'Toole, had a brother called Michael.

Maeve knew of her Uncle Michael, though she'd never met him. He'd been in Birmingham since early 1919, when he'd met and married his English wife, Agnes, in just a couple of months, and had never been home since. Maeve also knew that no obstacles had been put in the way of his leaving his home, but in fact the reverse. He'd served in the British Army in the Great War and had come back in late 1918, a bitter and disillusioned young man. Ireland was in disarray, the troubles at their height and rebel gangs roaming the country. His family, terrified he'd be caught up in it all, had encouraged Michael to accompany a neighbour catching the emigrant boat for England. He'd ended up in Birmingham and had got a job – a grand job he'd said, in a foundry. But he was still Annie's little brother and she wrote him regular letters of the family, and now was sure Maeve could lodge with him to see how she liked the place. In fact Michael had written *her* a very long, encouraging letter. Not only could she stay with them and welcome, he said, he could even get her a waitressing job in a café. He knew the owner, a Greek man by the name of Dolamartis, a good Catholic, and they went to the same church. He'd told Michael his assistant was leaving. Jobs were hard to find, her uncle said, and Maeve couldn't afford to be too choosy. Maeve had no intention of being choosy at all and at the mention of a job and place to stay, her parents' resistance finally crumbled. Maeve was on her way.

They were all there that early spring morning with the mist still swirling around the hills, to put her on the little rail bus that ran at the bottom of Thomas Brannigan's farm, to start the first leg of her long journey. She saw her mother holding little Nuala's hand and dabbing at her eyes with her apron, her father, his face still in stiff lines of disapproval, and the others staring at her as if they couldn't quite believe she was going. Maeve knew her father didn't want her to go, in fact he dreaded it, and in a way she understood why. She knew she had a special place in her father's heart, partly because she looked so like her mother and also because she was the firstborn. She also knew it had been her mother who'd persuaded her father to allow her to go, and if she hadn't supported her, it would have been far more difficult.

The way he'd gone on, it was as if he expected her to be leapt on by every man in Christendom as soon as she left the farm. She knew the lads all had an eye for her; she wasn't stupid. But her mother had talked to her, and anyway, she knew right from wrong. So though she felt sorry for her parents, she couldn't wait to be gone.

Maeve watched until the group by the farm gate had become like small dots and then she settled into her seat with a sigh of contentment. Excitement fizzed inside her so that she could hardly sit still. She wished she could snap her fingers and be in Birmingham, where she was sure everything that was good awaited her.

She sustained the excitement all the way to Belfast, though the size and noise of the station unnerved her. The clatter of the enormous trains that seemed to hurl into the station to stop with a hiss of steam and a piercing screech and a whistle made her jump more than once. She left the busy Belfast station for the ferry, feeling apprehensive about the journey across the water.

Maeve boarded with what seemed like thousands of other people crowding on to the gangplank, her case bumping against her knees. Once on board, she made her way on to the deck and, putting her case beside her, she held tightly to the rail as she watched the shores of Ireland fade into the distance and then disappear altogether. She felt quite suddenly unexpectedly desolate and a little frightened. The overcast leaden grey skies belied the fact that it was early April and although it was midmorning the light was as poor as dusk, which didn't help Maeve's mood. Nor did the roll of the ship and the churning of her stomach.

She leant over the side, overcome suddenly by nausea, and vomited all she'd eaten that morning into the white-fringed grey water crashing and foaming against the ferry's sides. She continued to retch over and over and she realised she wasn't the only one.

When eventually her nausea was over and as she wiped her mouth with a handkerchief she became aware of a dumpy little woman dressed in black watching her. The rain came then, not soft spring rain, but sharp shafts that stung Maeve's face and soaked her coat in minutes.

'Come away into the bar,' the woman told her, lifting her case as if it weighed nothing at all. 'You'll freeze to death out here.'

Maeve allowed herself to be led indoors, where she was met by a cacophony of people talking, laughing, shouting

4

and quarrelling, and here and there she heard snatches of songs, the laments of the emigrant Irish that brought tears to her eyes.

'Tch tch, that won't do,' the woman said. 'You need a brandy to buck you up. I'll send my Sean to get you one.'

Maeve's protests were waved aside and the woman escorted her to where a man also dressed in black sat on a suitcase just a little way from the bar.

'Sit down,' the woman commanded and, as the seats were all occupied, Maeve upended her case and sat on that.

The woman introduced herself as Minnie O'Rourke, and her husband, whom she dispatched for the drinks, as Sean. They were returning from a funeral for Sean's parents, who'd died within days of one another on the family farm in Galway. The farm now belonged to Sean, Minnie O'Rourke explained, though his three sisters ran the place. Maeve, having told her new acquaintance her own name, smiled politely and hoped the brandy would ease the cramps in her stomach.

The bar reminded her of Donovan's in her home town, with the tobacco stench that stung Maeve's eyes and hung like a blue fog over the room, together with the familiar smell of Guinness. Sean O'Rourke returned with two glasses of the black drink with the creamy white top for himself and his wife, and a large brandy in a balloon glass for Maeve.

Maeve looked at it fearfully. Never had she had any strong drink, except the odd sip of her father's Guinness, which he'd allowed her at Christmas and which she'd not liked. The brandy caught in her throat and caused her to cough and splutter, and Minnie O'Rourke patted her back and with a smile told her to treat the drink with respect and sip it.

And Maeve did sip it, grimacing at the taste as one might at foul-smelling medicine that promises to do some good, but she did like the warm glow that the brandy induced.

'That's brought the colour back to your cheeks anyway,' Minnie O'Rourke told her. 'Where are you bound for?'

'Birmingham,' Maeve said. 'To my uncle's place.'

'Well, isn't that good news?' Minnie exclaimed. 'We're going to Birmingham too. We have a fine house in Erdington. You'd best come along with us. It's desperate altogether travelling on your own.'

And Maeve was glad to have their company. It might stop her feeling fearful that she was making some dreadful mistake. She was also anxious to learn as much as she could about the city she was going to.

'Are you having a holiday?' Minnie asked.

'No,' Maeve said. 'I'm staying there. My uncle has got me a job in a café, near a place called Aston Cross.'

'My! You're lucky,' Minnie said, 'for God knows, jobs are few and far between at the moment, with the slump after the war, you know?' Without waiting for a reply she went on, 'My Sean had to have his gaffer's word that he'd have a job to go back to, or we wouldn't have been able to go to the funeral at all. Even then we could only take three days. His sisters wanted him to take three or four weeks, but we daren't, and he's a skilled man. He works in the brass industry.'

Maeve made no reply to this, for she was suddenly unaccountably weary and her head swam with the unaccustomed brandy on her empty and very sore stomach.

'Still and all, you have a job to go to, that's something,' Minnie went on.

'He knows the owner of the place,' Maeve said.

'That would be the way of it, right enough,' Minnie said. 'As I always say, God's good.'

Maeve opened her mouth to make some sort of reply, but all that came out was a large yawn.

'My, my,' said Minnie. 'You're dead beat, so you are, and no wonder after you being so sick and all. Lie yourself down across the cases and have a wee sleep, why don't you?'

What a relief it was, Maeve found, to lay her swimming head down, even across the lumpy hard cases, and pull up her legs to ease the cramps and close her eyes to ease the throbbing pain in her head. In minutes she was fast asleep.

She slept till the ferry docked. The O'Rourkes shook her awake and took her in hand, and she shambled behind them in the damp rain-soaked air, pushing her case before her as people thronged the decks in the rush to embark. They were waved through the customs sheds and into the noisy station in Liverpool that was teeming with people. Not that Maeve saw much of it, for the train was in and the O'Rourkes, seasoned travellers that they were, steered Maeve quickly through the crowds and on to the train to make sure of a seat, and Maeve was glad they had when she saw many passengers filling the corridors later, sitting astride their cases.

She was glad that on dry land once more she was feeling much better and able to face the picnic her mother had packed with such loving care early that morning. She shared it with Sean and Minnie O'Rourke while she plied them with questions about the city she was to live in. And as the train chugged its way southwards, they told her of Birmingham's cinemas and dance halls, which opened all year round. They described the music halls and the Bull

Ring, a huge shopping centre where great entertainment could be had, they said, on a Saturday night. Maeve was no longer nervous; instead she was in a fever of excitement to get to her uncle's house and begin her job. Then, she was sure, her life would take an up-turn.

When Maeve and the O'Rourkes finally alighted at New Street station, Maeve wondered if she'd ever find her uncle in such a loud and busy place. All around her was the noise of people. Porters pushing laden trolleys were yelling out warning to anyone in their way, and at a newsstand, a vendor shouted his wares, while beside her the gigantic train was giving little pants of steam, as if it were an untamed animal out of breath.

Her Uncle Michael told her afterwards he'd have recognised her anywhere from the one photograph she'd ever had taken, which she'd sent to him. He'd said the photo didn't do her justice and he'd commented on how like his sister Annie Maeve was. He could remember how stunning his sister had been at Maeve's age, and how she'd had the pick of the local suitors. He could see that Maeve had the same-shape face with the high cheekbones, blue eyes, straight nose and full mouth. They even had the same way of holding their heads and once had had the same-colour hair, but Maeve's mother's blonde locks were now peppered with grey. She wore it in a bun on the back of her neck and for the journey Maeve had copied her, feeling the style made her look more adult.

Maeve was pleased and relieved at her uncle's warm greeting. He pushed her extended hand aside and enveloped her in a big hug. His coat was scratchy and smelt of greasy dirt with a hint of tobacco, but none of that mattered. Maeve felt she was with one of her own, and tears of exhaustion and emotion welled up in her eyes. Not that she let them fall. This was her great adventure just beginning – no time for crying and carrying on, she told herself sternly.

She wiped her eyes surreptitiously and turned to the O'Rourkes, who were looking on in satisfaction at the respectable uncle, whom they thought a very suitable man indeed to look after the young Maeve Brannigan.

Michael shook hands with the two people that his niece had introduced him to, and thanked them sincerely for keeping her company. Maeve felt sorry to see them go, but had little time to dwell on it. Her uncle picked up her case and, holding her by the arm, he led her from the station.

She was shocked at the mean little streets, the houses pushed together, that her uncle took her through, after they'd alighted from the clanking swaying tram, which had frightened the life out of her. It wasn't at all what she'd expected. They alighted at a road called Bristol Street and her uncle turned from there into Belgrave Road and then into Varna Road, which ran off it.

'Here we are,' he said suddenly, stopping outside one of the doorways. 'Come away in and meet the family.'

Aunt Agnes, Michael's wife, had once been a pretty girl. She still had classic good looks, high cheekbones like Maeve's own, and deep-set dark brown eyes, with a well-formed nose and a full sensual mouth, and her brown hair fell in natural waves to her shoulders. But Agnes had always been easily offended and upset, and over the years her mouth had become petulant and surly. There was a hard glint in her beautiful eyes, as she'd wanted this niece of her husband's in her home less than she wanted to fly to the moon.

Maeve smiled, but the words of gratitude that sprang to her lips were stilled by the cold stare and compressed lips of her aunt. Behind her, her uncle was bustling as, she was to learn, he did all the time he was in the presence of his wife. He rubbed his hands together as if he was going to receive a rare and wonderful gift as he said, 'Aggie, Agnes, this is Maeve.' As if, Maeve thought, she could be anyone else.

Agnes made no response whatsoever. Afterwards, Maeve was to think the insult had been as bad as if she'd spat on her or ordered her from the house. Suddenly the room seemed to grow chilly. Maeve didn't know how to respond, and neither did her uncle, she realised. He turned his attention to the two children who were sitting playing snap on the rug placed in front of the hearth.

'Away out of that, Billy and Jane. Have you not a word of welcome for your cousin?'

The children got to their feet reluctantly. They knew the young girl before them was the one their parents had argued long and hard about. In that house, it was often hard to know whether it was better to please their mother or their father. It was impossible to have a situation that would please the two of them.

'Hello,' Billy said.

It was a lacklustre greeting, and Billy saw his father frown on him. He didn't care much. His father's hands might be harder than his mother's, but he never used them on him, whereas his mother . . .

Jane was older than her brother and thought this welcome was a shame for the girl. Her dad had said Maeve was eighteen, but Jane thought she didn't look it, so she smiled and said, 'Hello, I'm Jane. D'you want me to help you take your things up to the attic where you'll be sleeping with me and Billy?'

'That would be nice,' Maeve said awkwardly, not sure whether this was the right response or not. She glanced across at her uncle, who nodded at her and she picked up her case. Jane had picked up the other bag, opened the door to the stairs that went off from the living room, and led the way.

Barely had the door closed on the girls when Maeve heard her aunt's voice for the first time. It rose in an angry screech that she must know would be perfectly audible to them both. Maeve was to find out that in a back-to-back house, if you turned over in bed, the walls were so thin, half the street would be aware of it.

'How long has she been foisted on us?' Agnes demanded of her husband.

'Agnes, we've discussed this.' Though her uncle's voice was muted, Maeve had not to strain to hear his words. 'Till she gets on her feet, that's all.'

'Till she gets on her feet,' Agnes sneered. 'And how am I to feed her on the pittance you bring home?'

'Surely to God we can do so for a little time. She has a job she'll start in a few days and then she'll pay her keep. Isn't she my own sister's child?'

'Aye, and your sister has a tribe of them at home, by all accounts,' Agnes cried. 'Are we to fund the whole of them over here one at a time?'

Jane placed the bag on the attic floor. She was flushed with embarrassment, but no more than Maeve was herself. She knew her face must be brick red, for she felt her cheeks burn with it. She'd been going to ask the child why her mother didn't want her there, but the answer was now apparent.

Then she heard Agnes's voice again. 'Are they to be hanging to your coat-tails all the days of your life? My family don't make demands on you like this.'

'Your family live around the doors, woman.' Michael's voice was loud and angry. 'They're never away from the place. God knows, I've not seen my family since the day I left.'

Jane looked at Maeve and said, 'Mom's worried about money. It ain't just you, honest. See, our dad was put on short time three weeks ago.'

'Short time?'

'He only works three days a week, like,' Jane explained.

Maeve sat down hard on the bed. Her uncle had never told them that, though he'd written and told her about the job in the café just before she'd left. In fact, she thought, looking around the bare attic, what he had told the Brannigans had not been totally true.

Maeve was glad that she had a bag packed with goodies from the farm, and the five-pound note her mother had pressed her to take.

'Food will always come in useful, especially fresh stuff,' Annie had said. 'Though Michael will hardly need the money – him with his fine job and grand house – I'll not have it said you'd go anywhere and not offer to pay your way. Give Michael's wife the money and leave it up to her what she'll do with it.'

And Maeve knew, as she sat in that attic, that both the food and the money would be welcome, for the fine job was now not so good, and the grand house had never been. The downstairs room, though, was well furnished. Two upholstered armchairs were drawn up before the fireplace and two small stools stood in one corner. There was also a drop-leaf table and four chairs with padded seats, and a matching sideboard. Even the blue-patterned linoleum was not pitted or ripped, and the rug before the fireplace looked fluffy and expensive.

So, once there had been money. Not money enough, perhaps, to lift the family out of the house that had given

Maeve such a shock that day, to a better one. But there had been money enough for furnishing at least the one room. Maybe their bedroom too, for though they'd passed her uncle and aunt's room on the first floor, Maeve wouldn't have dared, even if Jane hadn't been with her, to open the door and peep inside. The attic room, with its two iron bedsteads and bare boards, had not been touched much, though there were crisp white sheets and clean blankets on the beds.

'That's why our dad was able to meet you today, like,' Jane said, breaking into her thoughts. ''Cos he's on short time.'

And Maeve had thought he'd taken a day off because he could, because he was one of the bosses – a foreman or some such – as Michael had indicated in his letters home. There had been no preparation for a man who worked only three days a week. Suddenly she felt sorry for her Aunt Agnes. Already managing on little money, she had now to feed another mouth.

She took off her coat and hat and laid both on the bed, then picked the bag up and said to Jane, 'I have some things here to please your mother. I think she'll be happier when she sees them.'

It had grown quiet downstairs and though Maeve knew it was probably the uneasy silence of an argument not resolved, she was still grateful for it. She took the parcel of food downstairs and presented it to Agnes, together with the five-pound note for her keep.

The change in Agnes was swift. She pocketed the money in her apron immediately and smiled at Maeve in a belated welcoming gesture. But Maeve noticed the smile didn't reach her eyes and she knew then that Agnes would never be a friend to her.

The meal was fine and filling enough, with the bacon and eggs and soda bread and butter from home, together with chips from the chippy that Billy had been dispatched for, and everyone tucked in with a fine appetite.

Maeve made pleasant small talk for courtesy's sake, but still couldn't take to her aunt, and it was obvious that her uncle was almost afraid of Agnes. Maybe he had reason, but the fact remained that the man who'd warmly welcomed Maeve at the station did not exist in this house, and that realisation saddened her. She resolved to get a place of her own as soon as possible.

The children fired questions at her about Ireland, the homestead she'd left behind and their daddy's family, and Maeve answered them as best she could. But the journey and the emotion of the whole day had tired her out, and she was glad when it was late enough to take to her bed. She lay beside Jane, and though Jane would have liked to talk more, Maeve was too exhausted and quickly fell into a deep sleep.

After a few fraught days, during which her aunt openly showed her displeasure in having Maeve there despite the five pounds, she was glad to begin work. Maeve was no stranger to hard work and she knew what the woman had told her on the train was no lie. Work was scarce, and she'd seen men, often extremely thin, and shabbily and inadequately dressed, lolling on street corners. She knew she was lucky to get a job, and probably wouldn't have it at all if her uncle hadn't asked for her. She had no wish for her boss to regret his decision to employ her and didn't quibble at the hours he asked her to work, but because they were so long she asked him to let her know if he heard of some place nearby that she could rent.

Mr Dolamartis thought this over. He'd never had such an industrious little waitress, and so beautiful too; she certainly drew the men in. But the hours were often from early morning to late night, and though she never complained, he knew sometimes Maeve had trouble getting there in time in the morning and back at night to her uncle's house.

Above the café there was a flat, basic and small, and though Mr Dolamartis had never used it as a flat but as a storeroom, he knew he could use the room off the kitchen for storage instead, and give Maeve the chance of having a place of her own.

Maeve was thrilled. She wasn't put off by the grime and neglect, and set to with a will to clean it all. Mr Dolamartis, amused at her industry, brought her some distemper to brighten the place up. There was a battered old sofa there already, and a table and chairs were supplied by the café. The bed was set into the wall of the living room and pulled out at night, but Maeve had no bedding, no crocks or cutlery, no curtains for the windows nor lino for the floor.

But though she'd paid over a good proportion of her wages to her Aunt Agnes, she'd kept her tips and sometimes they were sizeable. These she spent on essentials, then saved up for other household goods she wanted. She was often free in the afternoon for a few hours after lunch when Mr Dolamartis would take over. Then Maeve would usually take a tram to the city centre and stroll around the shops, enthralled by the choices available and particularly attracted to the Bull Ring, where she was able to find many of the things to make her flat more like home.

She joined organisations at the Catholic Church, St Francis's, that she attended in Aston, in a bid to make friends with some of the younger parishioners. She'd been to the pictures and dancing with some of the young single Catholic girls on one of her rare evenings off, but she seldom went to her uncle's house, knowing that she wouldn't really be welcome.

TWO

Maeve met Brendan Hogan as she came out of Benediction one late summer's evening in 1930, when she'd been in Birmingham less than six months. She thought he'd been to church too, but though he hadn't, he didn't enlighten her. He was struck by the beauty of the young woman and wanted to impress her, but though he never missed Mass or Communion – and certainly not confession, because that's where all his sins were absolved – he hadn't much truck with Benediction. He thought you could get too much of religion if you weren't careful and, anyway, Benediction cut into his drinking time. He was actually on his way to a pub at Aston Cross, which he knew many ladies of ill repute frequented, when he bumped into the luscious golden-haired beauty who introduced herself as Maeve Brannigan. If the lovely lady wanted to believe he was a good clean-living Catholic boy, he wasn't going to deny it.

Brendan was well muscled and handsome, with jet-black hair, a clear complexion, deep brown eyes and eyebrows that met across his broad forehead. Even the nose seemed to have little shape but sort of spread across his face, and his thick lips did not detract from his handsomeness, and

Maeve Brannigan could not believe that such a man could possibly be interested in her.

But he was, and he smiled at her and said he was very pleased to meet her. He asked her name and Maeve told him without any hesitation, for she knew by the man's voice that he was as Irish as herself and a good Catholic too, going to Benediction no less. She felt as if her heart had turned a somersault and Brendan knew he wasn't going to walk away from this girl who attracted him so much.

'Maybe you'd do me the honour of letting me walk you home, Miss Brannigan?' he said, admiring to himself her soft lilting voice, and added with another smile, 'My name is Brendan Hogan.'

Maeve was stunned. She wanted Brendan to see her home, but she wondered if she was being forward by accepting his offer. Maybe that's how things were done in the cities? If she refused because she was afraid, then she might as well have stayed in Ireland, she told herself.

'Thank you, Mr Hogan,' she replied. 'You can walk with me if you wish, but I don't live at home. I work in Dolamartis's café and live in the flat above it.'

Her own place, Brendan thought. This gets better and better. But he behaved impeccably, wanting to see Maeve again, and when he delivered her to the door of the café, he didn't even kiss her. Never had the walk home appeared so short, Maeve thought regretfully, and never had she chatted in such an uninhibited way to someone she'd just met.

'Can I see you again?' Brendan asked, and Maeve thought her heart had stopped beating altogether.

'Please?' Brendan said, misinterpreting Maeve's silence. He knew his cronies at The Bell public house wouldn't believe this was Brendan Hogan of love-them-and-leave-them fame, but his body was on fire for Maeve Brannigan.

He was sure she wasn't used to pubs, so their first date was to the cinema to see Charlie Chaplin. Brendan was the perfect gentleman, presenting Maeve with her first box of chocolates and taking her arm for the short walk to the Globe picture house at the junction of High Street and New Street in Aston. Maeve knew that was the entrance for the better seats. On her previous visits, when she'd gone on her own on a free afternoon, or with friends from the church, she'd bought cheap tickets from the little window in New Street. When she told Brendan this, he laughed and gave her a squeeze.

'Only the best for my girl,' he said.

Maeve felt dizzy. Was she really Brendan's girl or was it just the way he talked? She began to think it meant nothing as the evening wore on, for Brendan made no move to take advantage of the dark to put his arms round her, or steal a kiss.

Never could Maeve imagine what self-control it took for Brendan to keep his arms by his sides. He scarcely watched the film because he was wondering if he'd given Maeve a good enough time for her to reward him with something else afterwards. With some girls a couple of gins did the trick, but he had an idea Maeve might be more difficult and he had no desire to frighten her off.

They left the cinema arm in arm.

'Happy, darling?' Brendan asked, and Maeve nodded. She was happy, she supposed; she'd laughed uproariously at Charlie Chaplin at the cinema and had been escorted there by a charming and very handsome man. But she was also confused, for the same man had said she was his girl, and just a minute before had called her darling and yet had scarcely touched her. She thought it a peculiar way of going on and she wondered if Brendan's words meant anything at all.

It was brought home to her that they did when they got to Maeve's door and he pulled her into his arms. His kiss made her feel weak at the knees and she responded readily to the embrace. Brendan was delighted; maybe it wouldn't be so difficult after all. 'Why don't you ask me up for a nightcap, Maeve, my darling?' he asked, raining kisses on her eyes, her cheeks and her throat till she was hardly able to think straight.

She nodded eagerly. After all, the man had given her a good night out and presented her with a box of chocolates of her very own, and it would be churlish and against all she had ever been taught to refuse him a cup of tea. She wasn't anxious for him to leave just yet either and would love to talk some more.

It was when she realised that Brendan had neither tea nor talk on his mind that she became uneasy.

'I'm sorry, Brendan,' she said, pulling out of his arms with difficulty and regret. 'I just can't.'

Brendan was angry, but he hid it well. He told himself that Maeve was a decent girl, and he'd not met many of them, that was the trouble. She was not given to going too far on a first date. He'd just have to have patience.

'It's all right,' he said.

Maeve saw the angry glint in Brendan's eye and knew she'd put it there, but she couldn't have gone further than they had. She'd let him touch and fondle her breasts, and that was bad enough and not something she'd ever have done if she'd been in her right mind and if Brendan's kisses hadn't made her dizzy and aching with longing. Well, she thought, I've kept my virginity, but lost my man because he'll want no more to do with me after tonight.

But Brendan most decidedly did want to see Maeve again. She had few evenings off, though Brendan never complained about that. He had plenty of mates from the brass foundry where he worked who lived in Aston Cross and drank in the pubs there, and he'd stay there on Maeve's evenings at work, arriving at the café at about half-past nine. Maeve closed up officially at ten, but if there were no customers she could close earlier and then all her time was devoted to Brendan. She never minded that he was drunk. After all, she reasoned, what else was there for him to do? Nor did she mind the bottles of beer he would bring to wash down the little bit of supper she would always save for him.

'Let me stay the night, Maeve?' he'd pleaded time and again on these nights.

Maeve's answer was always the same: 'Brendan, I can't.'

'Oh, but you can, my darling,' Brendan said one day almost a fortnight after their first date as he caressed and fondled one of Maeve's breasts. 'It would be so good. You'd enjoy it.'

Maeve didn't doubt it. Already she was allowing Brendan more liberties than she'd ever dreamt of allowing anyone and, finding it so nice, it would have been easy, so easy, to let Brendan do what he wanted. But always her mother's face would be before her, sorrow-filled, or the disapproving visage of the parish priest, and both images had given her the strength to pull back.

'Wouldn't your mother worry if you didn't go home anyway?' she asked Brendan one evening when he was again wheedling to spend the night with her.

He gave a bellow of laughter. 'Maeve, I'm a big boy now. My mother has no say in my life. No one has. And that's how it should be for you. You shouldn't worry so much about other people. You should do what feels good to you.'

But despite Brendan's urging Maeve wouldn't be moved. Brendan tried harder than he'd ever tried with any other girl, and on Maeve's rare evenings off he would forgo his pleasures at the pub and take her somewhere special. They went to the cinema twice more and even to the theatre once. The highlight of that visit to the Hippodrome in Corporation Street was to see a young Lancashire lass called Gracie Fields singing wonderful stirring songs that she urged the audience to join in.

Brendan was opening up new horizons for Maeve, and she was grateful to him and said so as they made their way home.

'How grateful?' Brendan said. 'I know a way you could show true gratitude.'

'Ah, Brendan, if only I could.'

'You can,' Brendan said. His desire for Maeve seemed to be growing rather than diminishing. Often he had to seek consolation elsewhere after he'd left Maeve, for the limits she put on his lovemaking fuelled his frustration.

Maeve didn't know how Brendan felt, though she hoped he truly loved her as she did him, for no one should do the kind of things they were doing to each other, and wanting to do more, unless they loved each other. The natural outcome was marriage and she waited for Brendan to ask her, knowing if he didn't ask her soon, she'd give way to his urgings and her own body's needs anyway and let Brendan love her as he wanted to for she'd be unable to help herself. She didn't tell Brendan this, but he guessed a lot from the little moans and sighs she was unable to suppress.

Brendan wanted to take Maeve down the Bull Ring on a Saturday evening but she never had a Saturday free.

'It's hardly fair,' he said one night as she lay in his arms.

'It's our busiest night. Mr Dolamartis would never agree.'

'Bet he would if I asked him,' Brendan said. 'I'll tell him he's destroying my love life keeping you behind the counter, or over a hot stove every Saturday. It isn't as if he doesn't get his bloody money's worth out of you. And he's a right stingy bugger. I'll have a word with him, don't you worry.'

And Brendan had a word and Maeve thought she'd remember for ever the first sight of the Bull Ring on that Saturday evening, lit up with gas flares and looking like fairyland. The noise was tremendous – both from the people thronging the place and the vendors shouting out their wares. Brendan caught up Maeve's hand and they ran like children down the cobbled streets of Jamaica Row.

'Let go of me!' she cried, laughing at him. 'Let go!'

But though Brendan slowed down, he kept hold of her hand as they walked among the stalls, looking at the array of goods on offer. Maeve had discovered the Bull Ring on her first visit to the city centre, but she'd never seen it at night. It seemed a different place, a magical place.

She jiggled a hot potato from hand to hand as she watched a man tied in chains free himself, while others tottered on high stilts among the crowds. A bare-fist boxer was challenging the men for a fight, five pounds to be won if they beat him.

'Shall I try?' Brendan asked teasingly, but Maeve held him back.

'You will not, Brendan,' she said firmly. 'I couldn't bear it.'

Brendan laughed at her. He'd had no intention of offering himself, but liked to see Maeve's concern.

Maeve didn't like the poor ragged men selling a variety of things from trays around their necks. 'Old lags from the last war,' Brendan told her, but he wouldn't let Maeve dwell on their poor existence or buy their razor blades or matches. He steered her instead towards the man with the piano accordion, and they joined in with others singing the popular songs.

That evening Maeve had her first taste of whelks when Brendan bought her a dish. She wasn't sure she really liked them, but thought they were better than the slimy jellied eels that Brendan chose.

Brendan put his arm round Maeve, amused at her delight in everything, and as she smiled up at him he felt as if he'd been hit by a sledgehammer in the pit of his stomach. He didn't know if it was love or not, he just knew he wanted Maeve more than he'd wanted anything in his life before.

They stayed at the Bull Ring until the Salvation Army band marched in blowing bugles and trumpets, and singing hymns with great gusto. Maeve was amazed how many stood and listened and even joined in some hymns, and when the Salvation Army left, they had tramps and some of the old lags in tow.

'Where are they taking them?' she asked Brendan.

'To the Citadel,' he replied. 'They'll give them thick soup and bread, and try and find some of them a bed for the night.'

Maeve was moved by that. She'd never met people of different religions, or of no religion at all, before she'd come to Birmingham, but she thought those in the Salvation Army must be good, kind people and brave to go about in their strange costumes risking ridicule.

'Come on,' Brendan said. 'The only one in your head should be me, my darling girl, and certainly not those down-and-outs. My throat's as dry as dust and I want a drink.'

Maeve didn't very much like the pub to which Brendan took her, but she quite liked the port and lemon he bought her. In fact she liked it so much she drank it down almost at once and Brendan smiled at her.

'It's not pop, you know. Treat it with care.'

Maeve remembered the brandy she'd had on the boat and how the Irish woman had said something similar. 'I'm not used to alcohol,' she said.

'Well, that's obvious,' Brendan said. 'I'll buy you another and you sip it this time.'

Maeve did sip it, but the unaccustomed drink made her feel peculiar and a little giggly, and as they made their way to the tram, she confessed to Brendan that her head felt swimmy. Brendan was pleased; he wanted Maeve in a compliant mood that night.

The café was in darkness and there wasn't a soul about as they stole up the stairs to Maeve's flat, and once inside Brendan pulled Maeve on to the settee beside him. Suddenly it didn't matter to Maeve that Brendan hadn't asked her to marry him. He would, she was sure, in time, and until then . . . After all, he'd been so kind to her and so generous. She didn't repel Brendan's groping fingers, nor the kisses that she seemed to be drowning in.

But then at the last moment she pulled back and Brendan let out a howl of agony. He felt as if his crotch would explode and he knew by Maeve's wild eyes and breathlessness that she wanted it as much as he did. No pleading would shift her, and Brendan thought of taking her by force, but knew it would destroy everything between them if he did.

But Maeve too had been shaken and was frustrated and unhappy. It was getting harder and harder to refuse Brendan when she wanted it so much herself. She'd never in her life felt the hot shafts of desire that Brendan induced in her and knew that eventually she would give in to him.

Brendan knew it too, but he didn't know how long it could take to break Maeve from her upbringing and the moral confines of the Church, and wasn't at all sure he could last out that long. However, despite his deep desire for Maeve, he'd had no intention on God's earth of marrying her in the beginning.

He'd had no intention of marrying anyone. He'd never known a happy marriage – certainly his own parents' had been no advertisement for blissful contentment. All his brothers had gone down the same road and he'd seen the lifeblood squeezed out of them with their demanding wives and houses full of screaming brats. He had no use for children.

He was the eldest in his family and each child his mother had had after him had meant less attention for himself. He'd felt further and further pushed away as the younger ones got what care and love there might be, though there was precious little of either.

There had been no time at all for his father either. His mother just seemed to regard him as a walking pay packet. She'd never been satisfied with the amount he'd given her every Friday night. Small wonder, Brendan thought, his father had felt the need to smack her about now and then. Brendan had certainly seen no harm in it. She was a moaning bloody nag, like most women, and he agreed with his father that they all needed teaching a lesson a time or two. A man had to be master in his own house.

He'd decided long ago that he'd share his money with no woman. He worked for it and he'd choose how it was to be spent. Brendan was the only one left at home. His mother cooked his meals and washed and ironed for him, and he paid keep, which she was always bloody grateful for. He always had enough left to buy as many fags as he wanted, a bellyful of beer as often as he liked and to place a bet if he had the mind to. He thought his brothers fools and saw marriage as a trap.

He didn't live like a monk either. He had plenty of money to jingle in his pocket and buy drinks for those willing to please him, and he found there were women enough to accommodate him if he was that way inclined. He used to boast he'd never had to pay for sex. After a good night out most were only too grateful for a bit of slap and tickle, and Brendan always admitted to it later in confession and got absolution. He saw no reason for his life to change. That was until he met Maeve Brannigan.

That night, with his whole body on fire, he faced the fact that to have Maeve he had to marry her, for his need for her had got between him and his reason. And so he proposed.

Maeve was ecstatic that the man she adored, loved more than life itself, had asked her to marry him and soon they could love each other totally and fully as they both longed to.

However, Maeve's parents didn't want their daughter marrying a man they'd never seen, especially as she was under age. In desperation, Maeve turned to her uncle. Michael knew Brendan, had known him for years because they attended the same church and drank in the same pub when Michael ever had the money and Aggie's permission to do so. He thought Brendan Hogan a grand man altogether, but because Maeve seldom went near them he had not been aware that his niece was even seeing him.

He knew Brendan had a bit of a reputation with a certain type of woman, but he told himself there was no harm in that – many young men sowed their wild oats until they met the girl they wanted to marry. He wrote and told Maeve's parents Brendan was a good fellow altogether and would make Maeve a grand husband, and wasn't he not only a good Catholic, but as Irish as themselves and from County Clare? Reassured and relieved they gave their blessing.

Brendan knew there were ways of preventing pregnancies, for at the pubs he'd met many old lags, veterans of the Great War, who had told him about it. Not that the rubber sheaths they wore were necessarily to prevent pregnancy, but rather the clap that the French prostitutes seemed riddled with. But they would prevent pregnancy too, and that's what he was interested in. He wanted Maeve all to himself and not just for the tiny morsels of time that were all she'd have left for him if she had a houseful of weans to attend to.

But when Brendan went to see the priest before the wedding, Father Trelawney was shocked that he should even consider such a thing. Didn't Brendan realise that it was totally against the Church's teaching? Didn't Brendan appreciate each child was a gift from God?

Chastened and resigned, Brendan married his Maeve in late October 1930 at St Catherine's Church where he and his family worshipped. Maeve was coming up to nineteen. Her white wedding dress and the bridesmaid dress for her cousin, Jane, were paid for by her parents, and the wedding breakfast was paid for by Brendan's parents. They said they were glad to get him off their hands and especially to one of their own. 'Sure, didn't we think he'd be hanging round our necks for years?' his mother, Lily, said.

At first Maeve and Brendan were blissfully happy. For Brendan, little had changed except that now when he tottered home from the pub, he had a nice spot of sex thrown in after supper, and Maeve was always as eager as he was. Maeve waited on him hand and foot, much as his mother had done, and took joy in doing so, for she loved him very much.

Brendan had a good, well-paid job at Samuel Heath and Sons, the brass works in Leopold Street. Maeve considered them both very lucky with so many out of work at that time. When Brendan told her where he worked Maeve remembered the couple that had been kind to her on the ferry when she'd been so sick. That man had said he was a brass worker too. It seemed like a lucky omen that her husband worked in the same industry.

Mr Dolamartis was loath to let Maeve go and said he had no objection to her continuing work after her marriage. The flat was cramped for the two of them, but Brendan's mother said that many couples started on worse, and Maeve knew she spoke the truth.

Maeve was delighted to find herself pregnant when she and Brendan had been married six months. In her brief but passionate courtship, the subject of children had never been discussed. She'd barely noticed his indifference to any references she'd made to her brothers and sisters back home in Ireland. She'd met none of his nieces and nephews till the wedding and there had been virtually no contact since because Maeve worked such long and unsociable hours.

She'd always presumed the natural progression in marriage was children. She longed to be a mother and hold Brendan's child in her arms, and thought he would be equally pleased. But Brendan raved and shouted, telling her she was a stupid cow and the pregnancy was all her fault, and when, in tears because of the onslaught and not at all sure what she had done to deserve it, she remonstrated with him, he punched her in the face. Maeve gave a cry of alarm and put her hand up to ward off further blows, and tasted blood in her mouth.

Brendan saw the pleasant life they'd been enjoying slipping away from them. Like his father's, his life would turn sour and he'd have a child every bloody year bleeding him dry. He suddenly felt so hopeless about the future that he'd lashed out at Maeve.

Now he couldn't look at her bloodstained face; he couldn't believe he'd done that to his lovely beautiful Maeve. He went off to the pub, knowing his brothers would make fun of him when he told them the news and remind him they'd told him not to bother getting married. God, they'd say, hadn't he the life of Riley already? Just at that moment Brendan thought life was a bloody bitch and women the biggest bitches of all. Temptresses all of them, and Maeve no better than the rest.

Despite his brothers' taunts that evening, Brendan was bitterly ashamed of himself for what he had done. He thought about it all night and apologised to Maeve the next day. He told her he loved her and said he'd been shocked by the news that he was going to be a father and he'd lashed out in frustration. He said it hadn't been how they'd planned things. Maeve knew it hadn't, but thought Brendan must have known the passionate lovemaking they indulged in so often would eventually result in a baby. But she didn't blame her husband, feeling that in some way it must have been partly her fault, so she kissed him and told him that it was all right, confident that it wouldn't happen again.

Yet as her pregnancy had continued, Brendan often clouted Maeve, usually after he'd been drinking. She was far too ashamed to tell anyone about it and always thought up an excuse to explain the bruises that could be seen. And Brendan was always so sorry afterwards, full of remorse. Anyway, she thought, she must be at least partly to blame because Brendan was not the same man she'd courted or the same as he'd been in the early months of their marriage and she felt ashamed and saddened. Maeve would always forgive him and believe him when he assured her it wouldn't happen again.

As the birth got closer, Maeve knew she'd have to give up her job and therefore the flat too. Everyone was keeping an eye out for a place for them, and when she heard of the vacant back-to-back house in a court off Latimer Street in the Horse Fair, she'd been delighted. She was seven months pregnant then and felt the new house would be a fresh start for them both.

She told herself it was probably the cramped conditions of the flat getting to Brendan, causing him to hit out. His mother, Lily, though Maeve had not breathed a word of Brendan's violence towards her, said any man would be annoyed to see his wife working the hours Maeve did. 'You should be at home, dear,' she said, 'looking after your man properly.' Maeve immediately felt guilty that she'd been neglecting her husband and resolved to try harder to be a model wife.

Mr Dolamartis, in a fit of generosity at losing Maeve, had found her a second-hand gas cooker and a fellow to fit it in her new home, and Maeve had been thrilled with it. However, money was tighter than ever, for not only were Maeve's wages lost, but now they had to find the rent and money for the gas meter for the cooker and the lamps, and for coal too, for they moved in the middle of September and the evenings were often chilly.

Added to that, there were things to buy for the baby. The food bills had increased too, now that they couldn't be supplemented by café fare, and Brendan in consequence had to part with more of his wages. No longer were there tempting suppers for him when he got home from the pub. Sometimes, indeed, there was nothing at all, not that he had that much money to spend in the pub either.

Elsie Phillips, who lived in the house adjoining Maeve's, had been a tower of strength to her since she'd moved in. Maeve was glad of it, for since the move Brendan had become morose and moody, and often snapped at Maeve for very little. Without Elsie Maeve would have been depressed by the whole situation.

Elsie was very fond of Maeve. She and her husband, Alf, had never had children. Early in their marriage it hadn't mattered much, for Elsie had her hands full with her mother, who after years of caring for her husband, who had TB, eventually became ill herself with a tumour in the stomach.

Elsie tended to her mother in a bed brought downstairs and her father coughing his guts up in the bedroom above. She and Alf had the attic and she often wondered how she'd cope if she became pregnant, and at the time thanked God that she hadn't. Two years later, all that she had of her parents were the two wooden crosses in the church-yard. After they'd been married for seven more childless years, Elsie mentioned to Alf that perhaps they should see the doctor, but Alf said he was reluctant to discuss anything so personal. The priest Elsie went to for advice told her she had to be content with whatever God sent and if he intended her to be childless then she had to be satisfied with it. She hadn't ever been satisfied, but as she was unable to change the situation she had to accept it.

But when a heavily pregnant Maeve Hogan moved in next door to her some years later, Elsie's maternal instincts rose to the fore. Maeve was only nineteen, her twentieth birthday being in late December, and could have been Elsie's own daughter. Maeve, often confused and made unhappy by Brendan's behaviour, and missing her own mother, found Elsie's company very welcome indeed.

A strong friendship grew between them, and it had been Elsie's hand that Maeve had clung to as her son, Kevin, was born in November 1931, while Brendan went on a drinking binge and disappeared for two days. He returned looking like death, without a word of explanation or apology and took no notice of his infant son.

In fact Brendan's indifference towards Kevin seemed to be echoed among all his family, and even Maeve's uncle and aunt. Letters of congratulation from Ireland were all well and good, but not the same as her family visiting and taking delight in the child. So Maeve was glad of Elsie's support. She knew she'd get little from Brendan and she thanked God that she had such a kind and caring neighbour.

THREE

Brendan hated the child who'd supplanted him. One day, being unused to the demands of a young baby, Maeve hadn't quite finished feeding Kevin when Brendan walked in the door. He watched his son tugging at his wife's breasts and was so consumed by jealousy that he shook.

He strode across the room and dragged the child so roughly from Maeve that he began to wail, and Maeve got to her feet, terrified Brendan would hurt him. Not that he didn't want to, for he knew Maeve preferred the child over him. But in the end he almost threw him back to Maeve and told her to put him in the bedroom out of the bloody road.

Another night he came home to find no dinner ready because, she said, 'the baby wouldn't settle'. The resultant punch he gave her was to make sure that that never happened again.

'You look after me before any squalling brat,' he yelled, as Maeve wiped the blood oozing from her nose and her split lip. 'Maybe you'll remember that in future.'

No longer was Maeve so eager for him each night either, and would often turn from him if Kevin made a murmur, holding the baby in her arms and crooning while her husband grew hot with impatience and frustration. He never spoke of his feelings and fears, but instead grew moodier than ever, and often gave Maeve the odd punch or clout if he felt she was annoying him in some way.

Maeve didn't really understand what had happened to the husband that she still loved, who'd courted her with such consideration and professed his devotion to her often. She sometimes remembered with a pang of nostalgia how they used to laugh together over something silly, or the hours and hours they used to talk and never tire of one another, or the way she used to yearn for his hands on her body. Now such intimacy seemed to have slunk away from them.

Brendan worked hard, there was no denying that, and in the early days of their marriage he'd talked about his work and the sweltering heat he toiled under, turning copper and zinc into molten metal in white-hot furnaces so that they could be poured into crucibles. The sweat ran from him so freely that often the shirt he wore was still damp when he arrived home.

Maeve had witnessed the weariness on his face when he came in the door and saw the lines on his brow rimed with dirt, and the grime streaking his cheeks. She'd seen his cracked, calloused hands encrusted with black, and smelt the sour sweat of him. She'd often felt sorry for him, and because of it, had forgiven him his temper.

Then she'd always had the kettle on the boil for Brendan's wash. He said he always felt better with the muck sluiced off him and clean, dry clothes on, but since Kevin's birth all that had stopped. Now he was prepared to sit down at the table unwashed, reeking from stale sweat and with filthy hands and nails, and would shovel in his food as though he was a pig at a trough.

Because Maeve knew beer inflamed Brendan's temper, she tried talking to him after his meal when he was more rational and at least sober. She tried, as she'd done before, asking him what she was doing that so enraged him that he felt he had to raise his hand to her. Brendan never had an answer to give her. He felt she needed no explanation and the fact that she seemed to expect one angered him further. His mother would never have questioned his father.

When she tried to talk to him about the money he gave her, which was woefully inadequate, Brendan flew into such a temper Maeve was terrified. She produced a list of things she had to buy, or pay for each week, thinking it might help, and he tore it from her hands, ripped it into pieces and threw them into the fire.

The back of his hand sliced across Maeve's cheek as he hissed, 'All the bloody same, women, nag, nag, nag, and always about bloody money. Well, you'll just have to manage on what I give you, for you'll get no more.'

Maeve had been stunned by both the blow and Brendan's reaction. After that she didn't say anything more to him about the son of whom he seemed to take no notice. In fact, if it hadn't been for Elsie Phillips next door, who took as much delight in the child as she did herself, Maeve might have become seriously depressed.

It was Elsie's advice that Maeve sought one sunny morning in September 1932. Elsie listened and then said, 'You'll have to tell him, girl. For God's sake, pregnancy is one thing you can't hide.'

'Elsie, I'm scared.'

'It's his baby as much as yours, Maeve. You didn't do it on your own.'

'You don't know him, Elsie. He'll go mad.'

'Better you tell him than let him find out for himself,' Elsie said. But she spoke cautiously because she'd known for some time that Maeve's husband smacked her about a bit. The construction of the houses was not conducive to any degree of privacy, and she'd heard some of the blows Maeve had received, and seen the evidence with her own eyes the next day. But Maeve had not mentioned the violence so neither had Elsie.

Still, Maeve knew Elsie was right. Brendan had to know that she was three months gone with another child. When Maeve told him that night after tea, he flew into a temper and shouted and screamed so much, Elsie was tempted to go in, but Alf told her to mind her own business. She didn't breathe easy till she heard Maeve's door slam and knew Brendan had taken himself off to the pub.

All evening Brendan brooded, over the many pints he ordered, on the news he'd received that day. There would be a baby every bloody year, just as he'd imagined it, till Maeve hadn't a moment to bid him the time of day, and he hadn't two halfpennies to call his own. Every penny would go to feed and clothe bleeding kids he had never wanted. Some bloody gift from God!

That night Brendan staggered home from the pub consumed with the unfairness of it. It was Maeve's fault, tempting him like all women tempted men, trapping him into marriage by not letting him do what he wanted until she had the ring on her finger. Bloody bitches, all women. Maeve most of all, and it was about time she was taught a lesson she'd not forget in a hurry.

The next morning, when Brendan saw the mess he'd made of Maeve's face and hazily remembered what he'd done to her the night before, he felt guilty and ashamed, and angry with himself for feeling that way. He told himself she'd asked for it. He growled at her to get his breakfast and, alarmed and afraid, Maeve, without a word, eased herself painfully from the bed and went to do his bidding.

She was glad when he went to work, for only then did her limbs stop trembling, but when Kevin awoke and began to cry, she groaned as she mounted the stairs, for she was stiff and sore, and every part of her seemed to ache. She wanted to hide from the world, at least until her face was back to normal, she felt so ashamed.

She finished feeding Kevin, changed him and then rocked him in her arms until his eyelids drooped and eventually closed. She laid him in the pram and went into the bedroom, where she painfully dressed herself. Then, wrapping her shawl around her head and shoulders, pulling it well over her face, she made her way to the outdoor lavatory.

Outside the autumn sun penetrated the court in dusty shafts, and small children played around the doorways. Two women stood keeping an eye on them and having a chat and both looked curiously at Maeve. She muttered a greeting, but kept her head down and hurried past.

When she returned the women had gone, though the children still played on, and she was grateful that they took no notice of her. As she reached her door, she heard Kevin's plaintive cry, and she struggled with the latch, anxious to get in and see to him. She lost her grip on the shawl and it slipped from her just as Elsie Phillips's door opened. She stared at Maeve's face with a look of dismay and shock.

So she'd been right, she thought to herself. The brute had been smacking her about, but it was more than the odd slap or punch this time. 'You poor sod,' she said with feeling, and the sympathy started the tears in Maeve's eyes.

She stumbled through the door, the tears almost blinding her. Elsie stood undecided, not sure whether to follow her into the house or go out to the shops, as she'd intended, and mind her own business. But then, she reminded herself, the girl had no one belonging to her, except a sour-faced old cow of an aunt. She'd seen her just the once at Kevin's christening and couldn't take to her, nor her milksop, henpecked husband, who seemed to think the sun shone out of Brendan Hogan's arse.

Her mind made up, she put down her bag, took off her coat, closed her own door and went to Maeve's. The girl still cried, even as she held the baby, and Elsie's heart was smitten with pity for her. She knew the pattern Maeve's life would take from now on, for she believed once a man started beating his wife he would always do so, and she also knew Maeve would not get a lot of sympathy from anyone because of it either.

She took the baby from Maeve and sat him up in the pram, where he could watch what was going on, and pressed his mother down into a chair.

'I'm going to make us a cup of tea,' Elsie said, 'and then see if I can do summat about your face. After that if you need any shopping I'll get it for you. You'll not want to go out much for a day or two, I'd say.'

Maeve marvelled that Elsie seemed to know just how she felt and was very glad of the older woman's presence. For the first time she didn't feel so isolated.

Elsie had been right. Maeve's life took on a pattern from that first real beating, the first one that Brendan hadn't apologised for. She realised whatever she did or didn't do, however she pleaded, begged or tried to talk to Brendan, he would treat her as he saw fit. In his eyes that was grudgingly giving her money he could spare her after his booze, fags and bets had been accounted for, however inadequate it was, and clouting her whenever he felt like it.

'Write and tell your mother,' Elsie advised one day in early spring 1933.

'Tell her what?' Maeve demanded harshly, wincing, for she was recovering from another few hefty clouts which she had been given not long after her daughter, Grace, was born on 9 February. 'Tell her my husband doesn't give me enough money either to feed us or keep us warm, and beats me? What the hell could she do about it, but worry herself into an early grave?'

A further worry was nagging at Maeve's mind at this time and that was Brendan's treatment of Kevin. The child was fifteen months old when his sister was born, no longer a wee baby to be rocked to sleep, but an active toddler.

Maeve knew Brendan had to come first in everything and she'd learnt to accept that. Maeve made dinner for him every night, even if she lived on bread and scrape herself, or sometimes nothing at all, because it was healthier to do so. And while he ate, he wanted the children out of sight, but now Kevin was not always in bed when he came in and that seemed to enrage him, even if the child was doing nothing wrong.

She tried to protect him as much as she was able, but his father often gave him a hefty slap on the legs, or a swipe across the head for no reason that Maeve could see except that he wanted to do it. Remonstrating with him and protesting that Kevin was only a wee boy did no good at all. In fact all she usually got for her efforts was a slap herself. That wouldn't have stopped her if it hadn't been for the fact that she was afraid to protest too much in case the child got the brunt of it and she tried to keep them apart as much as possible.

Maeve herself got used to the way life was for her. She lived day to day, interested only in getting enough to eat for herself and Kevin each day. She fed Grace herself and Elsie complained she should be eating wholesome meals to do it properly. Maeve thought that was easy to say. Now she was a regular at the pawnshop, yet the first time she'd gone there she'd nearly died of shame. Ballyglen did not sport a pawnshop or anything like it. Poor people there could apply to the St Vincent de Paul for tokens to spend in the shops for groceries only. You were considered the lowest of the low to apply to them, but often Maeve would have welcomed something to put food in her mouth and her son's that Brendan could not convert to beer money.

The winter was the hardest, often with no money for either coal or gas, and little enough for food. They would have surely perished but for the odd shovelful of coal from Elsie, or the bit of stew or soup she said she had over. Maeve knew full well she'd done extra on purpose, but was often too hungry and dispirited to care.

'Elsie, I can see this life stretching out before me for years and years,' Maeve complained to her friend one day.

Elsie could see it too, but thought it wouldn't be helpful to say so.

'I've tried talking to him, but it does no good,' Maeve went on. 'Surely he can see how we live, what I'm left to eat, and the weans. Dear God, Elsie, if you'd known the type of man he was when we were courting, or even just married . . .' Maeve shook her head sorrowfully. 'He's not the same at all.'

Elsie had heard the story more than once and she still said nothing. She did all she could for Maeve, but to go

41

between man and wife – that was something she shrank from, and her Alf said she was not to get involved. He said Maeve had an uncle she could appeal to, or failing that she could go home to her mother.

But Elsie knew no such course was open to Maeve. On the rare occasions her uncle had braved his wife's wrath to visit his niece, he always had his kids with him. And her predicament was hardly a subject Maeve could bring up in their hearing. Anyhow, he'd never hear a word said against Brendan and still thought him a fine figure of a man.

As for her mother, Elsie knew she'd been told nothing, for even if she had, as Maeve said, there was little she could do. Maeve wouldn't leave Brendan unless something desperate happened altogether. She was a good Catholic girl and knew only too well that marriage was for life and you married for better or worse. Anyroad, Elsie thought, even if Maeve wanted to go to her mammy for a wee holiday, a break from the brute, how, when she barely had two halfpennies to bless herself with, would she find the money for the fare?

She didn't bother saying any of this. Her Alf was a good man, and a good provider. He'd never lifted his hand to her all their married life, and she knew if things had been different he would have been a good father to their children. Well, that was not to be and Elsie had faced that fact years before, but she often wondered what she would have done had Maeve been her daughter.

Would she have stood by just because of some words said at an altar and watched Maeve and her children being terrorised or half starved and frozen to death? No, by God, she wouldn't, and as Maeve hadn't her mother and father to stand up for her Elsie was determined to do all she could.

Maeve knew she couldn't have coped so well if it hadn't been for Elsie. Getting the children clothes and even some for herself had been a real headache. All the baby necessities had been bought from Maeve's wages when she worked at the café, but as the children grew problems arose. Elsie took her to jumble sales where for a few hoarded pennies she could buy jumpers and cardigans to be unravelled and knitted up again, or skirts that could be cut up to make something for the children, and then sometimes Elsie would bring a similar load from the rag market.

Maeve had been taught to sew and her mother had a treadle sewing machine similar to Elsie's, so Maeve knew all about cutting out and tacking together for Elsie to go over seams and hemming neatly. Knitting she'd never been shown, but she soon picked it up. 'Born of necessity,' Maeve said when Elsie commented on the speed Maeve was able to knit after just a couple of weeks. 'Anyway, it gives me pleasure to have the children dressed respectable. I only wish I could knit shoes like the booties they had as babies.'

Shoes were the very devil to get. There were adult shoes sometimes, and Maeve had got herself a pair at a jumble sale when her others had literally fallen off her feet, though the second-hand ones were a size too big. Any children's shoes were, in the main, worn through, the toes kicked in or the soles hanging off.

She remembered how she'd run barefoot all through the spring and summer of her Irish childhood and delighted in it, leaping over the spring turf and never feeling the pebbles in the dusty farm tracks. She thought there wouldn't be the same pleasure on the cobbles of the courts or the hard dirty pavements of the streets, but barefoot Kevin and little Grace often had to go.

Before school every September, Maeve and her brothers and sisters had all been fitted out with shoes. Sometimes they were handed down from an older child, but newly soled and heeled, and they all had new clothes made by their mother during the holidays. Maeve had little hope of finding a pair of shoes for each child that weren't too worn before the cold of winter, but if she was lucky she could sometimes get a ragged pair of plimsolls, the canvas worn and ripped and with paper-thin soles that she'd line with cardboard.

The spring that Grace turned two years old and Kevin was three, Maeve again missed a second period. She was terrified of telling Brendan. She didn't know why he appeared surprised by it and acted as if it was her fault. Surely to God he must have realised that what he did most nights was bound to lead to pregnancy in the end. She'd never complained or refused because she knew it was her duty to submit to her husband.

The little sexual forays and fondling that she'd enjoyed in courtship when she'd longed for Brendan to continue had stopped in the early months of her marriage, once she'd told him of her pregnancy. Brendan had seen no need after that to bring Maeve to the point of excitement and longing. He didn't really expect her to enjoy it and didn't really care whether she did or not. In the marriage service she'd promised to obey him and that's what she had to do.

At first, again and again Maeve had responded to Brendan, each time hoping to recapture the heady romance and embraces she'd enjoyed before she'd told him she was expecting a baby. She remembered how Brendan's fingers could touch, stroke and caress her body and send her senses reeling and a throbbing urgency she'd never felt

44

before beginning between her legs. Oh God, how she'd wanted him to go on and on. But now she felt nothing but the sensation of Brendan's body in the bed at night, his beery breath wafting across her and his thick tongue probing her mouth till she felt she might choke, and then he'd take her roughly and without any form of tenderness. It was, Maeve reflected, just one thing to be endured, but it had already resulted in two children, and now there was a third on the way. She no longer loved Brendan, she realised with an aching sense of loss; now she only feared the man she'd once have laid down her life for.

Another month passed and there was a definite rounding out of her stomach and Maeve knew any day Brendan would discover her pregnancy for himself. She tried to work out whether he would resent her even more for not telling him. Either way, she knew she was going to catch it.

Then one Friday night in April, with Brendan fed and sitting reading the paper with a cup of tea in his hand, Maeve began getting the children to bed. They always sat stock-still whenever their father was around and it wrung Maeve's heart to see them sitting so silent and quiet like no children should ever be – like only petrifying fear could make them. Poor little Grace only had to hear her father's boots ringing on the cobblestones for her to wet herself.

When Maeve got them up into the attic, unless it was the depths of winter, she'd often have a bit of a game with them – tickling them into laughter perhaps or telling them a wee story. However, that evening Maeve, having finished washing Grace, then picked her up to take her to bed. Kevin, who'd been washed first and was sitting on a cracket by the fire, got to his feet, having no wish to be left with a man who scared the living daylights out of him. In his panic to follow his mother, he stumbled over the fender, knocking against his father, causing him to tip the hot tea down his leg.

With a roar Brendan was upon the child and Kevin's resultant shriek stopped Maeve in her tracks. But she knew whatever had happened she could do nothing with Grace in her arms. She ran up to the attic and laid her in the bed, cautioning her to stay there, then flew down the stairs. She knew Grace would stay where she was for she was a timid little thing, and no wonder, and anyway, the screams and shouts from below would frighten the most stout-hearted.

What Maeve saw when she stepped into the room nearly stopped her heart beating, for Brendan had the belt unhooked from his trousers, Kevin's ragged underpants that he slept in pulled down, and he was whipping his little bottom. Maeve didn't know what Kevin had done, nor did she care. Whatever it was it didn't warrant what his father was doing to him and with an outraged scream she was upon him.

Brendan warded her off and then, totally enraged, he turned on her, the belt lashing her to right and left till she sank to the floor with a whimper. 'Let that be a lesson to you,' he growled as he pulled his coat from the rail behind the door and slammed his way out.

The next day, Maeve miscarried and she sent Kevin for Elsie. She looked at the stripes on her body where the belt's end had flicked and asked, 'Was it you telling him you were pregnant brought this on?'

'No, not this time,' Maeve said. 'This time I got it protecting Kevin. This time the bloody sod didn't even know I was pregnant.' The tears came then, hot and scalding as she cried for herself, her children and the little baby she had lost.

Elsie held Maeve tight as she went on, her voice muffled with tears, 'Kevin spilt his tea, that's all. An accident, of course – he never goes near the bastard if he can help it – and for that Brendan took his belt off to him.' She pulled herself out of the comfort of Elsie's arms, and though the marks of tears were still on her face, her eyes were dry and wide and staring. 'D'you hear me, Elsie?' she demanded. 'That child who's little more than a baby was whipped with a belt for spilling a drop of tea.'

That was the first time Brendan used his belt on Kevin, but not the last. Maeve fought for him when she could, but she was often stopped by Brendan's threat: 'Come nearer or lift a hand to help him and I'll beat him senseless.'

Maeve knew he was capable of it, for he truly seemed to detest Kevin and she was forced to watch. She thought of seeking advice at the church, but hesitated to involve the priest, Father Trelawney, who seemed anyway a great buddy of Brendan's. Brendan said it was a father's duty to chastise his son and Maeve was very much afraid the priest might agree.

Just before Kevin began school, Maeve miscarried again and Kevin indirectly caused that as well. Both children had caught measles, but Grace, who'd not been as ill as Kevin, was up and about while Kevin was still very poorly indeed. He lay across the chairs during the day with the curtains drawn to protect his eyes. Maeve used the rent money to pay the doctor's bill and buy the medicine and the meat for nourishing broth to spoon into him.

That day Maeve had Brendan's dinner cooking on the stove when Kevin began to vomit. By the time the nausea had passed and Kevin had lain back exhausted on the pillows and Maeve had wiped his face and given him a drink and taken the bowl to wash, the potatoes had stuck to the pan and the sausages were blackened.

Brendan's rage was terrible. 'But,' Maeve told Elsie later, 'he knew I was pregnant this time. I don't know how, Elsie. He seemed to concentrate on my stomach. Anyway he's got what he wanted, another little baby is lost.'

'Yes,' said Elsie grimly. Brendan seemed to be getting worse, both to Maeve and young Kevin, and Elsie was afraid for them all. She'd heard of women been killed by violent husbands and they were never brought to court for it. There was always some other cause registered on the death certificate. She wished that Maeve could get away somewhere, or else that Brendan could be run down by a tram.

In the dark of the night, Maeve, often hungry, tired and worn out trying to placate Brendan, would wonder about her life. And though she loved her children dearly and felt they were the only good thing to come out of her travesty of a marriage, she longed sometimes to be able to turn the clock back. She wished she could return to the cosy farmhouse where no one threatened another. Her father had never raised his hand to her, or any of her sisters. Annie had always said his hands were too hard and he might hurt them too much. Dear God, Maeve thought, if he only saw me now. He'd murder Brendan for laying a hand on me, let alone wee Kevin.

But Maeve didn't tell them – couldn't tell them. She wrote about the children and how they were and what they were doing, glad her mother could not see their pinched, impoverished faces, their patched, darned and ragged clothes and often bare feet. She told her of the miscarriages, needing sympathy, for Brendan had given her none. The first time he'd been surprised to find her in bed and Elsie in charge of his tea, for he'd not known of Maeve's pregnancy, but he'd said little about it except to tell Maeve it was probably all to the good since the two they had were enough to rear.

Maeve had turned her head away, too miserable to say anything. But the second time, she'd turned on him angrily. 'Are you satisfied now, you bloody brute?' she'd cried. 'Are you going to beat any child I'm expecting out of me? Dear God, Brendan, I hope your conscience is clear enough for you to sleep at night.'

She got a slap for her outburst, but it had been worth it to see how shocked he'd been that she'd actually answered him back.

Her mother, though, sent her back encouraging little letters that made her cry. She wrote as she spoke and the hurt she felt on Maeve's losses was genuine. It was as if she reached across the water to her and Maeve missed her more than ever.

In January 1936, George V died at Sandringham, and it was supposed his eldest son, the popular Edward, would succeed him, though it was rumoured that he was having an affair with a divorcee, Wallis Simpson.

'Can't have her as Queen,' Elsie commented, 'not a divorcee.'

'Why?' Maeve asked. 'It's only the Catholic Church that doesn't recognise divorce.'

'Aye, but he's the head of the Church of England, isn't he, the King?' Elsie said. 'No. Can't have him on the throne and then marry her.'

It seemed Elsie was right, for, as the days passed, there was no news of a coronation. 'I'd not want the crown at the moment anyroad,' Elsie said. 'The world's a dicey place and I think the whole thing's going to blow up in our face. I'd not want to be in the government or the Royal Family just now. I mean, look at them Germans again.'

Maeve nodded. Some dreadful tales were coming out of that country, things they'd done to the Jews that it was hard to believe. 'Warmongers, that's what Germans are,' Elsie said. 'Mark my words there'll be trouble. Why else are they building up their armies and that?'

Maeve couldn't answer her. Just a couple of years before, Hitler had been made Führer of Germany and conscription was brought in. Not the action of a peaceful country, surely?

Brendan said it wouldn't affect them anyway. 'It'll probably come to nothing,' he said. 'Germany was soundly beaten last time. They'll hardly come back for more.'

'What about the things people say they're doing to the Jews?'

Brendan shrugged. 'We're not Jews – what do we care?' he said indifferently. 'Things just as bad have been done to Catholics in the past.'

Maeve knew Brendan was right, but she didn't think that just because atrocities were committed against one group in the past they should be tolerated against another group now. But surely, surely it wouldn't come to war. The First World War was supposed to be the war to end all wars and over ten million had died to make sure it was. No country could want that carnage again; they wouldn't be that stupid.

Even when civil war broke out in Spain in July few Britons were bothered. What was Spain anyway? It was nothing to do with them. France and Britain were right to agree to a policy of nonintervention. But when news came that Hitler's armies and those of Italy under Mussolini were being sent to help Franco, the military dictator, two thousand British people joined the International Brigade on the side of the Republicans and sailed for Spain.

'Bloody fools,' Brendan declared. 'It isn't their fight.'

'Maybe they have a conscience,' Maeve retorted, angry with him because he had given Kevin a sound spanking for dropping a cup and breaking it. 'That's something you don't seem to have.'

Brendan grabbed Maeve's cheeks and squeezed them between his large muscular fingers. 'Watch that lip,' he said, 'or I just might split it open for you.'

'Oh Brendan, leave me alone,' Maeve said wearily, jerking her head away. 'Leave us all alone, please, can't you?'

'Aye, I can,' Brendan said with a humourless laugh. 'But maybe I don't want to.'

And that, thought Maeve, is the truth of it. He enjoys tormenting us.

But the international situation was more unsettling than Brendan's attitude, for wasn't she used to that? She listened to it on the new wireless with its accumulator, which Elsie and Alf had bought themselves, and knew that war clouds were gathering all around them.

Kevin began St Catherine's School the September before his fifth birthday. To Maeve's shame and distress, he had no shoes and his clothes were darned and ragged, but she couldn't even scrape up the coppers to buy better second-hand stuff. She was behind again with the rent and knew if some of the arrears weren't paid off she'd be out in the street.

Kevin wasn't the only barefoot or badly shod child at the school, and in October a man came to see them from the *Birmingham Mail* Christmas Tree Fund. Kevin came home a few days later clutching not only a pair of new boots stamped so they couldn't be pawned, and a pair of socks to go with them, but also a pair of brown corduroy trousers and a navy jumper and shirt. Maeve was glad of the decent warm clothing, but mortified that she was unable to provide them herself, especially when she knew her husband was in full-time work for which he was paid a living wage.

What made it worse were the two hundred men who'd marched from Jarrow in the northeast of England, where unemployment stood at sixty-eight per cent. They were demanding jobs and had marched to London with a petition, but the Prime Minister refused even to see or to speak to them.

Maeve felt she could have accepted her poverty better if Brendan had been unemployed and they'd had to exist on dole money. She'd read somewhere that the average family of husband, wife and two children needed six pounds a week to keep them above the poverty line. She knew many earned much less than that, but she was pretty certain that Brendan earned that much and more, for his job was skilled. But she was lucky if she saw the odd pound of it, and while her husband seemed to have money to do as he pleased, the rest of the family were definitely in poverty.

As the year drew to a close, Edward, the uncrowned King, abdicated. He said he 'found it impossible . . . to discharge my duties as King . . . without the help and support of the woman I love.'

Everyone was shocked at what he had done. 'Love, my arse,' Elsie said angrily. 'What's he playing at? He's the King and that should come first. As my mother would say, love flies out the window when the bills come in the door.'

'Well, that would hardly apply to them, would it, Elsie?' Maeve said with a laugh, amazed that her friend should care so much.

But most people had an opinion on the abdication and she found it was discussed everywhere. But however anyone felt, by 12 December 1936 Britain had a new King – Prince Albert, who would be known as George VI. He'd married a lady called Elizabeth Bowes-Lyon, who would be Queen, and he had two daughters. The elder, Elizabeth, who was then ten years old, was now heir to the throne.

Maeve listened to it all on Elsie's wireless and later read about it in the paper, but all in all she felt nothing in her situation was likely to change, whichever King was on the throne, and she looked forward with little enthusiasm to 1937.

FOUR

'Terrible world to bring kids up in, this,' Elsie said to Maeve one day in the spring of 1938. She was eyeing Maeve's swollen stomach as she spoke, because Maeve was six months gone again and when she'd told Brendan about it she'd borne the marks for almost a week. Still, he'd more or less left her alone after that. This was one at least she hadn't miscarried. And there was nothing to be gained by going on about it. The world was a dangerous enough place with enough to worry about, God alone knew. Elsie often thought it was as if the whole globe was like a tinderbox and ready to go up at any time. 'I mean, bloody civil war still going on in Spain,' she said. 'And that bloody Hitler and Mussolini like bosom buddies and now the Nips attacking the Chinese.'

'Yes, but none of it affects us,' Maeve said, 'not really. I mean, it's all happening miles away.'

'Don't you believe it,' Elsie countered. 'If you ask me, girl, we're teetering on the edge of war.'

Elsie wasn't the only one to think that way. 'Needn't think I'm fighting if it comes to war,' Brendan growled one evening.

No, Maeve longed to say, you'd rather fight women and weans. But she said nothing to him, as she often didn't these days, and carried on making a cup of tea. He'd finished his meal and began slurping at his tea while he read the paper. The children sat together on one of the armchairs watching him.

'I don't know why he insists on them being there,' Maeve complained to Elsie one day. 'I feed them before he comes in and if they're still hungry I try and give them a bite before bedtime, but he insists they have to sit while he fills his face with things they can only dream about. Grace is frightened enough to sit still and say nothing, but Kevin isn't. He'd rather be out in the street playing with the others and he's always fidgeting. One of these days there will be trouble, I can smell it, because although he's scared witless of his father, he hates him for what he does to me and to us all. Sometimes it comes out in his voice when he talks to him and the way he glares at him. The child isn't old enough yet, nor wily enough to hide his feelings.'

Just a couple of weeks after this conversation things came to a head. It was mid-June 1938 and six-year-old Kevin had been playing out in the street with his friends and his little sister when his father came home from work.

'In the house now, Grace, Kevin,' Brendan rapped out. Grace, in her haste to obey him, scurried along the street, down the entry and across the yard. But Kevin, though he acknowledged what his father had said, made no move to follow him straight away.

When he did leave his friends reluctantly and went in, it was to see his father unfastening his belt, and the child's face blanched with fear.

Hoping to distract her husband's attention from Kevin, Maeve hauled herself awkwardly from the chair, her pregnancy hanging heavily on her, and said sharply to the boy, 'Where have you been? You were called in ten minutes ago.'

Kevin looked at her and Maeve was sure he knew what she was trying to do. 'You'll go straight to bed this minute,' she said angrily. 'Maybe then you'll remember to come in when you're called.'

She knew if she could get him away, out of Brendan's sight, he had a chance. Afterwards, she intended to talk to Kevin, as she gave him a little supper after his father had gone to the pub, and tell him never to risk that situation again.

She thought – even Kevin thought – they'd got away with it. Keeping his eyes averted from his father's, for to look at them turned his legs to jelly, Kevin walked across the room and without a word opened the door to the stairs. It was then that he felt the wrench on his collar as he was yanked back into the room with such violence the buttons were torn from his shirt and the back of the material ripped open, and, as Brendan tore the rest of it from his body, Kevin began to shake.

'This young man's got too big for his boots,' Brendan said. 'I say he needs teaching a lesson. What d'you say, Maeve?'

'No!' Maeve had been knocked off balance by Brendan's actions, but she pulled herself away from the wall and cried, 'Don't you dare touch him, Brendan! Don't you bloody dare!'

'Dare! Dare!' While she was still holding Kevin, Brendan grabbed Maeve's arm and bent it up her back so that she cried out with the pain of it.

'Leave him, Brendan, for God's sake,' she pleaded when she could speak. 'He's just a wee boy.'

'Aye, and a wee boy who has to grow up with respect for his father,' Brendan snapped, and he pushed Maeve from him and laid Kevin across his knees.

The boy's anguished eyes met those of Maeve. 'Mom,' he cried, and jumped with pain at the suddenness of the belt on his bare skin.

The belt had come down on Kevin's back once more and his screams were reverberating through the house before Maeve recovered enough to throw herself against Brendan again. This time he was more furious with his wife, but he held on to Kevin tightly, knowing if he let him go he would scurry away. He tried to shrug Maeve off, but she wouldn't be shifted. Instead she lunged forward and raked her fingers down his face. Enraged, he turned round, holding Kevin tight in his arms, and aimed a vicious kick towards Maeve's stomach, and the force of it sent her cannoning into the wall. She banged her head, knocking herself dizzy, and slithered down to a sitting position with her head spinning and such severe shocking pains in her stomach that she doubled over in agony.

She saw that Kevin's back was crisscrossed with stripes, some of which oozed blood. Maeve lay, too stunned and sore to move, and screamed for help, and her screams matched those of her small son.

Maeve was never sure what would have happened that night if Elsie hadn't come in from next door. She ignored her husband's advice to leave well alone and went in unannounced. Afterwards, she described the scene to him. 'The child was beaten black and blue,' she said. 'The man's a maniac and needs to be locked up. Maeve lay there groaning in a corner, and Grace was sobbing too, her hands over her eyes and a puddle at her feet where she'd wet herself with fear.'

Brendan wanted no doctor fetched. They had, he said, no money for doctors. Maeve would be as right as rain after a night's sleep and he was only chastising the boy as it was a father's right.

Elsie thought differently, said so forcibly and dispatched her Alf to fetch the doctor. She filled a kettle with water, put it on to boil and ran up for blankets to wrap around Maeve and her son. She'd reached the bedroom when she remembered Maeve had pawned the blankets and hadn't yet got the money together to redeem them. Instead she grabbed two coats and put one round Maeve's shoulders. She pushed the two armchairs together and put Kevin's limp form down on his stomach and she gently placed the coat over his lacerated body. There was no sign of Brendan, for which she was mighty glad, and she drew Grace, still sobbing, into her arms and tried to soothe her.

Dr Fleming took in the situation at once. On his way to the house he'd passed Brendan Hogan and had seen clearly the man's scratched cheeks, but when he saw Kevin's injuries he was appalled. He examined Maeve and knew she was in premature labour and had to go to hospital. The unborn baby didn't stand a chance of surviving, but if the mother was going to live, she needed hospital care.

Some hours later, Maeve lay in hospital while doctors tried to save the life of her and her baby, who was struggling to be born weeks too early. As the night wore on, despite all their care, Maeve's pains became worse and by the morning she'd given birth to a small, premature and underdeveloped stillborn baby boy. Her scalding tears were of little comfort to her and hate for her husband festered in her soul. She was determined to leave him at the first opportunity. If not for her sake, then for the sake of Kevin because she was suffused with guilt that she'd been unable to prevent Brendan wielding his vicious temper on his young son.

But opportunity wasn't a thing that Maeve had in abundance. For two weeks she lay in hospital while Elsie cared for her children, trying to think of some way out of the dilemma she was in. Elsie had had to keep Kevin away from school for the first week while his back healed, though she thought he might carry the marks for ever. Grace had been sworn to secrecy lest the children be taken away. The doctor had wanted to inform the authorities, but Maeve had begged him not to. She was terrified her children would be taken from her and then she knew she'd have the devil's own job to get them back, and so reluctantly Dr Fleming agreed to say nothing. Brendan, however, was forced to return to his mother's house, for Elsie refused even to boil a kettle for the man she called a drunken bully.

For the fortnight, Maeve plotted and planned, but all her thoughts came to nothing, for she lacked that basic commodity – money. She came out of hospital at the end of June quite desperate and yet no nearer to achieving her objective.

'You can't stay with the man,' Elsie stormed.

'I can't leave him either,' Maeve cried back. 'Where in heaven's name would I go with two children and no job?'

There was only one place, Maeve knew it and Elsie knew it. That was to go across the water to her mother's. 'Surely to God, Maeve, when you tell her how things are, she won't refuse to take you in?'

'No,' Maeve said. 'She'd support me if she only knew the half of it.'

'Well then?'

'Well then nothing, Elsie. How the hell am I to find the money to take us all to Ireland? You know I haven't money to bless myself with.'

'Could you ask your mammy?'

'I could not,' Maeve cried. 'Don't ever think of such a thing. She has six others besides myself, and the youngest still at school.'

And there the matter rested.

But a couple of weeks later, it reared its ugly head again. In the first week of Maeve's release from hospital the doctor had told Brendan quite forcibly that he had to leave Maeve alone and for a good while, and even the priest, Father Trelawney, alerted by the doctor as to Maeve's delicate state of health, told him he must curb his natural desires and show patience.

He showed patience, though his temper was surly and he lashed out at Maeve often, but she could cope with that. It wasn't in the nature of an actual beating. But by the third week of July, three weeks after she'd been released from hospital, Brendan reckoned Maeve had had enough time to get over whatever it was had ailed her, and he began again demanding his rights. Maeve lay passive beneath him and prayed she wouldn't become pregnant again, but she was afraid of inflaming his temper further by refusing.

About this time, Elsie came in one day in a fever of excitement. The two children were out playing when she burst in. 'I've got a job for you,' Elsie said.

'What?' Maeve looked at her in astonishment.

'You heard. A job,' Elsie repeated. 'I've just been in Mountford's and the old man has had a heart attack. It wasn't serious, like – it was in the way of a warning – but the doctor said he had to take life easier for a bit and

Mrs Mountford asked me if I would work a few hours to help her out for a bit, or if I knew of someone trustworthy. I thought of you straight off, for this way you can earn enough to take you to see your mother in Ireland.'

'Elsie, I couldn't,' Maeve said. 'Brendan would never—'

'You don't tell Brendan,' Elsie told her firmly. 'And you certainly don't bloody well ask him.'

'But he'd know,' Maeve insisted, thinking how close and how public Mountford's corner shop was.

'How would he?' Elsie demanded. 'Mrs Mountford told me the hours. Ten to four, Monday to Friday except for Wednesday, when the shop closes at one o'clock, and nine till two on Saturday. You'd manage that, and still be home to cook the sod his tea.'

Maeve knew she would. Brendan left the house at half-past six in the morning and didn't come home till half-six in the evening – that was when he came straight home. On Saturdays he finished work at one and went on to the pub and didn't come home till at least half-past three. But still she hesitated. 'I couldn't, Elsie.'

'Why not? You just tell old George Mountford and his missus, Edith, that you have experience. They'll snap you up.'

'What about the weans?'

'What about them?' Elsie had said. 'You can take them to school in the mornings and I'll collect and mind them in the afternoons till you come in. Saturdays, you leave them in with me.'

'Ah, Elsie . . .' Maeve said. She knew she had a great deal to be grateful for in the older woman and to prevent her getting all tearful about it, asked in a jocular way, 'Are you dying to get rid of me so much?'

'Aye. You've guessed,' Elsie said, but her eyes were moist and she hoped Maeve wouldn't notice, and to prevent her doing just that she said sternly, 'Get yourself down that shop before I put my bloody boot behind you. I'll put the kettle on and we'll have a cup of tea to celebrate your new job when you get back.'

'Don't count your chickens,' Maeve said as she went out the door.

'You'll get it,' Elsie said to her retreating back.

'Sweet Jesus, let her get this job,' she whispered. Jobs were hard to come by and if Maeve didn't get this, there could be a long wait for another and anything might have happened to her by then. Elsie knelt down on the rag rug in front of the firegrate and said a decade of rosary for her and hoped no one would take it in their head to pop in and see her kneeling to pray in the middle of the morning.

Maeve loved working for George and Edith Mountford, and as the months passed, she realised she'd seldom been so happy. Around her people were talking about the war that everyone now knew was imminent, and yet she was feeling very content. Her life was even easier once Kevin passed his seventh birthday in November and took himself and Grace to school and back every day.

The children were looking marginally better than they had. Maeve bought a few nice things for them to eat and some new clothes they desperately needed, though most of her wages were stored in the tin cash box in Elsie's house, to buy the tickets that were to be her and her children's passport to freedom. As part of Maeve's wages, Edith always made up a basket for her on Saturday afternoon and Maeve was surprised by the Mountfords' generosity. She'd had to hide a lot of the produce in the wardrobe in the attic, only bringing out a few things at a time to stack on the shelves. It would never do to arouse Brendan's suspicions.

It surprised Maeve as time went on that no one let on to him that she worked in the corner shop, for everyone knew. She served neighbours in the shop every day and yet no one said a word about it to Brendan.

'Why would they tell your old man?' Elsie asked when she queried it. 'Most of the women don't like him. They know he keeps you short of money and knocks you about. They think you've got guts to put up with it and earn some money to provide for your kids. They won't split on you.'

And they didn't. And Maeve coped, although for the first week or two she found it tiring being on her feet all day and then dealing with the children and cooking a meal when she got home. But she watched the money rise in the cash box and it cheered her. The cash box had been her first purchase and she knew there was no place to hide money in her house. If Brendan even got a sniff there was any to be had, he'd tear the place apart until he found it and have it off her. It had to be left in Elsie's keeping, but Elsie had suggested the cash box with a key, which Maeve must keep.

Maeve had been working at the shop just over a fortnight when Brendan gave her such a beating one night that she was bruised from head to toe the next day. Every movement hurt, but she forced her stiffened limbs into action, for she wasn't missing a day from her job.

Edith Mountford looked at her bruised face and the left eye nearly closed and asked, 'What happened to you?'

'I walked into a door,' Maeve said.

'Some bloody door,' Edith remarked. 'Stick to that story if you want, but both you and I know what manner of door it was. You poor sod.'

The sympathy in her voice brought tears springing to Maeve's eyes, but she brushed them away and Edith said, 'You'd best work in the back for a couple of days till your face settles down a bit. You don't want folks gaping at you.'

Maeve was grateful for the older woman's understanding and she spent the next two days bagging up the flour, tea, sugar, currants and raisins, and doing the accounts and ordering new supplies, the tasks that Edith usually did. By the third day the bruising was more yellow than blue, but Maeve bought cosmetics in the chemist's that she hoped hid much of that, and the puffiness around her eye, and went back into the shop.

Many asked where she'd been, or looked at her rather curiously, but none asked outright what had happened to her face. Edith thought they didn't have to ask, for despite the repair job Maeve had attempted, most of her customers would know she'd had a good hiding. And it was a beating and a half. Edith had seen the bruises covering Maeve's arms when she'd pushed up the sleeves of her overall when she'd been bagging up in the back.

Maeve knew too, and decided in future she'd have to try to protect her face in some way. Edith, kind as she was, couldn't keep her on if she was unfit to serve in the shop.

These thoughts came to her mind the next time Brendan started on her, one night about three weeks later. 'Get up, you lazy sod, and get me a drink,' he growled.

Maeve sighed but that was enough.

'I said get up.' His hand reached for her and she felt the flimsy slip she slept in rip down the middle.

She saw his fist and ducked as she screamed at him, 'Leave me alone!'

Heedless even of the sleeping children in the attic, intent only on protecting herself, she stopped him for an instant with her cry, and she saw the cruel sardonic smile on his mouth. She knew it was useless to try to fight and so she tried threats.

Twisting from his grasp, she left a piece of her slip in his hands and she rolled off the other side of the bed and stood facing him. 'You touch me, Brendan, and I'll shout it from the rooftops,' she yelled at him. 'And I'll go down in the morning to St Catherine's and tell the priest. Do you confess it, I wonder, the times you beat me?'

'You're my wife, you stupid cow. I have the right to chastise you.'

'What right?' Maeve demanded. 'And your family? Do they know what manner of man you are?'

But even as she spoke, she thought they probably did. Brendan's four brothers treated their wives shamefully. Maeve wasn't sure if they knocked them about, but the women were kept as short of money as she was, and she'd seen Brendan's mother, Lily, with a split lip on one occasion and a black eye on another. In a household like that, she doubted they'd turn a hair if she complained to them about Brendan.

'Or I could tell my Uncle Michael,' she said. 'He'd sort you out if he knew the half of it.' But she knew that her uncle would do nothing, even if he believed her.

'You stupid bitch!' Brendan cried, and he leapt over the bed and gave Maeve such a punch that she was knocked off her feet. But she was up again quickly – she had no desire to be kicked senseless – and she tried to protect her face as the blows rained down on her.

Eventually Brendan stopped laying into her and pulled her hands from her face. She smelt the sour, beery stink of him as he yelled at her, 'Now do as you're bloody well told and get me a sodding drink.'

Maeve was glad to go, glad to get away from the man, but as she filled the kettle, she prayed she had enough gas to boil it and still have some for the morning.

But when she returned to the bedroom with the mug of tea in her hand, it was to see that Brendan had fallen on to the bed and now lay flat on top of the covers still in his clothes. His eyes were shut and snores were emanating from his open mouth. Maeve sighed in grateful relief and eased herself into the bed beside him, taking great care not to waken him.

After that night, he left her alone for a while. However, Maeve knew the situation wouldn't last. Brendan was essentially a bully, and a bully he'd remain. So when in the middle of March 1939 she missed a period, she knew the time had come to leave.

First though, Maeve took the children down to the rag market in the Bull Ring and bought them new clothes, for she'd not take them home to her mother in tatters. The clothes she'd bought them when she first started at Mountford's had been decent underwear to replace the ragged pieces they had, but these new things had to be hidden at Elsie's to allay Brendan's suspicions. She also bought them their first sandals and a little grey haversack each to carry their own clothes in.

Even after her purchases there were over twelve pounds in the tin. The train from New Street would cost a guinea altogether for the two children and one pound one and sixpence for Maeve, and the ferry would cost her fifty shillings and half of that amount each for Kevin and Grace.

'It will be over seven pounds,' Elsie said. 'It's a powerful amount of money.'

Maeve knew it was and she had yet to price the rail bus – the last leg of her journey home. But whatever it cost, she would pay it. She'd go home and raise her children – including the child as yet unborn – in dignity and free from fear.

It was hard saying goodbye to the Mountfords, but harder still saying goodbye to Elsie.

'He'll come round here, you know,' Maeve said. 'It'll be the first place he'll make for.'

'I'll just act dumb; it won't be hard for me to do,' and Elsie gave a wry smile.

'He'll know where I've gone,' Maeve said. 'God, he knows I have nowhere else.'

'Will you tell your uncle?'

'Not before I leave. He sees no harm in Brendan. Not that I've told him anything, because his wife, Agnes, is not the understanding type and I didn't want to be running to him with my problems. If I was to tell him now, he'd probably think we'd just had a wee bit of a row and it only needed him to come and have a wee chat with us both and everything would be all right again.'

'He'd do that?' Elsie cried. 'He'd tell him – even if you asked him not to?'

'He might,' Maeve said. 'He might feel it was his duty. Anyway, I'm not going to risk it.'

And she told no one else either. Barely had the door closed behind Brendan the next morning, before she pulled the case from off the top of the wardrobe and began piling her clothes in it.

She shook the children awake. She hadn't dared whisper a word of their escape before in case the children let something slip. Kevin was cranky because he was tired and Grace was still sleepy. But when Maeve told them where they were going, all thoughts of sleep sped from them. She said they were going on a train and a big ship over the water to Ireland to see their other gran, Granny Brannigan.

Then she gave them the haversacks and told them to put all their clothes in them. She then put out some of the new clothes that they hadn't been able to wear yet, the ones she'd kept hidden at Elsie's.

When they were ready to go, Maeve told them of the bag she'd filled for them with nice things to eat. There were sandwiches of jam, cheese and ham, with sausages and hard-boiled eggs that she'd cooked the night before to eat cold, and a swiss roll for afterwards. She had made two bottles of tea for herself, accepted a bottle of dandelion-and-burdock pop for the children from the Mountfords and packed a couple of old cups without handles to drink from.

'When can we start on the picnic?' Kevin had said, his mouth watering at the thought of it.

'We can have some of the sandwiches on the train,' Maeve had told him. 'But not all of them, and no cake and only a little bit of pop.'

'Oh, Mammy.'

'It's no good going on like that,' Maeve had said sharply. 'The food has got to last us a long time. It will take us all day to get home.'

Home! Just to say the word lifted her spirits, and she pushed her small son through the door, laughing gently at his disgruntled face.

There was no one about but Elsie to bid the family farewell. It was that hour in the morning when few women would be around; those husbands still in work would have left and the women would be busy organising their families for the day, and Maeve was glad of it.

She and Elsie clung to one another, though they weren't in the habit of it, and when they drew apart there were tears in both women's eyes.

'Write to me?' Elsie urged, and as Maeve nodded she asked, 'You have let your family know you're coming?'

'Aye,' Maeve said, but she didn't say she'd left sending the letter till the day before. It would arrive that morning and it would be too late for her mother to tell her not to come. She didn't expect a rapturous welcome in the farmhouse in Donegal, for her mother would never countenance a woman leaving her husband. She'd said a novena to the Blessed Virgin that she'd be able to convince her mother that she had a justifiable cause for walking out on Brendan Hogan. Anyway, that was it! She'd burnt her boats now right enough.

She straightened her shoulders, hoisted up her case, bid Elsie goodbye and walked down the street with a child each side of her.

FIVE

The children loved the train, as Maeve knew they would, and they ate their jam sandwiches, washed down with the pop from the cracked cups, almost as soon as they were settled. They were enchanted by the countryside they passed through. Now and again cows stared nervously at them over farm gates and sheep on the hillsides tugged on the grass relentlessly. Maeve told them the names of the animals and of the crops growing that they'd never seen before.

By the time the train reached Liverpool, both children were beginning to tire, but the excitement of going on a ship buoyed them up and the sight of it didn't disappoint them. 'Ulster Prince,' Kevin said, reading out the name on the side. 'Isn't this grand?' And it was grand, though the day had got duller as they travelled north, and rain began to fall as they went on to the gangplank. Maeve hoped it would stop raining soon so that the children could explore the ship without getting soaked. She peered over the rail and looked at the water lapping backwards and forwards as the vessel shifted slightly. It looked grey and scummy, not unlike the water that was left in the copper in the brew house after she'd done the washing.

The ship's hooter sounded, making the children jump, and Kevin watched the frenzied activities on the dockside. 'They're pulling up the gangplank,' he cried, 'and loosening those thick ropes.'

Maeve lifted Grace to look over the rail and the three of them watched the ferry pull away from the shores of England and from Brendan Hogan with relief.

The ferry had gone no distance at all and Liverpool was still a blur on the horizon when Grace began to feel sick. Kevin left his nauseous sister, tended by his mother, who was, he decided, a most peculiar colour herself, and went off to explore the ship.

He was back in just a few minutes. 'Mammy, there's a café here,' he cried, 'like a proper one with pink curtains at the windows and they're selling breakfast. Porridge, toast and jam and a pot of tea for one and six.' He'd watched some of the people eating and his mouth had watered.

Maeve badly wanted to dip into the store of money and give him one and six. It was cheap enough, for Grace was in no state to eat and she herself was trying to ignore the churning of her stomach to deal with her daughter. But, she didn't know how long the money would have to last them.

Regretfully Maeve shook her head. 'I have to watch the pennies.' Kevin didn't argue – hadn't it been the same all the days of his life? – but Maeve saw the disappointment in his eyes. She knew he was hungry. They'd not had much to eat on the train and to make it up to him she gave him a few sandwiches, a couple of cold sausages and a slice of cake. After it, Kevin ran around every bit of the ship that he was allowed in, along with other young boys as eager as he was to see all there was to see.

Maeve and Grace didn't share Kevin's enthusiasm and were glad to get off the heaving rolling ship and on to dry land once more, where Maeve shared out the rest of the food. Grace was very tired from all the travelling and once she'd eaten a little, she laid her head on her mother's knee and went fast asleep. Even Kevin allowed his eyelids to droop. He was becoming calmer the further they went from the house, and even Maeve was more relaxed.

'Lean against me, Kevin, if you're tired,' she said.

'Aren't you tired too?' Kevin asked her.

'No,' said Maeve. 'I'm too excited to sleep.'

She was apprehensive too, though she didn't share that with Kevin, but whatever reception she found at her journey's end, she knew it would be better than the life she'd left behind. Kevin was reassured and allowed himself to sleep, and so deep was his sleep that Maeve had to shake him awake when they got to Portadown.

The conductor on the rail bus they boarded for the last leg of their journey recognised Maeve. 'Well, hello there, Maeve Brannigan.'

'Hogan now,' Maeve corrected him.

'And these are your two?' he said, smiling at the children. 'Home for a wee holiday, are you all?'

'We are that,' Maeve said firmly, before either child was able to say anything else. 'And glad of it.'

'And I would be if I lived in Birmingham,' the conductor said, and added to Maeve, 'I bet your mammy will be pleased to see you. It's strange that she didn't mention you coming.'

'It was a spur-of-the-moment thing,' Maeve explained, and hoped her mammy would indeed be pleased.

In the dim evening light she could just see the green Donegal hills flecked with sheep, and dotted here and there with little thatched cottages that had plumes of smoke rising in the air. She closed her eyes in relief and happiness. She was nearly home. She pointed out the familiar things to the children and they listened eagerly as she described her parents' farm to them as the rail bus ate up the miles.

'Here we are, then,' the conductor said suddenly.

Grace and Kevin looked about them as they alighted. 'We can't be here,' Kevin said, 'because it isn't anywhere.'

Maeve didn't answer him straight away and instead pulled their luggage from the rail bus to lie at a heap at their feet. She'd helped the children on with their haversacks and picked up the case before she said, 'This isn't a proper station like those we passed; really it's not a stop at all, just the place nearest to the farm. We go through the gate and we're nearly there,' and so saying she opened the five-barred gate.

Maeve saw the children looking about them, and led them up the path that ran between two hedges bordering fields on either side. Dusk had fallen and suddenly Maeve felt the children's hands tighten in her own.

'Why isn't anyone here to meet us?' Grace asked, and Maeve could see Kevin's puzzled eyes on her too.

Maeve also wondered that. What if they wouldn't even see her? She told herself firmly to stop frightening the life out of herself and said as confidently as she could, 'I expect they're all busy, and anyway, it's only a step away now.' And then she laughed at the children's fright when two cows put their heads over the hedge and lowed at them.

They came to the corner of the cottage and as they turned into the cobbled yard in front of it there was a sudden terrific noise from a building beside the barn, but Maeve told her bemused children it was just the hens locked up for the night disturbed by their footsteps on the cobbles. The words had barely left her mouth when the farmhouse door suddenly opened and two dogs leapt out of it and around them, snapping and barking. Grace screamed and held tightly to her mother.

'Skip, Laddie,' said a stern voice from the doorway, and Maeve turned to look at the young man framed in the doorway.

'Colin?' she said in wonder and surprise. 'Little Colin?'

'Not so little now,' Colin replied. 'I'm sixteen.'

She'd known he was sixteen, for hadn't her mother written with news of the family? But in her mind Colin was still the wee boy of seven she'd left behind nine years before.

'You'd better come in,' Colin said.

Later the children told Maeve how pretty they thought the house was. It was low and painted white, with little windows all along the side of it and thatched with yellow straw, and grey smoke escaped from the squat chimney. The door was in two halves so you could open the top or the bottom. Both now stood open and Maeve led the children inside.

She had her heart in her mouth as she entered the dim farmhouse. It was just as if she'd never left. There was the press opposite the door containing all the crockery and a food cupboard to the side of it. Two pails of water stood on stools by the side of the bedroom door, while to the other side was the huge kitchen table before one of the windows with wooden chairs arranged around it. The settle and the armchairs were pulled up before the peat fire, and the curtained-off bed that belonged to Maeve's parents was in the far corner.

The only difference was in the group waiting for her. There was no Tom, for he'd been married two years before, and no Liam, away in Dublin, and Kate too was living there, in the nurses' home. Rosemarie was there, but Maeve knew she was engaged to be married, yet she'd been just twelve when Maeve had left home. Colin was still at home, and Nuala, no longer the wee child of just four striking out for independence, but almost a young lady of thirteen.

Her parents hadn't changed. There might have been a few more grey hairs in her mother's head, and more lines on her face and on that of her father, but they'd altered so little compared to the children. And across the room, in the silence that screamed around her, she saw them all staring at her.

Annie Brannigan waited for her daughter to speak, to explain to them why she'd done the disgraceful thing of leaving her husband and coming back home with her children.

Grace and Kevin were weary despite the snatches of sleep they'd had, and both were bone tired of getting on and off trams, trains, ships and rail buses. And now they were here in their mammy's old home and no one seemed to welcome them at all. Maeve saw the wobbling chin of her daughter and the obstinate scowl of her son, and she licked her lips nervously and said in a voice little more than a whisper, 'Hello, Mammy, Daddy.'

'Hello! Is that all you can say after nine years and you descending on us like this, and the only notice a scribe of a letter that arrived this morning telling us so?' Annie asked her daughter angrily.

'I'm sorry,' Maeve said. 'I had to come. There were reasons.'

She saw Grace's face pucker and the tears that had been threatening since she'd entered the farmhouse spilt down her cheeks. She sank to the flagged kitchen floor with a loud sob, crying, 'I don't like it here.'

The sight of the child crying smote Annie's heart. Whatever was wrong it wasn't the children's fault, and she went forward and gathered Grace into her arms. 'And you're Kevin, I suppose?' she said to the boy, who was scowling at her, and without waiting for him to answer went on, 'Take that look off your face, boy, and come away to the fire. If I know weans, a little food won't come amiss and will put a new complexion on the matter altogether.'

After that, it wasn't so bad at all. No one spoke of their unexpected arrival in front of the children. Instead Annie began to prepare a meal for them while Rosemarie and Nuala laid the table and Colin carried the cases and haversacks into the bedrooms.

Maeve saw the children were fascinated by the peat fire that everything was cooked on, the frying pan with the sizzling ham and eggs at the side of it, and the potatoes in a large pot fastened to a hook on a black metal bar that swung out from the wall.

The smell tantalised them all, and Maeve and the children were glad enough to scramble up to the table to eat the fine meal. It was served with butter yellower than the children had ever seen – not that they'd seen much butter at all in their young lives – and slices of bread that Maeve explained was soda bread.

Maeve was grateful to her father for keeping the conversation going around the table that first night. He didn't touch on the reasons for their being there, but instead asked the children questions about their school and friends, and told little stories and anecdotes of his own to put them at their ease. Maeve saw the children start to relax and open up to the kind man she'd always found her father to be. She saw his eyes light on her often and felt comforted, for she knew her father would be understanding and sympathetic when he knew the reason for her flight home.

Much later that night, Maeve sat and talked to her mother. They were alone. The children and young ones, Colin and Nuala, had all gone to bed, and Rosemarie had gone out with her young man, and her father was taking his last walk round the farm with the two dogs, as he was wont to do, checking on the beasts. Maeve had waited until she'd got her mother to herself before she began to explain, and once they were seated before the fire with a cup of tea apiece she began, 'I'm sorry to land on you like this, Mammy, but really I had to come. Brendan is . . . isn't the man I thought he was. I mean not like the man I married.'

'Then he's like many a one, cutie dear,' Annie said. 'How has he changed?'

'Well, Brendan earns good money, but I see little of it,' Maeve burst out. 'Sometimes I have barely enough to feed us. The weans go to bed hungry often. If it weren't for Elsie next door—'

'God, girl!' Annie exclaimed. 'Don't tell me you're telling your business to the neighbours?'

'Mammy, the neighbours would know even if I didn't say a word,' Maeve explained. 'It's not like here. We live on top of one another. The whole street, the whole neighbourhood, knows your business. But Elsie's not like that, anyway. She's a friend and she helps me. God, there's times I don't know where I'd have been without her.'

'Where is your husband in all this?' Annie asked her daughter, tight-lipped.

'My husband? Did you say my husband?' Maeve asked crisply. 'My husband, Mammy, is down at the pub every night, not caring if we go cold and hungry, as long as he has his beer money. Then, when he has his belly full, he comes home and takes it out on me, or wee Kevin.'

'He hits you?' Annie cried, at last incensed on her daughter's behalf.

'Aye, sometimes he just hits me. I can cope with that. It's when he really lays into me so my body is bruised everywhere and my face a swollen mess, with my eyes blackened and my lips split, that's what I find hard to bear.'

Annie's mouth had dropped open in shock as Maeve spoke, and when she'd finished she still stared at her, while her lips formed words, but no sound came out.

'I'm sorry, Mammy, for blurting it out like that,' Maeve said. 'But it's how it is often when he has the drink in him. But other times he can be sober, or nearly sober, and yet he takes his belt off to Kevin.'

'No!' Annie cried. The rearing of her children had in the main been left to her, although there had been occasions when Thomas had sometimes seen fit to discipline his sons for some serious misdemeanour. He'd used nothing but the flat of his hand across their backsides and they'd grown up with respect for him because of it. But a belt on a wee boy . . .!

'You'll see the marks yet across his back,' Maeve said. 'Brendan's been at him since the child was three years old. I get in between them and then I catch it. I think,' Maeve went on, 'he resents the weans and especially Kevin. Every time I tell him I'm pregnant, I know I'm for it.'

'Oh, Maeve, why didn't you tell us sooner?'

'After I'd made such a fuss to marry Brendan, I didn't want to admit I'd made a mistake and I didn't want to worry you. What in God's name could you do?'

'What about your Uncle Michael?' Annie asked. 'My heart was easier about you because he was there.'

'Well, he's not so near really,' Maeve said. 'It's not like Ballyglen in Birmingham, you know, where everyone in the town is just a stop away from one another. It's a tidy walk, but I do go and see him now and again. But his wife, Agnes, isn't so terribly welcoming.'

'What d'you mean?'

'Mammy, Michael hasn't got the fine house he'd have us believe. It's just a back-to-back like my own, though it's better furnished. Also, he has a job and a good one, but before this talk of war he was put on short time – three days a week, and some weeks only two. They were suffering themselves and very glad of the money and food you sent.'

Annie could scarcely believe what she was hearing. All the time Maeve had been in England, she'd comforted herself with the fact that she was being looked after by her uncle, who had a good job, a sizeable house and plenty of money to help his niece should she fall on hard times. 'Why didn't you tell me this?'

Maeve shrugged. 'It was Michael's tale to tell,' she said. 'Anyway, even if Uncle Michael had been better off it would hardly have mattered.' Maeve hated bad-mouthing Michael to her mother, the baby brother she had always loved, but she felt Annie had to know how it was.

'It would be no good complaining to him about Brendan. He likes him, Mammy. Brendan is a man's man. When Michael told you he was a fine figure of a man, he told the truth as he saw it. He still feels that. And, even if he

79

should want to help, Aunt Agnes wouldn't let him, for he does what she wants him to.'

'Does Agnes not like him helping his family?'

'No, she doesn't,' Maeve said. 'Her family live all around her and she sees them all the time, but she didn't want Uncle Michael's coming over from Ireland and making demands on him.'

'Is he still on this short-time work?'

'No,' Maeve said. 'Everyone's fully employed now, with war looming. Uncle Michael's even got overtime, more than he needs, really, in the foundry. His children, Jane and Billy, are both working too, both in munitions factories. There's plenty of work for everyone now and plenty of money. Even Aunt Agnes is thinking of getting a job.'

'Aunt Agnes?'

'It's not so shocking over there, Mammy, to see women working,' Maeve told her mother. 'Agnes says they'll need the women if the men get called up, as they're sure to like they did in the last war. I got a job in a shop and that's how I scraped the money up to come here, and kit the weans out with decent things.'

'I wondered how you managed it,' Annie said. 'I mean, with Brendan keeping you so short I know you couldn't have saved it out of the housekeeping.'

'God, no. It's bad enough to try and find the money to keep body and soul alive on what he hands over, and he would have it back off me if I didn't take it to the shops that very day. Mind, all it does is pay off the tick, for the things I've had in the week.'

Annie shook her head to think of her daughter suffering this way when they had plenty to eat for every meal. 'And not a word about a job in your letters?'

'I couldn't risk telling you, and you letting Michael know, and have him say something to Brendan.'

'Surely the neighbours knew?' Annie said. 'You said they knew everyone's business.'

'Oh yes, they knew,' Maeve said. 'At least the women did. I served them. But they knew the life I was leading. They knew the way the weans lived and knew they got little enough to eat. The women probably thought good luck to me if I managed to earn something to feed them properly. Anyway, whatever they thought, no one whispered a word of it.'

'And what made you decide to come home in the end?' Annie said.

Maeve was quiet for a moment and then she said, 'At first, at the very beginning, I used to get the feeling that somehow I deserved what was happening to me. That I must have done something wrong, or Brendan wouldn't have been so angry with me. I never felt that way, though, when he was hitting Kevin. Then I just felt angry, but for myself . . . Elsie said I was a fool, and that he'd kill me in the end, but I was so scared of him by then, I couldn't think straight.'

'Oh, my dear girl.'

Maeve hadn't been aware she was crying until her mother spoke. She scrubbed at her eyes impatiently and went on, 'It's all right, Mammy. I'm fine now. Let me tell you everything before Daddy is back, and you can then let him know what you see fit. You see, it was the first miscarriage when I realised I truly hated and despised the man I'd once loved so much. I felt sad about it too; it felt like a failure. I'd imagined Brendan and I would have such a rosy future ahead of us.

'Before we married and even in the first few months while we lived above the café and before I fell pregnant with Kevin, we were happy. So when he lashed out at me at first, I felt that in some way I deserved it. It seems crazy now, Mammy, but I hadn't realised anyone could change so much. And then he was always so sorry in the beginning. He always begged me to forgive him and promised it wouldn't happen again. It was when I became pregnant with Grace that I had the first bad beating from him and after that, he never bothered to apologise any more.'

She looked up at her mother and saw that her mother's eyes were brimming with tears. 'You must think I was stupid, Mammy.'

'God love you, not at all, at all,' Annie told Maeve, her voice husky with emotion and she clasped one of her daughter's hands in her own and held it tight. 'Go on, pet.'

Maeve sighed. 'After that, Mammy, I knew I'd married a bully and that was going to be the pattern of my life from then on, and fear had sort of taken over from love. But God, Mammy, when I lost the first baby – you mind, I wrote and told you about the two miscarriages early on?'

'Aye. I was heartsore for you, so I was.'

'Mammy, I lost those babies after a good hiding from Brendan,' Maeve said. 'I wasn't eating properly either because there was so little food in the house. The first time he hadn't known I was pregnant and I lay in bed, knowing there was no longer a baby growing inside me and I felt useless. I could do nothing about my own life and couldn't even protect my unborn child. I not only feared Brendan, but I also realised I hated him.

'Then I lost another at three months, in much the same way as the first, but this time Brendan knew I was pregnant and concentrated his attack on my stomach and seemed almost satisfied when I miscarried. The last one I lost because of a vicious kick in the stomach that I got from trying to protect Kevin. Then, with me out of action, because he'd nearly knocked me senseless – I still have the scars from the hobnails on my stomach – he really took it out of the child. He beat him black and blue. I think he might have beaten him to death that night if Elsie hadn't come in. She got the doctor in and he sent for an ambulance for me.'

'God, child, this is terrible,' Annie said, greatly distressed. 'And for you to tell not a soul . . .'

'I was ashamed,' Maeve said. 'I don't know what of, either. It wasn't me should have been ashamed. When the doctors asked me about the boot-shaped bruise on my stomach, I told them I'd fallen over the fireguard. They didn't believe me, but I stuck to my story. Then, when I missed my period again this month, I knew I had to get away. Can we stay, Mammy, till I get myself sorted out?'

Maeve saw her mother was moved by what she'd told her, but she also knew her mother didn't really want her there. You married for better or worse, richer or poorer, and that was how some would see it, regardless of what the woman had to endure. Her mother wouldn't turn her away, Maeve knew that, but in the same circumstances many would, and would tell Annie so. By receiving her daughter, Maeve knew Annie would lose face in the small community and that mattered to her.

But Maeve knew she mattered more. She'd always been assured of her mother's love and support, and she knew she'd not turn her back on her or the children.

And Annie could not, after all she'd heard, refuse them a place of refuge. She'd seen the lines of suffering on her daughter's white, gaunt face, and had been shocked by the sight of her grandchildren, pitifully thin and pasty-faced, and knew whatever it cost, they were welcome in her home.

She held out her arms and cradled Maeve as she hadn't done since she was a child. 'Why, child, of course you can stay here and for as long as you like,' she said. 'Where else would you come but home? And as for your father and the others, leave them to me. I'll tell them what I think fit.'

Tears of gratitude ran down Maeve's cheeks and she held her mother tight. Years later she could still remember the comfort her mother's arms and words had been.

SIX

It was just as her mother said it would be. The family all accepted her. Only her father spoke of it. 'I'm sorry for your trouble, Maeve,' he said, 'but you're home now and you're safe.'

'Thanks, Daddy,' Maeve said, and her eyes filled with tears at his words. She wondered that she hadn't come home sooner, but then she hadn't the wherewithal before, that was why. But her conscience troubled her because she had two children with her and was expecting another. She couldn't expect her parents to keep them and she decided she'd look round for a job to provide for them herself.

But when she spoke to her mother about it Annie had been adamant that if Maeve was determined to look for a job then she wasn't to do so until after the baby was born. 'You're not fit for anything, the state you're in,' she said. 'You're skin and bone. You need feeding up and making healthy.'

Her father said more: 'I'll not have a pregnant daughter of mine go out to work, as if I hadn't the means to keep her. When I need help to feed and clothe my own flesh and blood I'll let you know.'

Maeve didn't pursue the issue. The shock of what she'd done had got to her anyway, and she was worn out with it all. A peculiar lassitude seemed to affect her those first few days at the cottage as she was expected to do so little.

Elsie's letter jolted her back into life and reminded her that Brendan was only half a day's journey away. Elsie told Maeve that Brendan had been round to her house the first evening, as they'd thought he would, demanding to know where his wife and children were, but Elsie said she'd acted dumb and said she had no idea.

He didn't believe me, of course, and if Alf hadn't been by my side I wouldn't have fancied my chances with him. He was that mad, he was shaking with it, and his face was nearly purple. I tell you the truth, Maeve, if you'd walked down the road at that minute, he would surely have killed you. Anyroad, he left me and went round a few of the other neighbours, but of course no one knew anything – you were right to keep it all to yourself. He went out, to the pub I suppose or else your uncle's place. Anyroad, I didn't see him come home again that night. I haven't seen him since either. Trudy Gaskins, her that lives up the entry, said he's moved into his mother's place on the Pershore Road. She was up there the other night, because her daughter lives in the same road, and was on her time. She was with her all night and the next morning as she was getting ready to go home, she saw Brendan leaving his mother's door.

The day after Elsie's letter two more arrived for Maeve. One was from a confused Michael O'Toole. He said he presumed Maeve had run home and couldn't understand why she'd done it, and Brendan, who'd been to his door, was just as confused as he was. The second letter, ill-written and ill-spelt, was from Brendan, demanding Maeve's return. He reminded her she was his wife and therefore had a duty to him. Maeve barely finished the letter before she crumpled it in a ball and threw it into the fire.

She hoped any complaint and demands he was going to make would be confined to letters, for those she could handle. She'd had nightmares at first that he'd come straight after her, bawling and shouting, and was relieved as the second week drew to a close that that didn't happen. She was beginning slowly to relax.

Not willing to tell the neighbours the whole tale of Maeve and her children fleeing from a drunken brutal husband and father, the Brannigans said the little family were on a wee holiday as the weans had been ill. No one doubted that when they looked at their pinched faces and, as it was just two weeks to the Easter holidays, the story was easy enough to believe. Coming away from Mass the first Sunday, Maeve was greeted by Father O'Brien. He hadn't seen Maeve in years, but when he looked at the children's stick-like arms and legs and the city pallor on their faces he thought it was a good job indeed that she'd brought them home for a wee while.

'Come to get some fresh air in your lungs and some good food in your stomachs, have you?' he asked them heartily.

The children regarded the priest gravely. They were used to priests and the strange way they had about them, and knew the best and easiest practice was always to agree. 'Yes, Father,' they said in unison.

The priest said a similar thing the next week and the children made a similar response. By then, most of the parish knew Maeve was home and not before time, most said, by the look of them all. She was welcomed by women of her own age she'd been at school with and scores of neighbours and friends she'd known for years. Many asked her up for an afternoon or evening, but she always made excuses not to go. She didn't want to be asked any searching questions about her absent husband, or life back in Birmingham.

She was not unhappy. She was at peace and wanted nothing more than that.

The Easter holidays began and the days slid pleasantly one into another. The children followed their grandfather round the farm as he showed them the things growing in the ground, or lifted them up for rides on the tractor.

No animals frightened them now, not the barking boisterous dogs, nor the clucking hens, not even the strutting rooster, nor smelly pig and certainly not the cows that had startled them the first night. They thought their mournful brown eyes looked sad or wise or both, and when the cows stuck their heads over the fence to be stroked their fur felt like velvet and both children loved them.

All in all they were delighted with the place, which was as different from their own home as anything could possibly be. Also, for the first time, they enjoyed their lives free of stress and fear. Their faces had lost the wary look they'd had on arrival and Maeve marvelled at the difference in them after only a few weeks and knew she'd made the right decision to bring them home to Ireland.

The Wednesday before Easter, in Holy Week, Maeve went to confession one evening. It would be her second time, for she'd been to confession the first week she'd arrived, but she always went before Easter like all good Catholics.

She went through the usual litany of sins, feelings and expressing anger, small acts of spitefulness, the odd swearword or blasphemy, impatience, forgetting prayers, letting her attention slip at Mass and the odd impure thought that entered her mind.

When she finished, there was silence the other side of the grille and then the priest, his voice as cold as steel, said, 'Go on, my child.'

'I . . . I can't think of any more sins, Father.'

'Maeve, I'm ashamed of you,' the priest said sternly. 'You have shattered the sacrament of marriage in which God has joined you to Brendan Hogan for life. Yet you chose to walk out on him, depriving him of his wife and children. Don't you think that is something to repent of and ask forgiveness for?'

Maeve was stunned. She wondered for a moment how he knew, but Father O'Brien then enlightened her without her having to ask. 'Just this morning I received a most distressing letter from a Father Trelawney, whom I believe is the parish priest at St Catherine's where you both attend.'

Maeve wasn't even surprised. She might have known Brendan would go scurrying to his parish priest to enlist his help. He'd probably been urged on by his family, his domineering father and insignificant mother. 'See the priest, son. See if he can bring her to her senses.'

Maeve always thought Father Trelawney was Brendan's partner in crime, for whether it was beating her and Kevin black and blue, or spending every penny in the house on drink, leaving them cold and hungry, Father Trelawney wiped it out in confession. Brendan would return from church smug and certain that his soul was as white as the driven snow and begin his nefarious practices all over again. Well, as far as she was concerned they could all jump in the river. She was not going back to that life.

She swallowed hard and spoke firmly in an effort to explain to the priest. 'Father, I—'

'If you do not go back, Maeve,' the priest said, cutting off Maeve's attempt at explanation before she'd even begun, 'I can give you no absolution from your sins. You are committing a mortal sin and if you have no intention of returning to your rightful place beside your husband, God cannot forgive you. You will have to live in a state of sin.'

Maeve stumbled from the box, shocked to the core. She needed confession to feel cleansed from all her wrongdoings in order to be in a state of grace to receive Communion. Now she wouldn't dare to go up to the altar. For one thing, her conscience wouldn't let her and for another she'd be terrified Father O'Brien would refuse her the Sacraments and make a show of her.

At home she hid her distress until the children had gone to bed and then sobbed in her mother's arms. For twenty-seven years she'd been a good Catholic girl, attending Mass on Sundays and going to Devotions and Benediction often, and always going regularly to the Mission when priests travelled around Ireland preaching in the churches. She went to confession every fortnight and took Communion every Sunday and prayed as often as she remembered. The Church and its rituals were part of her life and now she'd been refused absolution because she wouldn't return to a violent sadistic man who terrorised her and her children and didn't give them enough money to live on. Yet she felt as if she'd lost a limb, as if she'd been cast adrift, and though she was glad of her mother's comforting arms, they could not solve the problem. She knew that she'd not heard the end of it.

After Maeve's experience, none of the rest of the family went to confession either, and for the first time ever, Annie didn't attend the Stations of the Cross on Good Friday.

And though they all went to Mass on Easter Sunday morning, no one went to Communion. Most of the congregation took Communion and they looked askance at Annie sitting with her daughters and grandchildren – Thomas and Colin had gone to early Mass – and wondered why they were not going to the altar.

Kevin and Grace were blissfully unaware of any dissension in the family, for nothing was discussed in front of them. By Easter Sunday they'd had a wonderful week with their Uncle Colin and Aunt Nuala, who spent a lot of time with their young relations whenever their chores on the farm enabled them to.

That Sunday Maeve's children didn't notice that the family scurried from the church without talking to any friends as they normally did, and they certainly didn't care. Their grandma had killed two chickens as it was a special day and a good dinner awaited them with pudding, as Lent was now over, and then they had the bar of chocolate each that Rosemarie had bought from the town for them to eat. They'd just discovered chocolate, which they'd never tasted before – not that they'd had much of it now either, for neither their grandma nor their mother approved of their eating too many sweet things, but both Kevin and Grace loved chocolate. They liked it to melt in their mouths and run down their throats, and to have a whole bar each was sheer luxury.

The Wednesday after Easter, Maeve was by the window when she spotted Father O'Brien striding purposefully down the lane and she felt her insides contract with fear. Annie was stirring a pot hung over the fire and hadn't seen him approach and she was glad they were alone, her father having taken the children, together with Nuala and Colin, in the cart to the peat bogs to cut turf.

'Mammy,' Maeve said, 'the priest's here.'

Annie straightened up, and her eyes met those of her daughter. The priest gave a tentative knock and lifted the latch as Annie cried, 'Come away in, Father.'

The priest seemed to fill the room. 'Will I take your coat?' Annie said. 'And will you be having a cup of tea?'

Father O'Brien didn't take his eyes from Maeve and she met them boldly, but he divested himself of his coat and said, 'A cup of tea would be very nice, so it would. Shall we sit down, Maeve?'

Maeve's legs were shaking and the top of her mouth was suddenly dry. She told herself she was a grown woman and this man before her couldn't make her do anything; he could hardly pick her up bodily and take her back to Birmingham. And yet she knew it was a mistake to under-estimate a priest's power.

He waited till Maeve was sitting opposite him, the kettle singing over the glowing peat and Annie busy at the dresser sorting out the best cup and saucer for the priest, and then he looked Maeve full in the face.

'Well, Maeve,' he said.

'Well what, Father?'

'Have you no idea why I felt it necessary to come out here and visit you?'

'Suppose you tell me?' Dear God, Maeve thought. What was the matter with her, answering the priest like that?

He didn't like it; she saw a frown furrow his brow and his eyebrows jerked up in surprise. 'Now, Maeve,' he said, 'there is no need for you to be like this. I told you of the letter I received from your parish priest. Last night I had a most disturbing call from the man.'

Maeve didn't reply and so the priest went on, 'Maeve, surely I do not have to remind you of your marriage vows?'

'No, Father. You have to remind me of nothing.'

'Father Trelawney said your husband is distraught, and with good reason, I'd say by your attitude.'

'My attitude!' Maeve cried. 'I'm sorry, Father, but you know nothing about it. It's Brendan's attitude needs to be sorted out.' Annie came bustling towards them then for the kettle was boiling noisily. She made a cup of tea for all of them, while Father O'Brien shook his head as he said, 'Father Trelawney tells me there were a few problems in your marriage, but that your husband is willing to meet you halfway.'

'A few problems! Is that what they call it these days?' Maeve said with a sneer. 'My husband, Father, drinks nearly every penny he earns, keeping me and the children short, and apart from that he is a vicious bully, both to me and my son.'

'Father Trelawney mentioned that you make trouble whenever your husband has seen fit to discipline the boy.'

'Discipline him? Using his belt on a wee boy, who even now is only just seven years old.'

'Boys, even wee boys, can be very bold. We both know that, Maeve,' Father O'Brien said. 'And, you know, it is a father's duty to chastise his children.'

Maeve shook her head in disbelief. What Brendan had done was not mere chastisement, but how could she make the man before her believe how it really was? 'All right then, Father. Let's leave Kevin for the moment. Is it a husband's duty to chastise his wife too?'

'It's a husband's duty to demand obedience from his wife. You promised to love, honour and obey him, you know.'

'I know what I said,' Maeve barked. 'And I was a fool, for the man is brutal. I have been bruised head to toe by my husband and my face has been such a mess, I've had to hide from my neighbours till the swelling has gone down and the black eye's not so noticeable. As for my son, he still has the stripes across his back from his father's attempts at disciplining him.'

'Your husband told Father Trelawney you are argumentative and undermine his treatment of the children. In other words, you provoke him.'

'Oh, so now it's my fault?'

'Not at all,' Father O'Brien said. 'Don't be so hasty, Maeve.' Annie had remained in the other chair during this time, completely silent. She saw her daughter become agitated and though she knew she had a point in everything she said, she was shocked to see Maeve attacking the parish priest in such a fashion. In order to give Maeve time to compose herself, she said, 'Would you like another cup of tea, Father?'

The priest handed the cup across to Annie. 'That would be lovely, thank you,' he said, and then he directed himself again to Maeve. 'Perhaps that is one of the problems here.'

'What is?'

'Your hot-headedness,' Father O'Brien said.

'My hot-headedness, Father, is because you want me to return to a brutal bully and I won't. You don't seem to have listened to a word I've said as to why I won't go back to him.'

'I have listened, Maeve,' Father O'Brien chided. 'I have also said your husband is so upset by your flight over here he has promised to change.'

'Oh yes,' Maeve said sarcastically. 'I bet.'

'Maeve, you're not being very helpful.'

'No, Father, I'm not, am I? That will probably be another black mark against me, won't it?'

Father O'Brien tutted in impatience. Maeve saw he was controlling his anger with difficulty. Without another word, he drained the cup of tea Annie had handed him and got to his feet before he looked at Maeve again. 'Is that your last word on the subject?'

'It is, Father.'

'Then, child, I'll pray for you.'

'Thank you. I'm probably in need of prayer.'

'Don't mock, Maeve. It doesn't become you,' Father O'Brien said sternly.

'Who's mocking, Father?' Maeve asked innocently. 'I don't know one soul in the land who would not value prayer.'

Again he tutted in annoyance. Annie had run before him to retrieve his coat and as he took it from her he said, 'And what is your view on this, Annie? Are you prepared to harbour Maeve and her children, although she is a married woman?'

Annie shrugged. 'She's my daughter, Father,' she said.

A little later they stood at the window and watched the priest stride angrily up the path.

Annie said, 'This won't be the end of it, lass. It's just the beginning.'

'I know, Mammy,' Maeve said with a sigh.

There was talk in the village when Maeve went to enrol her children in the village school after the Easter holidays. The headmaster, Mr Monahan, expressed surprise, and Maeve admitted that there were some problems at home that she needed time alone to sort out and she thought it better the children missed as little schooling as possible.

Mr Monahan was impressed with the young woman before him, softly spoken but with a decided lift to her chin. He remembered the cowed skinny children she'd arrived with and now saw them sitting each side of their mother definitely much improved even after a few short weeks.

He wondered what the problem was at home and hoped it wasn't serious, but taking the children into school could only benefit them even if it were for just a short time. He'd had to mention it to Father O'Brien, but he couldn't foresee any opposition there and he smiled at the children and welcomed them to the school.

They'd been there about ten days when Maeve received a letter from Father Trelawney. In it he expressed Brendan's regret for the way things had turned out. Father Trelawney said he was truly sorry and he promised things would be different if she returned. Maeve passed it over to her mother to read and when Annie gave it back to her she screwed it into a ball and threw it on the fire.

'You don't think he might change?' Annie said. 'You've given him a shock, leaving him – mightn't that bring him to his senses?'

Maeve shook her head. 'He was always sorry when he hit me at first,' she said. 'That didn't last, though. No, Mammy. I can't risk it. Not for me and the child I'm carrying, nor for Kevin and Grace. Do you want me to go? Are you worried that I've broken my marriage vows?'

'All I want is for you to be happy, child,' Annie said. 'And I'll abide by your decision.'

'I wonder what the priest would feel if he'd seen the mess Brendan has left me in after a particularly bad beating,' Maeve said bitterly. 'Or caught sight of the weals on Kevin's back. God, Mammy, I can't go back to that.'

'Calm yourself, child. Sure, no one's forcing you to.'

'Father O'Brien is having a damn good try and now the priest from St Catherine's has joined in.'

'Sure, isn't that their job?' Annie said placatingly. 'Are you going to write back to the man?'

'No, I'm not.'

'Is that wise, pet?' Annie said. 'Tell him how brutal Brendan is to you. Tell your side of the story.'

'It's too late for that, Mammy,' Maeve said resignedly. 'He and Brendan are great friends. Sure Brendan has got in with his excuses and he'll never believe different. I never went to him for help while I was there. Why should he believe anything I say now?'

Annie wasn't sure whether ignoring the letter was a wise course of action or not. But the decision had to be Maeve's and she said nothing more on the subject.

Just over a week later Maeve got a letter asking her to call at the school to discuss Kevin's progress.

'What have you done?' she asked her son that evening.

'Me? Nothing,' Kevin said. 'Why?'

'The headmaster wants to see me and whatever it is, it's about you.'

But Kevin couldn't enlighten her and Maeve saw no expression of guilt on his face as he said, 'I don't know, Mammy.'

Despite that, Maeve was sure Kevin was lying. She was sure Mr Monahan would tell Maeve about his misbehaviour in the classroom, his pranks in the playground, or his lack of progress in his studies. As she sat in the headmaster's stuffy little room, two days later, she was totally unprepared for what he did say.

'Remove him from the Communion classes?' she repeated. 'But why? I know he's not been here long, but he'd been doing the classes at St Catherine's in Birmingham since January. He knows most of the catechism. We test him on it in the evenings.'

The headmaster coughed nervously. He hated saying what he had to say and Maeve could see he did. She'd sensed his sympathy for her and Kevin too, but knew it would be Father O'Brien's doing. She saw it as clearly as if he were standing before her pontificating. He'd say the sins of the fathers are visited on the children as the Good Book said, even to the third and fourth generation. He'd remind Mr Monahan where his duty lay, and that wasn't welcoming to the Communion rails for the first time the son of a wife who'd upped and left her husband. He'd be sure Mr Monahan could explain that adequately to Maeve Hogan. That was, of course, if he wanted to keep his job.

Mr Monahan faced Mrs Hogan and coughed nervously. 'Mrs Hogan, it's more to do with influence in the home. Father O'Brien thinks that Kevin might not be picking up the right example. Maybe it would be better to wait for a year or so, when his future is more settled.'

Maeve felt her face burning with embarrassment at the same time as furious anger filled her being. She stared at the middle-aged man before her and knew he was just Father O'Brien's lackey. 'Do I have a choice in this?' she asked in clipped precise tones. 'Or has Father O'Brien already decided and his decision is final?'

'I . . . I could ask him for you,' the headmaster said.

'Don't worry,' Maeve said. 'I'll ask him myself.'

She swung out of the headmaster's office, her blue eyes smouldering and her cheeks red, and out into the church, where she found Father O'Brien in one of the pews reading his Office – the prayer book priests had to read every day. Even in her rage, she noted thankfully that the church was deserted. Early Mass was over, and no one was doing the flowers for the altar, or cleaning the place. The priest turned at her arrival and laid the book down in the pew beside him, and Maeve glared at him across the expanse of the church as she strode angrily towards him.

'How low can you sink?' she demanded.

The priest's brown eyes looked puzzled, but his mouth had a sardonic smile playing around it as he said, 'I beg your pardon?'

'You know full well what I'm talking about. I've just come from the school.'

'Oh, I see,' Father O'Brien said.

'What right had you to take out your spite against my son? It's me you're angry with, not him.'

'I assure you, I did not take the decision over spite against anyone,' Father O'Brien said. 'I am not angry with you either, more disappointed. You were always head-strong, Maeve, even as a wee girl, but I never expected you to do anything like this.'

Maeve ignored the things the priest said about her. In her opinion she was here to discuss just one issue. 'Mr Monahan said Kevin is to be removed from the First Communion class and it was at your suggestion.'

'He is correct.'

'What right have you?'

'I have all manner of rights, Maeve,' the priest said. 'But what right had you to uproot your children from their home and their father and bring them over here to Ireland, and once here, you refuse to either discuss it or consider returning? You are damaging your children.'

'I am not,' Maeve protested. 'I'm their mother and I'm doing what I think is best for them.'

'Ah, yes. I'm glad we've got to that point,' the priest said. 'Where is their father in all this?'

'Their father is—'

'Does he have no rights?'

'No. No, he bloody well doesn't,' Maeve cried. Her rage had reached boiling point and she could see sparks in front of her eyes. 'He has thrown them away. Do you know, you arrogant sod, that the bastard you want me to return to has killed, by his own brutality, a child I had carried for six months and one of the reasons I left this time was to protect the one I'm carrying now?'

'I know that is what you would like people to believe,' the priest said.

'What the hell do you mean?'

'I mean, your husband told Father Trelawney all about it. It appeared to be a tragic accident,' the priest said. 'Your husband admits he pushed you. He was administering punishment to young Kevin for not coming in when he was called, and what father wouldn't? He said you were like a wild animal, screaming and trying to rake his face with your nails and kick his legs. He pushed you and you fell against the fireguard. Next minute, you were on the floor groaning.'

Maeve stared at him open-mouthed. That wasn't how it was, but it was what the priest believed and from what he said, Father Trelawney did too. Whatever she said now, they wouldn't believe her.

Father O'Brien went on, 'And you must understand, I have no desire to punish your children, either of them, but the consequences of your actions will have to have far-reaching effects on your family – all of your family.'

It was uttered like a threat and Maeve shivered. She was filled with loathing for the plump self-satisfied priest with eyes full of condemnation and the pinched-in nostrils and hard cruel mouth. She wanted to put her hands over her head and scream in frustration, and her voice indeed rose in a scream as she cried out, 'You sadistic bastard, you're bloody well enjoying all this.'

The door of the church swung closed with a dull thud and the two combatants turned. Cissie O'Brien was the priest's sister. She looked after his house for him and had come to tell him his dinner was nearly ready. She glared at Maeve malevolently and Maeve knew she thought her circumstances of arriving at her mother's house with two children and no husband was very suspicious. Maeve had played into her hands for she knew she'd have heard clearly the abuse and swearwords she'd hurled at the priest even before she'd opened the door because Maeve's voice had bordered on hysterical.

Maeve looked at the older woman's eyes glittering with malicious dislike and knew she'd blown it. The rumours about them all had begun when she started the children at school and now she knew what she screamed at the priest would be all over the neighbourhood in twenty-four hours. Everyone would know that she hadn't brought the children for a wee holiday because they'd been ill at all, but that she'd actually left her husband. Cissie O'Brien would say her brother, the priest, had taken her to task about it, which after all was his job, and what a reaction he got. Maeve knew Cissie O'Brien would let people know what type of woman Maeve Hogan was and would take pleasure in doing it.

SEVEN

The following day, Kevin came home from school in tears. He'd held them in all day at school and most of the way home, but when he turned in the lane home, he broke down.

'Miss Kerrigan says I'm not to go into instruction for Holy Communion any more,' he explained between sobs to his mother. 'She says maybe I'll take it next year instead, but Declan and Martin are my age and taking it in July. Now everyone laughs at me in the playground and says I'm dumb and don't know my catechism, but I do.'

Maeve held her small angry son and could find no words to comfort him. At Mass the following Sunday, the Brannigans were all snubbed by friends and neighbours they'd known for years. Added to that, the brothers at Colin's school had made a few snide remarks about his family, and the lads had jeered at him a bit, and Nuala claimed she was almost ignored in the school yard.

Rosemarie said the bakery was busier than ever, but people didn't buy much, they just wanted to stand in groups and talk loudly, so that she would hear, about the Brannigan family they said had always thought themselves better than anyone else. Her future mother-in-law, a cow of the first order anyway, had expressed doubts about her Greg getting mixed up with such a family after the eldest of them had just upped and left her husband in that shocking way, and had Greg heard what she'd said to the priest? Maeve felt sick. She had brought all this on her family.

'Never mind, child,' Thomas told his daughter. 'They're ignorant. It'll blow over.'

But for Kevin and Grace, it didn't blow over. Grace said nothing about the girls who'd once been her friends, who now refused to play with her and who stood with others in clusters and taunted her, but she became quieter than ever.

Kevin, on the other hand, could not hide his skirmishes – like the time he came home with his knuckles skinned and a split lip, nor the time he had a bloody nose and a torn shirt, nor the marks of the cane across his hand.

'What did you get the cane for?' Maeve asked him.

'Fighting.'

'What's the matter with you?' she cried. 'All this fighting. You never used to fight.'

Kevin looked at the floor and said nothing.

'Well? What did you fight about?'

Kevin shrugged and Maeve had the urge to shake him till his teeth rattled. 'Kevin?' she said threateningly.

'It's because they say he hasn't got a daddy,' Grace said.

The look Kevin threw her was one of hate. 'Big mouth Grace,' he said.

'That will do,' Maeve said automatically. 'What do you mean, you haven't got a daddy?'

'That's what they said,' Kevin sighed, because now Grace had told their mother what it was all about there was no point in not explaining it all. 'They said if we had a daddy, he'd be here, someone would have seen him and no one has. That's why I fought. Then today they started again in the playground. I punched one boy in the face and told them we didn't want our daddy to live with us because he's a miserable old bugger, that's why I got the cane.'

Maeve glanced across the room to see her father and Colin trying to hide their smiles behind their hands, but Maeve didn't feel like laughing. She'd been living nine weeks at her parents' farm and had missed her third period, the morning sickness had almost stopped and although physically she felt well, mentally she was a wreck.

And how should she deal with it? Eventually she said crisply, 'Of course you have a daddy – everyone has a daddy somewhere and daddies don't have to live with their wives and children.'

'Ours won't, will he?' Grace asked fearfully.

'No,' Maeve said firmly. 'But that isn't the point. He still is and always will be your father, whether he lives with us or not. And, as for you, Kevin,' she added, turning back to her son, 'there's to be no more fighting about it and no bad language, or you'll feel my hand across your bottom.'

'Ach, he'll hear worse before he's much older,' Thomas told his daughter.

'Not from me, he won't,' Maeve said. But she knew the swearwords her small son unwittingly used were not the biggest issue here.

'Come away in, anyway,' Annie said. 'Let's not quarrel among ourselves.'

Maeve sighed. 'Aye.' Her mother was right. They had enough trouble with people outside of the family; they shouldn't fight each other.

'Don't worry so much, pet,' Thomas told his daughter. 'It'll just be a nine-days' wonder, you'll see.'

Maeve knew he was trying to cheer her up and didn't believe that any more than he did, but she gave him a watery smile anyway. 'I really hope so, Daddy. Oh, I really hope so.'

But the situation didn't ease. Other family members, although supportive, didn't understand what it was like. Tom, for example, was living far enough away from the family to belong to another parish entirely. He came to see Maeve and though he told her forcibly no woman should be forced to stay with a man who beat his wife and child and drank his wages, he couldn't help her at all.

Liam and Kate, away in Dublin, had almost forgotten what life was like in the small towns and villages in the north of Ireland, but in their letters to Maeve they urged her to stick to her guns after Annie wrote telling them all about it. And Maeve was glad of their support, for the only positive letters she got apart from theirs were from Elsie, who told her of the goings-on of the street. She also assured Maeve that while the tale of her taking off with the children was on everyone's lips for a while, in a street where one person's business is known to all, there were always new bits of gossip to chew over.

Her Uncle Michael, on the other hand, seemed totally confused by Maeve's flight. He expressed surprise that she'd returned to the very place that just a few years before she was mad to get away from. And he claimed Brendan was a broken man. He wrote to Annie:

Besides, I don't see that the problem between them could be so big, or surely I would have had some indication of it? Brendan, at any rate, is willing to forgive and forget and I think Maeve would be best to come home now. She has taught him a wee lesson and I'm sure he'll be a changed man after it.

'Why does no one see the man is evil through and through?' Maeve cried.

'You didn't,' Annie reminded her. 'It took you some time to get the measure of him. And when all's said and done, despite what you said about the house you live in, and how everyone knows your business, the man seen walking down the street might not be the same as the one within your own four walls.'

Maeve knew her mother was right. No one but his family had known Brendan as she had, yet she'd not seen through the veneer of his charm and had paid the price for nine years. Surely to God that was long enough?

Father O'Brien didn't think so. He was at the farmhouse the Saturday evening after Annie had received Michael's letter with yet another letter from Father Trelawney.

'This letter from your parish priest, Maeve, has your husband's assurance that things will be different. He promises that this will be so. He says also that you are unreasonable in some of your demands on him. Going for a drink after he finishes work is not unusual in a job such as his.'

'I know that, Father,' Maeve cried. 'I'm being made out to be a monster. I don't object to Brendan having a drink and never have had. But surely to God it's not right to take food from the weans' mouths for his beer money, or to give to the bookie's runner?'

Father O'Brien smiled and Maeve had the urge to smack him hard enough to swipe the smile from his face, especially when he said, 'Don't you think you're exaggerating just a little?'

'No, I bloody well don't,' Maeve said. 'I wish you'd all leave me alone and mind your own business.'

'Your spiritual welfare is my business.' Father O'Brien shook his head. Father Trelawney said Maeve was subject to exaggeration and, anyway, whatever Brendan Hogan had done in the past, he'd assured him he had changed, he'd been so upset by his wife's actions. 'You must give the man a chance, Maeve,' he said. 'You must forget the past. Things will be different now, I'm sure of it.'

Maeve didn't believe it, couldn't believe it, but Father O'Brien did and so did Father Trelawney. She was the wicked perpetrator who wanted to end their mockery of a marriage and Brendan the deserted husband, seemingly out of his mind with worry, and promising the moon if only his wife would come back to him.

She turned to face the priest. 'And can you guarantee that no harm will befall the child I'm carrying? And that no incident, however accidental, will result in a miscarriage? Whether you believe it or not, the child I miscarried was due to the impact of a hobnail boot in my stomach and I carry the imprint still. Whatever I told the authorities, they didn't believe me. I should imagine that they have me on some list or other, labelled "Suspicious Circumstances", don't you?'

Maeve had no idea whether this was true or not but, she guessed, neither would the priest. She was right, he didn't, and he made no attempt to answer her. Instead, he turned to Rosemarie, who was waiting for Greg to pick her up. Father O'Brien had chosen the time to visit the family with care, wanting them all to be there.

'Are you looking forward to your wedding, Rosemarie?' he asked.

Rosemarie was disarmed. Whatever argument the priest had with Maeve, she decided, did not concern her and she certainly couldn't be blamed in any way. 'Why, yes, Father.'

Father O'Brien smiled, and Maeve, seeing it, recognised the curl of the lip that had been the same as Brendan's just before he was to deliver the punch between the eyes. 'It would be a pity then,' the priest said, 'to postpone the ceremony.'

'But, Father, there's no need,' Rosemarie said, and Maeve could have wept for the naïvety and genuine bewilderment in her voice. 'Everything is arranged for August now.'

'Ah yes, but I wonder if you understand the sanctity of marriage, Rosemarie?'

'Yes, Father. Of course I do.'

'Your sister doesn't seem to.'

'Father, surely that's nothing to do with me?'

'Not directly, no,' the priest said. 'I just want you to fully understand the commitment you're making.'

'Stop this!' Maeve cried. 'Hound and harass me if you must, but for God's sake, leave my family alone.'

Father O'Brien's eyes sparkled with hatred. 'Leave your family alone,' he repeated. 'Like your family should have left you alone. Your mother should have shown you the door when you arrived, lest you corrupt your young brother and two sisters. But she didn't, so they share in your guilt and shame and will continue to do so, until you see sense.'

'Father, for pity's sake,' Annie cried. 'How could I turn my back on my own child?'

'When a woman is given in marriage, she and her husband should be as one,' Father O'Brien thundered. 'It was your Christian duty to point this out to Maeve.'

'Oh, you'd know all about it,' Thomas said sarcastically. 'Marriage, and all it means. Don't you come to my door again threatening my bloody family.'

'Thomas!'

'Don't you "Thomas" me, Annie. The man has a bloody nerve.'

108

'Shouting at me will change nothing,' Father O'Brien said. 'To come between a husband and wife is a mortal sin, and you should be aware of it. If you were to die with a mortal sin on your soul before you were able to repent and ask forgiveness, you would roast eternally in hell's flames.'

Maeve saw her mother's face blanch with fear, but her father's was red in temper. 'Is that so?' he said. 'Well, let me tell you, if welcoming my daughter, who was in dire need, is your idea of mortal sin, then I'd be glad to meet the others of like mind in hell and shake them by the hand. Not that I intend to see them for a wee while yet.'

'Thomas, you are making a grave mistake,' Father O'Brien said. 'God will not be mocked.'

'It's not God I'm mocking, you sanctimonious bugger,' Thomas said. 'And if you have nothing further to say, I'd like you to leave.'

'As I said, you're making a grave mistake.'

'No doubt. Good night, Father.' Thomas turned from the priest and sat down facing the fire with his back to the outraged man, then threw on another two peat bricks and gave the fire a poke.

It was up to Annie, flustered and upset, to see the priest to the door. 'I'm sorry, Father,' she said in a whisper as she opened it for him. 'He's . . . Thomas is a wee bit upset.'

'It's not to be wondered at. Everyone is upset when they go against God and what He wants,' the priest said, ducking his head to go out of the farmhouse. 'Think carefully about what I said back there, Annie. Good night to you.'

'Good night, Father.' She closed the door behind the priest.

Thomas turned to his wife and growled, 'Don't you ever do that again and apologise in my own house on my behalf.'

109

'I couldn't leave it like that,' Annie protested. 'You swearing at the priest and ordering him from the place.'

'You should think yourself lucky. If I'd had to look and listen to the hypocrite much longer, I would have punched him on the jaw,' Thomas said.

'That wouldn't have helped anyone, Daddy,' Rosemarie said, and she appealed to her mother. 'Do you think he meant it, about postponing the wedding? Only Greg's mother wouldn't like it.'

Maeve knew Greg's mother wouldn't, but then she liked so little. In many ways she felt sorry for Rosemarie, for Sadie Fearney was a widow and reliant on her son, Greg. She had no desire for him to take a wife and lose her place in the household, and Maeve guessed would make Rosemarie's life a misery unless she established herself at the very beginning. The last thing Rosemarie needed was for the priest to postpone that wedding indirectly because of something her elder sister did. Surely he couldn't do that, even though priests seemed to be a law unto themselves. Surely that was going beyond the bounds of reasonableness?

'I'm sure that was just an empty threat,' Maeve said. 'Just said to frighten and worry you.'

'I hope so,' Rosemarie said. Greg didn't have a very strong personality and was not able to stand against his mother at the best of times, and Rosemarie was not one for asserting herself either. She was frightened of her future mother-in-law, but she also knew if she wasn't to marry Greg, life would lose its meaning and if the priest were to succeed in blocking the wedding, Rosemarie knew Sadie would make hay out of it.

Maeve could see the worry of having a mortal sin on her soul was torturing her mother. Annie could never remember committing a mortal sin before. Mortal sin was for stealing, murder, adultery or missing Mass, but Annie had done none of those things and Maeve knew she would fret over the priest's words. Her father might be able to fend them off but her mother couldn't do that, she knew, and her heart felt like lead.

That night in bed, she lay long after Grace, Nuala and Rosemarie's even breathing told her they were asleep, and she thought about the trouble she'd brought to her family. Even the children were no longer carefree. Now Grace often had mysterious stomach aches before school, and both she and Kevin returned solemn-eyed and never spoke of the happenings through the day as they once had done. Neither indeed did Nuala and Colin, and Maeve guessed they were going through it too – and Rosemarie, behind the counter in a shop in the town, unable to hide away from people. Maeve supposed she should be grateful Rosemarie hadn't been sacked, but she knew she probably had to run the gauntlet daily.

Then, there was her mother, a prisoner on the farm for she couldn't face the townspeople. Thomas had to fetch her groceries, and though she went to Mass, she didn't go to confession, Benediction or Devotions and hadn't been to the Mothers' Union since Maeve had arrived at her door.

Maeve knew she had to return and, if necessary, live out the travesty of her marriage in her back-to-back hovel in Birmingham. Then maybe everyone else's life could go on as before. But she'd not take the children back to suffer with her. She couldn't do that to them for she knew full well what she'd be returning to.

She'd dreamt of starting afresh in Ireland, bringing her children up in peace and tranquillity and, in time, getting a job. Now the dream lay in tatters, and ahead of her, she had no doubt, lay a nightmare. She sobbed in the bed, muffling her tears in the pillow.

The next afternoon, she went to see Father O'Brien. She went alone, for she'd not told the family of her decision.

Cissie O'Brien, the priest's sister, looked at Maeve coldly. 'Yes?'

'I'd like to see the priest, please.'

'He's resting after his dinner.'

'It's urgent.' And it was urgent, Maeve thought, for if she didn't carry out the resolution now, having wrestled with it all night, she'd lose the courage to do it at all.

'Wait a minute,' Cissie said through compressed lips. 'I'll see how he is.'

A little later she was back, disapproval written all over her face. 'Come in,' she said reluctantly. 'Father will see you now.'

Father O'Brien was sitting before a fire, in a cosy-looking armchair in a comfortably furnished but very tidy sitting room.

'Well, Maeve?' Father O'Brien said heartily as if they'd never had a cross word in their lives. 'This is a surprise.' He got up from the chair and said, 'Sit down, sit down. I'll ask Cissie for tea.'

'No!' It came out louder and sharper than Maeve intended, and she went on, 'No, I'm sorry, I want no tea and I'd prefer to stand. What I have to say shouldn't take long.'

Father O'Brien's eyes narrowed but, undaunted, Maeve persevered. 'If I was to return to my husband,' she said, 'would you stop the harassment of my family?'

'Maeve, I object to the word harassment.'

'Call it what you like – your bounden Christian duty, if you like,' Maeve said impatiently. 'I've not come to bandy words with you but to ask for assurances. If I return, will you hear the confessions of my family and administer Communion to them at Mass? Will my mother be able to shop in Ballyglen again without folk whispering and sniggering behind her back? And will the children be free of taunts? And finally, will you allow Rosemarie's wedding to go ahead as planned and allow Kevin to rejoin the Communion class?'

'Maeve, that isn't all my doing.'

'A fair bit of it is,' Maeve said. 'And you could have stopped it all with one or two words to the parishioners from the pulpit. Isn't there a piece in the Bible, where Jesus meets the prostitute at the well, and when people would have stoned her to death Jesus stopped them and said that those who were without sin should cast the first stone? As I remember it, the woman got away without a mark on her. That's what my God's like, Father. Yours seems full of anger: "Vengeance is mine; . . . saith the Lord." Mine says, "Do your best, you're only human."'

'Maeve, you are blasphemous!'

'I'm not, Father,' Maeve said. 'My God is very real to me, but I can't see Him like you do.'

'Do you believe God speaks through me?'

Maeve shrugged. 'It's what we're taught to believe. I don't know, but whether you are answering for yourself or as God's mouthpiece, can you answer my questions?'

'And you will go back to Brendan?'

'Aye. And whether it's your God or mine, I hope one of them will help me,' Maeve said.

Father O'Brien pursed his lips, but didn't censure Maeve further. 'If your parents come and confess their sins in confession – all their sins – then there will be no problem with that, or allowing them to take Communion. Rosemarie's

113

wedding will go ahead as planned, but Kevin will be going back to Birmingham with you.'

'No, Father, he won't. Nor will Grace.'

'Oh, I'm sure Brendan—'

'Brendan, Father, won't give a tinker's cuss. In any case with all the talk of war, I feel the children will be safer over here in Ireland. He's never cared for them anyway, and they are scared witless of him. When he hears I am pregnant again, he will be furious. But this time, I want to carry this baby. Another condition is that Father Trelawney tells him that if anything happens to the child, he'll be held responsible.'

'Maeve, the miscarriage was an accident.'

'Well, I want no more of them,' Maeve said firmly. 'So will you do it?'

Father O'Brien looked at the girl before him and for all her twenty-seven years he thought, she was little more than a girl. Her body was slender despite the slight rounding of her stomach and her frame small-boned, her whole face was determined, but behind the determination he read real fear and apprehension in Maeve's face. He nodded. 'I'll see to it,' he promised.

'And, Father, Brendan can drink the pubs dry for all I care, as long as he tips up the rent and money for the gas and enough to feed us.'

'Didn't you say he beat you?' Father O'Brien said. 'Don't you want that stopped too?'

Maeve sighed. 'The age of miracles is passed,' she said. 'Brendan will never change. In fact, not having Kevin to torment and terrify might make it worse for me, but I am better able for it than a wee boy. I'll be all right.'

Father O'Brien suddenly felt immeasurably sorry for the woman in front of him. She'd been wilful and headstrong all of her growing up, a trial for the nuns who'd had the teaching of her since she'd been small. He was glad she was retuning to her husband, but for all that . . . 'Well, I'm glad you've seen sense at last, Maeve,' he said.

'Seeing sense, is that what they call it?' Maeve said sarcastically. 'I'm sorry, Father, but really I'm not returning to Brendan through choice, but because you've forced me. I'm not going to argue with you over it now. I've agreed to go back. Let it lie there.'

The priest gave a nod. 'When will you leave?'

'Oh, as soon as it can be arranged,' Maeve said. 'Now the decision has been made, there is no point in delaying things, is there?'

The priest nodded again and Maeve went on, 'And you will write immediately to Father Trelawney?'

'I will, I assure you.'

'So, I'll say goodbye, Father,' Maeve said.

The priest put out his hand and Maeve looked at it, but made no effort to take it. The silence stretched between them as her glance shifted from the outstretched hand to the priest's face.

'I'm sorry,' she said, 'I cannot shake hands with a man I have no respect for.'

She saw the priest's face flush with anger and embarrassment. She knew her words had shaken him and she also knew he'd probably never forgive her. She walked across the floor and opened the door. Father O'Brien watched her go but did not move, nor did he call his sister to see her out, and once outside Maeve let her breath out in a huge sigh and the tears rolled down her cheeks.

She tramped the hills for hours, seeing no one and glad of it, for the tears continued to flow and she gazed about her as she drank in the space and peace around her. She knew it might have to last her a lifetime.

Eventually, emotionally exhausted but with dry eyes, and her feelings so tightly in check that every part of her body ached, she returned to the farmhouse to tell her family what she'd done.

EIGHT

Brendan and Father Trelawney were waiting to meet Maeve at New Street station on the evening she returned home in the middle of June 1939. The journey had been horrendous and she'd been as sick as ever on the ferry, but as she'd been sick with misery and despair since she'd left, it hardly mattered. The vision of her solemn parents and tearful children haunted her throughout the journey back to Birmingham.

Father Trelawney treated her as if she was a valued guest and not an errant wife returning because she had to, and Brendan barely acknowledged her. Yet she was glad of the priest's presence, knowing while he was there Brendan could do little to her, and when he suggested going home with them both to talk things over, she accepted it, though never could she remember 'talking things over' with Brendan.

Everything looked dirtier and drabber than Maeve remembered as she came out of New Street station flanked by the two men and got into an uncomfortable tram for the short ride home. Latimer Street was full of children playing out in the summer evening, and many women stood at their doorways opening on to the street, talking

117

to their neighbours. As they became aware of Maeve, all conversation ceased and most of the women's eyes were sympathetic, but Maeve kept her head down and acknowledged none of them.

They turned down the entry into the court, where Maeve was surprised to see Elsie's door shut and the windows closed. She'd written Elsie a letter telling her that she was being forced to return but, knowing how she'd feel about it, had only posted the letter the previous day. But it should have arrived that morning, and Maeve was surprised her friend wasn't there to greet her and hoped it wasn't because she was cross with her for coming back. Maeve felt her spirits sink. She hadn't realised how much she'd been looking forward to seeing Elsie again.

Father Trelawney saw her glance at Elsie's house and said, 'Mrs Phillips is away at her sister's in Handsworth. She was taken bad and Mrs Phillips went over a couple of days ago.'

Maeve said nothing, but she saw the hard cruel smile on Brendan's face and was afraid. She knew it was the thought of Elsie next door that had saved her many a time. Brendan couldn't stand Elsie and told her so often, but she didn't give a damn and was one of the few people who seemed unafraid of him. When Brendan started on her Maeve knew those around would tut and say something should be done, but no one would interfere, and she shivered in sudden apprehension.

The step into the house was nearly black and the house itself smelt musty and was covered in a film of dust. Maeve remembered Elsie telling her that Brendan had been living at his mother's – not that he'd have done anything to clean the house even if he had been living in it; he wouldn't have had a clue where to start. Maeve longed to boil up some water and attack the place and knew she would as soon as she was alone, but for now Father Trelawney was there and wanting to 'talk things over' and she knew she'd have to humour the man.

She wondered if there was a bite to eat in the house, but before she was able to ask, Father Trelawney said, 'Brendan has got in a few basics, Maeve, and I suggest you put the kettle on, and Brendan and I will go out and treat the three of us to pie and chips.'

Maeve stared at him. Never had she tasted a pie from the chip shop. She'd seen them and smelt them, but never tasted one. Once she'd been in Elsie's house when her husband came in and Elsie had brought him chips and a steak-and-kidney pie from the chippy. The crust of the pie had been golden brown and when Alf cut into it, the sight of the chunks of meat in the thick appetising-looking gravy had made her feel faint. She'd had nothing to eat that day, her stomach had grumbled with emptiness, and she'd known there was little in her house to make a meal of. She'd had to make an excuse to Elsie and leave before she was tempted to grab the pie from Alf's plate and shove it in her own mouth.

'That would be grand, Father,' she said, her mouth watering at the thought of it. She was grateful, for everything looked better if you had a full stomach. And she was glad too that Father Trelawney was taking Brendan with him. She'd be on her own with him long enough, God alone knew, and she was terrified, bloody terrified, but she pushed such fears to the back of her mind, filled the kettle and laid the table for the meal.

Neither the incongruousness of the situation nor the presence of the priest and her brooding husband could take her enjoyment away from the delicious pie and crispy chips, which she forced herself to eat slowly. She hadn't known she was so hungry before she began, and the food and tea revived her. She was quite happy to let Father Trelawney carry the conversation.

It was with the meal over, the plates stacked for washing up and a second cup of tea before them that the priest began to talk about their 'marriage difficulties'.

Maeve had almost smiled at such a polite term. She knew this was her one chance with the presence of the priest to stay Brendan's hand, to improve even slightly the life she'd fled from and to put her side of the story. As she'd implied to Father O'Brien, Brendan was a violent man and this she could never change. She had to look at what she *could* do something about. Most of her problems related to money, because with the children out of the way, she could probably put up with Brendan's uncertain temper as long as she got enough to feed herself and the child she was carrying. 'Some of my "difficulties" as you call them, Father – really the main ones – are related to money, or the lack of it,' she said suddenly.

'Here we go,' Brendan said. 'Always bloody complaining.'

'Now, Brendan, let her have her say.'

Encouraged by this, Maeve said, 'Whatever Brendan earns, I'm never given enough of it to feed the family.'

'Is it my fault if she's a bad manager?' Brendan said, appealing to the priest.

'A bad manager?' Maeve exclaimed, and turning to Father Trelawney said, 'Father, I don't know exactly how much Brendan earns, but I know it's more than adequate for our needs. I know because of the amount he tips down his neck each evening, but he throws a pittance on the table on a Friday if I'm lucky, and I have a lot to pay out of it. It's never enough.'

'She's always bloody moaning on, Father,' Brendan put in.

'Let her finish,' Father Trelawney said. 'Go on, Maeve.'

'Father,' Maeve began, glad for once he appeared to be on her side, 'our rent for this place is six and six. I then have to pay one and sixpence a week for the clothing club and ten shillings for other things besides food: soap, soap powder and soda, money for the gas meters, candles and coal for the winter. I should pay sixpence a week for the doctor but I never have it, but those are the basic things before the food I have to buy.'

Father Trelawney had been writing the figures down as Maeve spoke and he looked up at Brendan and said, 'How much do you give Maeve each week?'

Maeve knew it was never a set amount she was given a week, only what she could manage to wheedle out of him, but she sat silent and waited for him to speak. He blustered at first and said, 'Well, Father, it's not so easy to say. Not just like that, you understand. I mean it's up to what I have to pay up and what I'm due.'

'What do you mean?'

'He means the gambling debts he runs up, Father,' Maeve said. 'And of course the little amount he wins back. Whether we all eat or not will often depend on how well the horses run.'

'You bitch!' Brendan cried, leaping to his feet, his fists balled by his side. He stabbed his finger in the air towards Maeve and appealed to the priest. 'You see how she is, Father. She's a sodding troublemaker – beg your pardon, Father.'

Father Trelawney spoke sternly: 'Sit down, Brendan.' And he waited till Brendan was seated before he went on, 'From my reckoning the very least Maeve can manage on is three pounds ten shillings. Are you giving her that sort of money?'

Maeve gave a snort of disbelief. Sometimes she was hard-pressed to prise a pound note out of her husband. Brendan turned hate-filled eyes upon her and said, 'A man has to have a drink, Father. You know in the job I have if you didn't drink you'd die, and what harm is a wee bet?'

'Jesus, Brendan, will you listen to yourself?' Maeve cried, encouraged by the priest's presence to speak at last. 'You can drink the pubs dry for all I care if you'll tip up your money before you go and spend what you have left. I don't give a tuppenny damn what you do with the rest if you just give me enough to warm and light the house and feed everyone.'

'Feed everyone!' Brendan mocked. 'You've no weans now. You've left them at your mother's to spite me.'

'There's a war coming, in case you hadn't noticed,' Maeve said. 'Our children are safer where they are. But I am pregnant again now and this one I want to give birth to and rear decently.'

'What does that mean?'

'Work it out,' Maeve snapped. 'I miscarried two after Grace in the early months and then lost a baby at six months.'

'Are you saying that was my fault?'

Maeve saw Brendan's eyes glittering and knew she was on dangerous ground but was too angry to care. 'Yes, I bloody well am. The first two were lost because I hadn't the food in my body to feed them nor any resistance against the clouts and punches you seem to think are part of married life. But the last one,' she added, 'was lost because of a kick from a hobnail boot in my stomach.'

She stood up and faced Brendan, her face crimson with temper and yelled across the table, 'You killed my unborn babies, Brendan Hogan, and near killed wee Kevin and me too. I returned to you only because I was forced. If anything happens to this child, I will hold Father Trelawney and Father O'Brien responsible for making me come back to you, and I've told Father O'Brien this.'

'Maeve—' Father Trelawney began.

'Maeve bloody nothing, Father,' Maeve snapped. 'You don't know how it is, neither of you priests does. I have to protect my children the only way I can.'

Brendan didn't speak. But the glare he directed at her and the way he licked his lips slowly made her insides somersault in alarm. She closed her eyes, shutting out his face. Oh sweet Jesus, she cried silently, protect me for pity's sake.

When she opened her eyes, Father Trelawney was regarding her gently. 'Maeve, to lose a baby must be appalling and very sad for you, but you must believe your miscarriages were accidents – tragic accidents, but just that. To apportion blame will not help you.'

'Apportion blame!' Maeve repeated. 'Father, I—'

But the priest cut her off. 'Let's return to the present and what can be done to help you both work towards a good marriage.'

Maeve stared at him, too angry to speak. Father Trelawney apparently was not going to talk about her miscarriages, nor agree that Brendan had had any hand in them at all. And as for the term 'good marriage', she'd stopped believing in that fantasy many years before. She didn't expect happiness; just to be free of fear for the safety of her unborn baby, and have enough money to feed the family was all she desired now.

'As I said before, I think Maeve should have three pounds and ten shillings a week,' Father Trelawney said. 'That will still leave you with a fair amount.'

Brendan gaped at him. 'Three pounds bloody ten?'

123

Maeve looked at the priest in surprise. It wasn't a fortune, but more than she'd ever got before, though she knew it wouldn't happen. Brendan would agree to it, maybe, while the priest was there, but Father Trelawney wouldn't be there on a Friday evening when Maeve risked a thumping to get some money off him before he left the house again to drink and gamble the night away. Often the amount he'd throw at her in the end was barely enough to clear the tick she'd run up in Mountford's.

But Father Trelawney surprised her. 'And I'd like you to bring it to the presbytery on Friday after work,' he went on. 'I'll bring it up to Maeve myself later that evening.'

Maeve felt the breath leave her body in a large sigh of relief. Not to have to fight for money would be like heaven. Even when she'd managed to get some money out of Brendan, she'd often gone to bed light-headed and aching with hunger herself, for the little food she'd managed to buy she'd given to the children. To think all that might be over was magic indeed; to think she might carry her baby to term and as well nourished as any other in that area was a relief.

Maeve saw by Brendan's glare that he was not pleased by what the priest said, but she knew he felt too awed by the clergy to go against him. 'Do you agree, Brendan?' the priest asked.

'There's no need for all this, Father.'

'Well, we'll see. But for now, do you agree?'

Brendan made an impatient movement with his head. 'Aye, aye. I suppose so. You've forced it on me.'

'And you, Maeve. Are you agreeable?'

'Aye, Father. It would be a blessing, so it would.'

'And why wouldn't it?' Brendan cut in sarcastically. 'She takes off when the notion takes her and returns without a bone of shame in her body and makes demands. And you, Father, you encourage her and with not a word about how she's behaved.'

'That's in the past, Brendan,' the priest said. 'The thing now is to look forward.' He got to his feet and nodded to the pair of them. 'I'm sure we can work something out.' And to Maeve he added, 'I'll be around with the money on Friday evening, Maeve.'

'Yes, Father.'

'And, Brendan?'

'I'll be there, Father,' Brendan growled. 'Leave it so.'

The priest said not another word and Maeve only waited until the door shut after him before beginning to tidy up the table, ignoring Brendan, who still sat there brooding.

'So,' he said at last, 'you conniving bitch, you have it all your own way.'

Maeve ignored him and he roared. 'D'you hear what I say?'

Her insides jumped with fright, but she answered him steadily, 'Yes, I hear you. I'm not deaf.'

Brendan shot up from his chair and, reaching his wife's side in a second, twisted one of her arms up her back until she cried out with the pain of it. 'Not deaf?' he said. 'Bloody insolent. I'll show you who's master here.'

He thrust Maeve from him as he spoke and she saw him fumbling with the loops on his belt. She cried, 'You touch me with that and I'll be off to St Catherine's in the morning and bring the priest up to you.'

The punch hit her between the eyes and knocked her off her feet and she stumbled against the hearth and lay against the mantelpiece, trying to pull herself together.

'Bring the priest,' Brendan sneered. 'There's not one man around these doors will blame me for the hiding I'm going to give you. You made a bloody mug of me, working in the corner shop to get the money to leave. I was told after you left me – in fact the whole bloody place knew about it but me. All laughing at me, they were, and you most of all. Well, you won't have reason to laugh when I'm finished with you.'

Maeve was more scared than ever. She wasn't surprised that Brendan had found out about her job once she was away from the place. She'd been surprised it had been kept from him for so long. But as he saw it, she, and indeed all the rest of the women, by keeping quiet about it had been laughing up their sleeves at him and he never could bear being laughed at. She also knew that however good her reasons were for leaving Brendan, every man would agree that a wife couldn't be allowed to walk out whenever she chose, and any that did should be taught a lesson they'd never forget to discourage others feeling the same way. She knew even if she were to scream blue murder those women would pretend they heard nothing.

There was no Elsie to save her this time, and Maeve saw with horror the glittering fire in Brendan's eyes. Violence brought out a frenzied excitement in him and she watched as he slid his belt through the last loop of his trousers and raised it in the air.

Maeve let out a yelp as the belt cut into her shoulder, and then with a sudden leap she was the other side of the table. The room, as she viewed it through her puffy eyes, refused to stay still, and Brendan appeared to sway in front of her as she spat out, 'Leave me be. If I lose this baby, I will be along to Father Trelawney so fast my feet won't touch the floor. I've told him I'll hold him responsible – him and Father O'Brien – and I'll show them what you've done to me.'

Maeve's words stayed Brendan's hand. He'd forgotten she was bloody pregnant again and if he was to beat her as he intended and she lost the child, he knew he'd be in trouble. He dropped his belt and, suddenly lunging forward, he grabbed hold of the front of Maeve's dress. He pulled her towards him and, slapping her hard on both cheeks, he said menacingly, 'You won't be pregnant for ever,' and he gave her a push so violent that she cracked her head against the wall.

She watched Brendan snatch his coat from a hook behind the door before leaving, slamming it behind him. She sighed in relief and sank trembling into one of the wooden chairs. Her head swam and her cheeks stung. She could taste blood in her mouth, her shoulder smarted from the lash of the belt, and she felt incredibly weary.

Her good intentions of cleaning the house as soon as Brendan had gone out were shelved, for she hadn't the energy. It had taken all her reserves of strength to stand up to her husband, and all she'd achieved was the postponement of the beating she knew she was in line for. God, but she was so scared of the man, and she sank her head into her folded arms on the table and cried her eyes out.

Two days later, when Elsie and Alf came home from Elsie's ailing sister's house, the swelling on Maeve's cheeks was not so obvious, but the bruising around her eyes and the bluish yellow colouring of them could not be disguised much. Elsie looked at Maeve steadily and said she wanted to bloody well shake her for coming back, and her reaction made Maeve weep afresh. Elsie comforted Maeve and told her she was sorry she'd upset her further and then went on to say that if she was to cry every time someone told her she was crazy in returning to the madman she'd been in such a hurry to leave, she'd spend her whole life in tears.

Just to have Elsie installed next door again lifted Maeve's spirits. And they needed lifting, for as well as her problems with Brendan, as the weeks passed she knew, as most of the world did, that war with Germany was almost inevitable.

Everyone said there would be rationing of foodstuffs to stop the rich stockpiling as they had in the First World War and causing shortages. Maeve said it would matter little to her – rationing or not, she'd live on bread and scrape, and not much of that either. The money Father Trelawney had insisted Brendan deliver to him had done little to ease her poverty. It would clear her tick and buy in a few basics from Mountford's, and get Brendan's suit out of the pawn-broker's. Brendan would take any she had left back off her when he got home from the pub. It did no good for her to protest that the rent man would be along in the morning and some money was needed for the gas meter.

Elsie said she should put it away in the cash box still in her house on Friday night before he got in, but Maeve was afraid to do that. Brendan knew she'd been given the money by the priest and she was afraid he'd kill her alto-gether if he couldn't find any on her, baby or no baby. In the end she was sure she'd have to admit where she'd hidden it and she didn't want Brendan terrorising Elsie, or finding out about the cash box.

So some weeks she had to hide from the rent man and often had little money for the gas and even less for coal. She made sure she had a meal for Brendan every evening and the means to cook it, for she was afraid of his temper if she hadn't anything in.

But now, realising the circumstances Maeve had lived in ever since she'd returned to Birmingham, Annie had sent money to her daughter. Maeve would have liked to refuse it, but to make such a proud gesture would have meant she lived on fresh air most of the time. Elsie was glad Maeve accepted the money, for despite the swell of her pregnancy, she'd become so thin she was almost scrawny.

Her uncle didn't seem to notice much change in Maeve. He came to see her as soon as he found out she was home and said he was delighted she'd seen sense in the end.

'It's a pity you left the children behind, though, Maeve,' he said.

'There's going to be a war, Uncle,' Maeve pointed out. 'They're talking about evacuating the children from the cities anyway. I'd rather mine stay with my parents than strangers I know nothing of.'

Michael could hardly argue with that, for by the middle of August, as Britain sweltered in a heatwave, preparations for war were all around them. Trenches were dug in parks and railings disappeared. The Government issued corrugated tin structures to those who had gardens to bury them in, and reinforced brick-built shelters surrounded by sandbags for the rest. A total blackout would be in force from 1 September, and Maeve asked Father Trelawney to tell Brendan she needed some extra money to buy material to make blackout curtains. Brendan paid up, as Maeve knew he would, when the priest told him of the two-hundred-pound fine he'd get if he didn't comply.

Elsie and Maeve went to the rag market, where the money went further, and Elsie made curtains for both houses on her treadle sewing machine. They looked horrid drawn across the windows, but far worse were the frightening gas masks everyone was to carry around in little boxes.

Maeve sat in Elsie's house on the morning of Sunday, 3 September, with so many of the neighbours clustered around the door had to be left open. They all listened to the proclamation that Britain was at war with Germany and no one was the least bit surprised.

And then nothing happened – nothing at all. Weeks passed and still nothing. There was no aerial bombardment such as they'd been told to expect, and eventually many mothers who'd agreed to their children being sent away went and brought them back again. People also wondered if the total blackout and the odious gas masks were necessary if no planes were going to fly over the Channel at all. But though they grumbled, most complied with the regulations.

Bridget Mary Hogan slipped into the world when the war was just six and a half weeks old, with the help of Elsie, and Lizzie Wainwright, the midwife, just before five o'clock on 21 October, puny and undersized in everything but her lungs. She yelled fit to burst at the birth without needing a smack, and Maeve held out her arms for her and was filled with a fierce protective pride.

She put her to the breast, which she took to immediately, and then the only sound in the room was the baby sucking. Maeve felt the small mouth tugging at her breast and Lizzie Wainwright gave a grim smile and remarked that the babby seemed to know what was what all right. Brendan, when he came home from work that night, was not interested in seeing either his wife or the daughter Elsie informed him Maeve'd given birth to. He waved away the dinner, said he was off to wet the baby's head, and didn't come back at all that night.

Maeve didn't care. Too buoyed up to sleep, she studied the tiny infant in the long dark hours by the light of a candle, looking for signs of the other two in her features. She decided the baby looked more like Kevin than Grace, but whichever one she resembled, holding Bridget in her arms helped ease the ache she still had in her heart for the children she'd left behind, and she resolved to write to tell Kevin and Grace about their new sister in the morning.

During Maeve's lying-in period, Elsie was a tower of strength and cooked nourishing broths to build up Maeve, insisting she have plenty of rest, while she herself took care of the house and did the washing and ironing. She cooked for Brendan too, thinking if she didn't he might take it out on Maeve.

Maeve felt well enough to take up the reins of the house again after two weeks. Elsie advised her to take it easy a while longer, for Bridget was a demanding baby and a hungry one. At first, Maeve felt she spent all day feeding her but she always tried to have her fed and asleep by the time Brendan came home so that she could have his tea on the table. She knew he resented the presence of babies and nothing annoyed him more than seeing a child at the breast. Maeve couldn't understand why. She couldn't understand much of the way her husband thought, but then she didn't have to understand it, just live with it for the sake of peace.

It was when she'd just got out of bed after Bridget's birth that she noticed how cold the house was. There was a nip in the air and she realised that it was November and somehow she'd have to get some coal in, but how to afford it was the problem. She shivered through two more weeks. Bridget was now four weeks old and each day the weather got colder. Maeve badly needed coal to warm the place. She knew it was no good appealing to the priest. Brendan would promise him all sorts and then not give her a brass halfpenny more. It wasn't like the business with the blackout curtains, when Brendan gave her the money to avoid a large fine; she had no stick to hold over him like that.

But still, coal had to be bought or little Bridget would freeze to death. The walls ran with damp as it was. And if the rent wasn't paid, and something paid off the arrears, they'd be out on their ears and she couldn't risk that.

Usually Father Trelawney brought Brendan's wages around at about seven, giving Maeve time to redeem Brendan's suit before the pawnshop shut at eight, and get as much food as she could at Mountford's, as they stayed open until nine or ten on a Friday night. Normally she didn't see anything of Brendan until much later.

So that Friday afternoon she went to the coal merchant 'Could you deliver some sacks of coal to me at about half-seven tonight?' she asked the man in the yard.

She saw the amazement on the grimy face of the coal man. She wished she looked more respectable, for she knew she was shabby in her shapeless old coat and second-hand down-at-heel shoes. She had bare legs, despite the coldness of the day, and the hands that pushed Bridget's dilapidated pram were red raw with the cold. She knew the man would think she had no money to pay him for his coal, as everything about her screamed poverty.

'Why the bloody hell should we deliver coal at that time of night?' the coal man demanded. 'It will be dark as pitch, 'specially in the bleeding blackout.'

'I'll have the money to pay then,' Maeve said, and added with a sigh, 'but I won't have it long. Once my husband is home from the pub, he'll take any money I have put by for coal.'

She saw a flicker of understanding flit over the coal man's face and knew she wasn't the only woman with a mean, selfish husband. The coal man asked tersely, 'How many bags?' Maeve let out a sigh of relief. 'Two,' she said. 'I have enough to pay for two.'

'Then two it will be,' said the coal man. 'I'll deliver them myself. I'd not trust the young lad; he'd never find the place and probably smash the lorry up too. Come inside and give me your address.'

The next call Maeve made was to Elsie's house. She gave her a ten-shilling note. 'Keep this till tomorrow,' Maeve said. 'It's for the rent and something off the arrears. I'm going to tell Brendan the rent man called this evening.'

'Think he'll believe it?'

Maeve shrugged, though her heart thumped in fear. 'He'll have to,' she said, 'and that's not all. I've ordered coal to be delivered this evening after Father Trelawney has given me my money and before Brendan has time to take it off me.' She saw the older woman's eyes widen with shock and said in protest, 'Elsie, if I hadn't, the baby would freeze to death.'

Elsie knew her words were true; she'd taken more than the odd shovel of coal from her own hearth to take the damp chill off Maeve's house. It had been so cold at times the breath escaped from her mouth in whispery vapour and her teeth had actually chattered. But Elsie also knew the risk Maeve was running, for she'd have little money left for Brendan to take off her that night and she knew he'd be furious.

'I'll listen out for him coming in,' she said. 'Call out if you need me.'

'I will, Elsie, and thanks,' Maeve said, and grasped the older woman's hand, so glad she lived just the other side of the paper-thin walls.

NINE

Years later Maeve could still remember sitting beside the crackly fire on that fateful night, warm for the first time since she'd left her bed after Bridget's birth. She'd fed her baby there and then, loath to take her to the freezing bedroom, tucked her into the pram near the fire, knowing she'd need at least one more feed before she went to bed anyway.

Once Bridget was asleep, she filled the kettle and stuck it on the embers of the fire, because she wanted to save as much gas as possible. She lit the gas mantles, though, for they threw better light around the room than the candles she usually had to resort to.

She cut herself two slices of bread which she smeared with jam and ate with a cup of tea. She'd had nothing to eat since that morning, when she'd eaten the stale end of a loaf; the rest of the bread she'd given to Brendan for his breakfast, along with the last of the tea too. Without Elsie she'd not have had a hot drink all day either. Really she knew it was no way to eat when she had to feed a child from her own milk. She needed to eat more than bread and scrape and the odd sup of tea to satisfy a baby, especially one with an appetite like Bridget's.

She hoped she might be able to hold on to the shilling she had hidden in her shoe. But out of what the priest had delivered into her hand that night, what with buying the necessary coal and putting the rent out and something off the arrears, she had a scant three shillings to appease Brendan with and that might not be enough. She was scared every time she thought of what he might do to her because of it.

She intended still being up when Brendan came in because she always felt more in control in the living room, but she'd have Bridget safely tucked in her cradle in the bedroom first so that she should be safe. She warmed the child's shawl and cot blankets at the fire so the icy chill of the room wouldn't matter so much.

But Maeve's plans came to nothing, for despite the warmed blankets and shawl, Bridget refused to settle that night after her feed. Desperate to quieten her, for she knew a baby's cry inflamed Brendan's temper more than anything, she cuddled her close as she walked the floor, patting her back endlessly. But Bridget continued to be fractious as the alarm clock by Maeve's side of the bed ticked the minutes away. She tried to calm herself, knowing the fearful tension she was feeling had probably been picked up by her daughter, making her more fretful.

Eventually the baby stopped drawing up her knees and her howls reduced to hiccupping sobs. Maeve's teeth chattered in the freezing air of the bedroom. Despite the baby's body pressed to her breast, her feet were like blocks of ice and she felt the intense cold seeping into her backbone. She thought longingly of the dying fire downstairs and vowed to get warm again before she returned to bed, even if it meant she had to put another few precious nuggets of coal on the embers. Bridget's cries had lessened to a snuffling whimper and Maeve was gently laying her in the cradle, continuing to pat her back, when suddenly she heard the front door thrust open and she imagined by the resultant crash that Brendan had fallen through it, as he'd done many times before.

Her stomach contracted in fear for she knew he must be very drunk and this certainty was increased as she heard him stumbling up the stairs muttering, 'No one makes a monkey of me. Going off like that. Everyone laughing – a laughing stock, that's what I am. I'm going to teach her a lesson she'll never forget.'

In the bedroom, Maeve trembled. She knew she was for it. She could almost see Brendan's cronies standing at the bar of The Bell, taunting him and making jokes about his manhood in allowing Maeve to get away with what she'd done, goading him and ensuring his temper was fully inflamed by closing time. Yet they'd know she would bear the brunt of it. She couldn't understand them. Grimly she remembered her first night home when he'd slapped her hard on both cheeks and reminded her she wouldn't be pregnant for ever and now she was pregnant no longer. She glanced at the baby, mercifully asleep, and hoped that she'd stay that way, for she couldn't guarantee even a baby's safety with Brendan in such a mood. She'd have to do her level best to placate him and she hoped he wouldn't start on about the money as well that night and find out what she'd done with it without his permission, for then he'd surely kill her.

Brendan slammed the bedroom door open with such force it crashed against the wall and rocked on its hinges, and he glared across the room at Maeve.

'Ah, here she is, my lady wife,' he mocked.

Maeve sat on the bed, but she'd moved away from the cradle, for she didn't want Brendan's anger directed there.

'H-hello, Brendan,' Maeve said, annoyed with herself for the stammer and wobble she couldn't keep out of her voice, knowing Brendan would be aware of it and realise how scared she was.

'"Hello, Brendan," she says,' Brendan mimicked. He spread his arms wide and swayed on his feet. 'Hello, Brendan, to the man she's made a monkey of for months.'

'Ah, come to bed, Brendan,' Maeve coaxed. She put out a hand towards him, but didn't dare touch him. Instead she began to unfasten her cardigan, but her fingers trembled that much, she could only fumble at the buttons.

'Come to bed?' Brendan repeated, lurching in front of her so that she smelt the stale scent of the beer on his breath and the sour stink of his unwashed body. 'I wouldn't come to bed with you,' he spat out. 'You whore! You bloody sodding whore!'

She didn't see the fist raised, but years later could remember the power of it slamming into her face, and she gave a strangled yelp at the smarting pain. Her nose and lips spurted blood, she tasted it in her mouth and she thought, maybe that's it, maybe now he'll be satisfied. She wiped the blood from her nose and mouth with the back of her hand. Then through her swollen lips she said, 'Come away now, Brendan. Let's go to bed.'

Brendan ignored her outstretched hand and said instead, 'Where's the bloody money? There was none on the mantelpiece downstairs.'

Oh God. Fear set her legs shaking.

'Let's . . . Let's talk about it in the morning,' Maeve urged. 'I'm tired, so I am. Come on to bed.'

But it was no use. Maeve knew Brendan would be well aware she was hiding something from him. She'd seen the suspicion in his eyes and knew what was in store for her as he growled again, 'What have you done with my bleeding money?'

Maeve licked her swollen lips. She knew this was it and when all was said and done, maybe it was as well to get it all over with. 'Brendan,' she said, 'there isn't much left.' She watched his eyes narrow and glitter with malice and she gabbled on while total and absolute terror gripped her like a vice. 'I had to buy coal – the house was like an icebox, so it was. Dear God, I was perished and the wean too. You have to keep them warm when they're small. The coal men wouldn't deliver without payment. Then there's the rent. We owe three weeks with this week, and the rent man caught me tonight and I had to give this week's money and something off the arrears.' She looked into Brendan's eyes and appealed to him. 'I had no choice, Brendan. I had to give him something.'

'You bloody sodding liar! '

His scream woke the baby and the resulting slap knocked Maeve to the floor. Mindful of Brendan's views on crying children, Maeve began crawling across to the cradle.

'Leave her!' Brendan snapped.

'Let me pacify her, Brendan?' Maeve pleaded.

'I said leave her,' Brendan said, and he kicked out at Maeve, drawing the breath from her body and knocking her legs from under her till she lay spread-eagled on the floor.

Maeve was too frightened for the child to argue further, but when she saw Brendan unbuckle his belt, she began to plead again, 'Please, Brendan, not that. Dear God! Please, I couldn't help spending the money. I have three shillings left for you.'

It was as if she hadn't spoken. Brendan slid his belt from his loops, hauling her to her feet as he did so and holding her with one hand by the upper arm, digging his nails into her flesh so that she was unable to pull away. As the baby's cries filled the room Maeve saw, by the light of the candle, the smile playing around Brendan's mouth as he lifted the belt and brought the buckle end down on Maeve's back. She'd struggled in panic, shrieking and screaming as she twisted in a futile effort to free herself. She was aware of her clothes being ripped to shreds as the belt continued to lash at her. Her efforts to escape seemed to excite Brendan further and she heard his breath rasping in his throat. A lash to the back of the legs caused them to buckle beneath her and she slumped on to her knees. Brendan, taken unawares, lost his grip and Maeve scarcely felt Brendan's nails tearing into her arm as she fell to the floor, because by that stage, she wasn't aware of much.

But her survival instinct was such that as soon as she hit the floor, she started to crawl frantically, her intention to hide under the bed. She was no longer screaming, but making little whimpers of terror. The sweat was running down Brendan's face, which was beetroot red – even his eyes shone demonic red in the flickering light of the candle – and he was gasping for breath as he dragged Maeve from under the bed by her arm and kicked viciously at her legs with his hobnail boots.

That's when Maeve knew she'd had one chance and it had gone. She was aware of deep groans as Brendan kicked her again and again till she vomited with the pain of it all. She thought she was going to die, there in the cold back bedroom of her house, lying in a bloodstained heap in her own vomit. Her last thoughts before she lost consciousness were for the children she'd left behind in Ireland and the wee baby wailing in the cradle.

It was the baby's continuous yells that eventually caused Elsie to investigate. She'd had words with Alf when she'd first heard Maeve's screams and had wanted to go to her. Alf said she should keep out of it; he'd even gone so far as to say if he'd given her the odd punch in the gob herself she mightn't be so keen to interfere in others' lives. At that Elsie had bristled and said she'd like to see him try, and as their argument grew fierce they yelled at each other so loud and furiously that the thumps and thuds from next door were not heard above their own anger.

And by the time they settled to an offended stony silence, there was no sound of Maeve or Brendan, only Bridget wailing like a banshee.

'See,' Alf remarked smugly to his wife. 'They've got over whatever it was and gone to sleep.'

'What, with that babby bawling its head off?' Elsie retorted. 'Well, I'm going round to see what's what, so put that in your pipe and smoke it.' And ignoring Alf's disapproving sniff she slid from her bed and, slipping an old coat on top of her nightgown and pushing shoes on her feet, she went next door.

The doors were seldom locked in the courts and Elsie didn't bother to knock. Apart from the baby's howls, the house was ominously still. There was no sound from the bedroom above, and that itself was strange. She expected to hear Maeve trying to pacify the baby, speaking to her or walking the floor with her because Maeve had told her that a crying baby irritated Brendan beyond anything else. That night of all nights, Elsie knew Maeve would be doing all she could to appease him.

But there was no sound from him either. He wasn't shouting or bawling at Maeve to shut the bloody brat up and yet Bridget's screams were piercing. Elsie opened the door to the stairs and crept up quietly until she stood at the open bedroom door, where she stood transfixed with shock. Brendan was sitting on the bed with his head in his hands as the baby's wails crescendoed. But Elsie took no notice, for she was horror-stricken by the motionless bloodstained figure that had once been Maeve Hogan lying on the floor. Elsie was convinced that what she had always feared had finally happened: Brendan had killed his wife.

'What have you done?' she said in an appalled whisper.

Brendan lifted his head to his hated neighbour and said, 'Bugger off and mind your own business. But I'll tell you one thing: she'll never run off on me again.'

Elsie glared at him, but didn't bother with a reply. She approached Maeve cautiously, though her senses recoiled from the sight, and took her limp wrist in her hand. Her relief was immense when she found a beating pulse and noticed Maeve's chest moving slightly.

She made Maeve as comfortable as she could, laying a pillow from the bed behind her head, but she hesitated to move her much. Elsie scooped the sobbing baby from the cradle, shocking her so much, her yells ceased, and without another word to Brendan she fled the house. Alf wasn't a hard man and once his wife stressed the seriousness of the situation, he got up, dressed and set off for Dr Fleming immediately.

Meanwhile, Elsie dressed herself hurriedly and tied the baby to her waist with a shawl. She sped through the night with the aid of a flickering torch until she stood outside the presbytery. The house was locked and in darkness, but undeterred, Elsie hammered on the door. She felt it had to be brought home to Father Trelawney what sort of a maniac Brendan Hogan was and she knew Maeve needed the priest's presence for she was seriously hurt.

The old housekeeper, Florrie McCormack, complete with curlers in her hair, came to the door at Elsie's frantic hammering, incensed that the priests she looked after should have their slumbers disturbed. Elsie demanded to see Father Trelawney in such a strident voice he was woken up and came to the top of the stairs. There was only the shielded torch to see by, but Elsie knew he was there.

'Will you come with me to my neighbour's house?' she called, and Father Trelawney descended the stairs and stood before her.

'Come on in,' he said, drawing her inside so that he could shut the door and turn on the light. It flooded the hall and showed Elsie the tousled-haired priest, a woolly dressing gown over his pyjamas, fleecy slippers on his feet and his face crimson with annoyance.

Elsie looked at the man who was so decently and warmly clad and thought of the tattered rags Maeve wore and the icy bedroom she'd left her in.

'Your neighbour, Maeve?' Father Trelawney asked. 'But I've already seen her this evening. She was all right when I left. What ails her?'

'What ails her?' Elsie screeched, almost bouncing on the floor. 'I'll tell you what ails her. She's been beaten half to death, that's what, and I'll tell you why.' She stabbed her stubby finger at the priest and cried, 'That money you bring her, d'you think the bastard lets her keep it? You know what type of man he is. You're not stupid. Well, tonight Maeve spent some of that money on what it was supposed to be used for, coal for the fire and rent money that she was owing because he takes every penny back off her that she hasn't already spent. He never even leaves her enough for the rent. God, you should see the mess he's made of her. Do you know what he said to me when

I found her? "She'll never run off again", that's what he said, the bastard!'

'How bad is she?'

'Bad enough,' Elsie said flatly. 'We've sent for the doctor. When I first saw her lying there, I thought he'd killed her.' She put a hand on Bridget's little head as if the baby understood her words and needed comfort.

'Is she asking for me?'

'No. But she probably would if she were able,' Elsie said, 'even if it were just to curse you from here to hell and back.' She saw the priest recoil slightly and knew he had no stomach for what she'd told him and probably didn't totally believe it was as bad as she said. 'She was unconscious when I left her,' Elsie said. 'Now come on. Get ready, she needs your prayers tonight if anyone does.'

Florrie McCormack came out of the kitchen as Father Trelawney came down the stairs. 'Are you away out, Father?' she asked with a disapproving look at Elsie.

'Yes. I don't know how long I'll be,' the priest answered as he packed a bag with the oils and holy water needed to administer the last rites.

'Wrap up well, for these nights are treacherous,' Florrie said solicitously. 'Shall I make you a hot drink before you go?'

'We've no time to spare,' Elsie said before the priest could speak, and she glanced up at Father Trelawney and said, 'Hurry. I don't like to leave Maeve alone for too long.'

The priest heard the steel in Elsie's voice and saw the glint of smouldering anger in her eyes and didn't argue with her. He grabbed the small black bag and they made the short journey to Maeve's house in silence.

When they got there, there was no sign of Brendan, but Alf was downstairs and the doctor was attending to Maeve in the bedroom above. The doctor was gently bathing the weals and bruises on Maeve's back and shoulders with warm water in a basin. He turned to Elsie and told her an ambulance had been sent for, and went on to say that any man who'd inflicted such punishment on his wife should be locked up.

'You found her, I believe?'

'Yes, Doctor,' Elsie replied. 'It was the screams of the baby alerted me.'

'The baby, yes, of course.'

Bridget, worn out with her tears and the dash to the presbytery, had been rocked to sleep and the doctor barely glanced at her before saying to Elsie, 'Could you put her down and give me a hand? We need to get as many of Mrs Hogan's clothes off as possible.'

'I'd be glad to,' Elsie said, and she was glad to have something to do for her friend. She began unwrapping the baby as she asked tentatively, 'Is she . . .? Will she . . .? Oh God!'

The doctor laid a hand on Elsie's trembling arm and said, 'She's very ill. We'll do our best.'

It had to do. In one way Elsie was grateful for the doctor's frankness. She glanced over at Father Trelawney, who was still standing at the door as though the shock of what he was witnessing had paralysed him. As she placed the baby in the cradle, he seemed to come out of it somewhat.

'Ah,' he said. 'You have Bridget, of course.'

Elsie stared at him. She had no time for him and the shock he might have suffered. 'Why of course, Father,' she said. 'Did you think I'd picked up any old babby just to keep me company?' And she added pityingly, 'Did you think I'd leave the babby with Brendan after I saw what he did to her mother?'

She didn't wait for the priest's reply and, laying Bridget down, she went over to the doctor, who was kneeling beside Maeve.

She'd never seen anyone, neither man nor woman, as badly beaten. Maeve's face had been beaten to pulp and the weals cut into her skin were crusted or dripping with blood on her shoulders and back and on the backs of her legs and even on her exposed breasts. Blackened bruising seemed to cover every part of her body. As well as this there was a large ugly-looking cut the length of her left leg and another from her head, both still bleeding.

Elsie hadn't been aware she was crying as she looked at the body of her young friend until she felt the tears drip on to her hands. She knelt beside the doctor and began to gently pull the ragged clothes from Maeve. Sometimes they were stuck, stiff with blood, and even easing them away with warm water brought some of Maeve's skin with it. The first time this happened, Elsie felt the bile rise in her throat, but she refused to be sick and bent to the task, knowing it had to be done.

And when it was done, and Maeve covered with a sheet, Father Trelawney came forward and asked the doctor, 'Is her life in danger?'

Elsie knew why he asked. If there was a chance Maeve might die, he would give her the last rites. The doctor looked the priest up and down, and with a face on him that showed he didn't like what he saw overmuch, then said, 'Do what you want. You and yours have brought this upon her anyway by making her come back to this man. I dare say you can do no further harm.'

Elsie wondered how he knew, but guessed he'd picked up gossip from the neighbours. Certainly, he seemed to hold Father Trelawney at least partially responsible for

Maeve being beaten by her husband. Elsie remembered the last time the doctor had been brought to the house. It had been to attend to both Kevin, who'd been beaten by his father, and then Maeve, who as a result of that particular beating had given birth to a stillborn premature baby. Obviously Dr Fleming had not forgotten that.

Father Trelawney made no comment to the doctor. He blessed the room with holy water before going forward to kneel beside Maeve, his stole around his neck, and began to mutter prayers as he held one of Maeve's unresponsive hands in his own. Elsie watched him dispassionately as he read from the Scriptures and anointed Maeve gently with the blessed oils and intoned a prayer for healing. When he had finished, he removed the stole gently, kissed it and turned to Elsie.

'I won't accompany Maeve to the hospital,' he told her as Alf announced the ambulance was outside. 'I was up all last night with a dying man.'

Elsie stared at him. 'Well, you just go home to your bed, Father, and rest yourself,' she said sarcastically. 'Next time Maeve is beaten up, I'll tell her to do it at a more convenient time for you. But I know one thing for sure, Maeve is not going to that hospital alone, and if you won't go, then I must.'

The priest was shocked at Elsie's reaction and she was surprised herself. She'd never spoken to a priest in such a way before, but then she'd seldom been as angry as she was that night. She lifted the baby from the cradle, wrapped her in the blankets and, without a further word to the priest, left the room.

Bridget was left in Alf's care as Elsie climbed into the ambulance after the stretcher behind Dr Fleming, who also insisted on going. All the way to hospital, she prayed for

Maeve. It would be all round the streets the next morning. In fact, if it hadn't been dark as pitch, the neighbours would have been out gawping that night too. Still, when all was said and done, they weren't a bad crowd and many, she knew, would be upset about what Brendan had done.

She grasped Maeve's hand, not knowing whether she could hear her or not, and whispered, 'Hold on, Maeve, we're nearly there.' And the ambulance sped on through the night.

TEN

Maeve felt she'd fallen into the pit of hell, and she groaned with pain more intense than she'd ever experienced before. She felt as if she were on fire and closed her eyes again wearily. She heard a movement beside her, forced her reluctant eyelids back and tried to focus.

And there, sitting in a chair at the foot of her bed, was a blurred image of Brendan. She didn't know where she was or why Brendan was there, and she tried to remember. Everything around her was very white and she was unable to move any part of herself. She turned her head and saw that drips fed into one of her arms and the other was in plaster from shoulder to fingertips and a monitor bleeped above her head. She realised she was in hospital and wondered how long she'd been there and where her baby was.

Brendan saw the flickering of Maeve's eyelids and got to his feet.

'Maeve?' he said.

Maeve saw him towering over her and she frowned. She was sure she was here because of Brendan! She couldn't remember. She shut her eyes tight and tried to focus her mind. Suddenly it came back to her, the terror of that night, the beating she'd endured, and now the perpetrator of it was by her hospital bed.

Brendan moved closer to her and she smelt the stink of him and even that set her teeth chattering. She opened her eyes again and saw his face inches above her own. 'Maeve?' he said again, and Maeve couldn't bear it. She couldn't stand any more and she opened her mouth and screamed. She screamed out all the petrifying fears that had trailed her through her shambles of a marriage and once she started screaming, she seemed to have no power to stop.

Brendan jumped back as if he'd been shot and as the unearthly sounds reverberated through the hospital, doctors and nurses came running and Maeve heard Brendan blustering, 'I didn't touch her! I didn't do anything! She just started! '

Maeve saw him being led away and his voice got fainter and fainter as her screams got louder and louder and more hysterical, and she tried to thrash on the bed but was anchored by the straps holding her wrists so that the drips couldn't be dislodged. She felt the bustle of staff all around her and with the prick of a needle she sank thankfully back into unconsciousness.

The next time she came to, Elsie was sitting beside her bed. She tried to smile at her friend, but her face hurt. Everything hurt. She opened her dry swollen lips and murmured, 'Elsie,' and tears ran down her cheeks.

'There, ducks, don't you upset yourself,' Elsie said, stroking her free hand. 'They'll put me out if they think I've made you cry.'

Maeve knew she was right and made a valiant effort to swallow the lump in her throat. She wished the pain would stop. It made her feel so weak and there were things she wanted to know. First and foremost was the whereabouts of her baby, but forming words was difficult.

'Bridget?' she attempted, and though the sound wasn't clear, Elsie knew what she was saying.

'Bridget's with me,' Elsie said. 'Has been since the first day,' and then she added, 'His mother came down and demanded to have the minding of her till you're better. You know what that Lily Hogan is like. I told her to sling her hook in no uncertain terms, I'll tell you. Told her she'd dragged her own kids up and she wasn't laying a hand on wee Bridget.' Elsie gave an emphatic nod of her head as she spoke and Maeve let go a sigh of relief. She wanted Bridget nowhere near her father or his people, and she knew Brendan would be staying with his mother.

Maeve moved her hand but winced as the needles in the back of her hand stung her, and Elsie said, 'They're to get some goodness into you, love. Help you get stronger, like. The doctors went mad when they brought you in. They said you were malnourished. Lord, Maeve, I've never seen anyone so blooming thin. You looked like one of those heathens the Church is always going on about saving. I'd no idea you was so bad. Course, I've never seen you without your clothes covering you before, but when I helped the doctor clean you up, Jesus! Maeve, your arms and legs were like sticks. I could actually see your ribs sticking out, though they were black and blue where that bastard had kicked the shit out of you.'

Maeve was too tired to answer and she was happy to let her friend talk.

'Proper shook the priest up, you did,' Elsie went on. 'I fetched him, you know.'

Maeve didn't know and her eyes opened wide in surprise.

'It was when I found you in such a state,' Elsie said. 'Alf went for the doctor and I went for the priest. He gave you the last rites.'

Last rites! That gave Maeve a jolt. They were given to people who were dying.

Elsie saw the consternation on her friend's face. 'The doctors kept going on about you having no stamina to fight anything,' Elsie said. 'It wasn't only the beating they were worried about.' Elsie gave her hand a pat and said, 'You look proper washed out, girl, and no wonder. I'll come and see you again tomorrow. You have some rest now.'

Maeve slept and when she next woke it was evening time. The winter's day beyond her window was dark and all the lights were on in the hospital, but around her she could hear the bustle of the tea trolley. Dr Fleming sat beside her.

'Hello,' he said when he saw her eyes were open. 'I thought I'd pop in before evening surgery and see how you are.'

Maeve concentrated hard and with difficulty, and slightly indistinctly asked, 'And how am I?'

'You're not very well,' the doctor said. 'You've been pretty ill, Maeve,' he said and added, 'You don't mind my calling you Maeve?'

Maeve shook her head. She didn't care what she was called. 'The point is, Maeve,' the doctor went on, 'the thing to do now is to look to the future.'

The future! Maeve wondered what he was talking about. She knew where her future lay and there were no options.

'You don't have to go back to him, that man, your husband,' the doctor went on as if he'd read her thoughts.

'No man has the right to treat a woman like your husband did.'

Maeve wondered if the doctor was a Catholic, if he knew the power of the Catholic Church. Probably not. In his circle leaving your husband because he beat you might be considered a reasonable thing to do. Maybe even divorce in such circumstances could be considered. But in the streets she lived in, women just got on with it and particularly so if they were Catholic. Divorce was not recognised by the Church and was unheard of.

She sighed and wondered if the doctor, who she could see was a kind man, would ever understand. She realised she probably owed him a lot of money. Elsie had told her he'd tended to her in the middle of the night. Maeve knew a house call, particularly at night, would be more expensive than a surgery visit.

She couldn't do anything about it now, not until she got out of hospital, anyway. She wondered, in her confused state, if Father Trelawney was still taking her money round and giving it to Elsie. She hated him. She partly blamed him for her being in hospital. Him and Father bloody O'Brien. She didn't want Father Trelawney near her again, nor Brendan either. Until she had to return home, she wanted no reminders of them.

'So, you just rest up,' the doctor was saying. 'Don't rush to get better. There's time enough.'

Maeve tried to smile at him because he was being kind to her again. He got to his feet hastily. 'I must be off,' he said. 'I hope I haven't tired you out.'

No, no, Maeve tried to say, but no sound came from her lips, and then despite herself, her eyelids shut. When she opened them, the doctor was gone and the ward was hushed and dark. Most patients were fast asleep and Maeve closed her eyes again.

The next day, they tried Maeve on solid food, though the intravenous drips still stayed in. Runny porridge in the morning and mashed-up broth at dinner time, with custard for tea. Maeve had to stay lying flat on her back and so she was spoonfed by one of the nurses and had to drink from a spouted cup. She was glad that nothing more solid was attempted, because her mouth was tender. Her lips smarted as the food was spooned in, and her throat felt as if it had half closed up.

The nurse told her some of her teeth had been loosened, but that they'd bedded down in her gums again. She felt them gingerly with her swollen tongue. But talking was a little easier.

'Thank you,' she told the young nurse after her teatime custard. 'You must be very busy. If I could sit up I'd feed myself.'

'Not yet awhile,' the nurse said. 'There's damage to your spine, you see.' She clapped her hands to her mouth. 'Oh God, I'm not supposed to say anything to you,' she said.

'Why not?'

'The doctors are the only ones supposed to discuss conditions with the patients,' the nurse said with a woebegone face. 'I'm always forgetting. The matron will have my guts for garters,' and she bit her lip nervously.

Maeve's senses were reeling. Damage to her spine? What damage? She told herself not to panic. She could feel her legs, feel them only too well. Sometimes, especially at night, they throbbed with pain. Underneath the bedclothes, she moved them gently slightly sideways and then up and down, gratified that she could, even if the pain was agonising as she did so.

'Don't worry,' she promised the nurse. 'I won't say a word. But you can do something for me too. Inform whoever you have to that I don't want to see my husband while I'm in here, nor do I want to see Father Trelawney. Will you do that for me?'

The young nurse said she would with pleasure. Most of the staff knew who had inflicted the injuries on Maeve Hogan anyway.

She wished she'd included Lily Hogan on her list of banned people, for the next day, when she saw Lily walking up the ward, Maeve felt her insides quail. She lay in the bed and thought that if she'd borne a child who'd turned out like Brendan, she'd be ashamed. But she knew Lily wouldn't be. And she wasn't.

Lily was a victim of her own husband's violence, and Maeve knew she would consider it a part of marriage, and she guessed Lily would convince herself Maeve was somehow responsible for it.

She wasn't disappointed either, for after Lily had regarded Maeve dispassionately for a moment or two, she said, 'You asked for it. You know that, don't you?'

Maeve gazed at her, not even surprised at her reaction, yet she asked, 'How do you work that out?'

'A husband can't take his wife running out on him without doing something about it. You must have realised; you're not stupid,' Lily said in the plaintive whine Maeve hated.

'Yes, well now you know why I was not that keen to come back.'

'Maeve, you married Brendan,' Lily said. 'You promised to obey him before God. You bore him children. You have obligations. You can't just run away whenever you have the notion. And when you did, he had to teach you a lesson. It's a husband's right.'

'He nearly bloody killed me!' Maeve cried. 'He married me for better or for worse as well, don't forget. The children I bore him are from his seed, his responsibility, and yet he would have them starve and freeze to death. Dear God, Lily, do you have no shame?'

'He's my son,' Lily Hogan said.

'And as such, can do no wrong?'

'I didn't say that,' Lily said. 'You don't go about things the right way, that's all. You antagonise him.'

'No, I bloody don't,' Maeve said through gritted teeth. 'It wouldn't have mattered what way I went about the business that night. He was determined to beat me to pulp.'

At the distress in Maeve's voice a nurse came forward anxiously. She saw the anger in Maeve's battered face and the tears that ran down her bruised cheeks from her bloodshot eyes and she said to Lily Hogan, 'I'm afraid I must ask you to leave. The patient mustn't be upset in this way.'

Highly affronted, Lily Hogan left and Maeve settled down again. But her mind kept jumping about. Obviously Lily thought it was a wife's lot to endure beatings, and either through upbringing, personal experience or both, had no reason to revise her ideas. Lily, by accepting violence throughout her own marriage, had passed on those values to her own five sons and two daughters. Brendan thought it was acceptable behaviour; it was what he'd grown up with.

Dr Thomas, the hospital doctor, came to see Maeve the next day. She kept her promise to the young nurse and didn't say a word about what she'd been told already, and listened intently as the doctor explained her injuries. As well as having lacerations and bruising throughout her body, one arm had been broken in two places, as well as a number of ribs. There was also damage to the kidneys and the spine, which could possibly correct itself with bed rest, he said. She also had a deep gash in one leg and her head, and both required stitching, while an X-ray revealed a hairline fracture of the skull.

However, when the doctor enquired if she would be pressing charges, Maeve's response was, 'No, I couldn't charge him if I wanted to. In the eyes of the law he has committed no crime. I thought you knew that. He is my husband and therefore thinks he has a right to chastise me.'

'But he hasn't. Surely you know that?'

'What difference would it make if I did?' Maeve said. 'It will change nothing.'

The doctor looked at the young woman aghast. He'd seldom seen or heard anything so monstrous and yet the woman spoke firmly, and though fear still lurked behind the eyes he had an idea that she knew exactly what she was talking about.

'So, that's that then!' the doctor exclaimed in exasperation. 'You just put up with it?'

'That's about the strength of it,' Maeve replied, but inside she quailed at the thought of going back to the house to live with Brendan again.

But there was little chance of going to live anywhere in the near future as one day slid into another and the weeks passed. Maeve was grateful to Elsie for caring for Bridget so well and looking after her house, even if she did urge Maeve to leave Brendan and go back to her mother every time she came. Maeve knew she wouldn't do that again. She'd gone down that road once and nearly destroyed those she held so dear. So not only did she not even consider going, she refused to let her mother and those at home know what Brendan had done, because Maeve thought it was silly to worry them about a situation they would be unable to change. Elsie didn't agree with her but knew it was pointless to argue. Elsie was just glad the post came after Brendan left for work. She always took the letters from Ireland to Maeve and if there was any money inside Maeve would give it back to her. At least Brendan never got to know about that. It would have been hard for Maeve if he ever got wind of it.

Maeve had been in hospital three weeks when she asked to see a priest about receiving Communion. She was surprised to see Father Trelawney, as he should have been refused entry, and she'd specifically asked for the old parish priest, Father Roberts, to attend to her.

Father Trelawney strode across the room and stopped by her bed. 'Hello, Maeve.'

Maeve let her eyes roll upwards. 'I don't want to see you, Father. I have nothing to say to you.'

'Then let me speak,' the priest said. 'Please believe me when I say how sorry I am for what happened to you.'

'What happened to me?' Maeve spat out. 'You talk as if I walked into a wall or was knocked down by a car. You know what happened to me as well as I do and by whose hand.'

Father Trelawney knew only too well, and why, and he asked gently, 'Why did you not say?'

'Look at me, Father,' Maeve cried. 'This is what happens when I defy Brendan and go against him in any way. And he thinks he's perfectly justified to beat me senseless. As his mother pointed out, in the marriage service I promised to obey him. I took him for better or worse, and that, as far as he's concerned, is that.'

Father Trelawney bowed his head and Maeve guessed he'd said those words himself to more than one distraught wife who'd hammered on his door for advice.

'That night I bought coal to prevent the child I'd given birth to from perishing with the cold. I also gave a ten-bob note to Elsie to keep for me – six and six for the rent and three and six off the arrears. If I hadn't, Brendan would have taken nearly every penny back off me again.'

'I had no idea this was happening, Maeve,' Father Trelawney said.

'Oh, I know that, Father,' Maeve said. 'Like you don't know that I often had nothing to eat or drink in the house but cold water. I make sure I have a dinner for Brendan, for I'd be afraid not to, but I live on bread and dripping or scrape or just bread by itself. I'm hungry and cold so often it's not worth talking of, and so were Kevin and Grace when they were home. We're not the only ones who live like this, I know. I'm not the only wife and mother who skulks around the Bull Ring on Saturday night to pick up vegetables my father wouldn't feed to the pigs and meat that's on the turn but cheap. Then I go home with my spoils and hope I have gas enough to make a meal. That, Father, is how it is.'

The priest was shocked at Maeve's words, there was no doubt. Not only had Brendan broken his word that he would try to control his temper, but he'd also taken the money that he took around to the priest on a Friday night. Father Trelawney was disappointed because he liked Brendan and they'd sunk a good few pints in The Bell together, and most men there moaned about their wives.

They were always saying he didn't know when he was well off and he had to agree. He had a very comfortable life. Florrie McCormack, their housekeeper, was a niece of Father Roberts's. She'd never been married and her sole purpose in life was caring and seeing to the priests in her care. She ran the house efficiently and well; their meals, even in wartime, were tasty, plentiful and never late; the house was spotless and their clothes collected from where they dropped them, washed, ironed and replaced in the right places. She never worried the priests over trifling matters and she never complained. Added to that, there was no worry over rent, or how to cope with the demands of a carping wife or a growing family, and Father Trelawney was glad of it when he listened to the men's grievances. But this behaviour of Brendan's could not go on. Difficult as it was he'd have to talk to him.

Maeve knew the priest had been moved and also knew he would probably have a wee chat about it with Brendan. It would be bugger all use, except to make Brendan angrier than ever. She wished she'd kept her bloody mouth shut.

Father Trelawney looked across at Maeve and asked gently, 'D'you want to make a good confession before I administer Communion?'

'No,' Maeve answered wearily. 'Not to you, Father. I've done enough confessing to you for one day.'

She never asked for a priest again, but Christmas was a bleak time. She cried for the baby she'd not seen in weeks, and had no appetite for her mashed-up Christmas dinner, which resembled something you'd feed to a baby you were trying to wean. Elsie and Alf tried to cheer her and brought in cards from the neighbours, which Elsie arranged around Maeve's bed in a bid to make her feel a wee bit better.

Maeve wasn't to know that Brendan would have liked the opportunity to see Maeve, for the hospital staff didn't mention the times he came because the doctors gave strict orders that she was not to be upset. But Brendan knew it was a form of madness that came over him at times that had caused him to attack Maeve so viciously. He had wanted to kill her and very nearly had. Father Trelawney had no need to seek him out at his mother's and take him to task as severely as he had. He knew what he'd done and was sorry, goddammit, but the bloody hospital wouldn't let him near her, apparently on her say-so. No wonder he got annoyed with the woman.

And then the priest going on about the war and all, saying everyone had to do their bit and pull together to beat the enemy – God, that stuck in Brendan's craw, for hadn't the bloody English been the enemy of Ireland for generations? Eventually, for the sake of peace, for the priest, when he put his mind to it, was a greater nag than any woman, he'd agreed to go bloody fire-watching a few nights after work. At least that was preferable to parading round the roads with a bloody broomstick over his shoulder, pretending that it was a gun.

When Elsie told Maeve she wondered what difference it would make to her. True, if he was fire-watching two or three nights a week, he couldn't be drinking, but she knew her husband: he would just use the extra money to back the horses, or spend it in some other dubious way. Anyway, the war was months old and no bombs had dropped. She knew the men in the forces might be having a hard time of it, but for the ordinary people, the worst thing they'd had to endure so far was the blackout and now, so Elsie told her, rationing, which had started in January 1940.

By the middle of January Maeve's back had healed sufficiently for her to sit up, and so it was one cold and gloomy day in the middle of February that Elsie came to the hospital with little Bridget wrapped in her shawl, for the ride home together in a taxi.

Maeve hardly acknowledged the luxury of the ride, for she was entranced by the baby she hadn't seen for weeks. Bridget seemed to have grown so much. Her eyes had changed from newborn blue to deep brown and her hair, light brown like Kevin's, lay like down on her tiny head. Maeve examined her features and counted her fingers and toes, awed as always by the tiny nails, the whole miracle of her. Suddenly Bridget seemed to scrutinise Maeve as if she didn't know quite who she was. A frown appeared on her little forehead and Maeve smiled at it. 'Hello, my precious,' she said, and the baby rewarded her with a big toothless beam that seemed to light up her face and almost caused Maeve's heart to stop beating.

She held her tight and vowed she would fight anyone, even Brendan and the entire clergy, for the right to a decent upbringing for Bridget.

Despite her promise to herself it was hard to enter her house again. But Elsie had been in and the place shone, and a cheerful fire burnt in the grate, warming the room and chasing away the shadows. Elsie had also left a stew simmering on the gas stove and the smell of it made Maeve's mouth water. There was little meat in it, as Maeve had expected, but plenty of vegetables and dumplings, together with a pan of potatoes and slices of bread to soak up the gravy. After a bowl of it, Maeve was revived, warmed inside and out and felt more able to cope with anything, even her husband.

And later that night she turned to face him as he came in the door.

'So,' he said at last, 'you're home again.'

'Aye. I'm home and I'll stay as long as you keep your fists and boots to yourself,' Maeve said, and her voice was firm, though her insides seemed to have turned to water.

'You asked for it.'

'I asked for nothing,' Maeve hissed, 'and I'll not stand it, not again.'

'Don't be so bloody stupid,' Brendan burst out. 'I'm your husband and it's my right to chastise you.'

Maeve didn't bother arguing. She knew that Brendan really did believe that, so instead she said, 'Well, you've chastised me now, let that be an end to it. If you leave me alone and give me enough to live on we'll manage well enough, I suppose. But if you don't, I'm off to the priest, Brendan.'

Brendan wasn't used to being spoken to like that, but he didn't slap Maeve like he once surely would have done because if she did actually go to tell the priest, he had the feeling he'd take a very dim view of it altogether.

Father Trelawney had been short and bad-tempered with him lately and said he really had to control his temper. Easy for him to say: he didn't have the aggravation of it.

'Elsie made a stew for us both,' Maeve told him. 'Sit up to the table and eat it now while it's hot.'

Brendan made no answer, but Maeve knew when he saw the stew in the bowl with a steaming plate of potatoes beside it, he'd realise how hungry he was, for he was always ravenous when he came in from work, and he made short work of the meal.

After he'd finished, he nodded at Maeve and said, 'All right, maybe I went a bit over the top and I was sorry

162

after. But you can't say you didn't ask for it, running off like you did.'

'I came back to you. Isn't that enough?'

'No,' Brendan snarled. 'No, it isn't because you only came back because you were forced to by the priest.'

'Aye. Can you wonder at it?'

Brendan said nothing. Instead, he just stared at Maeve and wished things could have been different, before weans had bloated her body and soured their lives.

Maeve didn't understand the look, but she was gratified that she'd had what almost amounted to an apology, something she hadn't had in years, and it gave her new heart. Maybe, things could be put right between them. She could only wait and see.

ELEVEN

Brendan hadn't radically changed at all, though over the weeks following the horrific beating he'd given her after Bridget's birth, his violence towards Maeve wasn't so bad, and she felt she could cope with the odd thump, clout or black eye that Brendan gave her every now and again.

More worrying to Maeve was the war news. For months and months it had seemed to meander along with nothing much happening, but by early June all that changed. The grumbles about the dreaded blackout and the rationing, paled into insignificance as the reports came in about the Expeditionary Forces' retreat from Dunkirk. Although many had been lifted from the beaches by small boats that had carried the marooned soldiers out to naval ships anchored in the deeper water of the channel, far too many had been left behind. In the streets around, many houses received the first telegrams sent out with dire news of their loved ones.

Nine months into the war, British people faced the dread realisation that for the first time they might be on the losing side and German paratroopers could soon be patrolling the streets, for now Britain was wide open for invasion. First, though, Hitler's plan seemed to be to subdue the cities, and as the Nazis pounded the ports with bombs to destroy the ships and sap the morale of the people, the RAF responded and the Battle of Britain was fought in the skies.

No one moaned now about the blackout restrictions, nor the rationing, even though meat was added to bacon, sugar, fat and tea, rationed to two ounces per person per week, by July. It was common knowledge that existence as they knew it depended on the boys in blue, who risked their lives daily to fight in the air. To moan about anything seemed disloyal and unpatriotic because the human cost was enormous and everyone knew it.

Maeve, in any case, couldn't afford even the basic rations on the money Brendan allowed her to keep. The priest still went on with the farce of bringing her the housekeeping that Brendan had given him, though he knew now that Brendan took most of it back again. She didn't bother complaining, in fact she spoke to him as little as possible. He knew the score now – God, she'd told him clearly enough – and he'd made it obvious whose side he was on, and it wasn't hers. Without the money from her mother she knew she'd be in queer street, though it filled her with shame being forced, through dire necessity, to accept it. As it was she could just about limp along from week to week.

Brendan was bored and bad-tempered. Though he'd had no desire to fight for the British Government, and as an Irish citizen couldn't be made to do so either, he didn't want to sit on factory roofs all night either, watching for nonexistent bombs. He complained, often taking his frustration and irritation out on Maeve.

It changed in the middle of the summer for all the citizens of Birmingham, including Brendan, who was on duty on the roof of an armaments factory on the night of 25 August. There had been one previous raid on Birmingham in early August, when a lone bomber, thought to be searching for Fort Dunlop, dropped his load over suburban Erdington. At the time Maeve had remembered the O'Rourkes, whom she'd met on the ferry. They lived in Erdington and she hoped they were safe. So far there had been many small raids, mainly on the east of the city, which had caused minimal damage, and people began to think that Birmingham was going to get off lightly.

But the night the bombers came to the city centre, Maeve leapt from her bed as soon as the siren began screaming. She dressed hurriedly and then picked the baby up, wrapping a blanket around her little body, for the night air could be chill. Brendan was fire-watching, but Elsie and Alf were at the door when she sped down the stairs and she was glad of their comforting presence and the wavering torch Alf had, lighting their way, though the beam was shielded as regulations demanded.

The drone of the planes was audible as they stepped into the street and they hurried as fast as they could to the shelter on Bristol Street, while behind them searchlights zigzagged across the sky.

The brick-built shelter, surrounded by sandbags, was filling up when Maeve, Elsie and Alf reached it, but Maeve was able to find an empty bunk to lay Bridget down. Although she'd stirred when she'd been lifted from the cot, she'd dropped off again.

For Maeve, as for most adults, there was no such respite. Every whistle and thud of explosion brought her bolt upright and eventually she gave up all pretence of sleep and accepted the sandwiches Elsie pressed on her and the hot sweet tea she had in a vacuum flask.

Two nights later, the situation was repeated. This time Alf was absent as he too was fire-watching.

'I expect Brendan will come in stinking of cordite and covered with black ash like last time,' Maeve said with a sigh, 'behaving like a weasel and beating the head off me for asking him a civil question.'

'I thought it was the drink that made him so violent, and there ain't that much of it about now,' Elsie said.

'So they say, all right,' Maeve said with feeling. 'Maybe lack of it makes him worse. I hear a lot of the pubs are short of beer now – perhaps that's the thing to be rationed next – and it's even rumoured some landlords water it down. Brendan doesn't seem to be affected by it, though. He seems to be able to drink enough of it to make him stinking drunk the nights he's not fire-watching.'

'Blokes like him would always find it,' Elsie said, and sent up a fervent prayer that the man would be burnt to a crisp on the roof of the factories one of these nights.

But after that second August raid there was a respite for about a month, and when the raids began again in late September they were the first in daylight too.

'Bloody cat and mouse,' Elsie declared as they hurried to the shelter one cold October night. 'Lull us into a sense of false security and then let us have it again. London's got it, and now us, thick and fast and every bleeding night. I met Deidre Bradshaw and she was telling me about her sister Daisy, who lives down by the docks in London. Deidre said her sister's all for going down the tube, 'cos there aren't enough shelters for the people. She's worried to death about her. I mean, she's got three nippers and all, and her husband away in the army.'

'I know, Deidre told me too,' Maeve said. 'And it's a terrible situation right enough.' There had been more than one report on the news and in the paper about unprotected Londoners bedding down in the underground stations and being moved on by the authorities. 'It isn't something you do by choice really, is it?' Maeve went on. 'Imagine dragging weans through the streets of London and trying to keep them safe in a cold draughty dirty station because it's the best you can do.'

She gave a sudden shiver for Deidre's sister, Daisy, and the thousands like her as they reached the door of their shelter and slipped inside. She'd never known Daisy Bullock, because she'd moved to London before Maeve got the house in Latimer Street. But her sister, Deidre, had moved to Grant Street as a new bride about the same time as Maeve, and the two women had become friends.

However, as the years passed there had been no sign of a child for Deidre and her husband, Matthew, and Maeve had become almost embarrassed because of her own evidence of fertility to see much of Deidre. She'd felt heartsore for her, especially as she'd always been so kind to Kevin and Grace, and had been one of the first to pop in with a gift for Bridget. Elsie had a special sympathy for her, recognising one such as herself and Alf with the barren childless years they'd had together.

At least she doesn't have to traipse down here every night like us,' Maeve said wearily, because she knew Deidre shared her parents' large cellar as they had a house that opened out on to Bell Barn Road.

Maeve wished she had a cellar she could use, because she was very weary, struggling down to the shelter night after night, with little or no sleep for herself. Bridget was getting more difficult to handle as she grew, and less likely to go to sleep once she'd been roused. Maeve was also always worried about her catching a cold, as her clothes were barely adequate for the approaching winter nights.

She was just coming up to her first birthday when Maeve opened the door one day to Deidre Bradshaw, holding a parcel. 'Baby clothes from my sister's youngest,' she explained, thrusting the parcel at Maeve. 'It's criminal to throw the stuff away these days.' And then with a glance at Maeve's face, 'You're not offended?'

'Offended?' Maeve wanted to give Deidre a kiss or drag her into the house and dance a jig. She was overcome with the woman's thoughtfulness for there was everything Bridget could need for the next year or two – dresses and cardigans and jumpers and leggings and vests and pants, warm fleecy nighties, and a blue siren suit with a hood trimmed with fur. It would be too big for Bridget yet, but she'd still put her in it, even if the cuffs did hang over her hands and feet. It would be a damned sight warmer than anything else she had. Maeve invited Deidre in and offered her a cup of tea.

On 26 October, in the early hours of the morning, there was an incendiary raid on the city centre. When the bleary-eyed people came out of the shelter to the reassuring sound of the all-clear, they stared at the brightly lit sky with crackling red and amber flames and sparks spitting into the night.

The August raids had mainly hit the Bull Ring, causing extensive damage and lifting the roof off the Market Hall. They'd left gaping holes and large craters behind them and reduced some shops to shells, but the October raid set whole streets alight in the city centre. The Luftwaffe returned the next night and the next until the morning of 29 October, when Maeve and Elsie stood in stunned silence outside their air-raid shelter in the early hours and watched Birmingham burn.

Maeve was too tired sometimes to remember to be cautious in her dealings with Brendan and often caught a clout from him for answering him back. But that morning, she hardly felt it, because she was far more worried about the war than she was about Brendan. She'd been stunned by the ferocity of the air attacks and wondered bleakly if anyone might be alive by the same time in 1941.

Maeve's mother urged her to come home, even if just for a wee while, but Maeve knew Brendan would never tolerate the idea. However, there were other alternatives. Many of the parents who'd brought their children home from their evacuated homes before Christmas 1939 were now regretting it. Further evacuations were being planned to safer areas, and mothers with babies, the pregnant, disabled and the elderly could be part of that programme. While Brendan ate his tea the following evening, Maeve broached the subject of her and Bridget going too.

He looked up at her under his bushy eyebrows. 'You'll go nowhere,' he said firmly. 'Your place is here, looking after the house and seeing to me.'

Maeve took a step back. The look on Brendan's face suggested to her that space between them might be a healthier option, but for Bridget's sake she went on, 'It's for the baby, Brendan. She's so small and I just wondered—'

'You just wondered, did you?' Brendan thundered, leaping to his feet and grabbing her. Maeve's words had incensed him. She was prepared to desert him, leave him to scratch about by himself because of a sodding baby, he thought. The children always came first with Maeve, just as they had for his mother. Bloody women were all the same. 'Listen to me,' he hissed. 'Let the bloody brat go if you're so bleeding worried about her, but you go nowhere. You get that?' And he shook her so hard that when he let go, she fell against the fireplace.

Maeve got it fine. No way would she allow her baby to go miles away in the charge of strangers, especially when Maeve had missed so much of her early babyhood.

'Maybe I'm selfish to keep her with me and in danger too,' Maeve said to Elsie, 'but I can't bear to let her go. I miss Kevin and Grace every day as it is, but Bridget's so small.'

'A baby is always best left with her mother,' Elsie said firmly.

'What if something should happen to her?'

'Something could happen to any of us,' Elsie said. 'Aren't we all in God's hands?'

And they were. The priests always said they shouldn't question God. He was all-powerful and loving and yet, thought Maeve, he allowed such suffering. It was a mystery to her.

Then, on 19 November, the sirens went off at fifteen minutes past seven. With a sigh of relief that at least the meal was over and done with, Maeve picked Bridget up. She was now toddling around the room and objected strongly to being grabbed and zipped into her siren suit, and over her wails Maeve said to Brendan, 'Are you on duty tonight?'

'No, I'm going down The Bell, but I might be called out. After the raid on Coventry they reckon this will be the big one.'

Maeve felt her limbs beginning to tremble. Weren't the raids they'd gone through already big enough?

'Can't you shut that brat up?' Brendan snapped.

'She's tired and out of sorts, that's all,' Maeve said. 'She can't help it.'

'I'll give her something to bloody cry for in a minute,' Brendan threatened.

'No, you won't!' Maeve said firmly. 'You touch her and I'll go straight to the priest. Anyway,' she said, taking her coat from the hook on the door, 'we're away now.'

She was out into the black inky night before Brendan could reply, glad of Elsie and Alf's company.

And there followed a night when Maeve doubted she'd see the dawn. Wave after wave of bombers attacked Birmingham and while few areas escaped damage, the city centre and the roads ringing it where the factories working for the war effort were situated were the prime targets.

That wasn't apparent to those cowering in the shelter, but what was, was the boom and crash of explosives, so powerful and so close they rocked the walls of the shelter. People screamed in fear and others cried or prayed, while one man with a mouth organ tried to organise a singsong, mainly for the children.

The noise was earth-shattering, what with the whistle and thud of bombs, the clatter of incendiaries and shrapnel that hit the walls and roof of the shelter like hailstones. This was answered by the ack-ack guns barking into the night and the emergency services' bells ringing crazily.

Maeve felt as if she was going mad. She wanted to cover her ears with her hands and scream her head off. She held Bridget tight, for the child screamed in fear and Maeve didn't blame her. She was aware of Elsie beside her, her face chalk white and her hands shaking as she poured tea. Alf was no longer with them. He'd been taken with other male volunteers as a rescue party to another brick-built shelter that had collapsed, trapping many people inside. Maeve looked at their own shuddering walls and wondered if theirs would be the next to go.

When the all-clear finally went at 4.30 a.m. and Maeve and Elsie left the shelter, they were met by billowing black smoke and swirling grey dust. It almost choked them, stinging their throats and causing them to cough till their eyes streamed. Bridget had fallen asleep from sheer exhaustion and Maeve held her tight against her to protect her throat and lungs.

The glowing amber and red sky showed up the buckled tramlines, the crater in the middle of Bristol Street and gaping holes opposite where shops had once stood. The rubble-filled pavements ran with water, and burst sandbags leaked on to the gleaming wet pavements.

Carefully, they picked their way over the debris littering the pavements, but when they got to the top of Bristol Passage they stopped dead and their mouths dropped open in shock, for Grant Street was there no longer, and neither was one side of Bell Barn Road. Instead, there was a vast sea of bricks, splintered wood and glass. Some houses had been sliced in half, spilling out the now dust-laden contents, and odd walls leant drunkenly and unsteadily against one another.

Even with the glowing orange sky, the swirling dust and smoke made it difficult to see much clearly, but Elsie and Maeve made their way resolutely up what little remained of Grant Street, wondering if Latimer Street, which led off it, still stood. Maeve wondered what she would do if she'd lost her home. Move in with Lily? Never! But what choice would she really have? The only alternative to that would be a shelter in a derelict building or a church hall somewhere, hardly ideal with a small child.

She was so taken by her own thoughts that she almost walked into Deidre Bradshaw, who was standing looking at the remains of what had once been her house. Even in the shielded light from the torch Elsie held, Maeve could see the tear stains on the young woman's face.

'Terrible, isn't it?' she said to Maeve. 'Dear God. But it's bad of me to cry like this over a house when others have suffered more. Pauline Dobson just two doors up was killed outright with her baby daughter last night.'

'No!' Maeve said in shock. She remembered the young woman had a baby born just three weeks before. The news would devastate her young soldier husband, of that Maeve was certain.

'Wouldn't go to the shelter, see. Said the baby was too small and she might catch something.'

'Bloody little fool!' Elsie said, but Maeve had sympathy for her. Sometimes even now she dreaded rousing Bridget when she looked so peaceful and she did worry that the baby would catch something from the air in the shelter, which grew fetid and stale with so much humanity crammed into it, and many of the people spluttering or coughing all the time.

'I asked her to come in with me tonight,' Deidre went on, 'but she wouldn't. Said it was too cold for the baby. Mind you, when the other side of Bell Barn Road went, I thought we were all goners. The whole place shook and plaster dust trickled down on us. I thought, this is it, we'll be entombed in a minute.'

'Oh God, don't,' Maeve said. 'Come on in and I'll make us all some tea.'

'No. I best get back,' Deidre insisted. 'My mom will be anxious. I had to see for myself, you know. I thought I might be able to salvage something.' Deidre gave a shrug. 'Fat chance, though.'

'What will you do?'

'Lodge with my parents,' Deidre said, 'till Matthew's demobbed, anyroad.' She put out her hand suddenly and stroked Bridget's cheek gently. 'Ain't she lovely?' she said. 'You know, times like this I don't mind not having kids.'

But Maeve heard the tone of Deidre's voice and saw the gentle way she touched Bridget and knew she hadn't really spoken the truth. She fervently hoped that when the war was finally over, she and Matthew might get it together and start a family.

Maeve yawned, suddenly aware of how tired she was. She was glad to reach the door of her house and hoped they'd get some sleep that night and the Luftwaffe would have a night off.

But they didn't. Maeve could hardly believe it. With Brendan on duty fire-watching again, she'd fallen asleep almost as soon as she had fed Bridget. But the sirens woke her just a couple of hours later. She stumbled sleepily around the bedroom, preparing to go to the shelter. That evening the attack was from parachute bombs and the first fell mainly in the Aston area of the city, but still Maeve and Elsie, with Alf this time, stayed in the shelter until the all-clear.

The following night, there was no raid, but it hardly mattered, Maeve thought, for she'd sat up half the night anyway waiting for the sirens, her nerves taut. She'd fallen across her bed fully clothed by the time Brendan stumbled into the room and she awoke to find him fumbling at her clothes, cursing that she had so much on. Maeve longed to ask Brendan to leave her alone and let her sleep but she couldn't take him starting on her. She undressed hurriedly and let him do as he pleased. Afterwards she lay sleepless for hours, her body aching from Brendan's rough handling, though her eyes smarted with tiredness.

On the evening of 22 November there was another raid, almost as bad as that on the nineteenth, when single attacks with high-explosive bombs were followed by wave after wave of bombers.

Maeve's heart was thudding against her ribs as the explosions went on all around them, but she tried to remain calm and blank from her mind all thought of the public shelter that had collapsed on the first major November attack, killing and crushing the people inside. 'If it's got your name on it, that's that,' was the general consensus.

The raid didn't finish till six o'clock, but the next day they found out how badly the city had been pounded. The pipes from three trunk water mains on Bristol Road had been shattered and the whole city was without water. Even draining the canals was not sufficient to cope with the fires, and the six hundred that had been started that night had to be left to burn. Although Brummies were not told how serious the situation was, the news filtered through.

For three days following this raid, water had to be collected in buckets from water cans until the mains were repaired and the taps connected up again, but during that time there were no further raids and everyone was glad of a little respite.

Despite this, most people could summon up the energy and enthusiasm for the second Christmas of the war, though the rationing was especially hard to take with the festive season to provide for.

It wasn't helped by two other major raids in December, both causing much destruction and loss of life. The first was on 3 December and the second a week later, starting at six o'clock in the evening and going on for thirteen hours.

The next day King George visited the ravaged city in an unscheduled stop and talked to the people suffering the raids, those in the rescue and emergency services and those made homeless. Despite herself, Maeve was impressed by the softly spoken King, who she'd heard had battled for years to control a stammer. Maeve thought he seemed genuinely upset at what the people had suffered. News of his visits spread through the city and people thronged the streets to see him, and the National Anthem was sung spontaneously in many places.

Over Christmas there was a lull in the raids and Maeve and Elsie went to the Bull Ring and took a look at their dilapidated, fire-gutted city. Whale meat was on sale but it was 2/6d a pound, too dear for Maeve, but Elsie bought some and the stallholder told her to cook it with onions and try to cut down the strong taste by mixing it with mashed potato. When Maeve tried a bit of Elsie's fish pie made in this way, she was glad she'd used the tip. It still tasted extremely fishy, but it filled her up and, anyway, no one could afford to be fussy.

'I hope 1941 is a better year than this last one, anyroad,' Elsie said to Maeve the day before New Year's Eve.

'And me. The raids terrify me,' Maeve admitted. 'Not for myself alone, but for Bridget and you and Alf and all the other neighbours and friends around.' Neither woman thought it strange that Brendan's name wasn't mentioned.

In January there was a call for more women to work in munitions and it was just after Maeve read this in Alf's paper that she met a neighbour, Maureen Dempsey, in Mountford's and they got to talking about it.

'Would you go, Maureen?' Maeve asked. 'I'd be a bit nervous about working in a factory. Anyway, it wouldn't do me a bit of good. Brendan would take every penny off me.'

'God, I'd go tomorrow if I could find someone to look after my two nippers,' Maureen said. 'I'd love to get out and get a job, and my old man can't take anything off me 'cos I don't even know where the bleeding sod is, but "somewhere in France". Mind you,' she added, 'if he tried that lark, I'd brain him with the bleeding frying pan.'

But an idea was stirring in Maeve's mind to earn some money of her own. She looked at Maureen's children, one just a wee baby and one a toddler, and she said, 'I'll look after the babies for you, Maureen.'

'Are you kidding?'

'Would I joke over something like this?'

'And would you take another nipper on?' Maureen asked. 'Only me mate and me was talking about it the other day and she said she'd like to do it and all, but her babby's nearly two. We could be set on together if you'd do it, like.'

And it was as easy as that. Maeve took on the three children, and as they arrived after Brendan left and were collected before he returned home, he was unaware of it. She got two pounds ten shillings a week for each child she minded, and so she normally received seven pounds ten shillings a week, plus what she tried to keep back from the money the priest still brought. And she continued to try because she couldn't allow Brendan to get any hint that she no longer had such a great need of it.

Fortunately, he was too caught up in his own affairs to notice any difference in Maeve or the children, so Maeve's source of income went undetected. Never one to waste money, Maeve put the cash box at Elsie's into play again, but she kept some money back to buy a few extras to add to the food cupboard on their weekly trip to the Bull Ring every Saturday.

Just after Maeve started minding the children she was issued with a Morrison shelter, which consisted of a steel table with steel mesh sides that she'd open to crawl inside. The bottom was sprung for a mattress to be fitted, which Maeve was given by the Red Cross.

'D'you think it's really necessary for us to have them?' she asked Elsie, because since the turn of the year, the raids had been light, short and infrequent, and had caused little damage. 'I mean, Hitler seems to have finished with us now.'

'Who knows what's on that madman's mind, ducks?' Elsie said. 'You hang on to your Morrison and I'll hang on to mine till this bloody war is over.'

Brendan kicked off about it right and proper when he came home and said it took up too much room, but Maeve let him rant, knowing he'd take no steps to remove it. Maeve soon found another use for it anyway, because it was a good place to lay the children down for a rest in the day, once they'd outgrown a pram. It was warmer than the bedroom in those crisp spring days and safer than a bed or chairs that they could roll off.

On 9 April Maeve was glad of her Morrison, because the Luftwaffe again attacked Birmingham in force, the sirens going off at nine thirty. Maeve soon found that one of the disadvantages of a Morrison was that the noise of the raid was all around you, not muffled like in the sand-bagged, reinforced public shelters. There was also no one to talk with, to take your mind off the terrifying noise, the drone of the planes with their distinctive 'burr burr' engine noise and the whistle of the dropping bombs and resultant blast of explosives that shook the walls and rattled the windows of the house. She clearly heard the shuddering crash of buildings collapsing, the screams and cries of people and the noise of ambulances and fire engines rushing through the night. She felt as if she were held in a vice of fear and she prayed that she and Bridget would be safe.

Surprisingly, Bridget did eventually fall asleep against Maeve's shoulder, but Maeve continued to sit and hold her, sure the house would collapse about them. A Morrison was supposed to stand up against that and Maeve was terrified that soon it would be put to the test, but when the all-clear went in the early hours of Good Friday morning, she was still alive and so was Bridget, and the house was intact.

Shortly after that raid, Maeve knew she was pregnant again and was scared stiff of telling Brendan.

'Oh, Elsie, what the bloody hell am I going to do?'

'Stand up to the bugger. Tell him straight,' Elsie said fiercely. 'Tell him it ain't your bleeding fault and he should learn to keep it in his trousers more often.'

'Oh, Elsie . . .' Maeve cried, and pictured the scene if she actually did what Elsie suggested. It really didn't bear thinking about. 'I wish I could just feel bloody well excited like I should be, instead of so frightened to tell my husband,' Maeve went on. 'I wouldn't mind how many I had if I was given enough money to rear them properly.'

But in the end she didn't have to tell Brendan, because he tumbled to it himself when he heard her being sick in the morning. The beating he gave her was so severe, she feared she would miscarry and though she didn't, she was too sore and bruised to move. She had to call on Elsie to look after the children until she was on her feet again and able to cope, because she'd been terrified of losing her source of income.

The childminding job was a lifesaver for Maeve. She wrote to her mother immediately she began earning, thanking her for the money she'd sent, saying it was no longer necessary and offering to contribute towards the cost of bringing up her children. Annie's reply was swift and firm. It would be a poor body indeed who needed payment for looking after their own flesh and blood, she said. And though she was glad things were better for Maeve, she didn't want another word said about money.

For Maeve, the money she earned made all the difference to her life, although much of it still was saved in the cash box. While others moaned about rationing, for cheese had been added to the grocery list and clothes were put on ration in June 1941, for Maeve the money meant now she could get decent food for Bridget and herself as well as Brendan. She could afford whale meat and horse meat from the Bull Ring on her Saturday outings with Elsie, and a bit of fruit, even if it was just apples and pears. There were no bananas or oranges, and grapes were far too expensive for Maeve's purse.

She was, however, able to buy some fairly good second-hand clothing that she could unpick to make something halfway decent for herself. Maeve often thought it was amazing the boost wearing clothes that weren't mere rags did for a person.

James David Hogan was born in November 1941, bigger and plumper altogether than his puny sister, Bridget, had been, and Maeve recovered quicker after the birth this time because she was slightly better nourished. She still saved as much money as possible and gave the best food to Bridget, the children in her care and Brendan rather than herself. But still, Elsie was glad to see the sheen back in Maeve's hair and the hopeless look leave her face that had lost its gauntness. Elsie could see again the beautiful woman that Maeve still was, that had been hidden beneath extreme poverty and the ragged clothes that hung on her sparse frame.

On 7 December Pearl Harbor was attacked and America entered the war. But all in all, in Birmingham life was more peaceful, at least on the war front, for there had been no raids since July. Maeve still had her own private war at home, but the house was warmer and the food more plentiful with the money Maeve earned. She hoped the end of the war would come speedily for the suffering of the people and yet when it did, she knew her source of income would dry up and she didn't know what the hell she'd do then.

TWELVE

In the spring of 1942, Elsie and Maeve saw their first American GIs in the Bull Ring. What surprised them most were the black ones. 'Jet-black, you know, shiny,' Elsie told Alf. 'And their eyes look so big in their head and their teeth so white.'

'Don't matter what they look like, as long as we're fighting on the same side,' Alf said.

Most Birmingham people thought the same, and couldn't understand the way some white Americans treated their black comrades. 'Ain't they all Yanks and all set to fight the bloody Germans and Japs, not each other?' was a typical comment.

But the GIs, both black and white, were soon a familiar sight in the city and the young girls found them particularly appealing. They spoke like most of the people they'd seen on the cinema screen, were dressed smarter than the average British Tommy and had more money to flash about, and they gave presents of chocolate, chewing gum and nylons to the chosen few.

Maeve was as intrigued by the Americans as anyone else, but in the main found them too brash and loud-mouthed for her taste. She was, however, as pleased as punch by the tins of dried egg that were imported from America in June 1942. Eggs were not and never had been on ration, but were extremely rare due to the slaughter of hundreds of hens to save on foodstuffs at the beginning of the war, so dried egg – though nothing like the real thing – was very welcome.

'Dig for victory' was the slogan nearly three years into a war that looked as if it would drag on for ever. Many of the parks and any waste ground were dug up and crops planted. People were encouraged to eat potatoes and root vegetables that could be home-grown rather than imported goods, putting the ships carrying such things at risk.

However, there was a limit to what people could do with potatoes, swede, carrots and the like. To help, a programme called *The Kitchen Front* was broadcast on the wireless just after the eight o'clock news and Elsie wrote down the recipes for her and Maeve to try out. The most famous of these was the meatless Woolton Pie named after Lord Woolton, who was the Minister for Food. It was fairly tasteless but most housewives had to resort to it, or something very similar, towards the end of the week when the rations were gone.

'Do us for Friday,' Elsie said, 'when we can't eat meat.'

'As a change from smelly whale-meat pie or dried egg,' Maeve said with a smile. 'Sometimes at night I dream about food. Isn't that a desperate admission?'

'It's a bit sad, all right,' Elsie agreed. 'Anyway, what's to dream about? Even with Lord Woolton and his brainy ideas, what we cook is hardly the stuff of dreams.'

'No, indeed,' Maeve agreed with a laugh. 'And it's not that sort of food I dream about. It's the stuff back home.

Rashers as big as a man's hand served up with an egg or two, or juicy pork with crunchy crackling, and chicken that would melt in your mouth.'

'People like you should be locked up for destroying public morale,' Elsie said in mock severity. She tipped the bag of second-hand clothes from the market they'd brought in with them as she spoke and began sorting through them. 'Come on, let's see if we can make something useful out of this lot.' She gave a wry laugh and said, 'At least it will be better than that damned Mrs Sew and Sew in my magazine. Making a blouse out of dusters, I ask you? Who the hell buys bloody dusters in the first place?'

Maeve smiled as she helped Elsie sort the big bag of clothes they'd got from the Bull Ring that day. Both women were soon unpicking seams and cutting off buttons and zips while Jamie snoozed away the rest of the morning and Bridget played happily with Elsie's button box. 'Make do and mend' was another slogan of the war at that time and the phrase 'waste not, want not' came into its own for to be a squander bug was the greatest crime in creation. But Maeve never took any sewing home with her, because it wouldn't do for Brendan to think she had spare money to buy second-hand clothes. But the bit extra had made all the difference to her.

Although the war carried on relentlessly, at least the raids had stopped. Then, towards the end of July 1942, Maeve was suddenly jerked awake one night. She lay for a few seconds wondering what had woken her. Then she heard it again, the steady drone of many planes and the distant thud and blast of the bombs. She jumped out of bed, pulled aside the blackout curtain at the window and saw the glow of incendiary fires.

Where are the bloody sirens? she thought, lifting the sleeping Jamie and wrapping the cot blanket around him before waking Bridget.

She was downstairs before the unearthly wail began, and realised that even those on watch had been lulled into thinking it was all over, for it had been a year since any form of attack. Even Brendan, on fire-watch duty that night, had remarked on how stupid it was when the raids had ceased.

But Maeve took no chances. Afterwards she heard of people roused by the sirens that had turned over in bed, thinking it was a false alarm, and had lost their lives because of it. Two days later, when the sirens screamed again, there was a rush for the shelters, but still nine hundred people were killed or seriously injured over the two nights.

'Do you think we're for another pasting?' Elsie asked Maeve after the second raid.

'I hope not,' Maeve said wearily. 'Bridget is the very devil to settle again now. She thinks she's up for the whole night if I wake her. If I tell her off, she makes so much row, she wakes her brother too. If there's many more raids I'll end up a gibbering idiot.'

'Oh,' commented Elsie drily, 'no change there then.'

But to everyone's relief, there were no more raids and though most people sat or lay for some days and weeks later waiting for the siren to wail again, eventually they began to relax.

In the spring of 1943 Maeve met Deidre Bradshaw at Mountford's shop, seemingly buying up the place. 'I've used some of Mom and Dad's coupons and points as well as my own,' she explained to Maeve. 'It's for a bit of a party. My Matthew is coming home for a while. He's been injured.'

186

'Oh, I'm sorry.'

'Don't be. I'm delighted,' Deidre said. 'It's only his leg. He was caught in a blast from a bomb but he's all right. They've patched him up, like, and he might be home for a fortnight, he said.'

There was no doubting Deidre's delight when Matthew did arrive, walking with a stick, his leg still heavily bandaged.

He returned to his unit in late April and Elsie, walking in on Maeve one day in June, announced with a smile, 'Seemingly, it was only Matthew's leg that was damaged then?'

'What?'

'The bloody woman's pregnant – Deidre Bradshaw. I've just met her coming home from the doctor's.'

Maeve couldn't have been more pleased and told Deidre when she saw her. She seemed to be floating on air and had a permanent smile on her face.

Angela Bradshaw was born in January 1944. Maeve left all the children in Elsie's care and went up to see the baby.

'She's lovely, beautiful,' she said to the proud mother, looking at the baby's down of dark brown hair and the deep blue eyes that she thought would probably turn to brown like those of her mother and father.

'Matthew's over the moon,' Deidre enthused. 'Oh, Maeve, I can't tell you how happy I am.'

'You don't need to,' Maeve said. She didn't tell Deidre she was pregnant herself. To do so would have brought to her mind the scene when she'd told Brendan, and the way he'd lashed out at her and split open her lip and made her nose pour with blood. 'Over the moon,' Deidre had said Matthew Bradshaw was. Maeve wished just once her own husband had reacted that way. But on no account would she take the pleasure from Deidre's eyes, and she pressed her hand fondly and said, 'You'll make a great mother, Deidre, never fret.'

Deidre did make a good mother, and the only sadness she had was that Matthew couldn't share in the rearing of their wonderful daughter.

Matthew was, however, back in late May of that year, along with many other serving men. Suddenly the area, deprived of men for so long, took on a different outlook, though most people knew so many men coming home together meant only one thing. It was the big push, everyone said. Make or break. God forbid another Dunkirk! But the Allies were winning, surely?

No one really knew and everyone was fearful. Matthew Bradshaw was not the only one at the station when the time came to leave, who hugged his wife and kissed his child and wondered if he'd ever see either of them again.

But D-Day was successful, if anything that caused so much loss of life as that could be deemed a success. But at least now people could see light at the end of the tunnel.

It didn't help Maeve. She gave birth to Mary Ann Hogan in July, aware that now she had three children to provide for and soon her income from childminding would dry up completely. She only looked after one child full time now, and another part time, for munitions production was easing. But Maeve wasn't at all sure how her family would survive without the extra money.

Still, others had problems too, she thought, one nice summer's day in late August when she met a distraught Deidre in the street. Her sister Daisy's husband had been killed in action, she said, and she had to go and see her. She was only glad that the blitz was over and it was safe to go. But for all that, she'd not take Angela, feeling sure her sister and the children would need all her attention.

'Mom will look after the babby till I come back,' she told Maeve, and added, 'I'll bring some clothes back with me for your two. My sister's told me she's just had a sort-out.'

But Maeve never got the clothes. The news filtered through slowly. Deidre, Daisy and the three children had all been killed outright by some pilotless rocket called a V1, and rechristened a doodlebug, that had landed on the house.

A white-faced, strained and trembling Matthew Bradshaw came home on compassionate leave. Angela had been left in the care of neighbours, for her grandparents were prostrate with grief. It was Matthew who had to organise the return of the remains of his wife, her sister and her children to Birmingham where they were buried together in Witton Cemetery.

'Don't it make you count your bleeding blessings?' Elsie said as they watched the cortège move off from the house, and even Maeve, recovering from yet another clout from Brendan's fist, agreed.

And then, at last, it was all over. Hitler killed himself in his bunker in May 1945 and the war was ended. Despite the hostilities in Japan continuing, people's joy could not be contained. They spilt out from the houses into the streets and parties were held everywhere.

Maeve celebrated with the rest. Now at last they could stay in their beds at night, bring their children up in peace. The telegraph boy would no longer be viewed with dread, and the family unit would be complete once more. After almost six years of austerity and hardship and tragedy, it was hard not to be euphoric about the thought of peace.

And yet Maeve's life had got harder since the previous December, when production of munitions ceased and she was back to the poverty of those earlier years of her marriage. She had dipped into her savings again and again, for now she hadn't even her mother's money to keep her afloat and, despite Elsie's urging, would not write her a begging letter telling her how bad things were.

By April there had been nothing left in the tin and despite pawning everything she could spare, by the time the war ended Maeve was very much afraid they were either going to starve to death, or else be put on to the street. Extreme and relentless hunger stripped her of any shred of dignity and confidence and she watched the children grow thin and pasty, their little faces pinched. She was in despair. She begged and pleaded unsuccessfully with Brendan to let her keep more of the money the priest brought, and earned many a clout or punch because of it. He said he'd give her what for, and properly if she kept moaning. He seemed neither to know nor to care that the children were often hungry and always cold.

'Tell the bloody priest,' Elsie advised.

'Father Trelawney? Talk sense Elsie, the man's as good as useless,' Maeve cried. 'Anyway, d'you expect him to sit here every night and protect me from Brendan when he comes home bottled from the boozer? You know he'll tell the priest all sorts and then lay into me afterwards and in the end it will make little or no difference.'

Elsie said nothing. She knew every word Maeve said was true and she also knew that she was very near the end of her tether. There was no money now for a bag of second-hand clothes and none either to have worn boots cobbled. Without the issue of boots and stockings from the *Evening Mail* Fund, Bridget would have gone barefoot to school.

190

Grateful though she was for the things from the *Mail*, Maeve was ashamed, just as she had been when the two older children had been issued with them. But she knew pride wouldn't keep a child's feet warm and dry and that fact she'd flung at Father Trelawney the previous Friday evening.

In the middle of this abject poverty, Brendan suddenly demanded their older children return. But Maeve soon realised it wasn't due to any love for them that he'd harboured over the years. 'Kevin will be fourteen soon,' he declared. 'It's about time he was out and earning. I'll get him set on alongside me.'

Maeve hesitated sending the letter. She didn't want her son in the same brutalising industry as his father. True, the wages were high, or at least acceptable, but it made old men out of young ones. But when had her views or wishes counted for anything?

She couldn't say with honesty she'd never missed her children, and she had longed for them every moment they'd been away from her, but she didn't know how she was going to feed an extra two on the pittance Brendan left her. But she knew she had to do as he commanded so she drew the writing pad towards her.

The night before Grace and Kevin's return, Maeve was too excited to sleep. She eased herself out of the bed carefully, so as not to disturb Brendan, and crept down the stairs. She would have liked to have made herself a cup of tea, but she only had enough to make Brendan a drink for the morning and she dared not use it up. She'd have to buy some more tomorrow before meeting the children.

Bridget and Jamie were as excited as she was about their brother and sister's imminent return. Jamie had seen the advantages of having a big brother around from other young boys like himself who had one, and on more than one occasion Maeve had heard him yell at a tormentor, 'You don't touch me, see, 'cos when my big brother comes home, he'll kick your head in.'

But though Maeve longed to have the children home again, she was worried how she would cope, even with the family allowance the Government had introduced. She'd almost wept in relief when Elsie had told her about it. That day she'd been desperate, for despite eating nothing herself, all she had for the children was the hard heel of a loaf they had to share and they'd been crying with hunger when Elsie came round all excited. She'd seen their distress and swept all of them into her house where she'd fed them reviving tea and toast, while she'd told Maeve of the news that she'd heard on that morning on the wireless.

'It's for mothers,' she'd said. 'Mothers like you, who never get a decent amount of money for their families.'

'But what good is it? Sure Brendan will have it off me the minute I get it.'

'Don't tell him. He don't listen to the news and it comes in an order book you cash at the post office. He'll never know.'

Maeve had hoped he wouldn't. He didn't listen to the news, right enough, and she'd prayed none of his cronies in the pub would find out and tell him, or he'd kill her altogether. But then what were the odds? She'd had many a beating for less and she wasn't prepared to let her children starve or perish to death. Damn him and men like him, she'd thought, and went straight to the post office to see about it.

Maeve had been astounded at money just given out for nothing. It was, as Elsie said, given to the mothers to help them bring the children up, and though she got nothing for Bridget, because there was none for the eldest child, she got five shillings each for Jamie and Mary Ann. And, the lady had told her, there'd be another ten shillings when the older children returned, until they reached the age of fourteen and left school.

The family allowance had been a great help, a godsend, but Maeve trembled every time she thought of Brendan finding out because she needed that money. He was seldom in the house where the children huddled in front of glowing ashes on a winter's night, with one candle balanced on a cracked saucer as the only light in the room and went to bed in their icy attic with hunger pains cramping their stomachs and without even the comfort of a hot drink.

But she was too wearied and scared to argue with him any more. She dreaded the thought of him really going for her again. At least, though, he'd laid no hand on the children recently. She'd promised herself that if he ever hit them as he had Kevin, she'd be off to St Catherine's so fast her feet wouldn't touch the ground. She'd bring the priest to the house herself to talk to Brendan. Funny that he was still nervous of the priest. She had no time for them, any of them, though she still went to Mass, for she had her immortal soul to think of.

She didn't blame Kevin and Grace for not wanting to return to the life they'd been glad to escape from. They hadn't actually said as much but their reply to her letter, though civil and polite enough, was stilted and lacked warmth, and Maeve's heart had ached as she'd read it. She sincerely hoped that they'd settle down at home eventually and that Brendan would leave them alone.

She took out the scrapbook filled with photos taken and sent by Annie, which Maeve had kept hidden underneath a threadbare cushion on one of the chairs in the room. Over the years she'd looked at it with the young ones around her, building up a picture for the little ones of their older brother and sister. That night, though, she wanted to look at the scrapbook alone.

Brendan had never cast his eyes on it, for she knew if anything were to upset him at all he'd be capable of flinging the book into the fire. And that would have torn the heart out of her, for it was the only record she had of the children growing up.

Maeve had only been back home from Ireland three weeks when, in early July 1939, Kevin had made his First Holy Communion. Her mother had bought a camera for the occasion and sent photographs of Kevin wearing smart grey trousers and the shirt and sash that had been as white as snow, and he'd held a white missal in his scrubbed hands. Maeve's own hands had trembled as she'd held the pictures of her son and she'd cried her eyes out because she couldn't be there by his side.

But still she was grateful to her mother for thinking of taking the photograph and over the years many more had come. Rosemarie's wedding was just a month later and she saw the whole family dressed up again, with Grace in a bridesmaid dress to match Nuala's and Colin and Kevin in suits and both as smart as paint.

A year later, it was Grace's turn to put on the white dress of the First Communicant and the veil held in place with a headdress of rosebuds. Maeve saw her blonde hair framing her earnest little face, trying to take in the enormity of it all. Then there were more casual photographs taken around the farm, out in the fields or in the milk shed, or cutting peat in the bog, and Maeve stored them jealously.

Interspersed with them was news of the family Annie was determined Maeve would not forget. Maeve knew when Liam passed his accountancy exams and Kate qualified as a nurse. She heard about the births of her brother Tom and Peggy's children and later those of Rosemarie and Greg, and she often felt as if her mother was reaching over the sea to her.

The last formal picture of the children was the one taken at their Confirmation. They'd travelled to the town for it the previous year and Kevin had written to describe his blue suit with his first pair of long trousers and Grace told of her dress of purest white satin caught up with white roses and the layers of lace underskirt beneath it.

Maeve held that photograph in her hand for a long time the day it came. There were tears of pride in her eyes for her children and also for the goodness of her parents, who'd looked after them so well. But she was filled with shame that she'd had little hand in their rearing.

She didn't know what they remembered of their early years with their father. Not wishing to frighten them, she told no one of the life she was living with Brendan, even when her mother asked her specifically, knowing she would be unable to do anything about any of it.

She'd also made few references to the war raging about them, no mention of the petrifying fear she often felt at the explosions, so loud they rocked the buildings, or of the people who found they had no homes to return to, the neighbours that would be neighbours no longer and the numbers of ordinary civilians dying. But Annie and Thomas were not fools. They'd listened to the wireless and read the papers and had known some of what Maeve had been suffering.

In the early spring of 1941, Maeve had written to her mother and told her that she'd been issued with a Morrison shelter, and now they'd all be as safe as houses and she'd even had Elsie take a photograph of it to reassure her.

Annie had looked aghast at the photograph and thought it looked little larger than a dog kennel and just as uncomfortable, but Thomas had said tetchily if it kept them all safe what did it matter a damn what it looked like? Annie had known he had a point and she'd written to Maeve and said she was delighted that she had such a shelter.

Maeve often left her mother's letters around for Brendan to read or she'd read little bits out to him, or the little notes from the children to remind him he had others growing up, but he'd never expressed the slightest interest. He didn't know for example that Kevin had a rare feel for the land, but Maeve did, because her mother had told her in a letter written a bare two years after he'd arrived in Ireland.

It's strange and him city bred. You'd scarce believe he's only nine, he's able to get through so much work. Your daddy says he couldn't manage without him. He's his right-hand man, especially as Colin is up in Dublin lodging with Liam while he studies to be a vet at the university.

Now Maeve wondered how her son with a feel for the land would cope with being enclosed in the stupefying heat and noise of a brass foundry.

She gave a sigh and closed the book, replacing it under the cushion, and went back to bed. But once there, she couldn't get comfortable somehow, and she felt the small mound of her stomach under the bedclothes and wished she'd not fallen for yet another child. It was a wicked thought and against the Church's teaching. The priest said you must be grateful for what God sent you but Mary Ann would only be seventeen months when this one would be born, and Maeve wished God had waited a wee while. To Maeve it would be yet another mouth to feed.

Not, of course, that she'd ever have done anything to get rid of it, for that would be an abomination under God and a mortal sin too. She knew of those who'd tried, including one desperate young girl just sixteen, who'd bled to death at the hands of a back-street butcher.

If Brendan had been a different sort of father, she'd have welcomed any number of children, but the way he was . . . Well, it was better to have as few as possible.

Away in Ireland, Grace and Kevin sat on the five-barred gate where they'd sat so many times before. In front of them were the narrow tracks of the rail bus that ran at the bottom of their granddad Thomas Brannigan's farm and Kevin was hurling pebbles at them with savagery. The pebbles zinged on the iron rails, the odd one raising up the occasional spark. Grace said nothing, sensing that the anger and frustration in her brother needed some outlet.

Eventually, Kevin tired of the game. He let the pebbles trickle through his fingers and he turned to Grace. His round, open face was almost scarlet and his blue eyes, strangely moist, seemed to stand out in his face as he cried desperately, 'Don't you care? Do you want to go home?'

'Don't be stupid!' Grace snapped. 'What do you think?'

'How would I know? You never say a damned word.'

'Well, you said plenty,' Grace replied. 'And what good, in God's name, did it do in the end?'

Kevin didn't reply, for his sister was right. When the letter had come he'd raged and roared. He'd declared loudly he'd not go home and no one could make him.

Eventually, his granddad had sat him down hard on the settle and said solemnly, 'Kevin lad, the man's your own father. You must do as he bids you for now. But you haven't to stay for ever. You can come back.'

His words were for Kevin alone and Grace realised her grandda spoke as if Kevin had a claim on the place. Yet Grace was just as bereft, but quieter in her distress, and what good would it have done for her to make a fuss as well? It would just be putting off the inevitable.

Kevin leapt down from the gate. 'Come on,' he said angrily – most of his words these days were angry now – 'it's nearly time for milking.'

Grace got down without a word and they went up the path, silently at first, busy with their own thoughts. Then Kevin suddenly said, 'This is going to be my farm one day. Grandda's going to leave it to me in his will.'

Grace stopped dead on the path and stared at him. Now she understood why her grandda had spoken as he had and yet she cried, 'He can't.'

'Who says he can't? It's his farm.'

'I know, but—'

'Who's to take it on after him if I don't?' Kevin said. 'Uncle Tom, married to Peggy Lunney, whose father's farm is three times the size of Grandda's farm already?'

Grace hadn't thought about that, but of course he couldn't. She remembered Grandda saying Old Francie Lunney was delighted when his only child took up with a farmer. The rheumatics had got him fair crippled, and young Tom had things mostly his own way and was in charge in everything but name. No, Tom wouldn't want her grandda's farm.

Nor, she realised, would Liam. He'd never pretended to be a farmer and, after passing his accountancy exams, was

198

now in a high position in a bank in Dublin. Then there was her Aunt Rosemarie, living with her husband, Greg, above the grocery store in the town, and Kate nursing in a Dublin hospital. And of the younger children, Colin was training to be a vet and Nuala had it in her head to be a nun. It was sad, Grace thought, that her grandma and grandda had struggled to bring up seven children, and yet it was a grandson that wanted the legacy that had been the means of those children being reared at all.

'You know why he wants us back, our dad?' Kevin cried, his words breaking in on her thoughts. 'D'you know the real reason?' He didn't wait for his sister's reply, but went on, 'It's because I'll be fourteen in November. He wants to put me in some God-awful factory, but I'll not stay. I can't stay, Grace. I'll die in some factory. I'll come back here when I'm sixteen and he can sod off.'

Grace knew if their father was to find out about Kevin's inheritance he would do everything in his power to take it from him. Not to farm it himself. Oh no! That would be too much like hard work. He'd sell it, and without a moment's qualm that it had been in the family for genera-tions. And once he had the money the family would see little or none of it. The pub and the bookie's runner would dispose of the money from the sale of Thomas Brannigan's farm quicker than the speed of light.

'But, Kevin,' she said, 'Daddy will never let you have the farm.'

'He'll have to,' Kevin said, tossing back his head, shaking his light brown hair from his eyes. 'Grandda's going to see a solicitor. He says there's ways to go about it so that our dad can do nothing.'

Grace hoped he was right. Kevin looked so sad and there was nothing she could do to make the situation better. So she said, 'Come on, then. If this is all going to belong to you someday, you can't be late for the milking,' and so saying, she strode off towards the cottage, and her brother, without another word, followed her.

Annie Brannigan watched her two grandchildren come round the side of the cottage. She knew that when they left her home in the morning the light would go out of her life, and that of her husband, Thomas. Kevin, she saw, was making for the milking shed. It would be for the last time, because the children would have plenty to do in the morning before catching the rail bus, the first leg of their journey home. Annie hoped and prayed devoutly that things would be better for them at home than they had been. Maeve would never say, though she'd asked her.

She knew neither wanted to go back; Kevin had made that very clear. Dear God, she could see problems there because Kevin despised his father. He wasn't too good at hiding his feelings either. He was a good lad, none better, and straight as a die, but he'd seen things no little lad should see and she had a feeling he'd stand up to his father when he got back. She could see sparks flying there, as he was a fine strapping lad too, not so easy to bully now, she'd have said.

Grace came into the cottage. She could have told her granny she remembered a lot from before she'd gone to live in Ireland, and most of it unpleasant. When she looked back, it seemed shrouded in misery. She'd often been hungry and cold and terrified, and when she was younger she'd only have to hear her father's boots cross the cobbles to their door, or his bullying voice downstairs, and she'd wet herself with fear.

The memories she had of her mother, on the other hand, were good ones. She remembered the feel of her arms around her, and her lilting voice singing nursery rhymes or telling her and Kevin stories, and the clean soapy smell of her better than she could remember what she looked like. Even in the photographs she'd sent, she'd been shadowy and half hidden by the babies she had in her arm. Bridget first and then Jamie and now Mary Ann.

But, Grace told herself, things must be better now. Their mother had written them long cheerful letters all through the war and surely she couldn't have done that if things had been as bad as before.

'What are you thinking about, Grace, to have such a frown on your pretty face?' Annie said, pressing her granddaughter into a chair in front of the fire and placing a thick earthenware mug in her hand. The tea was so strong it was orange-coloured. But still Grace was glad of it, for even with the door and window open, the heat in the cottage was intense because of the fire that had to be lit and tended every day.

'Going back,' Grace said, and added, 'I want to see Mammy, but I just wish she could come and live here like she did once before.'

But Grace knew that would never happen. It was a dream and dreams were for weans only. She drank the strong tea and swallowed the lump in her throat, and if her grandmother saw the tears glistening in Grace's eyes she made no comment.

THIRTEEN

Despite the photographs Annie had sent, Maeve was totally unprepared for the young man who got down from the train the next day at New Street station. Nor was she prepared for the young lady he'd helped down to stand beside him.

Surely, Maeve thought, they couldn't be Kevin and Grace alighting. She always imagined she would feel a rush of love for them immediately and run to hug and kiss them, telling them how much she'd missed them and it would be like it had always been. But the two who stood staring at her across the platform were strangers. She didn't know them, she realised, and you couldn't hug and kiss people you didn't know.

Kevin and Grace thought Maeve looked awful. She was wearing an old dress that hung on her sparse frame, covered with a shapeless cardigan, her legs were bare and her feet encased in a pair of flat laced shoes like a man's, scuffed, dirty and down-trodden at the heel. Her face was as they remembered it, but sort of jaded, her skin so pale it was almost white and her eyes had lost their shine, so even the blue appeared dimmer. They seemed also to be sunk in her head and had black smudges beneath them.

Kevin thought his mother looked fragile, as if she needed looking after. Beside Grace, his mother looked like an inferior copy, despite the fact Grace had been incredibly sick on the boat.

Grace thought her mother looked ill. Surely no one could be so pale and not be ill. And where on earth, she wondered, did her mother get those awful clothes she had on?

Maeve had forced herself to walk down the platform towards the children.

Kevin stepped forward. 'Hello, Mammy,' he said, and bent and kissed her on her cheek.

Maeve almost recoiled, for Kevin, as well as looking like a man, spoke like one, and it threw her completely. Also the kiss had been perfunctory and lacked warmth, as if it were the thing to do.

'Hello, Kevin,' Maeve said, recovering slightly. 'It's grand to see you, and you too, Grace.' She gave her daughter a hug and a kiss on the cheek, but didn't clasp her tightly as she wished to. She sensed the girl's reticence.

'Hello, Mammy,' Grace said as soon as Maeve released her, but she said it in a flat tone.

God, Maeve thought, this is awful. She forced herself to say cheerfully, 'I've missed you both so much. You don't know how I've longed for this day.'

There was a strained silence. Kevin knew he should say that he'd longed for this day too, that he wanted to come back home, but he bloody didn't. He hated being dragged back to the grimy city, where the houses were crowded one against the other and factories belched smoke into the air. He'd seen it all from the window as the train neared the station. It tugged on the memories he had of it all from when he was a young boy and he'd felt misery and almost despair begin to gnaw at him. It went too deep to give false assurances to his mother, who despite the fact she'd given birth to him and reared him for seven years was now a stranger.

Grace knew how Kevin felt. She was the one he'd poured out his heart to. She was the one who'd seen him tramping the hills, his eyes wild, or sobbing heartbrokenly when he thought he was alone. She felt for her brother, but she suddenly felt sorry for her mother too, for she looked so forlorn and lost standing in those ragged clothes on the windy platform, making an effort.

She had missed her mother probably more than Kevin had, but she'd never told anyone because she knew there was no good complaining about a situation she was unable to alter. But now as the silence stretched between them, she felt a rush of sympathy for Maeve. She was not to blame. Grace knew as well as Kevin who'd demanded their return and why.

'We're both tired, Mammy,' she said by way of explaining their behaviour. 'We'll be all right when we're home.'

'Yes, yes, of course,' Maeve said as if in relief. 'What am I thinking of? We'll go home and have a feed and it will put a different complexion on it altogether.' She looked at their luggage. They had a bag between them and two new shiny leather suitcases. She remembered the little grey haversacks she'd bought when they first went to Ireland, which had easily carried all their worldly possessions. She marvelled not only at the cases, but the fact that they obviously each had enough clothes to fill them.

Kevin saw his mother's eye on the suitcases and said gruffly, 'Grandda bought them, the cases. A sort of going-away present.'

'I know Bridget and Jamie will be impressed. Indeed the whole road will be. I don't think anyone around here has anything so fine,' Maeve said. She knew she'd have to keep the cases away from Brendan's probing eyes or he'd insist she pawn them. She couldn't do that. She guessed for her two older children it would be viewed as a betrayal.

'Where are they?' Grace said. 'The children? I thought you'd bring them.'

They'd thought so too, Maeve remembered. Bridget had turned sullen and Jamie mutinous when Maeve told them they were to stay with Elsie. She'd ignored their unhappy, angry faces, glad of the gurgling baby who didn't know what an important day it was. She'd wanted the time alone with Kevin and Grace, to welcome them properly and say what was in her heart. But it had all gone terribly wrong and she wished she had brought the children with her now. Bridget, after a few shy moments, would be asking them questions and Jamie, who'd never had a shy bone in his body, would be full of life. He'd have loved the station, the bustle and rush of it and she knew he'd have been entranced by the big steam engines.

'I left them with Elsie,' she said in answer to Grace. 'You mind Elsie?' And without waiting for a reply went on, 'Come on now. Let's away home.' She picked up a case in each hand.

'Leave them, Mammy,' Kevin said firmly. 'I'll carry them. They're too heavy for you.'

Maeve looked at her son. She'd hauled big bags of shopping home, carried buckets of coal, manhandled sheets from the copper in the brew house and big kettles of water for bath night on Saturday evenings before the fire. Never had she been helped in these tasks and never had she expected any help. 'They're not too bad,' she said.

'Bad enough,' Kevin said. 'I'll carry them. I'm stronger than you.'

There was no denying that, and Maeve relinquished the cases to Kevin, who lifted them with ease. She led the way from the station.

As they emerged from the entrance, Grace and Kevin thought they'd never before heard such noise nor seen so many people. Belfast had been busy, but they'd seen little of it, and this was different. There were crowds of people on the streets and more cars, lorries and vans on the road than they'd ever seen, vying with large buses and clanking trams. Grace glanced at her brother. She didn't think either of them would ever get used to the place.

In the tram they looked out of the windows and were staggered at the bomb damage they saw. They'd known about the raids, listening to the wireless that their granddad had bought especially to keep up with the war news. They'd been nervous and frightened when they heard of any that had centred around Birmingham and were always glad to get a letter from their mother afterwards to show she was alive and well, but they had not been prepared for so much destruction.

When they left the tram to walk to their house, they saw that whole streets had disappeared and it had a sobering effect on both of them. They knew from the damage they saw around them how much the area had suffered, and could imagine how difficult and often terrifying it must have been for everyone. Grace felt almost guilty that she and Kevin had been safe while others had suffered so much.

They all turned down the entry to the courtyard and Maeve opened Elsie's door without knocking. Kevin and Grace did remember Elsie and also knew how much they and their mother owed to her. She'd always been there when things were bad, and had taken care of them when their mother couldn't, like when she lost a baby one time. Kevin couldn't remember much about it except for the severe beating that, in the end, had rendered him unconscious.

He had no memory of Elsie coming in, or his mother going to hospital, but he'd come round in a soft bed in Elsie's house and she'd been putting soothing ointment on his back. Both he and Grace had been kept away from school, he remembered – Kevin, because he hadn't been fit to go, and Grace in case she should say something about what had happened at home. The doctor had come a couple of times and had given Elsie ointment for Kevin's back. The doctor had talked in a grave voice about infection and Elsie had got all het up and talked about something called Welfare, which she'd seemed scared of.

But all that was over, Kevin told himself. There was no need for Elsie to try to protect them all now, for he would, at least until the time he returned to Ireland. Many times as a child growing up and seeing the brute his father had turned into, he'd wished he could grow quickly and be able to stand up to him. Well, now he had and he'd better watch out.

Elsie hadn't changed much from Kevin and Grace's memory of her. Her grey hair was still frizzed up in tight curls and she still had little pouches of skin beneath her warm brown eyes. The crinkle lines to the sides of her nose were deeper and pulled at the sides of her mouth, and the skin round her neck had more folds in it than they remembered. The apron the children had seldom seen Elsie without encircled her waist over a flowered dress that looked far better than their mother's, the children noticed, and on her feet were soft slippers.

Her smile was as broad and genuine as ever and the light danced in her eyes as she surveyed the children with delight. 'Will you let me look at you?' she cried, hugging them both to her. 'My, you're a sight for sore eyes.'

Maeve, watching her, wondered why she herself couldn't have been so natural.

But if Kevin and Grace had been pleased to see Elsie, they were appalled by Jamie and Bridget and wee Mary Ann. They didn't say a word to one another about it, but they had no need. The look that passed between them at the children's pale pinched faces with their sticklike arms and legs spoke volumes.

They'd been well used to children in Ireland, for their Uncle Thomas and their Aunt Rosemarie had them and they were expected to mind their cousins often, and soon as Grace was of an age she'd always been roped in to mind Rosemarie's weans in the holidays while she served in the shop.

But neither Grace nor Kevin had seen children as thin and undernourished as their brother and sisters. Mary Ann hadn't even the dimples in her knees and backs of her hands that Grace had always found so endearing in Rosemarie's youngest child, Philomena.

But if Grace and Kevin were shocked by the little ones, Jamie was astounded by the size of his big brother and he said in awe, 'You're even bigger than our dad.' Then he looked up at Kevin and added, 'And I bet you could knock his bloody block off if you wanted.'

'Jamie, I've told you before about bad language,' said Maeve sternly, though it was difficult to be stern with Kevin, Grace and Elsie trying not very successfully to control their laughter.

'He'll hear worse before he's much older,' Elsie said, and it sent an echo through Maeve of a similar sentiment expressed by her father in Ireland, and she shivered suddenly.

* * *

Maeve watched Kevin holding Jamie's hand and Grace holding Bridget's as they went into the house. She hitched Mary Ann higher on her hip and said to her friend, 'Will you not come in, Elsie? You see how they are with me. It will be better if you're there.'

'What do I see but two confused children who need to get to know you all again?'

'Children! Kevin is almost a man.'

'No, he isn't,' Elsie said. 'He's not yet fourteen. He's still a boy, but in a man's body. He still needs you and will do for some time, but in a different way from the small child that went away to Ireland.'

Maeve realised Elsie was right. She couldn't expect to take up the relationship where she'd left it six years before. She had to get to know the personalities that had begun to develop in these adolescent children and go from there.

In the house, Grace had begun unloading the bag her grandma had packed and though Kevin was watching his sister, his thoughts were elsewhere. How the hell could he return to Ireland, even if such a thing were possible, and leave his mother and sisters and brother in such poverty without lifting a finger to help them? It was obvious from a scant look on the shelves that there was little food in the house and the family were evidence to the lack of nourishing food they had. Added to that, they were in rags and the two youngest were barefoot. He'd not worn smart clothes on the farm – they wouldn't have been practical or comfortable – and he'd always felt happier when he'd changed from his respectable clothes for Mass into those more fitting for farm work, but his everyday garments didn't hang on him in tatters.

The poverty in this house was so strong, you could almost smell it. Kevin suddenly remembered going to bed with griping hunger pains in his belly and the freezing cold that would seep into his very being so that his fingers and toes and even his backbone would ache with it. Neither the thin inadequate clothes of the day, nor the coats haphazardly arranged over the beds at night had gone even partway to keeping him warm, and the rattling draughty windows had often been coated with ice by morning.

And all this he'd forgotten. Well fed, well clothed, warm and secure on his grandparents' farm, he'd put such thoughts behind him. Even when he'd known about his brother and sisters, and seen them from the odd photographs his mother had sent them, never had he given a thought to their welfare. Well, he would now, he decided, even if it meant working in a damned factory. He'd told Grace it would kill him but now he knew it wouldn't. Not if his wages meant everyone could eat a little better and have warm clothes to wear in the winter and coal for the fire. And no way was his father getting a penny piece off him, he resolved. His money was going to be given to his mother to benefit all of them.

Maeve saw the frown on her son's face and wondered what he was thinking about so intently. She imagined he was thinking of his home and comparing it unfavourably with the farmhouse they'd left that morning. But the house was the last thought in Kevin's head except in the way it affected the people who lived in it.

Maeve might have commented on the expression on Kevin's face, but her attention was then taken by her daughter Grace and the goodies she was spreading out in front of her – delicacies she hadn't seen for years: rashers of bacon, slices of ham, eggs that had been carefully wrapped in tissue paper and then placed in a tin for safety. There was also barmbrack and soda bread, small tomatoes and butter wrapped in layers of newspaper to keep it from melting.

Maeve felt her mouth watering and tears stung her eyes. Just for once she decided she'd give them a meal to be proud of and now, before Brendan could take it from them.

Never had Bridget, Jamie and Mary Ann had a meal like it, and Maeve hadn't eaten so well for a long time. She'd forgotten how being properly fed and really full made her feel so optimistic and positive about things.

Maeve wasn't aware how shocked her older children had been at the appearance of their younger brother and sisters, nor how Kevin's priorities had changed, but she was grateful for the pleasant conversation around the table. She liked the way both of her elder ones were with the younger ones and how they answered the many questions fired at them by Jamie and the more tentative ones by Bridget. Maeve hoped when Brendan came home he'd be proud of Kevin, who stood so tall and muscular, and his daughter who seemed to be teetering on the edge of womanhood.

By the time he did return, Grace had helped her mother clear away all signs of the meal they'd enjoyed and Kevin had carried the cases upstairs. He stood at the door and regarded the attic which he would share with Bridget, Jamie and Grace. It was a cheerless place, a dim room with little light entering through the grimy window. There was no gaslight in the attic; a stub of a candle was stuck on to a cracked saucer with a wad of wax and he remembered the smell of those candles from when he was a little boy.

Not having gaslight didn't bother him; they didn't have it at his granny's in Ireland. There they had Tilley lamps filled with paraffin. But the bedroom he'd originally shared with Colin was a cheerful place with bright rugs on the floor and colourful bedspreads on the beds. There had been a wardrobe to share between the two of them, with a mirror in the door and a large chest of drawers. And at the table by the bed there was always a jug of water and a bowl.

His new bedroom had bare floorboards and housed two metal-framed beds with two orange boxes beside them for clothes. There was nothing else. He decided to leave his and Grace's things in the cases. But first he took out his suit, the one he wore for Mass with the pristine white shirt and the striped tie. He was so proud of that dark-blue suit. He'd gone into the town with his grandfather to have it made for him for his Confirmation, and he was glad his grandma had insisted he take some hangers in the case, though he had nowhere to hang the things but a hook on the wall. Then he pushed the cases and bags well underneath the bed, as his mother had told him to, chinking them against the chamber pots.

He'd just done this when he heard the sound of the front door being flung open downstairs. He knew his father was home and he felt his stomach contract. Despite his size and earlier positive thoughts, such deep-seated terror that the man had evoked in him as a small child couldn't just be wiped out. He knew he'd have to pretend it had, though, if he was to survive here. He squared his shoulders and made his way downstairs.

Brendan stood in the doorway, transfixed by the sight of Grace. She'd been sitting at the table with her mother, drinking tea, but she'd got up at his entrance and he'd read the trepidation in her eyes.

'Hello, Grace.'

'Hello, Daddy,' Grace said, glad that her father seemed so reasonable and normal and not at all drunk.

Her mother crossed the room to stand behind her daughter and Grace was glad of her support. Her limbs still trembled and she told herself to stop being so silly. Her father might have changed, and if he hadn't, she had and wouldn't be scared of her own shadow any more like she had as a child.

Behind her, she heard her mother let out a sigh of relief, 'Come away in, Brendan,' she said. 'And see the feast of things my mother has sent from Ireland. I'll make you a good feed tonight, so I will.'

And Brendan came in and hung up his coat and Maeve closed her eyes and prayed silently, please, please, God, make it go all right tonight.

Kevin opened the door from the stairs and stepped into the room, and Brendan's mouth dropped open in shock. He hadn't even had the photographs to prepare him for the way his son had grown and the stunned surprise on Brendan's face helped to still the panic that had been threatening to overwhelm Kevin at the thought of seeing his father again for the first time in years.

Brendan had been so taken up with Grace's resemblance to Maeve, he'd not noticed how tall she was, nor how fit and healthy. But Kevin, he saw, despite his tender years, was almost a man, and as he shut the door behind him, Brendan recovered himself slightly. 'So you're back then?'

Kevin stared at his father across the room. 'Aye.'

Brendan remembered when Kevin had been scared shit-less of him and with good reason, but the young man in front of him showed no fear. He should have insisted on their return earlier, war or no bloody war. If he had, his bloody son would be quaking in his boots now, not looking at him in that defiant way. He'd have to establish control;

he was still the boy's bloody father and it was time Kevin knew that, so he said, 'I'll see about a job for you in the morning. I'll have a word with the gaffer.'

Kevin couldn't believe his ears. The man hadn't been in the house five minutes before telling him he'd sort him out a job. Kevin was no stranger to work and not afraid of it either. He'd only been home a little while when he realised he'd have to stay for some years in order to help his mother. He knew he'd have to get a job, and soon, to contribute to the family's keep and he couldn't understand why he was so angry at his father's words. The point was he supposed he wanted no help from him. Anything obtained by his influence would be tainted, he felt. He knew he had to make his position clear immediately.

He faced his father across the table and said with a note of disdain, 'No, thanks, I don't want to work in the brass industry.' Brendan's mouth dropped open again. He hadn't realised how deep his son's voice would be. In the gruff 'Aye', the only other word he said, it hadn't been apparent, but he was further shocked by Kevin's words.

'So, I've bred a work-shy brat, have I?' he sneered.

'No. You bloody haven't. I'm not afraid of hard work,' Kevin burst out. 'I've worked on the farm alongside me grandda since I was nine years old.'

'"Worked alongside me grandda,"' Brendan mimicked. 'Call that work? You don't know you're born, boy. When the sweat runs off you so that you could wring out the shirt you're wearing, and you're so tired you can barely put one foot in front of the other, you can tell me you know about hard work. And that's what my son is going to do, because I want that for him and I make the decisions round here.'

'Not for me you don't,' Kevin spat out. 'Not any more. I'll get a job, don't worry, but I'll choose what it is.'

Maeve wasn't aware she was holding her breath in fear for her son. Everyone else was absolutely still, Grace chewing her bottom lip in consternation, while Bridget wondered if Kevin knew what he was doing and Jamie looked at the manic light shining in his father's eyes and trembled for his brother.

'You bloody upstart!' Brendan cried, and sprang across the table and grasped Kevin by the arm, his fingers cutting into his flesh viciously.

'Get off me,' Kevin cried, pulling away with force. 'Don't touch me. Don't you dare! You did enough of that in the past.'

'You're not too old for a bleeding good hiding.'

'Ah, but I am, you see,' Kevin said. 'I'm no longer the frightened wee boy you used to terrorise and beat half to death, and if you lay a hand on me again, I'll knock your bloody head off, father or no father.'

'That's a fine way to speak to me,' Brendan blustered, taken aback by Kevin's words. 'And in front of your wee brother and sisters too.'

'It's the only way to talk to a bully,' Kevin said, and he heard his mother's sharp intake of breath, but still he continued, 'And that's what you are really, a bully. I came back here because I had to, but I won't be bullied, or harassed, or forced into a job I don't want. I think it's better to get that clear, so we know where we stand from the start.'

'Stand? Begod, it's a fine thing when a son tells his father what to do,' Brendan yelled. 'I give the orders in this family, I'll tell you.' He turned to Maeve and pointed his finger at her. 'This is your doing. You have made them like this,' he said.

'It's nothing to do with Mammy,' Kevin said, crossing in front of her because he saw her limbs begin to shake as Brendan shouted at her. 'None of this is her fault. It's how I feel, that's all.'

'It's still your mother's fault,' Brendan said. 'If she'd not sent you away, I'd have seen you kept a civil tongue in your head.'

'By the power of the belt, I suppose,' Kevin sneered, 'and by starving me half to death into the bargain?'

Maeve could see the tic working at the side of Brendan's face that showed her he was controlling himself with difficulty, and his big hamlike hands were balled into fists. She knew she had to try to diffuse the situation. 'Come on away to the table, Brendan. I have your tea ready,' she said, and Kevin hated the conciliatory tone in which she'd spoken to his father and the slight tremor in her voice that showed her fear of him.

'I have potatoes on the boil in their skins,' she went on, 'and butter to have with them, fresh eggs and thick ham you've seldom seen the like of.'

Despite himself Brendan's attention was diverted as any person subjected to rationing for six years would be. He glared at his son but said nothing more and fell upon the heaped plate of food that was put before him as if he hadn't eaten for a week. Everyone breathed a little easier.

Kevin was a hero in the eyes of Bridget and Jamie, for not only had he stood up to his father, he also didn't seem the least bit afraid of him. They knew Grace was scared; they could both recognise it because they both felt the same way.

And Grace was scared. She'd forgotten how truly terrifying her father was and it came as an unpleasant shock that being a young lady of twelve years was no defence against it.

Brendan finished his meal, scraping his knife across the plate over and over in a way that set Maeve's teeth on edge. He then looked across at Kevin and snapped, 'You haven't heard the last of this. You don't call the tune here, whatever you were allowed to do in Ireland, and the sooner you realise that the better.'

Kevin didn't answer. He had nothing further he wanted to say. Maeve, watching him, knew whatever he said and however much he protested, if Brendan wanted him in the brass foundry then that's where he'd end up. She tried explaining this to him later, after Brendan had taken himself off to the pub and the small children had been put to bed.

'Mammy, I'm not stupid,' Kevin replied. 'With all the servicemen returning, work in a brass foundry might be all that's on offer and I would be daft altogether then to give it up, but I'll do it on my own. I don't want a job on the say-so of a man I despise.'

'Kevin, the man is your own father,' Maeve said.

'Some father!' Kevin cried. 'I never remember him saying a pleasant word to any of us all the years of my growing up. The life I led at his hands before you took me to Ireland destroyed something between us that will never be repaired now, and I can't pretend feelings for the man that aren't there.' He covered his mother's poor, work-roughened hands, with the swollen and misshapen knuckles, with his own large weathered ones and felt suddenly protective towards her. 'Don't fret,' he said gently. 'I don't care what I do as long as it brings in some money to benefit you all.'

Maeve considered telling him she'd hardly have chance to see the colour of anything he earned but decided to let him keep his dream a little longer.

'As a matter of fact, I'll look for something in the next few days,' Kevin went on. 'I don't think there's any point in me going to school for just a couple of months. It would be better for me to look around for something to earn a few coppers until then.'

'Have a wee rest first, though,' Maeve urged.

'I'm not used to being idle,' Kevin protested. 'Grandda used to say that a farm carries few passengers. Both Grace and I had our jobs to do from the start.'

'We didn't mind it though, Mammy,' Grace put in, anxious that her mother should understand that. 'Kevin especially enjoyed it.'

'I did that,' Kevin said, and Maeve heard the sadness in his voice and guessed given the choice he'd be back there tomorrow.

But then I suppose I would myself, Maeve thought, but in this life we can't always have what we'd like, and she gave a sigh, and neither Kevin nor Grace had to ask what the sigh was for.

FOURTEEN

Brendan spoke to the foreman about setting his son on the day after his arrival, but the man had shaken his head. 'More than my job's worth, Brendan, to take the lad on when he's not fourteen.'

'He's as near as makes no bloody difference.'

'Aye, and what if he should injure himself before he is? God, the company would be for the high jump.'

'Perhaps you should have left him in Ireland another few months,' added a workmate who was no friend of Brendan Hogan's. 'You could have had him travel back on his birthday and then he could start here the next day.'

'Shut your gob.'

'Aye, I will. I've said all there's to say on the matter,' the man said, and though Brendan longed to take a swing at him, he didn't dare. He risked dismissal doing that, so he had to curb his temper at work.

Anyway, there was no way round it: like it or lump it, Brendan had to wait another few months to get money out of his son. That knowledge made him surlier and more bad-tempered than ever and he clouted Maeve about a bit when he got home that night, but, she noticed, not on her face, where Kevin might see.

219

Brendan never mentioned the brass foundry again and though Kevin thought it odd, he wasn't going to bring the subject up. He never spoke to his father if he could help it. Maeve knew Brendan's plans had been thwarted in some way because he was so bad-tempered, yet he could only go so far, for he felt Kevin's eyes watching him all the time. He never raised his hand to any of them in Kevin's presence and if he gave Maeve the odd clout or punch in the privacy of their bedroom, she was sensible enough not to make a song and dance over it. But Kevin often felt the man's violence simmering just beneath the surface and he always felt better when he was out of the way, at work or at the pub.

Kevin himself felt very unsettled in the small cramped house, and the endless grey streets and pavements depressed him, but his goal of getting a job in just a few days eluded him. He knew too, despite the family allowance his mother had told him about, he and Grace would eventually be a further drain on Maeve's meagre resources.

By the end of the first week, he'd tried most of the shops he considered might have work in the area around his home, and had also tried towards the city centre and the markets where he thought he might pick up casual labour, but always the answer was no. It was hard not to get despondent about it. Maeve, in fact, was just delighted to have the two children back home again and didn't want Kevin rushing to find a job, but Elsie could understand the boy's frustrations.

'Let the lad be,' she advised Maeve, and added, 'The chances are he'll not find a job at all, for they're not easy to get.'

It certainly seemed that way as the days passed. The holidays drew to a close, and Grace and Bridget returned to school. Kevin was more lonely and bored than ever. Most of the lads his age were still at school and those a little older were working. He missed Ireland and the farm so much some days, he felt he could scarcely bear it.

He was in this frame of mind one morning and he snapped at Jamie. He'd thought him asleep in bed when he'd crept out of the attic after hearing his father leave the house. He wanted some time to himself before the house was astir and he badly needed some space on his own. However, he'd barely set the kettle on the gas before Jamie came down the stairs asking, 'What you doing, Kevin?'

Kevin turned, his face red with anger. 'For Christ's sake, will you leave me alone?' he cried.

He saw Jamie's face crumple and felt bad about it. He told himself he was no better than the father he hated, yelling and bawling at a little boy who'd done nothing wrong.

'I'm sorry, Jamie. I'm out of sorts today,' he said.

Jamie drew his fist across his face, wiping the evidence of tears away and said, ''S all right,' and he smiled a watery smile, and Kevin felt even worse. But below the surface he still felt impatient with the child, with everybody, and he knew he'd have to leave the house early and walk the bad humour out of him.

This time, though, he decided to go away from the city centre and he strode along Bristol Street towards Belgrave Road. His uncle and his family lived that way, but he had no intention of visiting them. He didn't mind his uncle, though he considered him a poor specimen of a man not to look after his mother better and see what manner of man it was she'd married. His mother always said it wasn't Uncle Michael's fault; that Brendan could be charming if

221

he chose. Kevin doubted it. He'd never seen evidence of any charm.

But at any rate, he'd visited his uncle's house just once since he and Grace had arrived home. They'd never been frequent visitors before they left and had few recollections of it. Their cousin Jane, who'd come to meet them, was now married and the mother of a three-year-old and they had little in common with her. Kevin thought he might have got on better with Billy, but he was still awaiting his demob from the navy.

Altogether it was a stiff, uncomfortable visit and not one that either Kevin or Grace was anxious to repeat. They wondered why they'd been asked at all, for their aunt seemed positively hostile and her mouth seemed set in a permanent sulk.

Both children thought if their Uncle Michael wasn't exactly afraid of his wife he certainly seemed cautious of rousing her temper, and perhaps with reason. They were glad that, though he'd called at the house a couple of times later to see how they were getting on, he didn't bring his wife, or issue another invitation to his own house.

Anyway, invited or not, Kevin had no intention of going that morning or any other, and he stood for a moment or two deliberating whether he should make for Calthorpe Park. But the feel of grass beneath his feet and the smell of the earth in the flowerbeds would only increase his frustration.

Instead he made his way up Wellington Street, past the police station. A little way along the road he came to a small line of shops. He studied the first one from the outside. One side of it sold papers, magazines, chocolates, sweets and cigarettes, while the larger area comprised a sizeable grocery shop. He scanned the adverts in the window as he always did. This one was advertising for a paperboy, he noticed, with the first stirring of hope he'd had in days. He was sure he could push papers in the doors as well as the next man and he squared his shoulders and opened the door.

Syd Moss of Moss's Select Stores was an unhappy and embittered man. Often he was loath to wake up in the morning, for once he opened his eyes he was reminded almost immediately of the fact that his only child, Stanley, would not be returning with the demobbed servicemen, as his body was lying under foreign soil somewhere. The news that the Mosses had received the previous year had caused Syd's dear wife, Gwen, who'd worked by his side for many years, to take to her bed. Even now she seldom left it.

Syd tried to be strong for her sake and also for the good of the shop, though sometimes he wondered why he bothered. But he'd been born in the rooms above it and knew nothing else.

Syd had little time for most of the modern youth. He'd seen the decline of moral standards over the war years. With many fathers away in the forces and mothers engaged in war work, the children had often been left to run wild. He'd seen girls, not long out of the schoolroom, dressed in tight skirts and skimpy tops, their faces plastered with make-up, tottering on high heels and draping themselves indecently over servicemen. And he had to admit they seemed to have had a preference for the American servicemen, the ones the British Tommies claimed were oversexed, overpaid and over here.

The young boys growing up without their fathers' influence appeared completely undisciplined. Syd found most of them rude, cheeky and totally lacking in any form of respect. That very day he'd had to sack his paperboy for dipping his hands in the till. It wasn't the first time either. He'd suspected it had been going on for months. Cigarettes had disappeared too when Syd's back had been turned. The lad hadn't shown the least bit of remorse or regret, except for the fact that he'd been found out. Syd felt bitter that his son – respectful, polite and as honest as a die – had given his life for the likes of the dishonest paperboy and the flashy-looking girls.

He was in no mood then for the young lad who stood facing him. He wasn't sure either that he was a lad. He was tall and well-muscled, almost a man, Syd would have said, and he wondered morosely why he wasn't in uniform. Every other bugger seemed to be.

The scowl he turned on Kevin wasn't welcoming, but what odds? Kevin thought. He already knew he'd not get the job, but he might as well try now he was here. He stared at the man steadily and said, 'Good morning, sir. I've come about the job advertised in the window.'

Syd stared at him. He liked his manners. He'd not been addressed as 'sir' for some years. The second realisation was that his voice was deep and had an Irish accent. Syd didn't like the Irish generally – load of papists the lot of them, having babies they couldn't afford to keep because the bloody Pope said they had to. Made no bloody sense to Syd. And light-fingered wasn't in it; he had to watch them like a hawk in the shop. The last paperboy had been Irish and look how he had turned out. He frowned at Kevin, who shifted his feet uneasily.

But what was it the lad said about a job? The only job advertisement was for a paperboy that Syd had put in himself. Surely he was too old to want to take that on.

He screwed up his eyes. 'What age are you, boy?'

'Thirteen, sir.'

'Thirteen!' That shook Syd. He'd have said the boy was eighteen, or at least seventeen. 'Then why aren't you at school?' he barked.

This question had been asked everywhere else Kevin had applied, but he tried not to show any exasperation as he explained, 'I'm not long returned from Ireland, where I spent the war years. My mother didn't think it was worth my going to school for just a couple of months.'

'So when are you fourteen?'

'November.'

'So if I give you this job, you'll up and leave me in a month or two?' But even while Syd snapped at him, he was sizing up the situation and wondering what the alternative was if he were to send the boy away. He'd been worrying all morning how he was going to do the evening paper round when he had the shop to see to.

He couldn't afford to offend the affluent customers in the big houses who were the only ones who had their papers delivered. They were the people with money in their pockets, not like those in the mean streets around the shop, who mainly lived on tick. If he looked after the richer customers now, then when the war was just a memory and a thing of the past, these people would be the big spenders and he'd like his to be the shop they spent their money in.

Even now most of them took a great many papers and magazines in the week, and coming to pay for their papers on a Saturday morning brought them in to buy more. When rationing was finally over, he'd make sure his shelves were well stacked. But if he should offend them now by not being able to offer a delivery service for their papers,

225

they'd buy them elsewhere and a sizeable chunk of profit would go down the drain.

And somehow that still mattered to Syd. It was the only thing he had. The shop was once everything to him and Gwen. They'd bought the shop next door to them when it became vacant in the late thirties and enlarged the grocery side of the business. As each shop had a flat above it, they'd got an empty flat too next to their own. Gwen was as pleased with the flat as she had been acquiring the shop. She thought Stanley would be able to have his own place when he left the army if he wanted, and could still be near them. The blitz of Birmingham had put paid to her plans and over the war the three-bedroomed place was home to many destitute frightened families bombed out of their own homes.

Syd, however, was proud of the enlarged shop, though looking after it single-handed was hard and he couldn't deliver the papers morning and evening as well. He decided he'd take on the Irish boy who looked and spoke like a man, but only because he was in a fix. Woe betide him if he turned out to be light-fingered too or, big as he was, he'd be out on his ear with Syd's boot in the seat of his pants helping him. But if he was good enough, it would give him a breathing space, a couple of months to get a decent lad from a good home to take on the paper delivery.

Kevin knew nothing of Syd's thoughts as he studied the man in front of him. He was smallish and slight, and his hair was greying at the temples and going slightly thin on top, but it was his long mournful face with the mouth in a constant droop and the brown eyes without a spark of life in them that betrayed his age most.

Kevin watched the man's face working as Syd let his mind wander. Kevin thought he'd reject him like all the others. He only wondered why he was taking so long over it. He was surprised when Syd said, 'You ever done work like this before?'

'No, sir, never,' Kevin said. 'But it can't be that difficult.'

'Not difficult, no. But you have to keep your wits about you,' Syd said stiffly. 'Nothing riles folks more than having the wrong paper at breakfast or not getting a copy of the magazine they're following a serial in. Have you a bike?'

'No.'

'It will be some hike.'

'I'm used to walking, sir,' Kevin said, but he knew it might take him some time at first, because he didn't know the area at all, but he knew he couldn't show any nervousness.

'It's an early start in the morning. They don't want their papers delivered with their elevenses. You must be here by seven.'

Kevin grinned. Getting up early had never been a problem to him. His grandda's cows had to be milked at six in the morning and he'd never let him down. 'I'll be here,' he said.

'And you can start immediately?'

'Aye.'

'Where do you live anyway?' Syd asked.

'Latimer Street.'

Syd stroked his chin. 'That's quite a way. You sure you'll manage it?'

'Quite sure.'

'Right. I'll give you a try,' Syd said, almost grudgingly. 'This afternoon at four. Don't be late.'

'And the wage?'

'Three and six a week. Take it or leave it.'

'I'll take it. Thank you, sir,' Kevin said, and his smile of relief at getting paid employment nearly split his face in two.

He went home as fast as he could to tell his mother the good news, but Maeve was worried as to what his father would say.

'Why should he say anything, Mammy?' Kevin asked. 'I won't tell him.'

'He'll know.'

'How would he?' Kevin said. 'My early-morning round will start after he goes to work and I'll have done my evening round and be back in the house before he's home in the evenings. Saturday evenings he'll be sleeping it off as usual and Sundays he never gets up until about ten o'clock so that he can go to Mass at eleven. He'll not know a thing about it.'

'If he should find out, Kevin, he'll kill you,' Maeve said and gave an involuntary shiver. 'He'll kill the pair of us.'

'There will be no more talk of killing, Mammy,' Kevin said, putting an arm around Maeve's shoulder. 'He'll not touch you, nor me either. I'm home now and not a wee boy any more and I'll see he never hurts you again.' Maeve saw the determination in her son's face but she felt no relief, only a further dread, for she knew Brendan as Kevin didn't.

Kevin found delivering papers more difficult and tiring than he'd imagined. The houses the paper shops delivered to were the large ones, usually spaced well apart behind high privet hedges and approached by sweeping drives. It took Kevin quite a few days to find his way around with the help of the notebook Syd had given him. It had the roads marked on it and the houses, with details of papers and magazines they had each day.

Sunday, Kevin soon discovered, was the most difficult day of all. People who'd never normally have a paper might have one or more on Sunday and consequently the round was longer and the bag heavier, and he was glad there was only one Sunday in a week.

Brendan had assumed Kevin had returned to St Catherine's school, like Grace, until his birthday. He never asked, nor expressed the slightest interest in what any of the children did. He sensed too that since the lad had come back he'd lost some power over Maeve, over them all, and it enraged him.

One evening he heard them all laughing as he neared the house, a sound he'd seldom heard in his home. Elsie had heard it too and it cheered her, but it annoyed Brendan and especially that, at his entrance, the hilarity was turned off as if it were a tap. He'd glared round at them all, sitting cosily before the crackling fire, for Maeve had fed the children earlier and cleared away all evidence of the meal before Brendan came home. Bridget and Jamie lowered their eyes to the floor at the look on their father's face. Grace glanced at her mother nervously, and Maeve got to her feet with a sigh, which irritated Brendan, just as if she'd prefer to be sitting by the fire laughing and carrying on with the weans than seeing to him.

Only Kevin showed no sign of fear or nervousness for his father and contempt shone in his eyes. By God, Brendan thought, it was more than enough to rile a man, the defiant look the lad had. 'Get that scowl off your face, boy,' he commanded. He'd see how defiant he would be when he'd sweated his guts out in a brass foundry. He'd work him till he was ready to drop. Then he'd know who the master was in this house.

Kevin watched his father, wondering at the malicious smile playing around his mouth, but he said nothing. He could hardly bear to speak to the man. Even to be in his company oppressed him and he heartily wished he could take his mother away from him, but knew that wasn't in his power yet.

Kevin soon got a reputation for being a good and conscientious worker. Maeve insisted he keep sixpence of his pay back for pocket money, but he never used it for himself. Instead he bought comics for the children, or sweets if he had points enough. He wished he could buy them all some decent clothes, especially his mother, because even the dress and coat she wore for Mass were threadbare and shabby. One of the first things Kevin was determined to do with his wages once he was working full time, rationing or no rationing, was to see them all dressed decently.

Mary Ann wasn't so badly off, because she still had the things Deidre Bradshaw had given to Maeve for Bridget years before. But Kevin and Grace insisted some of their clothes be altered for the others, so Jamie now had a couple of pairs of short trousers his bottom wasn't sticking out of and Bridget had a plaid skirt and at least one warm dress for the winter.

But Kevin knew that while warm clothes were important for the children, they weren't much in the way of presents for little children, and so for Bridget's sixth birthday in October, he searched every shop in the area with his sixpence, and in the rag market he found a skipping rope, and bought a yo-yo in a shop up a side street selling second-hand stuff. He'd seen children in the street playing with both toys and noted the fact that Bridget had neither. In fact the Hogan children seemed to have no toys at all.

Maeve was touched by Kevin's consideration, and glad he had something to give Bridget for the children had so little. After his birthday, she knew life could and probably would change for the worse. Brendan would have Kevin down the foundry where, he'd threatened, he'd volunteer the lad for any overtime going and strip him of his wages before he left the place. So she tried not to rely on his paper round money, but put as much away as she could in the tin box in Elsie's house. But she'd taken some out of it that week to give Bridget a decent birthday for once in her life.

She'd planned a little party for the child. It would be her first and as her birthday was on Sunday they decided to have it on that day, but in Elsie's house, lest any sound of merriment rouse Brendan, who'd be sleeping off the effects of his Sunday lunchtime binge.

It was the best afternoon Bridget could remember having and she was entranced by Kevin's gifts to her, because in her short life she could never remember being given anything to play with before. Then she surveyed the table with delight and cried, 'It's like V-E Day.'

Grace and Kevin both remembered their mother's account of V-E Day. She'd told them of people's relief and elation, and the street party when shopkeepers broke into their stock to give everyone, and especially the children, a day to remember. A party tea was laid on for them such as they'd not had in six years. Their grandfather had said that they were being premature celebrating before the war with Japan was finally over too. He'd said it was as if the servicemen fighting in the jungle were of no account.

But just before they left in August, the war against Japan had been won by two atomic bombs and an attack on Tokyo by over a thousand aircraft. The numbers killed shocked the world, but when the skeletal survivors of the Japanese POW camps were liberated and they heard of their suffering and those of their fellow inmates who'd not made it, most people had little sympathy for Japan's citizens.

'I didn't have a cake then, though, just for myself with six candles on,' Bridget cried, her eyes shining. 'Not at the V-E Day party I never,' and Grace, moved by the child's delight in everything, bent down and gave her a hug.

Syd Moss knew that Kevin's birthday wasn't that far off. He would miss him as his paperboy because he was the best he'd ever had and he'd done nothing about finding a replacement. He guessed at the poverty of his home and knew that money would probably be fairly tight. He had no doubt that once Kevin passed fourteen, he'd waste no time being set on somewhere.

Syd considered the matter. They'd never hired anyone for the shop. For years he'd worked side by side with Gwen, and then Stanley as he grew. He'd always prided himself on the fact it was a family business and he'd imagined it would stay that way.

Now it often seemed as if he'd lost his wife as well as his son, for the depression she'd sunk into at the news of Stanley's death had deepened. She had no interest in anything any more and least of all the shop. But the fact remained Syd wasn't as young as he had been and he needed help. If Gwen was not able for it, that meant looking outside the family. Why then should he look further than the lad they had already that they could trust? True he was young, but that might be all to the good: he could train him in his ways.

He got on with him all right and that in itself was unusual, for he had to admit his track record with boys was not good and it wasn't always the boys' fault. He'd discussed the matter with Gwen and she'd been against it as he knew she would be, but not enough for her to agree to go down into the shop herself.

'I need a hand down there, Gwen,' Syd had said. 'The food will be coming off ration now, bit by bit, and though we won't have the bother of coupons and points, in another way we'll have more stock to order and shelve. As it is, I can barely cope with the tobacco and magazine counter and the grocery side too. I can't have eyes everywhere either.'

'The boy might not want it.'

'He might not,' Syd agreed, 'though I doubt he'll be too choosy. His family seem as poor as the rest.'

Kevin knew that himself. Soon he'd have to see about a job. It wasn't enough just to say he wasn't going to work in the foundry. He had to decide where he was going to work.

Syd glared at him as he returned that night after his round, but Kevin knew that Syd's baleful look was not always directed at him, nor was the snap in his voice, nor the frown that furrowed his brow. Outside, dusk had begun to fall, the weather was bitterly cold and Kevin was glad to reach the comparative warmth of the shop. He hung his bag on the hook behind the door leading upstairs and blew on his cold fingers. 'I'll be off then, Mr Moss,' he shouted.

'What? No, no . . . Wait on a minute.'

Mystified, Kevin hovered while Syd served a customer, wondering what he'd done now. He was totally unprepared for his employer's proposal.

'Serve in the shop?' he repeated. 'Full time, you mean?'

He couldn't believe it and at first was delighted. It was a much better job for him than being shut in a factory and he didn't even mind Syd Moss and his moods. Many

233

people around the roads had told him about Stanley and he thought it understandable that the parents of a lad, only a little older than himself killed like that wouldn't be the same after it. Small wonder Syd often looked thoughtful and sometimes downright miserable.

However, Kevin had his own worries and only one thing mattered. 'How much money are you offering, Mr Moss?'

Syd hesitated. He deplored the modern method of giving youngsters high wages but he knew if he wasn't to offer Kevin decent money he would go elsewhere. And yet he had no experience and he might turn out to be bloody useless. He wasn't going to hand money over for nothing. 'Well, let's se how you shape up first,' he said, playing for time. 'There are two Saturdays yet before your birthday. You come and give me a hand those days and we'll go from there. I'll give you three and six for the day, eight till six. Then we'll see.'

'I'll take it and welcome,' Kevin said.

Kevin and Grace had been unused to rationing until they came to Birmingham, but Kevin knew he'd have to try to understand both the rationed goods and those on points before he went to work at Moss's Select Stores. But he found it was a complicated task.

'Everyone over the age of five has a buff-coloured ration book containing coupons for fifty-two weeks,' Maeve told him. 'And another green book if you're expecting, to give you extras. Children under five have green books too and they can have extra milk and orange juice on it and stuff like that. But,' she added, 'despite your entitlement on the rations, it depends on whether the stuff is available. For example, we're supposed to have one egg each a fortnight and we'd think ourselves lucky to see one a month.'

Kevin found it totally confusing. He discovered, though, as many people do, that trying to learn something cold from a book is much harder than actually doing it. The women knew exactly the amount of food they were allotted, and were only too willing to help him, and on that first Saturday he was kept busy from the moment he hung up his paper-round bag at eight o'clock until about half-past nine.

'There'll be a bit of a lull now,' Syd told him. 'I'll pop upstairs for a bite to eat. Will you be all right?'

'Aye. Sure I will,' answered Kevin, trying to ignore the hunger pangs in his own stomach. It had been a long time since he'd struggled into his clothes in the dark that morning before drinking the cup of tea his mother had had ready, together with the bread spread with whatever she had in. He knew he had another couple of slices of the same for his lunch wrapped in the bag the bread came in.

He wished his mother could have a lie-in in the morning instead of having to get up at the crack of dawn to see to his bloody father. He was worried about her, because he thought she was far too thin to be so heavily pregnant, though her ankles were huge and she slopped about in men's shoes three sizes larger than she usually took, as they were all she could get on.

Elsie also knew Maeve wasn't right, and she urged her to see Dr Fleming, because somehow this pregnancy, above all the others, had managed to do what all the years of neglect and abuse had failed to do and that was suck the very heart from her.

But Maeve hadn't the money for doctors, so no way was she going to ask Dr Fleming to call. 'What the hell could he do for me anyway?' she demanded. 'I'm pregnant and that's that. I haven't money to throw away to be told what I already know myself and be given a bottle of tonic that does no good at all. Don't fuss me.'

Maeve was more bothered about Kevin at that time than she was about herself because she couldn't understand why he'd been so keen to work in the shop on Saturday. He wouldn't tell her anything until it was decided, so she had no idea Syd was thinking of offering Kevin a full-time job. He just said the money would be useful, and in truth Maeve couldn't argue with that. But after he'd gone to work that first Saturday she realised he hadn't answered her when she'd asked if he'd told the Mosses that he'd have to give up the paper round, and anxiety for her stubborn, slightly headstrong son began to niggle at her.

FIFTEEN

They had Jamie's birthday party next door, as they'd had Bridget's, and on Sunday too, primarily because Kevin was working on Saturday and Jamie wouldn't have considered his birthday complete if his brother couldn't be there.

Kevin was feeling very happy that day. He'd worked hard the previous day, and at the end of it Syd, never given to praising people and in particular boys, said, 'You did well, Kevin. You do as well as that next week and you'll have a job the following Monday. What d'you say?'

There'd been no discussion of wages and Kevin knew he wouldn't mention a figure until he saw how he was the next Saturday. He trusted Mr Moss to treat him fairly so he smiled and said, 'Thank you, sir. I'd be pleased to work for you.'

He wanted to say a lot more, but Syd seemed satisfied. 'Hmph,' he said gruffly. 'Glad you have manners, at least. Now I think I've solved the problem of a present for your young brother's birthday. How old will he be?'

'Four,' Kevin said, wondering how Syd knew the problem he was having finding something in the practically bare shops to please a four-year-old. He'd only mentioned the matter that day to a customer, who, knowing who

Kevin was, asked to be remembered to his mother, as early in the war she had minded her baby for her while she went to work. Kevin had told her it was his young brother's birthday that day and although they were having a party on Sunday, he hadn't found anything in the shops to buy for him.

Kevin hadn't been aware Syd had even been in the store at the time. The customer sympathised and said it would be a bleak Christmas indeed for all the children that year. 'You wouldn't think we'd won the bleeding war, would you?' she'd said with a grim laugh, and now it seemed Syd had listened to the entire exchange, and as Kevin was getting his coat on he came forward with two miniature cars, one black and one a dull red and both in pristine condition.

'Used to be Stanley's,' Syd said, his voice gruffer than ever. 'No sense in hanging on to them.'

'Oh, thank you, sir,' Kevin said, genuinely touched.

Kevin came home with his three and six in his pocket and the certainty of a full-time job at the shop if he worked as hard the following Saturday as he had that day. He also had the two cars to make Jamie's fourth birthday special and the knowledge that Syd Moss, often querulous and bad-tempered, was underneath it all a very kind man.

The party was a great success and Jamie was as entranced as Bridget had been the previous month. He was bright-cheeked with excitement and happiness as he tumbled into their house. He'd had a better time than he could ever remember having.

Maeve heard Brendan's steps on the stairs and she hoped they hadn't woken him, for then he'd be furious. She grabbed the presents from Jamie's arms and threw them under the cushion of the settee and Jamie, knowing why

238

she was doing it, made no protest. He knew, until they knew what humour his father was in, no one would risk incurring his displeasure.

Maeve realised with a sinking heart, catching sight of her husband framed in the doorway, that he was in a temper over something or other, as he often was. His mouth was turned down and he had an ugly scowl covering his face.

Maeve wished there were no icy spears hitting the pavement outside, or that the attic was less of an ice box, for she'd have liked to get the little ones out of the way of what she sensed would be a nasty confrontation. She could have sent them back next door to Elsie, but guessed that that would make the situation worse.

'Well, Kevin,' Brendan said, before he'd stepped fully into the room. 'No more lie-a-bed for you after next week. You're fourteen on the Friday and you start alongside of me on Monday morning.'

Kevin licked his lips and was glad of the long trousers covering his quaking legs. He stood straight, taking comfort from the height that topped his father's, and said, 'I already have a job starting Monday week.'

'You have, begod? Where's this job then?'

'Moss's grocery and tobacconist shop in Wellington Street.'

He glanced at his mother and saw her stricken face. He'd told her what Syd had said the previous evening and she'd meant to talk to him that night, to explain that his father wouldn't tolerate his working there. He had his son's life planned. She'd make Kevin see sense, she was sure. She had no idea the boy would throw it at his father in this way.

Kevin watched the blood drain from his mother's face and Brendan's mouth drop agape. 'What the hell do you know about serving in a bloody shop?'

239

'Enough, it seems,' Kevin answered mildly.

'You insolent young pup!' Brendan cried, jumping forward and clouting Kevin's head with the palm of his hand, and he heard a cry of protest from his mother.

The blow knocked Kevin sick and off balance slightly, but as he leant panting against the mantelpiece he faced his father seemingly unafraid. 'You do that again and I'll give you the same back.'

Brendan was stunned. Never had he expected one of his children to talk to him that way. 'D'you all see what I've bred?' he appealed to the rest of the family ranged round him. 'The most ungrateful bugger in the world and turning on his own father.'

Kevin was white with fury and Grace could have told anyone that was a bad sign. Her hands were curled into fists so tight the nails were digging into her flesh. She badly wanted to use the toilet – her bladder continued to be the barometer of her feelings – and she bit her bottom lip so hard it was bleeding. She seemed unaware of it as she seemed unaware of Bridget hiding behind her, covering her face with the folds of her skirt as she whimpered in fear. Jamie had retreated from his place beside Kevin when Brendan lashed out at him and leant for comfort against his mother's side and his face was crumpled up with the effort of not crying. Maeve lifted Mary Ann, who'd begun to grizzle, higher up her hip, mindful of her swollen stomach and put her hand on her young son's head. The air was electric. Maeve could almost smell the violence.

'Ungrateful!' Kevin spat at his father. 'What the bloody hell have I got to thank you for? You led me and Grace a life of misery and, while you tried to beat me to death, you terrified the life out of my mother and sister. Mammy was so frightened what you'd do to us, she ran away and my grandparents brought us up for the last six years. You haven't had to put your hand in your pocket much for us,' Kevin said, and added with a sneer, 'Our upkeep hasn't affected your beer money any.'

The punch took Kevin unawares and he staggered against the hearth, signing his mother away, as she would have come to his aid. 'I've warned you,' he said as he drew his hand across his mouth and it came away covered in blood.

Brendan knew his son had the advantage of height and possibly brawn, though Brendan's shoulders and arms were well muscled from the work he did, and he also had the advantage of weight and surprise. Kevin would be unused to fighting except the odd skirmish in the school yard maybe, and totally unused to the fighting of the streets.

Before Kevin was able to right himself, Brendan's hobnail boot caught him squarely between the legs. Kevin, clutching at himself, gave a cry and sank to his knees, but Brendan hadn't finished with him and lashed out to either side of his face until Kevin fell forward on to the floor, and then he gave him a hefty kick in his stomach.

The children were screaming in panic and Maeve knew she had to get them away. She handed the baby to her white, trembling, elder daughter and said, 'Take them in to Elsie.'

But Grace seemed to be in shock, staring transfixed at the scene before her as if she couldn't believe it, tears trickling down her face. Maeve gave her a shake. 'Grace!'

Grace didn't want to leave. She wanted to stay with Kevin, who lay so still he might have been dead. 'Is he . . . all right?'

He was far from all right, but Maeve knew what she meant and she gave her husband a hefty push. Strangely, he didn't retaliate, but after a glance at Kevin, slumped into an armchair. Maeve sank to her knees beside her son.

'Yes,' she assured her daughter, seeing Kevin's chest rising and falling, 'but get the weans away, for God's sake.'

She wished with all her heart they'd not been there. She glared at her husband as the door closed behind the distressed children. He sat before the fire as if the unconscious boy on the floor was nothing to do with him. He'd not any concern about him or taken any part in the exchange she'd had with the other children. A wave of hatred for the man she'd married, who seemed almost subhuman, rose in her.

She got to her feet, went across to Brendan and looked him full in the face. 'You're a monster, Brendan!' she hissed. 'A bloody sadistic monster and I won't stand this starting once more. Lay one hand on him again and I'll see the authorities.'

Brendan laughed a low malicious laugh. 'About a man chastising his son?' he cried. 'You're bloody barmy, woman.' Leaping to his feet he slapped Maeve's face with such force, she almost staggered into the fire.

She righted herself and yelled at him, 'Try it on, Brendan, and we'll see who's barmy.' And she went past him to put the kettle on for warm water to bathe Kevin's face.

'Silly bugger had to be shown who's master in this house,' Brendan said, glaring at Maeve. 'You've always spoilt the lad and taken his side against me. No father would put up with being spoken to like that. No bugger in the land would blame me for laying into him.'

'Well, we'll have to see about it, won't we?' Maeve said, too worried about Kevin to care about herself. 'But I'm warning you, Brendan, that's the last time you'll beat him like that.'

Brendan stared at her, amazed at her defiance and her answering back. It would never have happened before that sod Kevin had returned.

'You watch what you're saying to me or you'll get the same.'

'And just who are you but a brute and a monster, and attacking me will change nothing?' Maeve bawled. 'You're the boy's father; you should be helping him, not beating him up.'

'Aye,' Brendan said with a sneer. 'I'm glad you remembered he's my son at least. When he wakes tell him he'll get more of the same if he defies me again, and you'll do nothing about it if you know what's good for you.'

The slam of the door as Brendan left made Maeve jump, but she busied herself making Kevin as comfortable as she could with a rolled-up coat beneath his head. He came round as she bathed his face, and Elsie, coming in at that moment, saw the injured boy on the floor and Maeve's swollen cheek and the trickle of blood running from one side of her mouth, and sighed in exasperation.

Kevin felt as if he'd been run over by a tram, but the warm water was soothing. There was a searing pain between his legs that worried him most of all and he couldn't help his face screwing up because of it, though he stifled the groan.

Maeve guessed what was bothering him. She'd seen the power of the vicious kick and hoped there was no lasting damage. She knew Kevin wouldn't mention it to her, so she said, 'Do you want the doctor to look you over?'

If Kevin agreed, she would take the opportunity to have a quiet word with Dr Fleming first and tell him why Brendan had attacked his son. She saw Elsie look at her strangely. Maeve knew she'd think it odd that she'd not think of having the doctor for herself, but was suggesting it for Kevin, but then she hadn't witnessed what Brendan had done.

Kevin shook his head. 'I want no doctor,' he said through gritted teeth and added, 'And he needn't think he can punch and kick me into a job I don't want. This has made me more determined to make my own way.'

Maeve blanched. 'Kevin, lad, don't fight him, for God's sake,' she pleaded. 'I know it's not right. It was to protect you as well as myself I fled that time. He'll kill or cripple you before he's finished if you try and stand up to him. He has it in for you anyway; he has done from the day you were born.'

'Why?'

Maeve shrugged. 'I've given up trying to work out what goes on in his mind,' she said. 'I think it's something to do with you being the first.'

'Well, I don't care if he hates my guts,' Kevin stated, 'because I hate his. I always have and I'm sorry, Mammy, but I won't be bullied. I start at Moss's full time a week on Monday and as far as I care he can jump in the canal, but he'll not stop me.'

Maeve heard the decisive words, but also saw the determined lift to the chin and the set to Kevin's mouth. He reminded her so much of Brendan that she caught her breath. She wondered afresh what had soured that young man she'd once loved with all her being who'd courted her with all gentleness and consideration.

Whenever she'd voiced these thoughts to Elsie in the past, Elsie would pooh-pooh the idea of her having any blame. She'd say that Brendan was from a violent home where his own mother and the wives of his brothers were often abused.

'But did that mean he'd definitely be the same?' Maeve would ask. 'We all know of decent families where one child goes off the rails, or the other way round.'

'Even so, if they're from bad stock . . .'

'God, Elsie, what does that make my children?' Maeve had cried. 'Will Kevin and Jamie become wife beaters because their father is, and Grace, Bridget and Mary Ann endure it because they think it's normal and acceptable behaviour?'

'Of course not, Maeve,' Elsie had said. 'Your children have you as a model.'

It was on the tip of Maeve's tongue to say Brendan and his brothers had Lily, but she knew Lily was no model for anyone. Maeve knew whatever the circumstance, she herself would never look totally unmoved and without a jot of sympathy at the battered wife of Kevin or Jamie lying on a hospital bed and blame the woman as Lily had.

But the look on Kevin's face showed that he had a lot of his father in him, though she knew better than to say so. 'Help me up, Mammy,' Kevin said, and both Elsie and Maeve lifted him to his feet and sat him in the chair by the fire. Maeve saw the way Kevin bit his lip to stop any cry escaping and she was filled with pity for him. 'D'you want a bath, son?' she asked.

Kevin would have loved a bath. The warm water would soothe him and he could have a good look at himself down below, but his mother would first have to get the bath off the hook from behind the scullery door, drag it before the fire and fill it first with large pans and kettles of boiling water and then the same of cold water. He wouldn't ask her to do that. She wasn't strong enough and it wouldn't be right in her condition, and Elsie was too old. Since his return he'd always filled his own bath after his mother had gone to bed. Once he had a job he hoped he'd have the money to go to the public baths, but that would be in the future and wouldn't help that night.

So he said, 'No, Mammy, I think I'll just be away to bed.' He pulled himself to his feet gingerly and, stooping like an old man, he stumbled to the stairs.

'Can you manage?'

'Aye, Mammy. Don't fuss.'

Elsie waited till she heard his stumbling progress up the stairs before she said, 'Like mother like son. That boy's in agony. What in Christ's name has the bugger done to him?'

'What hasn't he?' Maeve said bitterly. 'He kicked Kevin between the legs so hard it disabled him totally. Brendan then was able to lay into him with his fists and boots.'

'And this was all about the job Grace told me he has got for himself?'

'Aye,' Maeve said, and added, 'Well, at least that's how it started, and then Brendan told Kevin he was an ungrateful bugger and Kevin let him have it.'

'I admire him, but it was a foolhardy thing to do,' Elsie said.

'Don't I know it?' Maeve replied. 'And he seems as determined as ever. I'd send him back home to my mammy, but I don't think he'd go. Anyway, Brendan would just up and fetch him back, and likely after half killing me first.'

'He could stay with me a wee while,' Elsie offered.

'No,' Maeve said. 'I couldn't heap that on you. God, you'd not want Brendan constantly round your door, yelling and performing.'

Elsie couldn't say she did and so the two women talked on, but neither could find a solution to the dilemma, and Maeve went to bed with a heavy heart.

When Kevin opened his eyes the next morning, he felt as if he'd dropped into a burning furnace and the pain between his legs was worse than ever. He sat up cautiously and eased himself out of bed, gasping as he tried to stand upright. Downstairs he could hear the rumble of voices and knew one was his father's. Soon he'd be gone to work and then Kevin would slip downstairs and have a comforting cup of tea.

He began to scramble into his clothes, which he left in a certain order every night so he could put them on in the semi-dark to avoid waking the others.

He was pulling up his trousers when Grace suddenly sat up in the other iron bed and said, 'Kev?'

'Whisht, you'll have the wee ones awake,' Kevin whispered. 'What d'you want?'

'How do you feel?'

'How d'you think? Bloody marvellous, so I am.'

'What are you going to do, Kevin? About Daddy?'

'Hate his guts, what d'you think?'

'I mean—'

'I don't want to talk about it, OK?' Kevin said. He heard the door slam behind his father and added, 'Anyway, I've got a paper round to do.'

Grace listened to her brother's laboured descent of the stairs and the little gasps and groans he was making as she slipped out of bed and dressed herself. Kevin tried to compose himself before he stepped into the room, but he felt breathless with the pain of it all. Sweat stood out on his forehead and his face was brick red.

Maeve turned as he came in and saw the pain lines creasing his face, which was glistening with sweat. 'Kevin?' she said. 'I was going to let you lie in today.'

'I have a paper round, Mammy.'

'You're in no fit state,' Maeve said. 'We'll get a message to Mr Moss.'

'No, Mammy, he'll give my job to someone else,' Kevin protested.

'Kevin, you can scarcely walk.'

Kevin made an effort to straighten up, but a wave of nausea washed over him. Maeve saw the colour drain from his face and she sat him down, pressed a cup of tea into his hand and began toasting bread on the fire's embers. She was spreading the second slice liberally with dripping when Grace entered the room.

She was usually up early on Mondays to help her mother with the weekly wash, so Maeve made no comment on her entrance, but Grace looked at her mother and said, 'Could you cope with the wash on your own today, Mammy?'

'Why?' Maeve asked. 'What have you to do?'

'Kevin's paper round.'

'No you don't,' Kevin cried. 'It's my round; I'll do it myself.' So saying, he tried to spring to his feet, but spasms of pain ran through his body at the sudden movement and he sank to the floor into an undignified heap with a moan of despair.

'See sense, Kevin,' Grace said, nibbling at the toast meant for her brother and watching Kevin being helped into the chair by their mother. 'If I don't do it till you're better, your boss will just get someone else, and that's the end of your job, isn't it? And maybe your career as a shop-keeper too will be over before it's begun.'

'He'll not be able to do that, anyway,' Maeve said, and added to Grace, 'You best tell that to Mr Moss. Tell him he'll be starting with his dad instead a week today.'

She still thinks I'm going into the foundry, Kevin thought. After all that has happened, she still thinks that, and he shook his head at his sister.

Grace caught his line of thought and had no intention of telling this Mr Moss anything, but she didn't bother arguing with her mother. Instead, she said, 'OK, Mammy. But it will leave Mr Moss in a hole today if Kevin just doesn't turn out at such short notice. I mean, he's been good to us. Look at the cars he gave Kevin for Jamie's birthday.'

Maeve frowned. 'I don't want to let the man down right enough.'

'Then let me go,' pleaded Grace. 'After all, three and six is three and six.'

Maeve nodded. 'All right then, but have a cup of tea before you go.'

Kevin, accepting the inevitable and feeling guiltily glad that he didn't have to go out into the icy morning said, 'What will you tell him?'

'That you're sick, what else?' Grace said. 'Do you want me to tell him all about our family problems?'

'Hardly,' Kevin said. But Kevin knew Syd Moss might well become involved in them if he was to work there full time. Brendan would be sure to make his presence felt sooner or later and, Kevin thought, in all fairness he ought to make Syd Moss aware of the risk he was taking by offering him employment. Maybe it was fairer to have a word with him and put him in the picture when he was well enough to take up his paper round again.

That was not until Thursday morning and even then the bruises were still evident on his face. The puffiness had gone down a little and the throbbing ache between his legs had settled down to a bearable pain level.

Kevin was glad he had a thick coat with a scarf and Balaclava and strong boots to keep out the winter chill. He knew he was better dressed than many round the streets and he kept his scarf pulled up and his Balaclava down when he entered the shop, although he knew Syd probably wouldn't have time to study him properly. That time in the morning was the busiest as men on their way to work called in for their daily paper, baccy or ciggies, and even sweets if they had the points for them.

Syd just looked up from where he was serving a customer and grunted, 'You're back then?'

Though he didn't show it, Syd was glad to see Kevin. His sister had done the work well enough and he was grateful she was ready to do it when she said her brother was sick, but he didn't think a girl was right for a paper round. The bags were heavy and if he'd had a daughter as well as Stanley, he wouldn't have let her go out in all weathers with the heavy bag dragging her shoulder down.

'He was all right Saturday,' he'd said to Grace that first Monday morning.

He'd seen the flicker of Grace's eyes. Just a second and the look had been gone, but Syd had known in that second Kevin was not sick. Something else was keeping him away. But he'd said nothing to Grace. This was something he'd have to have out with Kevin himself.

When Kevin got back from his round, the first rush had gone, and then the occasional shopper was buying one or two items. Finally the shop was empty. Syd followed Kevin to the door leading to the living quarters where he hung his bag and said sharply, 'What was the matter with you the last three days?'

Kevin, taken unawares, said, 'Didn't my sister tell you?'

'Your sister told me you were sick,' Syd Moss said grimly. 'I know you weren't and I want you to tell me why you saw fit not to turn up for three days.' He peered closer at Kevin and saw the discoloured face and puffy eyes and added, 'Have you been fighting? Is that it?'

Kevin considered lying, but what would happen then if he began work and his father was to come raging into the shop? Kevin knew if he told him now Syd might think it was a bad risk employing him. But then he hadn't a chance of keeping his job if he kept quiet. His father thought he'd beaten him into submission. When he realised he hadn't, he'd be round raising Cain, he knew.

'Not exactly,' he told the shopkeeper. 'My father did this.'

He was unaware of the curl of his lip as he said this, but Syd was well aware of it and angry at the implied insolence. 'And what did you do to merit it, boy?' he barked.

'Nothing,' Kevin snapped back and then seeing Syd's outraged face said, 'Sorry, sir, but I really did nothing bad. I just told him I wanted to work here.'

'Why should that make him angry with you?' Syd asked in genuine bewilderment.

'Because he wants me to work in the brass foundry with him.'

All of Syd's life he'd been taught respect for his elders and betters and most of all for his parents, and he glared at Kevin. 'You're Catholic, aren't you?' he asked. 'Haven't you been taught to honour your father and mother?'

'No . . . I mean yes, sir, but it's hard to honour my father, Mr Moss. He's a bully who beats my mother and keeps us all short of money.' Kevin hadn't wanted to blurt that out and he knew his mother would be ashamed at a stranger being told their business, but it had burst unbidden from his lips. He hung his head. 'I'm sorry, sir,' he said. 'I know this isn't your problem.'

251

Syd didn't like the sound of the boy's father and wondered if he could be exaggerating. Fathers, in his opinion, were a funny breed. Some miners, for example, would insist their sons follow their trade because it was the thing to do, regardless of how dangerous it was. Others would move heaven and earth to give their sons a better start. Maybe it was the same in the brass industry?

But in truth the man sounded a brute, the very type of man Syd detested, the sort who raised his hand to his wife. But the lad was sorry he'd told him that bit, he'd seen it in his face, so he decided not to take that tack, but concentrate on the boy. 'Was your father upset that you didn't want to do the same job as him? Was that it?'

'Yes, sir. But not for the reason you might think,' Kevin said. 'Not because we've ever got on or anything and he wants to show me the ropes. It's because he wants to take my money off me.'

'Is the money good?'

Kevin didn't know yet how much his wages were to be for working in the shop, let alone the foundry, but he guessed not that much. 'No. I don't think so,' he said. 'At least not unless I work every hour God sends. But whatever I earn, my father will take off me on pay day,' he cried out. Suddenly it was important that Syd Moss knew how bad it was at home. 'I don't want my wages for myself,' he said. 'They're for my mammy. She's nearly always short of money and has been for years, and her and the younger ones have often gone without. My father,' he said with contempt, 'spends all his wages on beer, fags and betting. My mother needs every penny, Mr Moss. Christ, the weans would have starved to death if my father had had his way.'

Syd couldn't help but be moved by the emotion in Kevin's voice and the worry on his face. 'And when your father was told you wouldn't join him in the foundry, he punched you?' Syd asked.

'If he'd only punched me I'd have been able to come to work; I'm taller than my father, Mr Moss, but he fights dirty. He kicked me . . .' Kevin stopped and wondered how he could explain. He couldn't bring himself to say where he'd been kicked. His face flushed crimson at the thought and Sydney Moss deduced a good deal by the flush. 'He kicked me all over,' Kevin finished lamely. 'I couldn't walk too well. That's why Grace offered to do the round for me.'

Syd was shocked. He'd spanked Stanley when he was a child and he'd like to bet there wasn't a boy in the land who hadn't had one good spanking, but it was always with the flat of his hand. And when he got to an age to understand, corporal punishment was needed less and less. He'd never have laid into Stanley at thirteen or fourteen years old.

But what should he do about Kevin? 'How do you feel about your father now, Kevin?'

'I hate him. I'm sorry if that shocks you but I don't remember a time when I didn't hate him.'

'So when does he want you to start at the foundry?'

'Monday.'

'The very same day as you were due to start here?'

'I'll be here.'

'How will you do that? What if your father refuses to let you come?'

Kevin felt a moment of despair. He knew his violent father would try to show him who was master in the home. But he couldn't physically drag Kevin down the road to the foundry as if he was a child in a tantrum. He was too big now for his father to manhandle him. But really he shouldn't involve Syd Moss in his quarrel with his father. So he sighed and said, 'I know it's asking a lot. You shouldn't be mixed up in this. I'll understand if you don't want to employ me now.'

'That's my decision, boy,' Syd said. 'You just turn up for the papers this afternoon.'

'You mean I still have a job here?'

'Let's see how you shape up on Saturday,' Syd said, and Kevin smiled for the first time. 'Yes, sir,' he said, and he went out of the shop whistling.

SIXTEEN

Kevin couldn't believe his eyes. It was almost four o'clock and dusk was settling already on that second wintry Saturday he'd worked for Syd. He was just about to call to him that he would be off on his paper round, for he'd insisted he keep that up too, when he caught sight of his father outside the door.

His father was never around at that time of day; on Saturday he was sleeping it off usually, but he must have been made suspicious by the fact that Kevin refused to be drawn into an argument about his future employment. Since Monday evening, Brendan had been at him, goading and taunting him and reminding him who it was who made the decisions in the house, who was master, who he was answerable to. Who indeed, Brendan claimed, Kevin owed his very existence to.

God, it had been hard to be silent, but Kevin had managed it just as he'd managed to hide from his father how much pain he was in. Maeve thought because Kevin hadn't reacted to Brendan's jeering comments he'd given in to his father's demands. Only Grace guessed he hadn't, for she knew her brother well and was scared for him, even though she was also proud.

Friday was his birthday and that morning, as Maeve made him his cup of tea before the paper round, she presented Kevin with a card and a parcel wrapped in tissue paper.

'A wristwatch, Mammy!' he exclaimed with pleasure on opening the parcel. 'You shouldn't have gone to such expense.'

'Ah, Kevin, you give me so much,' Maeve said. 'It's a pleasure to give something back, so it is. And you'll need a watch now that you'll be a working man from Monday.'

'Aye,' Kevin said, 'but I'd always know the time as Syd has a clock on the wall.'

Maeve's face paled. 'Surely to God, Kevin, you've given up all thought of work in the shop?'

'No, Mammy. You didn't seriously think I should because my thug of a father demands it? Did you think he'd beaten the notion out of me? Oh no, Mammy. He's had his own way too long.'

'Kevin, for Christ's sake, please will you listen to me?'

'No, Mammy, not in this.' He kissed his mother's cheek and went on, 'He got the better of me last time because I didn't realise the dirty fighter he was. Next time I'll be prepared.'

'Kevin—'

'See you later. I'll have to go, I'll be late,' Kevin said. And he made sure there was never time later that day to speak of it.

The second Saturday morning Syd told Kevin to go up for a bite of breakfast as he came into the shop after having his own.

'I had my breakfast before I came away.'

'It's a long time since then,' Syd said. 'Go on up, for God's sake. If there's one thing the missus goes off about it's good food going cold for the want of an appetite.'

He watched Kevin go up the stairs and hoped he'd never know what a battle he'd had for Gwen even to see the boy, let alone give him a meal. Syd had taken to Kevin Hogan and had plans for him, but his plans needed Gwen's approval because it was her home too. The first step to it all was for her to meet the boy, which up until now she'd refused to do.

'The family are as poor as church mice,' Syd had said. 'He's lucky if he gets a crust spread with dripping for his breakfast and that would be just after half-six because he's here well before seven.'

'He's no different from any other boy round here then.'

'No, except that this one is working for us and till six o'clock tonight,' Syd had said. 'Come on, lass. We don't want the lad fainting in the shop.'

'You don't know what you're asking me.'

'I do.' He'd put his hands on his wife's shoulders. 'For God's sake, Gwen . . .'

'I don't want other people here, and especially a boy,' Gwen had spat out.

'It isn't Kevin Hogan's fault Stanley died,' Syd had said, and heard Gwen gasp at the mention of their son.

And then Gwen had crumpled and the tears she'd not yet shed had poured in a torrent from her, coming from deep within. Syd had comforted her, but when her tears were spent, Gwen had looked at her husband and though her eyes were still bleak and sorrow-laden, she'd said resolutely enough, 'All right, Syd. Ask the boy up for a bit of breakfast.'

Despite her brave decision, she was apprehensive that Saturday, but when Kevin burst into the kitchen she was glad she'd asked him. He looked nothing like her son and for that she was glad. His hair was lighter than Stanley's and his eyes blue, his skin paler and freckled and his frame larger and more muscular where Stanley had been small and slightly built, like Sydney. She found herself thinking Kevin would have made a much better-looking soldier than Stanley had.

Kevin gazed at Mrs Moss. Her hair was iron grey and compressed into a bun at the nape of her neck. The skin on her face looked paper thin and it had lines scored across it, round her mouth and down her nose, that made her face appear longer than it was. Her eyes were dull, and her face full of sadness. Her mouth was thin and compressed, and an undetermined chin hovered above her sagging neck. Kevin looked her full in the face and knew that for Gwen to ask him to her home had taken great courage.

The thought made him feel great compassion for the sad woman before him. 'Mr Moss asked me to come up, Mrs Moss,' he said. 'I hope I'm not disturbing you.'

Gwen was impressed by Kevin's manners and told Syd so later, and Kevin couldn't help but be impressed by the breakfast she set before him. The eggs were dried, it was true, but made up like scrambled eggs and piled on the two thick slices of toasted bread, there was a mug of strong tea to wash it down, and Kevin tucked in with relish.

The food gave him energy and he worked tirelessly in the shop. Syd was delighted with him. Many of the customers remembered him from the previous week and greeted him, and most seemed pleased when Syd said he'd be working there full time from Monday.

Kevin wondered when his employer would mention the question of wages, for nothing had been decided between them as yet and he'd have to have it all arranged between them before he left that day.

He needn't have worried: Syd had it all in hand. Generally shop work wasn't as well paid as work in a factory, and here Kevin would also get his meals thrown in. This wasn't totally altruistic on Syd's part. He knew how hard it was to work on an empty stomach and he knew he'd get more out of Kevin if he was well fed. This would have been difficult to do with rationing as tough as ever if the Mosses hadn't owned a shop. As it was, they were able to wangle quite a few under-the-counter items and so the breakfast and dinner Gwen would supply would not pose much of a problem to them.

And really Syd didn't want meals taken into account with regard to Kevin's wages because he liked the lad himself but, more importantly, because Gwen had taken to him. Syd knew Kevin had broken through the icy barrier she'd put round herself and Syd saw it as a small step towards her recovery. For that reason alone he would like to keep hold of Kevin. The fact that the lad was a good worker and polite to everyone, even the most obnoxious of customers, was a bonus.

So it was over their dinner of creamy mashed potatoes and fat brown sausages that Syd talked to Kevin. 'Now, young Kevin, we'll have to decide on your wages.'

Kevin swallowed the piece of sausage in his mouth and said, 'Yes, sir.'

Syd glanced at his wife, whom he'd already discussed the matter with, and said, 'A pound all right for a start?'

Kevin nearly fell off his chair. He'd thought the man would offer him perhaps twelve and six, he might be persuaded up to fifteen bob, but never in a million Sundays did Kevin imagine he'd get so much. He could still do the paper round, which would mean he would earn one pound, three and six a week.

The surprise and shock of it almost took away his power of speech. 'It . . . that . . . would be . . . would be grand, Mr Moss.'

'You'll have to work for it, mind, seven o'clock to six most days. Wednesday you'll finish at one o'clock, but Friday we don't close till nine or ten.'

'I don't mind hard work, Mr Moss.'

'I've seen evidence of that, lad,' Mr Moss said, and as any praise from him was unusual, this further silenced Kevin. The man went on, 'If I didn't think you'd work, you'd not have been offered the job in the first place.'

Kevin rejoined the shop full of good food and gratitude to the Mosses, who had been so kind to him. It had been a lucky day when he'd gone inside and asked Syd Moss to give him the job of paperboy.

He surveyed the shop with pride. It was a fine place to work, light and airy, and in the main the customers were fine, always ready for a chat and a joke. Some took the mickey out of his accent, but he didn't mind that. He often felt if he had to choose between an Irish brogue and a Brummie accent, he'd know which one he would pick, but not wishing to offend, he didn't share his thoughts.

He couldn't wait for the afternoon to end. He wanted to go home and tell his mother that soon her money worries would be over. He knew better than to leave her money, but he could do other things like buy the coal for the family and many things could be picked up cheap at the Bull Ring. He could go down there on his half-day, or on Saturday after work, for the Bull Ring stayed open till late. It was lit with gas flare lights now, but his mother had told him that during the war a strict blackout had had to be observed and he'd thought it must have been a dismal place then.

He wondered whether he should go down that night and squander some of his three and sixpence on a treat for them all, if he could find anything. He always gave it complete into his mother's hands, but now there would be a proper wage packet at the end of the week.

But his ponderings fled from his mind when he saw the figure outside. The sky had been overcast all day. Dusk had come early and a fine mist had begun falling as drizzle. But even in the murky gloom, Kevin was pretty sure who it was and as the figure swayed his way forward, he was lit up for a moment in the light from a streetlamp outside the shop. Kevin knew his father was well aware of where he was and had come to settle the score with him.

He felt the sweat break out under his armpits and the palms of his hands grew sticky. He knew his father would be drunk, possibly very drunk, and he was glad there were no customers in the shop. He turned to the slight figure of Syd Moss and knew he'd never match up to his father's bulk, but he had to be warned.

'Mr Moss,' he said, 'my father is outside.'

Syd looked up. He knew after what Kevin had told him on Thursday that this moment would come. It had come sooner rather than later, that was all, and maybe just as well. He looked out at the man just the other side of the shop window and wondered why he hadn't come blundering in and why he stood staring that way.

But Brendan was biding his time, checking there were no customers, for he wanted no witnesses to what he intended to do. It was pay-the-price time and, by God, he'd enjoy extracting his dues from his lily-livered, work-shy son. His bloody son had made a laughing stock of him, as his mother had years before, and that had been brought home to him that very lunchtime at The Bell.

'Thought your lad was following you into the foundry?' one man had asked.

'So he is. What of it?'

'Well, what's he doing serving at Moss's shop in Wellington Street?'

'What the bloody hell you talking about?'

'Straight up. My missus saw him last Saturday, large as life, him and the old fellow running the place. The bloke said your lad was his new assistant.'

There was a burst of laughter from the others listening. 'Got one over you again, Brendan, eh, man?' one of them said. 'You d'aint know a thing about it, did yer?'

Brendan had reddened. He remembered the name Kevin had thrown at him. Moss's tobacconist and grocery, he'd said, on Wellington Street. Sly sod hadn't said he'd already started work.

'Brendan don't know a damn thing about what his family are up to, seems to me,' another man put in. 'First his wife takes off and now his son goes his own way.'

Brendan's fists balled at his side. He longed to punch the man grinning at him on the jaw.

'You want to be the master in your own house,' the first man said. 'Like I am. You wouldn't see my wife and kids deciding things. I'd give them what for if they started that game.'

Brendan's answer was to lunge forward at the man, grasp him by the throat and punch him between the eyes. Restraining hands pulled him off and the burly landlord came bustling from behind the bar, manhandled Brendan out of the door and kicked him into the street. He unsteadily got to his feet and leant against a house for a moment till the dizziness in his head abated. Behind him, ringing in his ears, was the laughter from his so-called mates.

By the time he reached Syd Moss's shop the words that had been thrown at him across the bar had whipped him into a frenzied fury. He wanted to tear his son limb from limb and that excuse for a man that he worked with. He remembered what Maeve had threatened to do to him if he touched her precious son again. Well, she could go to hell! She must have known all along about Kevin and his job. By the time he'd finished with her she'd be in no fit state to go anywhere or tell anyone anything. Then they'd see who had the last laugh.

Syd Moss studied the man who burst through the shop doorway. He was powerfully built and stood a full head above him, with muscular shoulders and arms. However, the rest of his body looked flabby and soft, and as he had his donkey jacket unfastened, Syd plainly saw the beer gut hanging over his belt. His face was red and bloated, and damp from the rain droplets that shook from his thick hair as he turned to look at Syd through bleary bloodshot eyes.

'So,' he said, 'you're the little squirt that turns a son against his own father?'

Syd was scared, there was no denying it. Brendan Hogan had frightened better and bigger men than he, but he also knew better than to admit any sense of weakness and his voice was firm. 'I assure you, Mr Ho—'

He got no further. With a roar, Brendan lifted the man from his feet and his hands locked around his throat. He'd deal with Kevin later; first he'd teach this excuse for a man that it would be unwise and unhealthy for him to employ Kevin in any capacity.

Kevin leapt on his father with a yell and tried to tear his arms away. He'd seen Syd's frantic gasps and grunts cease and his hands that had clawed at Brendan stop their useless struggle and fall to his sides, and the boy was panic-stricken. He pummelled at his father as he desperately tried to make him relax his hold on Syd's neck. He saw the small man's eyes bulge and a trickle of blood dribble from his mouth, and then he slumped, seemingly lifeless.

Brendan dropped Syd to the floor where he fell into an unconscious heap.

'For Christ's sake!' Kevin cried. He wanted to go to Syd and check that he was all right, but knew if he was to drop his guard for one instant his father would take full advantage of it.

He faced his father unafraid, surprised he wasn't shaking with fear. He felt angry but calm, and knew he'd have to remain so in order to outwit him, because to be free of him he would have to fight him and win. Force was the only thing his father recognised.

Brendan said sneeringly, 'Seems you didn't have enough of a hiding on Sunday. You're asking for another one.'

Kevin said nothing and Brendan went on, 'What's up with you? Scared, are you? Come and get me then.'

Kevin longed to do just that, to throw himself upon the man and punch his filthy mouth for him, but he knew that's what Brendan wanted him to do and he forced himself to keep his head.

'Lily-livered mammy's boy!'

Out of the corner of his eye Kevin caught sight of Syd struggling to a sitting position, rubbing ruefully at his scarlet neck. His face was deathly pale, he had blood running down his chin and the white of one of his eyes was crimson. Kevin felt sorry for the man hauled into a situation not of his own making and he glared with pure hatred at Brendan and said tantalisingly, 'Come on, big boy. Pick on someone your own size for a change, or are you only able for beating women and weans?'

Brendan charged him like a bull, his fists swinging like hammers and Kevin knew if one of them were to catch him full in the face or the mouth, he'd be knocked halfway across the shop and the fight would be finished before it had begun. Even the glancing blows he parried had him partially winded. He was glad his father's drunken state made the swipes wide and were slow enough to enable him to get out of the way.

He tried to keep an eye on his father's feet, knowing and still feeling the damage they could inflict and Brendan, reading Kevin's thoughts and sensing his caution, grew reckless. He was staggering, literally, from the first full right-handed blow Kevin landed on his face while the second left him dazed and disorientated. Kevin's blood was thoroughly up by this time, he followed it with two body blows. Brendan began to sway, and at Kevin's punch between the eyes he slumped to his knees, keeled over and was still.

Kevin gazed at the still figure dispassionately. Perhaps he should feel some shame that he'd raised his hand to his own father, but he felt none. In fact, when Brendan had fallen to the floor, Kevin had had to resist the desire to put the boot in, kick the shit out of him.

Perhaps Syd knew some of the thoughts tumbling around Kevin's head and wished to distract him for he cried huskily, 'Help me up, boy.'

Kevin helped Syd on to the stool behind the counter, where he rubbed at his damaged throat before commenting, 'There could be trouble over this. We'd best get the police.'

'I only hit him when he went for me.'

'And d'you think that's how he'll tell it when he comes round?' Syd said, and Kevin knew he wouldn't. His father would endeavour to put the blame on him and Syd, possibly more on Syd. Kevin knew how his mind worked. Syd glanced at Kevin. It would be the easiest thing in the world now to say to the boy that he'd decided he didn't need help in the shop. He'd made a mistake and he didn't need a full-time assistant. The boy would know he was lying, but he wouldn't blame him. He'd accept the inevitable and work alongside his father and no doubt fight to keep part of his wages from him. But that part wouldn't be Syd's problem any more – none of his concern. Kevin Hogan would only be one of many.

The difference was he'd met the boy and liked and admired him, and if he was to ignore him he felt that Stanley's death would have been in vain. He and many others had gone to war because of a bully: Hitler had threatened to overrun and control Europe. Because of the brave servicemen he'd been defeated and Sydney knew if he were to give in to Kevin's father he would be besmirching not only his son's memory but also all the others who gave their lives.

'We'll need to get the police,' Syd said, 'and we need to get a doctor, young Kevin, to look at his injuries and ours.' He laid a hand on Kevin's shoulder and went on, 'If you want to get out of your father's clutches this is the only way.'

Brendan Hogan was still bawling at the policeman when Dr Fleming came down the stairs from the flat where he'd been examining Kevin and Syd Moss. Brendan had claimed Sydney had enticed his son away and encouraged him to defy his father, who'd a job ready and waiting for him, and when he'd come to discuss the matter that afternoon, Kevin had gone for him like a tiger, encouraged by the shopkeeper.

Dr Fleming looked at Brendan coldly. 'Mr Moss said you went for his throat.'

'Well, I might have . . .' Brendan began. He was flustered. 'I wasn't myself. Maybe I was a bit hasty. I mean, when a man deliberately sets a son against his father . . .'

'I agree you probably weren't yourself, Mr Hogan,' the doctor said stressing the 'Mr', 'because you were drunk, stinking drunk. I'm sure the landlord at The Bell could verify that if he had to, and I have to tell you, you almost killed Syd Moss. There are bruises all round his neck and such was the severe pressure you applied, blood vessels have ruptured in the neck, which is why one of Mr Moss's eyes is badly bloodshot and there has been bleeding from his mouth and nose. It is, Mr Hogan, a serious assault, so serious that I've advised Mr Moss to file an assault charge against you.'

Brendan, mouth agape, was looking at the doctor as if he couldn't believe his ears. He shook his head from side to side in an effort to clear it. 'Now look here,' he roared, 'I was the one assaulted. Bloody hell, it's a fine thing, this, assaulted by my own son. I could file a bloody charge, I can tell you.'

'Oh, could you?' the doctor remarked sarcastically. 'Well, I'll tell you and this police officer here that I've been attending the results of your handiwork on your family for years. Once before, many years ago, you attacked your son with a belt with such ferocity, I was tempted to tell the authorities. It was only because of your wife I desisted, the same wife who often bears the marks of your violent assaults on her.'

'She's my wife, and he's my son,' Brendan yelled. 'It's my right to chastise them.'

'Chastise! Chastise, did you say?' the doctor cried. 'You laid into Kevin only a week ago with your fist and your boots. His face has calmed down a little and will heal eventually, but his body is a mass of bruises and lacerations where the hobnails in your boots have torn into his skin. The kick you administered between his legs was so ferocious it split one of his testicles. Kevin should have received hospital treatment for it. You may have rendered the lad sterile; only time will tell. Is that your idea of chastisement?'

The policeman, who'd been listening quite horror-stricken at the doctor's words said, 'Shall we take him down the station then? They will be making charges against him, I suppose.'

'Get your hands off me,' Brendan cried, pulling himself from the policeman's grasp. He stared at the doctor. 'Aye, well, if they make a claim against me, I'll do the same to them. I was knocked unconscious by my own son. That's worth something, surely?'

'Oh yes, it's worth me thinking with satisfaction that you've got your just deserts at last,' Dr Fleming said. 'Kevin attacked you to protect Mr Moss, isn't that right, Constable?'

'If Mr Moss is injured like you say, sir, I would say this man's son wouldn't have a case to answer,' the policeman said.

'And as for being knocked unconscious,' the doctor went on, 'though Kevin admitted knocking you down, I would say the amount of beer you consumed had some-thing to do with you lying comatose on the floor.'

They were laughing at him and Brendan felt anger flow through him so that his whole body felt on fire and he saw red lights before his eyes. He couldn't bear being laughed at. Someone would pay for this tonight, he prom-ised himself, and he knew who it would be.

'We'll take him down and charge him then, sir,' the policeman said.

What were they talking about? Brendan thought. They couldn't take him anywhere. They hadn't the right. What the bloody hell were they doing, the pair of them?

Dr Fleming knew there would be no charge facing Brendan Hogan, for Syd and young Kevin were willing to do a deal. They wouldn't press charges if he left them alone. Syd had also decided that it would be far too dangerous for Kevin to continue to live at home after this latest fiasco.

Even Gwen had agreed he should move in with them when she looked at her husband's bruised and swollen throat and realised that, but for the boy, he could have been strangled to death. The boy's father was obviously a maniac and Kevin couldn't return home to that. Stanley's bedroom had remained a shrine to his memory, but now she realised someone else had greater need of it than her dead son. She'd prepare it for Kevin, and the nice doctor offered to take Kevin home later to collect his things and explain it all to his mother.

But Dr Fleming wanted Brendan locked up, at least for the night. He'd been humiliated and made to feel small and it had angered him, and knowing Brendan Hogan even as little as he did, he guessed that left on the streets he'd take his anger out on his wife. He'd rather he cool his heels in a police cell than use his wife as a punchbag and he told the constable as much.

Brendan was led away handcuffed, still struggling and proclaiming he'd been set up and someone would pay for it. The door had barely closed on him before Kevin appeared in the shop and the doctor said, 'I'll pop along and see your mother and explain things. I'll come back for you at six and you can collect your clothes.'

Kevin nodded, but he hoped his mother wouldn't be too upset. She was bound to feel it, for she'd missed most of his growing up as it was and now for him to choose somewhere else to live would hurt her, he felt sure. But, if he'd agreed to his father's demands, his mother would have descended again into the grinding poverty that he knew had been her lot for years. This way he could lift her out of it even a little bit. His wages, a fortune to a lad like him, would be a great help to his mother and the rest of them at home.

He was glad the policeman had taken his father away. But he knew he would make no case against him even if it were possible for a son to speak against his father in a court of law, and he wasn't sure that it was. What if he'd tried to do just that and his father had got off? Then none of their lives would have been worth living and his mother's least of all. The doctor had suggested working out some sort of deal with him, and both Kevin and Syd had thought it the safest thing to do in the circumstances. God, Kevin thought, how he hated the man. He wished he would die and leave them all alone and he didn't care if that was a mortal sin or not. One day he'd earn enough to take care of them all and then his father could jump in the canal.

Elsie was in Maeve's house that evening when the doctor called and neither was prepared for the news he brought. Maeve listened open-mouthed.

'Let's get this right,' she said almost disbelievingly. 'Brendan went to the shop, had some sort of set-to with Syd Moss, and our Kevin knocked him down?'

'He did indeed.'

'Won't he get into trouble for it?'

'Oh no,' the doctor assured her, 'for you see it was in the nature of self-defence. After all, your husband almost choked the life out of the shopkeeper, Mr Moss.'

'Oh, I see,' Maeve said, though she did not see at all. She couldn't take in the fact that her husband was locked up in a cell for the night, nor that because of the attack the Mosses had offered Kevin a home with them and he'd accepted. She knew it was best and sensible. Hadn't she already come to the decision that her son and husband could not live together? Of course she had, and this was the only answer.

But in reality she felt as if she'd lost her son all over again and was irrationally jealous of this Mrs Moss, who would have the pleasure of Kevin's company. She'd wash and iron his clothes, prepare his meals, make his bed and clean his room. She'd be the one to hear Kevin's confidences and worries, and share his happier moments too. She was the one he would always be grateful to.

And when in later years he looked back on his life, Maeve had the feeling he'd think his mother had let him down and it was only the presence of Elsie and the doctor that prevented her crying out against this latest hurt that seemed to pierce her very soul.

SEVENTEEN

All the next morning Maeve waited for Brendan to appear. She knew he'd be released that day sometime and presumed it would be in the morning, and the only time she left the house was to go to nine o'clock Mass.

By dinner her nerves were stretched to breaking point. 'Go out for the day, you and the babbies. Let him take his bad humour out on someone else for a change,' Elsie advised.

'You know I can't do that,' Maeve said. 'From what the doctor said yesterday, Brendan was attacked by Kevin. It doesn't matter why or how or who was in the right – not to Brendan it won't. If I wasn't here when he came home . . . well, let's say I'd be afraid to face him ever again.'

'That mightn't be a bad thing.'

'God, Elsie,' Maeve cried, her eyes flashing angrily, 'd'you think I'd still be here if I had any sort of a bloody choice?'

And Elsie knew she wouldn't and so her advice was worse than useless. 'I know, Maeve,' she said more gently. 'But it would be better if I stayed with you.'

'No, no, that would be worse!' Maeve cried. 'If you care for me at all, get the kids out of it. He'll be raging,

I know that, and they don't have to witness it. I'll try and calm him down before they come home. I have a bit of dinner saved for him. I'll heat it up over a pan of water. Food always puts him in a better mood.'

Elsie knew as well as Maeve that nothing would ease Brendan's temper that day because he'd been humiliated, and that he couldn't take. But then the man had to be faced sometime, and Maeve was right to try to protect the children.

'Stand up to the brute, Maeve,' she said. 'Don't let him have it all his own way.'

'I intend to,' Maeve said grimly. 'I'm fed up being used as Brendan's punch-ball, believe you me.'

Elsie looked at her for a few moments at her gaunt face and the huge distended belly and swollen legs and feet. God, she thought, if she was my daughter I'd batter Brendan Hogan into the ground with whatever I could lay my hands on. 'I'll take the babby over to me sister's for a bit,' she said. 'And I'll see if Alf will take the others to the flicks.'

The children were wild to visit the Broadway and see *Dumbo,* the cartoon film the American Walt Disney had made some time before. Only Grace expressed disquiet.

'What about Daddy?'

'What about him?' Maeve asked. 'God alone knows when we'll see him.'

'Why don't you come with us?' Grace urged. 'He may come home and you'd be on your own.'

'What if he does?' Maeve said. 'It won't be the first time. Go on, Grace. I will go to no pictures. I want a chance to put my feet up for five minutes.' Grace allowed herself to be persuaded. She did want to see the film. All the girls were talking about it and her mother didn't seem worried. She knew what had gone on at the shop and why because her mother had told her, but neither Jamie nor Bridget knew anything. Maybe being in a prison cell all night would have frightened her father into behaving himself. She'd love something to frighten him for a change.

As soon as Maeve glimpsed Brendan weaving across the yard that afternoon, she felt her insides quail and she hurried through the scullery and lit the gas under the pan of water she had ready to reheat Brendan's dinner. She knew from one glance at Brendan's glowering face that, far from cooling him off, the night in the cells had given him time to brood on the injustices he imagined he'd had heaped upon him. She also noted that whenever the police had released him, it had given him enough time to get bottled. Anger and alcohol spelt trouble for Maeve and she knew that however she handled the next few minutes, she was in for a good hiding and was pretty certain that this time even her pregnancy would not save her.

She glanced at him as he came in and saw the darkening under one eye and the grazed cheeks and thick lip, and knew that Kevin had indeed hit his father as the doctor had told her. The fact cheered her, despite her knowing she'd probably pay dearly for it.

He made no reply but a grunt to her greeting, and watched her laying a place for him at the table without a word. But when she encouraged him to sit and eat his dinner, he leapt up like an enraged animal, picked up the plate and hurled it across the room. Maeve watched the meat, potato and cabbage soaked in gravy slide down the wall in glutinous globules to mix with the pieces of plate smashed to smithereens on the floor, and felt such anger towards Brendan that she almost shook with it.

'You can keep your sodding dinner,' Brendan bawled at her. 'You knew what the little bastard was doing all the time. Together you made a fool of me and I'll not stand that.'

All night that fact had coursed through his mind as he'd paced his prison cell, and after his release this anger was now fuelled by beer. When he lurched into the house that day he was determined to beat the living daylights out of Maeve. Since Kevin's return, she'd become difficult, even defiant at times. Well, she'd know who was master by the time he'd finished.

Maeve couldn't deny she knew what Kevin was doing, and even if she'd claimed not to know it would have made no difference. She could almost feel Brendan's rage – the violence emanating from him – and as he made a grab for her, she twisted out of his grasp. Elsie was right, she knew. She should have got out. One day she knew Brendan would be so angry with her he'd beat her to death. Well, whatever he did to her that day, she'd leave her mark on him. She was fed up of being a punch-ball, as she'd told Elsie, but it was more than that. From what the doctor had told her, he'd almost done for Syd Moss and might have finished the job more thoroughly if it hadn't been for Kevin. She couldn't stand up to him like Kevin but, by God, he wouldn't have it all his own way either.

She fought like a cornered tiger, beating at him with her fists and biting at the hands trying to bind her, scratching his bruised face and trying to protect her stomach. Her retaliation seemed to give Brendan some malicious pleasure and her efforts were in any case futile. Her cumbersome, heavy body didn't help, but she felt a measure of satisfaction that, even as he punched her to the floor, his face and arms bore the evidence of her nails and teeth.

She lay long after Brendan had stumbled up the stairs to bed. She was too weary and sore to move and too bloody fed up with it all. Eventually, with a sigh she got to her feet and staggered into the scullery to put the kettle on, hoping at least to have a chance to bathe her face before the children saw it.

However, the water hadn't even come to the boil before Elsie was in the door with Mary Ann in the pushchair. She nodded at Maeve's face and said resignedly, 'He's back then?'

'Aye. And he's left his calling card.'

Grace, who came in later, laughing with the others over something in the film, was struck dumb by the sight of her mother's swollen, battered face. Elsie had helped her bathe it by then, but in all truth there was little they could do and Grace was annoyed for allowing herself to be persuaded to watch the antics of a flying elephant instead of being home to support her mother. She knew what manner of man her father was, she well remembered from before their flight to Ireland and he'd shown his true colours since they'd been back. Did she honestly think a man like that would have taken a beating from Kevin and not make someone pay for it? No she didn't, she wasn't a fool, but she'd gone out and left her mother unprotected.

Whatever Brendan had done had seemed to knock the stuffing out of Maeve, Elsie noticed, but Maeve dismissed their concerns and said she was just tired and she'd be as right as rain with a cup of tea inside her. Elsie was far from convinced, but Alf said he wanted his own fireside and a bite to eat and Elsie had no option but to go home.

'I'll pop in later,' she said as she passed Maeve, pressing her hand.

'Don't bother yourself,' Maeve said. 'I'll make an early night of it. Once the wee ones are in bed, I'll likely follow them. Brendan will sleep on till morning, if I'm any judge, so at least I'll be free of his attentions tonight.'

'If you're sure.'

'I'm sure.'

It was later, in the dark night, that Maeve, trying to find a position that eased her battered body, realised she hadn't felt the baby move since the beating she'd endured hours before. The worry nagged at her tired mind and took all thought of sleep from her. Next morning she felt like a piece of chewed string as she dragged her aching body from the bed and made her way downstairs to get Brendan's breakfast.

She wished it wasn't Monday and the washing to do. She could have done without it, but she knew wishing was a waste of time, and began collecting the clothes together as Brendan ate his breakfast in a surly silence that Maeve had no intention of breaking.

Just minutes after Brendan slammed the door behind him, Grace was downstairs to help her mother. She saw the laboured way she moved around the room and said, 'I'll start on the washing, Mammy, if you like, and you can see to the weans.'

Maeve could have kissed her, for every movement she made was painful and every step agony, and the pains around her stomach gripped her like a tight band.

Grace carried the bucket of slack down to the coal house and then she filled the copper up, bucket by bucket, from the tap by the door. She lit the fire beneath it, sprinkled in soap powder and left it to boil up while she fetched the clothes.

'Why didn't Kevin just agree to work in the foundry?' Grace had asked the previous evening. 'I don't see I'll have much choice when it's my turn.'

'It's not the job alone,' Maeve had explained. 'You see, pet, Brendan would have every penny off Kevin if they worked in the same place. His wages would benefit us not a jot.'

'What about mine when I go to work next year?' Grace had asked.

'Who knows?'

'I'll not give anything to him, Mammy. My wages will be for you.'

She knew her mother had been surprised and she was still scared of her father, but she wouldn't give in to him, not on this question of her wages. He expected them to do everything he said and when he said it, but she and Kevin had been raised by firm but loving grandparents who'd given them self-respect and taught them to stand up for what they thought was right.

She poured the bubbling water into the maiding tub and began pounding the clothes with the wooden dolly to loosen the dirt. It had been as black as night when she'd crept down to the brew house, but now as the grey morning chased the dark away, the yard came to life. Men's boots clattered on the cobbles as they made their way to work and the sleepy-eyed children stumbled down to the lavatory. Elsie was glad to see Grace doing the washing as she passed, for she didn't think Maeve would be up to it that day at least.

'I'll pop in and see your mother when I get Alf off,' she called to Grace.

Grace nodded, but didn't speak. She hadn't breath to. As she'd come across the yard to the brew house early that morning, the intense cold had seeped into her bones and caught at the back of her throat, for the day was raw. But now the sweat ran down Grace's face as she bent over the steamy water. She had good strong arms from the work she'd done to help her grandparents, particularly making the butter in the dairy, which meant pounding the cream in the creamery barrel in a similar way to that of maiding clothes.

The action though did nothing to soothe her emotions. She imagined she was bashing the dolly in her father's face. She wished she were as big and strong as Kevin and able to knock him down as her mother told her he'd done, and then, she thought, I'd stamp on his bloody face. Let him see how he'd like it for a change.

The maiding over, she drew a hand across her clammy face for although the door stood sagging open on broken hinges and the icy wind gusted through broken windows, the brew house was damply warm. Moisture ran down the walls and hung in the air that was tinged with the smell of soap powder.

She had the whites soaking in a bucket of Becket's blue when her mother appeared in the doorway. 'Get yourself away,' she said. 'There's porridge on the stove for you.'

Underneath the bruising, Grace saw the white pallor of her mother. Her eyes were almost totally closed up and had smudges of black beneath them. Her unpinned hair lay in rat-tails around her face and she had her old coat wrapped around her, while her feet were pushed into an old pair of boots that would normally have been three sizes too big. Grace thought she looked awful – worse than awful, ill.

'Are you all right?'

'I'm grand. Go on now, or you'll be late and getting the strap.'

Grace knew her mother was right. There was no excuse acceptable for lateness at school. All latecomers had the strap. And yet she was loath to leave her.

'You could write a note,' she said. 'I could stay home today.'

'Will you go, Grace?' Pain that she was unable to cry out against caused Maeve to speak harshly. And then she felt ashamed, especially in view of what the child had accomplished that morning. 'I'm sorry,' she said, but Grace shook her head.

'It doesn't matter, Mammy,' she said, left the washhouse and crossed the yard.

Maeve leant against the mangle and groaned as another intense pain gripped her stomach.

'D'you think it's the babby?' Elsie said much later when Maeve could no longer disguise the fact she was in pain.

'No. It's not due for another month,' Maeve said. 'Besides, it's not that type of pain.'

'Well, summat's gripping your innards, bab,' she said. 'I think we should fetch the doctor.'

'Not bloody likely,' Maeve said as she sat at the table cutting up vegetables for a stew she knew she wouldn't be able to eat. She'd eaten nothing all day, knowing she'd be sick if she tried. She'd existed on cups of weak tea, but she didn't tell Elsie that either. 'It'll just be another bill to pay, won't it?' she said. 'I'll be as right as rain when it's all over. And for God's sake say nothing to Grace. It's hardly worth worrying her to death.'

'I ain't bloody stupid altogether,' Elsie said testily.

'I'm sorry, Elsie,' Maeve said. 'I know you're not.'

Mollified, Elsie, who'd finished the washing for Maeve and was now ironing it, laid the flat iron down and said, 'I'm just away to make Alf some dinner. I'll come in later.'

'No, Elsie, you've done enough,' Maeve said. 'I'll be fine. Anyway, Grace will be in soon and she'll give me a hand.' She glanced over at the children, who'd been so good all day, almost as if they'd been aware she wasn't well, though Elsie had been with her most of the time. Now Jamie lay on his stomach before the fire, playing with the toy cars Kevin had brought him for his birthday and Mary Ann played with cotton reels Elsie had saved for her and strung together with a piece of string.

Maeve felt sorry for both of the little ones, especially Jamie. She'd told him Kevin was going to live elsewhere to make it easier for him to get to work in the shop each day, but she knew she hadn't fooled him. He'd wept bitterly and Mary Ann had cried in sympathy, and Maeve had felt like joining in with the pair of them.

Jamie glanced up at his mother's bruised face and wished they could all go somewhere else, away from their father, so she didn't keep getting her face bashed in all the time. He'd noticed it straight away the evening before, when they came back from the pictures, but he hadn't bothered saying anything.

He lifted his head as the door opened and Bridget and Grace stepped into the house, bringing with them the cold settling in for the night. It had turned their faces bright pink and set their fingers and toes tingling with it. But even as Grace removed her coat and moved closer to the fire, she watched her mother. Maeve, being aware of it, tried not to make a fuss, even when she had a pain she wanted to double over with. Really, she thought, maybe I should get Lizzie Wainwright to take a look. It would do no harm and put my mind at rest, if nothing else. If she was no better after dinner, she would ask Grace to pop along to see the midwife.

Grace was worried when Maeve vomited back the small amount of dinner she'd eaten, but Maeve told her not to fuss. 'I had a big meal with Elsie before you came in,' she said. 'It's no wonder that my stomach objected to another load being deposited in it. I'm too full of baby to eat like that,' she said with an attempt at a smile. But the baby was ominously still. There was so little room now, any movement it made was apparent, even under the tent-like smocks she wore, and sometimes it made her feel sick. But that night she would have welcomed any amount of gymnastics.

It was with the washing-up done and the children being prepared for bed that Maeve suddenly had a pain that made her say to Grace, 'I have to go to the lavatory and quickly.'

She pulled her coat from the hook behind the door as she spoke. 'See to them, will you?'

'Aye. Of course, go on,' Grace said, and Maeve left without another word passing between her and Brendan, though he sat just feet from her, gazing into the fire with a cup of tea in his hand.

The cold took Maeve's breath away when she stepped out into the yard. She was glad of the pool of light from the gas lamp that showed up the icy patches lying on and between the cobbles that scrunched as she walked on them.

She knew, once she passed behind the brew house to where the lavatories were, that the light would be much dimmer and she'd have to go carefully, for she didn't own a torch. She also knew that with everyone in the court using the brew house that day, there were bound to be pools of water around it.

She clutched her coat around her as she hurried just as fast as she dared, for the cramps in her stomach suggested urgency, until she was in the darkest part of the yard. Suddenly her foot shot from under her on a patch of ice and she twisted awkwardly, gasping with pain that shot through her back as well as her stomach. Suddenly there was a feeling between her legs as if someone had pulled a plug and water gushed from her.

'Oh bloody hell!' Maeve cried out. 'It isn't cramps, it's the baby. It'll be Lizzie Wainwright for me tonight, and the doctor too if she advises it,' and she felt comforted because everyone said the baby stopped moving just before birth.

Maeve turned quickly, forgetting in her need to get indoors to be careful, and she skidded on one of the large frozen pools from the brew house. She felt herself falling, but could do nothing to stop herself and fell heavily to the floor, cracking her head on the cobblestones, and felt darkness overwhelming her. The water that had spilt from her body soaked the coat she had wrapped around herself and began to freeze.

Back in the house, Grace was too busy to miss or worry about her mother. She'd filled the children's hot-water bottles and put them in the bed and had refilled the kettle for the wash Maeve insisted they have before bed, and for their drink of cocoa from the tin Kevin had bought them. She was thinking of the comfort the hot-water bottle was and how it took the chill from the icy sheets. In Ireland, as the winter took its icy grip on the cottage, her grandma used to have a stone bottle which she would stand up in the bed and fix it in the position with the bedclothes, so you crept into a cocoon of warmth.

The rubber hot-water bottles were nearly as good, but where Kevin had got the three he'd brought home the week before was anyone's guess. He'd said he'd been down the Bull Ring, but everyone knew anything made of rubber could not be had for love nor money. Even Maeve had not asked him where they'd come from; Grace guessed her mammy would rather not know. She needed them too much to have a conscience about it.

'Where's your bloody mother?' Brendan suddenly snarled, startling Grace so much she nearly tipped the kettle she was pouring into the basin all over herself.

'She's out at the lavvy,' Grace said.

'All this bloody time?'

'She has an upset stomach,' Grace said tersely. 'She's been bad all day.'

'Always something bloody upset in that woman,' Brendan said, lifting his jacket down. 'Well, I'm away out.'

Grace was glad. His brooding silence had got on her nerves and had scared Bridget and Jamie. They'd been afraid to make a noise when their father had been in, but almost as soon as the door closed behind him, they began clamouring for a story from Grace.

With Mary Ann sucking a bottle on her knee and the children sitting either side of her in the armchair, Grace began. Although they enjoyed the fairy stories she'd told them first, they really enjoyed the stories of Ireland and of the life she and Kevin had had when they'd lived there.

The minutes ticked away without Grace being aware of it. Mary Ann dropped off to sleep and Grace took her upstairs and laid the baby in the cot in the bedroom, and it wasn't until she came back downstairs that she realised how long her mother had been gone.

She put her coat on and wrapped her scarf around her neck before she set out to see if she was all right, but even so the cold made her gasp and she pulled her scarf up over her mouth and edged her way carefully, mindful of her slithering feet. She peered through the gloom as she stepped out from the lamp that lighted up the yard as far as the brew house, expecting to see her mother coming back, walking with the peculiar waddle pregnant women tended to develop.

There was nothing, so she picked her way, cautiously waiting for a moment for her eyes to adjust to the more intense darkness and then moving forward again. She almost stumbled over the prone figure of her mother before she'd realised what it was that she'd tripped over.

Then her scream filled the air as she threw herself down beside her, her mother's sodden coat soaking her knees as she cried, 'Mammy, Mammy?' And then as her mother didn't respond she raced up the yard, unheeding of her feet skating over the ice, yelling for Elsie.

Moss's shop had been officially shut for over two hours when there was a hammering on the door. Kevin looked in enquiry at Syd and he shook his head.

'Leave it, boy. We've been open since seven o'clock this morning. If people can't get their things between seven o'clock in the morning and six in the evening, then it's hard luck to them, they can do without.'

Kevin was inclined to agree with him. It always amazed him the number of people who'd come in at one minute to six and then take an age over their purchases. He'd noticed it the two Saturdays he worked and this, his first full day. Closing at six was a joke. And now someone was hammering, and it was past eight o'clock in the evening.

'They'll get fed up when we don't answer,' Syd said.

But whoever it was didn't get fed up. In fact, the hammering got worse, and eventually Syd was forced to heave himself from the chair and put his stockinged feet in his slippers. Remembering his father's visit on Saturday, Kevin strode down the stairs after Syd as Gwen hovered on the landing.

But when the blind was shot up it revealed a frantic and very agitated Grace, who almost fell into the shop as Syd opened the door. Kevin saw his sister's face was swollen and blotchy from crying and tears still ran down her face.

'What is it?' he demanded urgently as apprehension seemed to grip his stomach. 'What is the matter?'

Syd, tutting at the distress of the child, ushered her inside. Grace made an effort to control herself. She scrubbed at her eyes with her coat sleeve and though her tears were wiped from her face, she'd cried for so long, her gulping sobs continued. She also panted breathlessly, for she'd run all the way from her house, but for all that she struggled to explain.

'It's Mammy . . . She's . . . The baby's coming. But that's not all,' she went on, catching the look of relief on Kevin's face. 'That's not the worse thing at all. She collapsed in the yard and knocked herself out. She lay there for ages.'

She could say no more. She couldn't tell Kevin about the water Elsie said lay inside her mammy's tummy around the baby to protect it that had soaked Maeve's clothes into a sodden freezing lump, surrounding her as she lay on the icy cobblestones. You couldn't explain that to a boy and, knowing the power of his temper, she didn't tell him either of the doctor who'd been so angry at the mess of her mother's face, nor of the ambulance men who'd loaded Maeve on to the stretcher and turned to Grace and Elsie as they passed under the lamp and asked Elsie, 'Has this woman been assaulted?'

No, she couldn't tell Kevin that, for he hadn't known that their father had laid into their mother the previous day. Kevin should have known that would happen, and she should have known too. In just a few short weeks, they'd remembered what manner of man their father was.

Elsie knew, and Alf, and that's why they'd taken the kids out of the way, but good as they were, it wasn't their problem. If either she or Kevin had been around it might never have happened.

But it had, and the doctor and one of the ambulance men had remarked on it. They wouldn't let Grace in the ambulance, but Elsie got in with her. 'Stay with the weans,' she told Grace. 'Alf is with them now. Go in to him.'

But Grace never went near the house. Instead she made for Moss's shop and Kevin. She looked at her brother now and said, 'She's in a bad way. It's lying out in the cold for ages, and with the baby coming as well.'

'Where did they take her, the General?'

'Aye, but they won't let us in.'

'They will, by God. Even if we can't see her, I'll find someone to tell us how she is.'

Kevin knew this was one time when his height and voice could be used to his advantage. He knew he could pass for a lot older than his years and decided to do just that, at least for this one evening.

'I'll come along with you,' Syd said. Kevin opened his mouth to argue but Syd went on, 'I'd like to know how your mother is myself and another adult on your side will be no bad thing.'

Kevin gave a brief nod. Syd was a good sort and whatever he saw and heard that night, Kevin knew it wouldn't be bandied about as gossip in the shop. 'I'll just go and get my coat,' Syd said, and added, 'I'll just clear it with Gwen; tell her what's what.'

He hurried from the room and Kevin uncharacteristically crossed the room and put his arm around his sister's heaving shoulders. It was a gesture he hadn't done in years, but at that moment it was the thing Grace appreciated

287

above all others. She'd felt so afraid for her mother, and she'd heard enough snatches from the ambulance men to know they were concerned for her – so concerned, she'd heard one say, he doubted she'd make it. Grace had wanted to scream out her denial at that, but she hadn't, and when Elsie had stepped into the ambulance and left her on the pavement she'd felt so alone. She'd needed Kevin and felt comforted by the reassurance of his support and the hug he now gave her.

EIGHTEEN

When Maeve was eventually pronounced out of immediate danger, her family weren't the only ones to sigh with relief. The doctors did too, for they hadn't been at all sure she would survive. The baby, which they'd taken from her by Caesarean section while she was still unconscious, had been a little girl and she'd been stillborn.

The doctor explained this gently to Maeve the day after she'd regained full consciousness.

'I know you have other children,' he said, 'for two of them have been here every day and, I may say, badgering the life out of me for news of you.'

'That will be Kevin and Grace, I expect,' Maeve said.

'Well, I'm sure your children will be a consolation for you.'

'What do you mean?'

'I mean, Mrs Hogan, your internal organs have been damaged and therefore it will be highly unlikely that you will ever carry a child again. I think you know how that happened. I had a talk with your neighbour when you were admitted.'

If the doctor expected tears, or a grief-stricken woman, he was surprised. Maeve felt only mild regret for the baby girl that she'd never wanted. In fact she felt relief, although she felt guilty for feeling that way. The doctor wondered at her lack of emotion and he remembered the agitated neighbour who'd travelled in the ambulance with her. He'd been worn out and had been on duty for eighteen hours when Maeve had been brought in. A quick examination plainly showed a young woman in the throes of labour who'd been beaten badly, and recently too, for the bruises were fresh. She was also suffering from hypothermia and a nasty crack on the head, needed stitching, and added to that she appeared to be suffering from extreme malnutrition. He hadn't been the only one in the examination room who'd been shocked at the thinness of her and knew he had a very sick woman on his hands.

Elsie, seated in the grim hospital corridor, saw the grey-faced doctor approach, his mouth in a tight line, and knew the news was bad.

'Are you a relative of Mrs Hogan?' he asked.

'No, but a good friend and neighbour,' Elsie stated stoutly, 'and have been for many years. How is she, Doctor?'

'Poorly, very poorly,' the doctor said. 'She's been prepared for surgery now.'

'Surgery?'

'The baby has to be taken away,' the doctor said. 'I'm afraid it's dead. The woman has been badly beaten too. Can you throw any light on that as you know her so well?'

Elsie was in a turmoil. She didn't know how much Maeve would want the doctor to know and, anyway, she thought the doctor was talking of the marks on Maeve's face, for it was all she'd seen and so she said, 'Maybe she bruised her face when she fell over.'

The doctor raised his eyebrows. 'Both sides?' he questioned. 'And managed to split her lip and black her eye?

290

No, I'm afraid her injuries are consistent with punches, but I'm not just interested in her face.' He looked steadily at Elsie and said, 'You may not be aware of it, but apart from her legs, there's scarcely a part of her body that is not severely bruised, with the skin broken in some areas.'

Elsie didn't know and the doctor could see that. 'Did a beating damage the baby? Is that what you're saying?'

The doctor shrugged. 'Probably. It has certainly damaged the mother and is the most likely cause of the birth being brought on.'

Anger coursed through Elsie's veins and she didn't care any more what Maeve wanted her to say, the hospital should know. 'The bugger she's married to did this to Maeve,' she burst out. 'And this isn't the first time, nor the first time he's landed her here in hospital either.'

She didn't care how cross Maeve would be with her – that was if she ever recovered – for Elsie knew her condition was very grave. But, she promised herself, if Maeve didn't pull through, she'd shout from the rooftops the type of man Brendan Hogan was. She'd do her best to bring him to justice. She'd see someone about it. He'd not get away with it.

The arrival of Kevin and Grace, with a man they introduced as Syd Moss, put an end to the revenge Elsie was planning for Brendan Hogan. She answered the children's question about Maeve's condition and about the baby that had died inside her, but she said nothing of her other injuries. She knew instinctively that Maeve would not want Kevin to go looking for his father seeking retribution and, knowing Kevin as she did, she guessed that was exactly what he would do if he knew. Even in Elsie's desire for revenge she did not envisage involving his son.

But it soon became apparent that nothing would happen to Brendan this time either. The subject was broached by the hospital doctor when Maeve had been in hospital little more than a week.

'Have you considered what you'll do when you leave here?' he asked.

'Do?'

'Well, you don't intend to return to your husband?' the doctor said. 'You could have died. You could sue him for assault.'

'Doctor,' Maeve said wearily, 'the police don't take action against domestic assaults.'

'But surely . . .?'

'Doctor, it's not a crime for a man to assault his wife,' she went on. 'The police would laugh in my face if I tried. Maybe they could have a nice quiet word with him – and a fat lot of good that would do.'

'But you realise he shouldn't be able to hit you like this?'

'I'm not a bloody fool altogether,' Maeve snapped. 'But in the dead of night, who the hell could stop him? When he gets so drunk that he can hardly stand, and so angry that he wants to kill me, who the hell will protect me and my children then? And if I asked the police to speak to him, it would be worse for me when they'd gone.'

The young doctor saw that the woman might be correct in her assumption of how her husband would react, but her injuries had been appalling. She could easily have died. Surely there was something he could do. 'What if I was to speak to the authorities? I'm sure they would rehouse you in a safer place away from him.'

Maeve had actually laughed then. She regarded the young earnest doctor with exasperation as she said, 'Doctor, be realistic. We've just fought a war when

292

Birmingham, along with many other cities, was bombed to pieces. Housing people was a problem before. It will be a nightmare now. They won't look kindly on a request from you or anyone else to find me somewhere different to live because I've had a row with my husband.'

'So you'll go back to him?'

'I have no alternative,' Maeve said wearily. 'I tried to leave him once before. I was forced to go back by the Church. I couldn't go through it all again.' She remembered Brendan's threat that if she tried that again, he'd find her and bring her back and he'd kill her. She knew he was capable of doing just that.

She gave a shudder at the thought of it. The young doctor noticed, but didn't understand. He'd also noticed the naked fear in her eyes, but she saw his gaze upon her and her voice was steady when she said, 'I have living with me a twelve-year-old girl and another just six, a boy of four and a baby less than eighteen months. There is nowhere I can go where he won't find me.'

Maeve stopped then and tried to think of the level of Brendan's rage if she was to try to flee from him and what he'd do to her when he found her. It would be impossible anyway with four dependent children and without a half-penny to bless herself with. 'If I could go, if I had the wherewithal to leave him,' she told the doctor, 'wherever it was he'd seek me out and then . . . then it really would be only God that could help me.'

The doctor heard the touch of despair in Maeve's voice, but also the resignation. 'So is there nothing we can do to help you?'

'I know you mean well, Doctor,' Maeve said, 'and I appreciate it. Living with my husband is not a bed of roses, not for me or my children, and I'll not pretend it is, but

I married him and that's that. If you really want to help, keep him and Father Trelawney away while I'm in here.'

Dr Fleming could have told the young doctor he was wasting his time. He knew whatever the provocation, Maeve Hogan would not, could not, leave her husband. He glanced at her pitiful bruised face and thought back to the night he'd seen her lying in the yard after her frantic daughter had come pounding on his door. He'd thought for one moment she was dead and she hadn't been far from it. He could never understand why women put up with it and yet, realistically, what could they do about it? Maeve Hogan was just one of many.

He'd actually popped in to see her twice before she regained consciousness and did so again just after the junior hospital doctor had made an abortive attempt to talk what he termed 'sense' into her.

'She doesn't want to see either her husband or the parish priest,' the young doctor complained to Dr Fleming. 'It's pretty obvious they frighten her, but she won't inform the police.'

'So, have you banned them?'

'You can be damned sure I have,' the young doctor said vehemently. 'After seeing the mess the husband has made of his wife along with the perfectly formed baby that was born dead, I wanted to send his teeth down his throat, never mind ban him from the hospital. And as for the priest, if she doesn't want to see him, then she doesn't have to.'

Dr Fleming knew how the junior doctor felt. Brendan Hogan and the priest always evoked the same feelings in him. He sincerely hoped Hogan at least would eventually get his comeuppance, and before he inflicted more harm on his wife. But he shared none of the conversation he'd had with the young doctor with Maeve when he sat by her bed a little later.

Two days later, Maeve's Uncle Michael came to see her. He understood, he told her, that she would be upset about losing her baby, but to hold it against her husband and the priest wouldn't help her.

Maeve gazed at her uncle and wondered why he'd never seen through Brendan. If she blurted out what Brendan had done, he'd scarcely believe her anyway. Only Elsie, Alf and the hospital knew the true facts, and she wanted it kept that way. She certainly didn't want Kevin getting wind of it. He didn't even know her face had been battered, for though he'd come every day since she'd been admitted, it had been almost a week before he'd seen her. By then her face had calmed down a lot; any swelling or discoloration he might have noticed he put down to her fall in the yard.

So Maeve didn't want to tell her uncle about her hatred of Brendan, nor that of Father Trelawney, who she believed was in collusion with him. So being unable to say any of this, Maeve said nothing and eventually Michael said testily, 'Maeve, have you listened to a word I've said?'

'Of course.'

'I expected an answer.'

'You didn't ask a question,' Maeve pointed out. 'You said the priest couldn't understand what I have against him. That didn't need an answer.'

'Maeve, you are being deliberately awkward. I know you've been very ill, and so I'm prepared to make allowances.'

'I don't want allowances made for me,' Maeve hissed. 'And I don't believe for one minute that Father Trelawney is confused by my attitude. He's not that stupid.'

A hovering nurse, hearing the heated interchange and seeing Maeve's flushed angry face, came forward and suggested that Michael leave. All the nurses knew about Maeve and what had happened to her and she had their sympathy. Also, the doctor had issued strict instructions that she was not to be upset in any way, so the nurse said to the man, 'I'm afraid Mrs Hogan is far from full recovery yet,' and she led him from the ward.

At the door, Michael glanced back and, checking that Maeve was too far away to hear, asked, 'What exactly is wrong with her? I mean I knew about the baby, but what else?'

'We can't discuss individual patients Mr . . .?' the nurse said reprovingly.

'O'Toole. I'm Maeve's uncle.'

'You'd have to make an appointment to see the specialist, Mr O'Toole,' the nurse told him. 'And even then it is up to the patient whether she wants you to know or not.'

The same information was given to Lily Hogan. The woman thought the whole thing ridiculous. So what if their Brendan's wife had had a stillbirth? It wasn't the end of the bloody world. She wasn't the first and wouldn't be the last. Other women would have got up from their bed this long time and seen to their homes and their husbands, not lie in hospital wallowing in sympathy and being waited on hand and foot and feeling sorry for themselves. She told Brendan to put his foot down and insist she come home and do her duty, and send that interfering sod Elsie Phillips back where she came from. But Brendan, who'd had a sound ticking off from the doctor, who'd told him he could think himself lucky he wasn't on an assault-and-battery charge, for once seemed reluctant to do that.

'The doctors know what they are doing, Ma,' he said.

But did they? That's what she asked the nurse and they refused to tell anything. 'I'm her mother-in-law,' she snapped at the matron, whose face was so stiff it might have been dipped in the same starch as her apron and cap.

'I don't care if you are the Virgin Mary,' the matron replied crisply. 'Not only do we have to have the patient's permission, but you'd also have to see the doctor.'

Lily was outraged. Fancy speaking to her like that and saying that about the Virgin Mary. It was blasphemous, that's what. She made the sign of the cross to be on the safe side before going in to see Maeve.

'It doesn't do to dwell on it,' she told her sharply. 'After all, you can try again.'

'I can't, Lily,' Maeve told her. 'There is damage to my insides. I can't have any more.'

That had Lily nonplussed for a minute, and she thought it probably explained why Maeve was in hospital. Brendan hadn't told her any of that. 'Still and all,' she said at last, 'sure don't you have five fine weans already? That's enough for anyone to rear.'

Especially married to your son, Maeve might have said, but instead she just agreed with her.

Only with Elsie could Maeve be herself. With everyone else she put on an act. Even those in Ireland were not told the whole story and though the sympathetic letters were a comfort to her, in her replies there was much she couldn't say.

Elsie had the running of the house again, and though Grace helped as much as she could she knew she'd find it hard without their good neighbour next door.

As Maeve's third week in hospital drew to a close Elsie said, 'You have kids to be proud of, Maeve. Grace is like a mother to the little ones and getting to be a first-class cook. Even little Bridget is doing her share, washing the dishes and seeing to Mary Ann and Jamie – when he'll let her, of course. As for Kevin, well, he's a lad and a half. He orders the coal for you, and pays for it too. Says he'll do the same every Saturday after work. He called round to me on Wednesday and asked me if I wanted any money, but I'm all right. Brendan can't try any of his tricks on me like he does you, and that Gwen Moss gives Kevin a basket of food every Friday. I don't know where she gets some of the stuff from. It does you good to see the kids tucking in like they do.'

Maeve wondered bleakly if anyone missed her at all – certainly everyone seemed to function perfectly all right without her.

Elsie saw the drop in her friend's spirit and, guessing the reason, said reassuringly, 'Of course, they talk about you all the time. It's not the same place without you at all. Mary Ann is the worst, because she's too young to explain to. She often cried in the beginning, and Bridget and Jamie never give over asking when you'll be home again.'

Maeve wondered herself as day followed day. She realised how close Christmas was when the nurses began decorating the wards. She definitely didn't want to spend Christmas in hospital and asked the doctor when he came on his rounds.

'Oh, I see you're fed up with us,' he said in a bantering tone. 'We patch you up, wait on you hand and foot and as soon as you feel better you can't wait to go home again.'

'My weans are missing me,' Maeve said. 'I feel fine now.'

'You're certainly better than when you came in,' the doctor agreed. 'I think you can go home in the next day or two.'

Maeve said nothing about this to Elsie. She saw no point in raising the children's hopes only to have them dashed. She decided to wait until she had a definite date for her discharge. But the doctor was true to his word and just four days before Christmas Maeve went home, determined, despite everything, to make it an especially good one for her children.

She was scared meeting Brendan for the first time, and flabbergasted that he seemed determined to ignore the whole incident. She spoke to him as little as possible, but when she did, she made sure her voice did not tremble. She was determined, however she felt inside, she would not let the monster she was married to be aware of her fear.

However, Christmas was quite a grim time, despite the decorations Kevin bought to brighten the place up, and the piece of pork Grace had got from the market in the Bull Ring.

Kevin came round on Christmas Eve night, loaded with presents for the children, knowing his father would be out. Maeve was speechless, for the shops were bare and she, like many other mothers, had nothing but a good meal to offer the children on Christmas Day. But Kevin hadn't bought the toys: they'd been donated by Gwen Moss and had once belonged to her son.

Gwen Moss loved having Kevin live with her. She envied his mother giving birth to a son she would be able to watch grow into manhood although she felt sorry that after his years in Ireland his mother had got him back only to lose him again. And for that reason, knowing Kevin's brother and sisters would have nothing for Christmas, she'd taken him into the storeroom at the back of the shop and had found the strength to part with Stanley's old toys.

On Christmas morning the children gave whoops of delight as they opened the stockings Kevin had helped fill.

He'd saved his sweets rations to buy a bar of chocolate for each of them and he added a silver sixpence and an orange, which he'd queued for two and a half hours to get the previous Saturday evening, when he was given the nod by one of the stallholders he'd got to know that there were some due in. In all their lives, the little ones had never had an orange and Maeve could hardly wait till morning to see their faces.

But there were more delights: marbles and more cars for Jamie, a whip and top for Bridget and colouring books and crayons for both, and a book about someone called Little Black Sambo for Jamie, and *Brer Rabbit* for Bridget. Mary Ann had the truck full of bricks that had been Gwen and Syd's present to their son on his first birthday. Gwen had felt a pang giving it to Kevin, but it was her way of trying to make it up to Kevin's mother.

But Kevin hadn't forgotten his mother or Grace either. He'd bought Grace a box of white hankies, lace-edged and with a G embroidered in one corner, and Grace thought they were far too lovely just to wipe her nose on and wondered if she'd ever use them for that purpose. Maeve, on the other hand, was delighted with the Minster silk stockings he gave her. They'd cost him three and eleven-pence and some of his precious clothing coupons, but he thought his mother well worth it. He hadn't let either his mother or Grace open their presents on Christmas Eve, but when he woke in his bedroom at the Mosses' on Christmas morning he could imagine their pleasure and surprise.

He walked to St Catherine's as he'd done every Sunday for nine o'clock Mass and met his family after it. He'd rightly guessed that his father would not be attending the early service. His mother was glad to see him and despite the crowds around her, gave him a hug and wished him Happy Christmas, and Jamie and Bridget danced around him, holding his hands and crying he must come to the house and see what Santa had brought them.

But Kevin knew he could not do that. Promising he would come and see their new toys soon, he walked away from the family. Maeve watched him go and willed herself not to cry, knowing it would be noticed if she did. But Bridget and Jamie grizzled all the way home, and even Grace had a lump in her throat.

After that the day felt flat. Maeve tried to regenerate it and so did Grace, building up towers of blocks for Mary Ann to destroy and reading the two books the children had been given. And it might have worked. But the minute Brendan stepped over the threshold, after eleven o'clock Mass, sober, for the pubs were closed, and furious because of it, the atmosphere changed. Maeve felt as if a leaden weight had been attached to her innards and knew by the children's muted excitement and lack of chatter that they were similarly affected.

The meal was eaten in almost total silence and it was Jamie that lit the blue touchpaper.

'D'you think Santa left Kevin summat too, Mammy?' he said. 'Or is he too old now?'

Brendan leapt to his feet and lifted Jamie up by his shirt front, while his fist banged the table so that the crockery jumped. 'I'll not have that name mentioned in this house,' he yelled into Jamie's terrified face as he shook him like a rat. 'Do . . . you . . . understand? He's no bloody son of mine.'

Both Maeve and Grace were on their feet to protest, and Bridget and Mary Ann were crying and Jamie was screaming when he had the breath to do so.

Maeve saw Brendan's face was almost purple and a pulse beat in his temple and she thought it was a pity he hadn't killed himself before now in a fit of apoplexy. 'Leave him alone!' she yelled, beating at Brendan with her fists.

'Leave him alone, did you say?' Brendan said. 'Leave him alone? Oh, I'll leave him well alone. Will this satisfy you, you stupid barren sod, you excuse for a woman?'

And so saying, he threw Jamie from him. The child hit the wall and Maeve heard the sickening thud of his head knocked against it and he slithered to a heap, his face grey and his eyes rolling in his head. With a cry, Maeve and Grace ran to him and Bridget crawled under the table, dragging Mary Ann after her as the row raged above them.

Afterwards, Maeve knew the happy anticipation they'd woken with that morning and the wonder of the toys Santa had brought them had been wiped out. Only the ugly scene at dinnertime would be remembered. That saddened her, but she knew it could have been worse. At least Jamie had not been seriously injured, as he could have been. The cruel words Brendan had thrown at her were only what she was becoming used to, and she'd bawled back at him, 'I wish you were dead, do you hear? I wish you were dead!'

Later she gathered the children around her. 'You're not to breathe a word of this to Kevin,' she said. 'Sure you won't? Now promise me.'

'Ah, Mammy! ' Jamie said. He wanted to tell Kevin all about it and get him to feel the duck egg on the back of his head and at least sympathise with him, but his mammy looked at him sternly.

'Don't you remember what your daddy did to Kevin last time?' she asked.

Jamie nodded. He remembered only too well.

'Well, do you want him to go through that again?'

No of course he didn't. Jamie shook his head vigorously.

'Then keep your lips buttoned,' Maeve said firmly and, glancing at the others, added, 'And that goes for you, Grace and Bridget, as well.'

And Grace sighed. The pleasure had drained out of the day for her too, and she wished it were over.

'You go down to that bloody shop today and get some money off that son of yours,' Brendan growled out to Maeve the second Friday in January as he ate his breakfast.

'What?'

'You heard.'

'Brendan, we can't take money off Kevin.'

Brendan slapped Maeve across the mouth. 'I don't want to hear his name.'

The sting in Maeve's cheek enraged her. 'Don't you tell me what to say now,' she cried. 'God help me if I can't say my own son's name.'

Brendan grabbed her by the throat. 'You do,' he said, 'and I'll bust your mouth for you so bad, you'll not be able to say anything for some time.'

Maeve was frightened, but she twisted from his grasp and faced him across the table. 'Aye, that's your style,' she taunted, 'bullying women and weans. Last time you came upon Kevin, you came out the worst and he's just a boy yet. If I were you, Brendan, I'd be trembling in my shoes, for Kevin might easily come looking for you when he's a man.'

The smile on Brendan's face was one of pure evil. 'There's more than one way of killing the cat,' he said, 'and you'd do well to remember that.' He saw the blood drain from Maeve's face with satisfaction and went on, 'Now, you go down to that shop today and get some money out of the bloody sod. He owes us, and he should give something into the house.'

Maeve knew that Kevin already gave plenty to the house, as well as the odd bits and pieces he brought from the shop and the things he bought in from the Bull Ring. But none of this could she share with Brendan and she had no intention of doing so. 'Tell him you need the money,' Brendan said. 'He'll believe you.'

'But it won't be for me, will it?' Maeve said. 'Let's face it, Brendan, I'll not have it long enough to see the colour of it. Kevin will know that as well as I do.'

'If you mention that name just once more, I'll knock your teeth down your throat,' Brendan growled. 'Do as you're bloody told. If your precious son is as canny as you think, he'll know what will happen to you if you come back empty-handed. Oh, and tell him you'll come every week and you'll be wanting the same.'

Kevin knew full well what the money was for when Maeve saw him later that day, and yet he couldn't send his mother back with nothing. 'Tell him I earn twelve and six,' he said. 'He'll believe it. It's a good enough wage for one my age.'

'Why then, do you earn more than that?'

'Maybe,' he said with a sardonic grin, 'Mr Moss recognises quality when he sees it.'

'Aye, maybe he does,' Maeve agreed with a wry smile, and added, 'Modesty too, I'd say.'

'Whatever,' Kevin said with a shrug. 'The point is, getting my father to believe twelve and six is the wage I earn, with half a crown of that going towards my keep.'

'Do you pay keep?'

'No, like I said, they recognise quality,' Kevin said.

'We've gone down that road once,' Maeve said. 'So, as far as your father is concerned, you're left with ten shillings?'

'Aye, and half of it is all he's going to get,' Kevin said grimly. 'And if he argues, tell him to take the issue up with me.'

That was the last thing Maeve wanted. 'Be careful, Kevin,' she said. 'Your father has it in for you. He's made threats.'

'He's a windbag.'

'Aye, he is, but he has friends who are out-and-out thugs. Don't underestimate him.'

'Jesus, Mammy, it's you there in the firing line day after day. Don't be worrying about me too,' Kevin cried.

He pressed his mother down in the armchair in the living room of the Mosses' flat. Syd had insisted Kevin take his mother there when she asked if she could have a quiet word with him, but Kevin could see she was uncomfortable. 'Wait here, Mammy,' he said. 'The money is in my room. I'll get it.'

Maeve sat and looked about her. The furnishings, she noted, were comfortable without being lavish. There was a carpet on the floor, well worn and obviously bought years before, like the brown moquette-covered suite with cushions of dull yellow and orange. It was pulled before a tiled fireplace where a cheerful fire was burning. The mantelpiece was filled with ornaments and photographs in silver frames.

Maeve strolled over and studied them. Every one was of the same child at varying stages as he grew up. Sometimes he was alone and sometimes with one or other of his parents. In the last one he was dressed as a soldier and Maeve knew he was one of many who'd not come home from the war, and she recognised the depths of Gwen Moss's pain, though she'd never met the woman or her son.

Maeve knew that there was another flat, the same as the one she was now standing in, on the other side of the wall. Kevin had told her that the door for the adjoining flat, which had once led down to the grocery section of the shop, had been blocked off because the flat had tenants in it. But apart from that, the two places were identical, and Maeve marvelled at the spacious and comfortable home Kevin was living in.

As Maeve stood musing, Kevin came back with the two half-crowns. Maeve took the money home and hoped it would be enough to placate her husband and get him to leave her alone. It would indeed have to be enough, and he'd have to realise that, for it was all Kevin was going to hand over for him.

Brendan did roar and rant about the amount, and the ungrateful sod of a son he had, and Maeve had a split lip and an eye blackened for her trouble, and wasn't at all sure he wasn't really going to let her have it again. But, scared though she was, she stuck to her guns and stated forcibly that the lad could give them no more and Brendan had to be satisfied with it. He recognised a determination in her that he thought he'd beaten out of her years before and he guessed whatever he did to her, she'd ask for no more money from Kevin, so with a final punch that sent her reeling against the wall, he pocketed the two half-crowns and decided to say nothing else for now. He'd cook Kevin's goose one of these days, see if he didn't. But for now five extra bob a week would suit him nicely.

NINETEEN

In late March 1946, Brendan heard something that drove all thoughts of getting back at Kevin from his mind. He learnt of the deceit of his wife that so enraged him he could see only red before his eyes and he burnt as if with a fever at her duplicity. If she'd stood before him that day at the bar of The Bell when a man told him of the family allowance that she'd been receiving secretly for months, he'd have broken every bone in her body with his bare hands.

'Are you sure?' he asked the man.

'Course I'm sure, man. My missus gets it. Gets five bob for each kid 'cept the eldest, till they're fourteen, like. It comes in an order book. D'aint your missus tell you owt about it?'

'No she didn't, the cow.' If she had have done Brendan would have given her less and she'd known that. She'd taken money off him, money he'd near sweated blood for, when she'd not needed it, because she was getting fifteen shillings from the bloody Government. Well, she'd pay for cheating him like that. He'd make her sorry she'd ever been born.

Maeve was still downstairs when Brendan came home that night, glad the winter was nearly over at last. She hoped now she'd be able to clear Jamie's cough for it had persisted through the winter months, not helped by the dampness in the whole place.

There were supposed to be big changes planned for the whole country. Everyone was going to be better off and healthier, it was said. Family allowances were just part of it. There was to be a health service so that you wouldn't pay to visit a doctor or a dentist, and prescriptions and spectacles were to be free too. Maeve thought it would be wonderful if it happened. Then perhaps she could get the doctor to give Jamie something and not have to pay for it.

It had been a depressing winter really, and most women were fed up to the back teeth with rationing and restrictions, which was why the Housewife's League had become so popular. It had begun with just a few hundred members and swelled to thousands. Maeve had read all about it in Alf's paper and listened to the report on Elsie's wireless as the women converged on Westminster, complaining about bread rationing and the threatened abolition of dried eggs. They spoke for every woman in the land and Maeve felt a sense of empathy with them. She heard the chants of others in the background and wished she could have joined them on their pilgrimage to London.

Suddenly Maeve heard Brendan's boots on the cobbles and she glanced up at the clock, surprised that he was home so early, and as he came in the door, she could see that though he was drunk he wasn't staggering. Yet he was angrier than she'd seen him in a long while. She knew she was going to catch it again, but try as she might she couldn't think of anything she'd done recently to inflame him so.

His face was blotched bright red and purple, his mouth turned down in a sneer, his eyes glittered with malice in his face and the whites looked red in the light from the flickering fire. Maeve was scared. She'd been scared many times before, but she realised she was bloody terrified by the look of Brendan now.

She felt her legs tremble and tried to infuse some determination into her weary and frightened body. Why the hell should she have to put up with being knocked senseless because something had annoyed her husband? Well, she wouldn't – not any more. If she couldn't fight him she'd run. She'd get past him, at least into the yard, and if he reached her there she'd yell her bloody head off, and she thanked God she hadn't undressed.

Before she could move, though, Brendan was upon her. He'd seen her eyes flicker towards the door, and guessing her intention, blocked her way out with his body while both fists punched at her face and body and she staggered under the blows.

'And that's just for starters, Maeve Hogan,' Brendan said, holding her tight with one hand and unfastening his belt with the other. 'I'm going to flay every stitch you have from your body before I'm done. You'll think twice before you cheat me again, you lying whore.'

'I didn't, I haven't.' Maeve knew it was no use. She felt the first lash across the shoulder-blades and gasped as the power of it cut through the thin cardigan covering the even thinner dress to her body underneath. 'What have I done?' she cried. 'For God's sake, Brendan.'

'Family allowance, that's what. You lying, thieving sod . . .' And the belt cut into her right and left.

Maeve twisted and turned and tried to escape him, but the lashings went on and Maeve's screams were coming from deep within her.

'Stop it!' cried a voice suddenly from the stairs, and Grace stood there in one of the full-length winceyette nighties her grandma had made before she left Ireland. Her golden hair was in two plaits down her back, her feet were bare and the sight of her checked Brendan. He stopped with his arms raised.

Maeve was in agony, but her worry was all for her daughter. 'Get away,' she said. 'Go back to bed. Go on.'

'You heard your mother, girl,' Brendan snarled. 'This is no place for you.'

And Grace wanted to do just that. When the row began she'd wanted to wriggle down in bed and put the blanket over her and her hands over her ears and pretend it was happening to someone she didn't know and care about.

But she told herself that was all she'd ever done. Even as far back as before the flight to Ireland, the time her father really laid into Kevin, all she'd done was wet her knickers. She could have run next door for Elsie as soon as it began. She doubted either of her parents would have noticed her.

But that was understandable perhaps as she was small. But since she'd come back, she'd allowed her father to beat Kevin, and then to beat her mother so badly that she'd given birth to a stillborn baby. And still she lay in bed, shivering in fear and allowing her bullying father to tear into her mother again.

But as the screams went on this evening, she'd forced herself to get up and creep stealthily down the stairs. Then, before she could frighten herself into running back again, she'd opened the door and stepped into the room. She saw the clothes her mother had on lay in shreds across her back and shoulders and even across her breasts where the belt had curled round. Much of her body was exposed and blood was seeping from the raised purple weals, and Maeve's face showed the agony she was in. Grace was suddenly furiously angry, and knew she wasn't going to walk away. Not this time.

'Leave her alone!' she screamed.

'Want a taste of it yourself?' Brendan sneered, and he raised the belt threateningly. 'Come on then, miss.'

'No! No!' Maeve screamed, but Grace faced her father seemingly unafraid and said, 'You do that and I'll go straight to Dr Fleming.'

It had been Dr Fleming she'd gone for the night her mother had fallen in the yard, and she'd found him a nice, comfortable sort of man. He'd chattered away to Grace as he'd driven her back to Latimer Street, phoning for an ambulance before he left. He was only able to make a very brief examination of Maeve, but he'd seen her battered face by the light of his flashlight and seemed annoyed about it.

'Never let this happen to you, Grace Hogan,' he'd said sternly. 'You can come to me at any time. Do you understand?'

She hadn't been able to make a reply then, for the ambulance had arrived, but it was good enough to throw this at her father now. 'He said to tell him if you ever hit me.'

'Go away to bed, little girl,' Brendan said sneeringly as if she'd not spoken, and he pushed her hard so that the stair door flew open and she fell back on to the bottom steps. He raised the belt again and she flew at him, clawing uselessly at his powerful arms and he smiled, he actually smiled as he held her from him with one hand and beat her mother with the other, and Maeve was so terrified that he'd lash at Grace with the belt, she just stood there and took it, though her body bounced with each stinging blow.

Grace twisted from his grasp. 'You're evil!' she screamed at her father. She didn't know what to do. Would Elsie

311

come in? Without a doubt, but could she stop him? Anyway, Grace could hardly run into the yard in her nightdress, and her father probably wouldn't let her anywhere near the door.

She glanced round the room, her eyes lighting on the poker. 'Stop it!' she screamed again, grasping it and brandishing it above her head. 'Stop it or I'll bloody brain you.'

She saw her father turn to face her, and she saw his mouth open in surprise and he laughed. She realised in that moment that he wasn't totally sane. He enjoyed inflicting pain and he'd go on doing it. She felt sick, but knew too that if she didn't hit him, he could kill her mother, and if she didn't attack him with all the strength she had in her, she'd never get another chance.

Brendan never thought his daughter would have the courage to carry out her threat and in the back of his mind, he thought he'd teach her a lesson or two when he'd done with her mother. Grace saw the look on her father's face, and, trembling for herself, brought the poker down powerfully. She saw fleetingly the mocking disbelief change to startling realisation as if in slow motion. Then the poker caught him with a resounding crack to the left side of the head and he fell to the floor.

'Oh God, Grace, what have you done?' Maeve cried.

'Mammy, he would have killed you if I hadn't stopped him! ' Grace screamed, and her mother held the distraught child in her arms, though every movement pained her greatly.

'Oh God . . .' Maeve felt suddenly weak. Her knees buckled under her and Grace helped her to a chair.

'Is he . . .?' the child asked.

Maeve glanced across to her husband, lying prone and apparently lifeless on the floor, and said fervently, 'I hope so, love, for all our sakes.' She was sure Grace had administered a fatal blow and felt only relief that Brendan would never hurt her or her children any more. But just now there was her daughter to protect. 'Look,' she said, 'you must say nothing about any of this. You heard nothing and you don't know what happened, d'you hear?'

'Yes, but—'

'Listen to me, for God's sake,' Maeve cried. 'We haven't much time. We'll have to say it was an accident. We were both in bed. I heard him stumbling about, heard him cry out and came downstairs where I found him with his head against the fender. Now have you got that?'

'But, Mammy, anyone would understand why I hit him. He's evil! Bad! Wicked!'

'God, Grace, will you listen to me,' Maeve cried out frantically. 'His family will get clever lawyers that twist around any damn words you say, and it's the death sentence for murder, let me remind you. Maybe you would be spared because of your age, but could you imagine what your life would be like for you in this street?' She took Grace's face between her hands. 'Child dear, this is the only way. Now you get your clothes on, because you'll need to fetch Dr Fleming. Hide your nightgown because it's got blood on it. Don't let the others see it.'

Grace was in a daze. She saw the crimson stain running along one sleeve and she had the urge to tear it off her and thrust it into the fire. But instead, she allowed herself to be propelled to the stairs. When Grace went for the doctor Maeve intended to bathe her face and change her clothing. She'd have to wear something with a high neck, she told herself, for it would never do for Dr Fleming to catch sight of Brendan's handiwork, for then their story would fall apart.

She turned from the stairs to where her husband lay, the poker beside him where it had fallen from Grace's hand. She had to steel herself to go near him, for even dead, the man still terrified her. But to protect Grace she had to get the poker and clean the blood from it, and she leant across Brendan's body to reach it. She saw the gaping wound oozing thick dark blood down the side of his face, matting in his hair and forming a puddle on the lino, but she hadn't a thread of sympathy for the man. Her thoughts were all for her daughter. Then she nearly jumped out of her skin as Brendan's eyes suddenly opened and he stared at her.

With a cry of terror, she leapt away from him, petrified of his powerful arms that at any moment might encircle her. He wasn't dead! She stood trembling, almost unable to believe it. The man was alive to continue to terrorise them again. Any minute she expected to see him lumber to his feet and this time she knew he would finish the job he'd started on her and then it would be Grace's turn.

No, she cried inwardly, I won't stand it, not any more. Grace was right, the man was evil. She felt sick with fear and yet she was unable to turn away from the compelling eyes that seemed to bore into her, but he made no move to rise. Oh dear God, she cried silently, what should I do?

Brendan's lips moved, but no sound came out, just a dribble of bloody saliva that ran down his chin. 'It's the death sentence for murder' – the words she'd spoken to Grace echoed in her head and yet, she knew this was her only chance to make sure he never got up again. If he recovered from this he would kill her and then God help the others growing up under his brutal tyranny.

She shook like a leaf, but knowing what she had to do, she dropped to her knees and, grabbing a cushion from the chair, she pressed it over Brendan's face, holding it down tightly, shutting out the sight of his startled eyes as if he realised her intention as she approached him.

She couldn't have held him if he hadn't been stunned from the blow Grace had dealt him. Even then, he threshed from side to side and his back arched in protest. But she held her hands as steady and tight as a vice. It seemed an eternity she knelt there, willing him to stop fighting, terrified Grace would come down and see what she was doing, or Elsie would come to see the reason for the commotion. Eventually, Brendan lay still, but Maeve forced herself to count to fifty before she removed the cushion.

Brendan's eyes were still staring, his look one of surprise and his mouth agape. Maeve laid her head on his chest, bracing herself to do so, dreading even now the thought of his arms suddenly crushing the lifeblood out of her.

But no more would he do that. There was no heartbeat. The man was dead at last. At that realisation, the nausea rose in Maeve's throat.

As she vomited into the sink she told herself she'd killed Brendan for the sake of the family. She'd liberated them from a life of fear and deprivation. What shocked her most was not that she'd killed a man, but that she was justifying the reasons for doing so.

Upstairs, Grace was dressed, but sat on the bed she shared with Bridget, her hands clasped tight between her knees, unable to stop her body shaking as reaction to what she had done set in and she rocked her body backwards and forwards in agitation. She groaned aloud but quietly, mindful of the sleeping Bridget and Jamie.

'Grace, are you ready?' Maeve called softly from the door, surprised at how steady her voice was, and then as Grace entered the room, she said, 'Help me move your father across to the fender and then you go to Dr Fleming and tell him to come.'

'Are you sure he's really properly dead, Mammy?'

'Absolutely sure, pet,' Maeve said, glad she'd closed Brendan's eyes and mouth before calling her daughter. She said nothing about her part in the demise of her husband. She'd explain it all later. Instead she put her arms round her daughter, gave her a squeeze and said, 'Don't worry, pet. Away with you now and get the doctor.'

Dr Fleming knew the gash on Brendan's head was consistent with being hit by a blunt instrument, and he saw clearly the bluish hue of his face that indicated suffocation but he wrote the death certificate as accidental death, thereby falling in with Maeve's explanation of how Brendan injured himself. He also saw the bits of lint around Brendan's mouth and noticed they were the colour of the cushions of the chairs. He made no comment and only removed them carefully with his handkerchief, in case others should be more curious as to how they got there, and he chose not to notice the damp patch on the lino.

He knew Brendan had not died accidentally and, looking at Maeve's bruised and battered face and swollen lip, he didn't need to be a genius to guess what had happened in that small back-to-back house that night. As a doctor he was committed to saving lives, not covering up for those who'd taken the life of another. Therefore he was risking not only his job, but also his liberty, for it would be viewed as an offence if he were found out.

He thought back to a comment he'd made at the hospital, just a few months earlier, when he'd remarked on Brendan Hogan getting his comeuppance. That night, as he gazed at the lifeless man sprawled over the floor, his head placed strategically on the fender, he knew he'd paid the price all right for his years of tyranny.

He pushed any misgivings he may have had to the back of his mind and said to Maeve, 'Do you need anything, sleeping tablets or something of that sort?'

Maeve stared at him steadily and then shook her head. 'D'you know,' she said, 'I think I'll sleep better tonight than I have in a long while.'

But, despite Maeve's apparent calm, the doctor was pleased Elsie was in with the woman and child. She was such a sensible woman, he'd found. Alf had been sent to fetch Kevin, and the doctor was pleased about that too, but he'd arranged for the body to be collected pronto. He didn't want Kevin to see it at all. He had an idea that he would know his father's injury had been caused by no fender. Not that he'd knowingly put his mother in danger, but really the fewer people that knew of their deception, the better he'd like it. Despite this he was glad that Kevin was coming. He liked the boy and he was mature beyond his years and would be of great support to his mother and sister for in his opinion they were both suffering from shock that could manifest itself in various ways.

Elsie, who knew Maeve so well, also knew she was in shock – and young Grace too – and she knew that the story given to the doctor, of their both being in bed asleep and then wakened by Brendan stumbling about, and then finding him out cold with a large gash on his head, was untrue. She was glad she was there, if only to stop either of them blurting out something that was better left unsaid.

Elsie didn't blame Maeve one bit for fetching Brendan Hogan one. She herself would have done it long before, and she'd do all in her power to see Maeve didn't suffer for it. In a way she blamed herself, for she'd heard Maeve's screams that night: they were such that the whole court would have been aware of them. She and Alf had gone early to bed, and the noise had roused her from sleep. She'd been all for going in, but she hadn't because the house had suddenly gone ominously still and quiet.

No one would betray Maeve, Elsie thought. After all, the man was dead and hounding his battered wife wouldn't help. Anyway, most people feared the police. Maeve Hogan was one of their own, and all things considered, had one hell of a life of it. Good luck to her if she'd clouted the fellow that had terrorised her for years.

So thought the women of the court. The men, Brendan's drinking partners, might have had more to say on the subject if they'd been home to hear the to-do in the house, but Brendan had been in such a rage he'd left the pub early. When they heard the news, the general consensus was that while there was no doubt Brendan had had a load on him that night, they'd all seen him worse and he'd never fallen then. It all went to show that when your number's up that's it, they remarked sagely, and none of them thought of anything more sinister happening to Brendan Hogan.

Kevin, when he arrived, told them he was glad the old bugger was dead where he could harm no one any more, and he didn't care who heard him say so. His mother's face was battered, he noted, and it enraged him. 'Pity he didn't die before he started on you again,' he said, and Maeve was glad of the clothes covering up the weal marks on the rest of her. The same weal marks made Elsie whistle when she saw them later, as she bathed Maeve's back and put salve on.

But though Kevin was worried about his mother, he was more concerned about Grace, who was jumpy and agitated. Elsie, who'd guessed at the events of that evening from seeing the gash on the side of the malicious bugger's head that had been caused by no fender, told Kevin his sister was in shock.

'It's seeing her father lying dead like that. Bound to upset her.'

Kevin knew that wasn't it. He agreed it might have shocked her at the time, but, God, you'd think she'd be over it all now and be pleased the old bugger was dead and where he couldn't petrify the life out of her any more, and he said so.

'God, Grace, I'd thought you'd be getting ready to dance on his bloody grave like I am.'

Grace turned troubled, sad eyes upon her brother and said, 'Ah, but you can, Kevin. That's one thing I can never do.'

Maeve heard her daughter's words and stepped between them. She wanted Grace to say nothing to anyone else about the events of that evening. She'd explain her own part in them as soon as she got her alone, and she felt Kevin's eyes on her as she led Grace away.

But Kevin's attention was soon taken by Bridget and Jamie. They'd slept through the entire incident, but when they stirred in the morning Maeve wondered what to tell them.

'Tell them the truth, Mammy,' Kevin said. 'That the man was so full of beer he fell and bashed his head in.' He missed the panicky look that passed between his mother and sister, but Elsie didn't. 'Don't think they'll be upset, or anyway near it,' Kevin went on. 'They'll more likely be overjoyed.'

And they were. Bridget tried to hide her relief but Jamie didn't. He couldn't. He was ecstatic! It was the best news he'd heard in years and his smile nearly cut his face in two. 'I'm glad,' he declared just as Kevin had. 'Now he can't hurt nobody no more.'

Maeve didn't chide him. She remembered the way Brendan had thrown him against the wall on Christmas Day. To protect him and the others, as well as herself, she'd killed a man who'd terrorised them all. What other reaction could be expected? she asked herself, and instead of correcting Jamie she caught him up and sat him on her knee. Bridget threw herself on her mother too and even Mary Ann tried to climb up her legs. Maeve encircled her arms around her younger children while her eyes met those of her elder children and she knew not only was she well blessed but that what she'd done to Brendan had been worth it.

After the initial relief that Brendan was dead, shock set in. The worry of it drove sleep from her mind each night, but she was also afraid to sleep. In her dreams, she relived the minute when she'd held the cushion over Brendan's face and the memory of it terrified her.

In the day Maeve was often unable to concentrate, often didn't hear when someone spoke to her and was given to almost uncontrollable bouts of shivering. Elsie was all for calling the doctor, but Maeve would have none of it. 'It's reaction, nothing more, and not to be wondered at.'

Grace's white face with black smudges beneath her bleak, sorrow-filled eyes also haunted Maeve, and she knew she was suffering too, but Maeve was just about stumbling through the days herself. She just couldn't bring herself to talk about that dreadful night, and yet she knew the burden of guilt lay heavy on Grace's slender shoulders. Maeve felt as if she was walking a fine line between sanity and insanity. She could talk to no one about it, but in the dead of the night, when she paced the floor for hour after ceaseless hour, she honestly thought she was losing her mind.

She was grateful for the support of the neighbours – mainly Elsie, of course, but others were always popping in to see how she was. Brendan's mother, Lily, had been to see her as well, to lament the loss of a son and plan for a funeral he would be proud of. Then Kevin was never away from the place, Gwen Moss stepping in to take his place at the shop so that he could help his mother.

There was so much to do and Maeve was totally unable to deal with most of it, and she was glad of Kevin and Elsie's constant and unwavering support. Kevin wrote letters to the family in Ireland while Elsie contacted the priest and those at the Abbey in Erdington, where Brendan was to be buried, St Catherine's having no graveyard of its own. There were the coffin and flowers to order, the cars to book and food to put on to refresh the mourners, and Maeve was terrified of the debt she was getting herself into just to put Brendan into the ground and cover him up.

No one from Maeve's family was coming over from Donegal for the funeral, as springtime was not a good time to leave a farm, and it was also a desperate journey for just a couple of days. Instead, Liam and Kate came over on the ferry from Dublin to Holyhead in North Wales and down by train to Birmingham to represent the family. Maeve's mother sent her love and support and forty pounds to cover the funeral costs, knowing how expensive it would be, and Maeve had cried with relief.

Elsie liked Liam, the smart businessman in the black suit, and the no-nonsense sister Kate in the black woollen dress and matching coat. 'If you'd had that pair at your back these past years you wouldn't have suffered as you did,' Elsie said, when they'd all departed with her ineffectual Uncle Michael, at whose house they were staying until after the funeral. 'That brother of yours would have settled Brendan's hash and no mistake.'

Maeve agreed he probably would have. 'Let's not go on about it now though,' she said. 'The man's dead. Leave it so.'

'Oh, now he's a bloody saint, is he, now he's snuffed it?'

'Not at all,' Maeve retorted. 'I'm not a hypocrite altogether. Lily has him in the house above now, the coffin in the front room with candles all around him and people saying the rosary all the night through for the repose of his soul like they do in Ireland. I couldn't go along with that.' She looked at her friend and went on, 'To tell you the truth, Elsie, if all these prayers have managed to get Brendan into heaven and I should meet him at the pearly gates, then I would turn round and take my chance with Old Nick himself and rather do it. I couldn't stick Brendan Hogan throughout all eternity.'

'That's the first time I've seen you crack your face in years,' Elsie said, seeing the ghost of a smile playing around Maeve's mouth, 'and you've no need to worry yourself. According to the priest, we're all a load of sinners anyway. There'll be enough of us in hell to have a party, I'm thinking.'

Maeve laughed with her friend, because she expected her to, but the word 'sinner' tugged at her.

She knew she was destined for hell, because she was a murderer and God couldn't help her, for she wasn't a mite sorry.

TWENTY

The funeral was over, the coffin had been lowered to the ground, the prayers intoned, the clods of earth thrown on top, then neighbours, friends and those others after a good feed filed into Maeve's house where they demolished in one half-hour the table of food that it had taken two days to prepare. Maeve provided tea for those that wanted it and Syd Moss sent a couple of bottles of lemonade for the children. The Hogan family produced the whisky and beer and Elsie brought a bottle of sweet sherry for any ladies that might like a drop.

Maeve hadn't tasted sherry since V-E Day and was surprised at how pleasant she found it. 'You're turning me into a lush,' she complained as Elsie poured her a second glass.

'Hardly,' Elsie replied. 'Just a little sustenance that might help you cope with the brave fellow's family.'

Maeve hoped a couple of drinks would do the trick because Brendan's parents and brothers were hard to take, while the women of the family seemed afraid of their own shadows and far too cowed to have a conversation with. As the drink flowed freely, Maeve had to listen to what a fine fellow her late husband was, endorsed by her uncle, who was as drunk as she'd ever seen him.

'I could tell them another thing he's good at,' Elsie whispered in Maeve's ear. 'Kicking the shit out of people.'

Oh God, Maeve thought, I want to laugh. What's the matter with me? It must be the sherry; I'm not used to it.

'Steady, sis,' Liam said in her ear. He'd been shocked by the sight of his sister and his niece when he'd arrived in Birmingham. They'd seemed incredibly thin and frail, and their stark red-rimmed eyes with the blue smudges beneath them looked huge in their white faces.

They were jumpy and nervous too, and both he and Kate had been worried about them. But then, they agreed it must have been an awful shock to see the man lying there dead.

They hoped they would feel better after the funeral. Liam particularly felt sorry for his sister having to deal with the awful members of her late husband's family. He could see the incredible strain she was under and he said quietly, 'It's nearly over. Hang on.'

Oh, how glad Maeve was to have Liam and Kate beside her. She wished they could stay longer, but they had to go back to their busy lives. But when they were saying goodbye to her the following day, Liam pressed two ten-pound notes into Maeve's hand. 'From Kate and me,' he said. 'I don't know how you'll manage now. You'll have to look into it, but this money I'm sure won't come amiss either. Mammy is writing to you. She'll help you all she can, but I don't really have to tell you that.'

'Oh, Liam' – tears stood out in Maeve's eyes – 'it's too much.'

'Not at all. You have a lot to do with it,' Liam said. 'Now have it to please us both.'

And she had it, not only to please her brother and sister, but to take the haunted resigned look from Kevin's face. She'd seen it at the funeral in a moment he thought himself unobserved. She knew what he was thinking. His dream of ever going back to Ireland lay in tatters around him. He was now the man of the family and would have to support them all.

It couldn't be right. With all these reforms they were planning, surely there was something put aside for widows? She'd see about it, she decided, and she tucked the money away without telling another soul of it, and reached up and gave Liam and Kate a hug and kiss that told them of her gratitude more than words could have done.

The day after the funeral, after saying goodbye to her aunt and uncle, Grace didn't go back to school. Instead, without telling anyone, she'd gone to St Chad's Cathedral in the city centre to confession. She couldn't face telling Father Trelawney what she had done, yet she had to admit it to a priest somewhere.

'Bless me, Father, for I have sinned. It is a week since my last confession,' Grace began bravely – the words she'd known since she was seven years old. Then there was silence.

Father Casey of St Chad's shifted in his seat. 'Go on, my child?'

'Father . . . Father, I've got just the one big sin.'

'A sin is a sin in the eyes of God, my child.'

'No, no. Please listen, Father. This is murder. I murdered someone.'

Grace suddenly realised she hadn't lowered her voice and any of the people waiting for confession might have heard her, and her limbs began trembling.

The priest was repeating, 'Murder, my child?' and Grace could tell he didn't believe his own ears. 'Did you say murder?'

It was important to Grace that the priest should believe her. 'Yes, Father,' she said, but though her tone was definite, she'd lowered her voice.

'Do you know what you are saying?'

'It gets worse, Father,' Grace said, impatient to get it over with once she'd started. 'The person I murdered is, w-was, my father and . . . and another thing: I've prayed and prayed, but I can't be sorry I did it.'

Father Casey sat up in his chair. 'Have the police been involved in this? I presume you have told the police? Really this shouldn't be dealt with in confession.'

The child, and from her voice the priest knew her to be a child, said in a voice so quiet he strained to hear, 'I'd hardly tell you this face to face, Father, that's why I came to confession. He was an awful man, my father, and the whole family were frightened to death of him, and my mother most of all.'

'Dear, dear.'

'He'd cut my mother's back to ribbons with his belt,' Grace went on. 'I really believe he would have killed her if I hadn't gone down and hit him with the poker.'

'Could you not get him to stop?'

Grace sighed. 'Don't you think I tried? I yelled and shouted and pulled at his arms, but it was no good.'

'So you hit out to stop him?'

'No, Father.' There was a small silence. Grace could say that and she'd get absolution and everything would be all right. Except she would have lied to a priest and in a confessional box too. But if she told the truth, the priest could do nothing for her. She knew that and yet she said,

'I'd like you to believe that, but it's not true. I knew if I just stopped him, it would be my turn next – if not then, certainly later. I hit him to kill him, Father. Then I knew then everyone would be free of the fear we carried around in us all the time.'

'And you're not sorry?'

'No, Father, and I don't think I ever will be.'

'Then you know I can't give you absolution?'

'Yes, Father, I thought you might not,' Grace said. 'But if God's everywhere like we're told,' she went on, 'He'll know how it's been for my mother over the years. She sent us to Ireland more to protect us from our father than the war.' She stopped for a minute and went on, 'Anyway, if God is all-seeing and -knowing, maybe even if I can't be forgiven for killing my father, He'll think it partly justified.'

'I don't think so, child. Murder is never justified.'

'Would you say that if Hitler had been murdered?' Grace burst out. 'Especially if it had saved millions of other lives? I bet everyone would have clapped their hands off if Hitler had been done away with. Well, my father was a madman like him. He gave us all hell, Father. Why should his life matter more than my mother and my family?'

And Father Casey couldn't answer. Those stock phrases that he had off pat did not seem to have any relevance here.

'Pray for me, Father,' the child said, and the priest prayed that God should have mercy on her soul, and when he'd finished, Grace left the confessional box feeling that at least she'd put her side of it to God.

At St Chad's, before Benediction that same evening, there was half an hour given over to prayer, contemplation or confession, if someone was in urgent need of it. Father

Casey sat in a pew, his Office unopened on his knee. He was still puzzling over the child's visit that morning, and turning it over in his mind, when a woman he'd never seen before approached him and asked him to hear her confession. She was a poor woman, he could tell by her threadbare, shapeless coat and bare legs, her feet thrust into old worn-out shoes, with a shawl thrown over her head for propriety's sake.

He wasn't to know that Maeve had already walked the streets for hours trying to come to terms with what she had done. Eventually, she faced the fact that her husband was dead through her hand and nothing on God's earth could change that. The point was, could she live with herself after it or not?

At the time she'd felt it to be justified and she knew if she was to go under now, her children would have nobody to turn to. Suddenly she knew she had to confess this to someone. Give it to God and let Him deal with it. But she'd not tell Father Trelawney. Good God, no! She'd go to St Chad's.

The old priest was totally unprepared for what Maeve told him from the other side of the grille. 'You killed your husband?' he repeated incredulously.

For a moment or two Father Casey thought killing family members might be a form of sickness sweeping the parish. In all his years as a priest, no one had ever confessed to murder in the confessional box and now he'd heard two in one day. It was likely surely that the poor unfortunate was one and the same. But that being so, to kill a man once was usually enough. To kill him twice was carrying things too far. He told himself not to be flippant over a murder and brought his mind back to the woman on the other side of the screen.

'Can you explain what happened? How this terrible thing came about?'

'Yes, Father. I . . . He was beating me.'

'Was this usual? I mean, did he do it often?'

'He was always cruel, Father. A punch or kick was normal for him and happened often. But this time I knew he meant business, because I'd been drawing the family allowance and not told him anything about it.'

'Had you a reason for this secrecy?'

'Oh yes, Father. Bre— My husband kept me desperately short of money. If I'd told him about the family allowance he'd have kept that off the amount he gave me. That night somehow he found out. But my daughter was wakened in her bed and came downstairs and tried to make him stop. When he wouldn't, she hit him with the poker.'

Then Father Casey knew it was the same man the child had told him she'd killed. For some reason, she didn't know the whole story. The woman had stopped speaking, but the priest knew there was more for him to hear.

'Go on, my child.'

Maeve swallowed the lump, but her wobbly voice was husky with unshed tears as she went on, 'We thought he was dead, Father. He fell unconscious to the floor, but when my daughter went upstairs to get dressed so that she could fetch the doctor, he opened his eyes and looked at me. And . . . and I knew if he lived, then next time he'd kill me, Father, and possibly my daughter too, because she'd struck out at him.'

'So?' prompted the priest.

'So, I put a cushion over his face and smothered him to death,' Maeve said, and added defiantly, 'I was glad I did it. I don't want absolution, Father, and I know you can't give it. I just wanted to confess to someone. I'll let God judge me, Father.'

'My child?'

But the woman had opened the door and left, and by the time the priest had collected himself and followed suit, he saw her scurrying from the church. That night he went to bed a troubled man. He'd never had a clash of loyalties before as far as rights and wrongs went, but now he was totally perplexed. A man of his parish or some adjoining one had been killed and he'd been a brute of the first order. The child thought she'd brought about his end and really it was the mother. If the police were involved, whatever he'd done to her previously she could hang for her actions that night. One of the commandments stated forcibly 'Thou shalt not kill', and he'd always thought murderers should hang – an eye for an eye, as it were. But not in this case. Oh, definitely not if all the woman and child had said was true.

He wondered what they'd told the doctor, how they had covered it up as an accident. Surely the doctor wasn't fooled. He should have informed the police. But there'd been nothing in the paper and anything like this would make headlines. But then Father Casey didn't know when it had all transpired. But even if he'd had the faintest desire to inform the authorities, he couldn't do so, because both the woman and girl had used the secrecy of the confessional box to whisper their guilty secret, knowing he could speak of it to no one else.

Strangely enough, although Maeve hadn't asked for absolution, nor received any, her heart felt definitely lighter as she left the confessional and she knew the time had come to speak to Grace, for the poor child was whipping herself. When Maeve entered the house, Grace made no comment on her absence, though she hadn't known where she'd gone, nor did she give her mother any form of greeting. She seemed almost removed from normal life and Maeve knew she could wait no longer to be told the truth.

She was glad for once they were alone and the wee ones would be well asleep by now. She made them both a cup of tea and they sat before the fire and drank it together.

'D'you ever think of the night your father died, Grace?' Maeve asked.

Grace's troubled eyes slid across to her mother and Maeve knew she didn't want to think about it, let alone talk of it. She was silent so long Maeve thought she wasn't going to answer at all and when she did it was in a whisper. 'All the time.'

She could have gone on to tell her mother of the times she'd woken from a terrifying nightmare with a shriek and found herself bathed in sweat, or the times she'd threshed about so much in an effort to escape the petrifying fear she'd roused Bridget as well as herself. She could have told Maeve she was now often too frightened to sleep and would lie wakeful and tense, just as scared by the thoughts tumbling around in her brain.

But she couldn't load all this on her mother and she was staggered when she heard Maeve say, 'I know how it is, Grace, for my guilt lies heavy on me.'

Grace stared at Maeve, her blue eyes seeming to stand out in her head. 'Your guilt, Mammy? You did nothing but try to protect me.'

'Oh, but I did, Grace,' Maeve said, and she put her cup down and crossed to kneel in front of Grace's chair. 'Listen to me, Grace,' she said, holding on to her hands tight and forcing her unwilling eyes to look into her own. 'You didn't kill your father. I did that.'

Maeve felt Grace's movement to pull her hands away, rejecting her words, but she held on tighter, knowing Grace had to believe her or guilt would destroy her life. 'You stunned him only,' she went on. 'I thought he was dead, right enough. You mind we both thought that?' She waited for Grace's mute nod before going on. 'But he wasn't, pet. When I leant over him to get the poker, he opened his eyes and looked at me.'

She heard Grace's loud gasp. The fear had leapt into her eyes and voice as she said, 'What did you do?'

This time Maeve hesitated. She'd killed a man in cold blood, not in the heat of passion, a man who lay helpless on the floor. She was tortured by it and imagined always she would be and yet she had to admit to Grace what she'd done. 'I thought of what you said earlier,' Maeve began, 'about Brendan being bad, evil. That night he intended beating me to pulp as he's done before and then probably would have started on you because you stuck up for me. He also had something especially nasty planned for Kevin – he kept hinting at it. Suddenly I was angry. Why should he do as he pleased and just get away with it?'

'Mammy, weren't you scared?'

'God, Grace, I thought my heart had stopped beating altogether,' Maeve admitted. 'But I knew it was a chance to finish it for good.'

Grace gave a gasp. Her eyes were wide and scared-looking and her voice a horrified whisper as she asked again, 'Mammy, what did you do?'

Maeve shut her eyes for she couldn't bear to see the condemnation in her daughter's. She was back in that room, that terrible awful night with her bullying brute of a husband lying prostrate on the floor and herself leaning over him. She stammered as she tried to explain to Grace.

'I-I c-caught up one of the cushions on the settee and smothered him, holding it down till he stopped breathing.'

Grace pulled back from her mother. 'You're not just making this up?'

'Christ, child, why would I make up such a tale?' Maeve cried. 'The guilt of what I did is killing me. I would have told you sooner if I could have done.'

'But you couldn't have held anything over Daddy's face,' Grace said. 'He'd have pushed you off. I must have nearly half killed him for you to be able to do that.'

'I'm not saying you didn't hurt him,' Maeve said. 'I'm just saying you didn't kill him. You might have wanted to, but you didn't. If I hadn't attacked him too and we'd have brought the doctor, he might be alive today.'

A long shudder ran through Grace's body. 'I'm glad he isn't,' she said.

'It might have been my funeral you were attending a few days later if he'd lived,' Maeve said. 'Never forget that, Grace. You saved my life and you never need feel a moment's shame for your part in it.'

Maeve sensed the burden slide from Grace's shoulders, but she didn't see the intense fear that replaced it, not for Grace herself, but for her mother, for the child knew her mother could hang for what she'd done that night. Only the two of them knew what had really happened and that's how it must stay. Dr Fleming had guessed, Grace felt sure, but he didn't know.

What if one of them was to blurt it out, or the doctor were to have a sudden fit of conscience? Bodies could be exhumed; Grace had read about it. Would they know just by looking at her father's body what had happened to him?

'Mammy,' she said urgently, 'we must never tell another living soul about this.'

Maeve gathered her daughter into her arms and hugged her tight and assured her that it would always be a secret between them.

Brendan had been dead nearly a fortnight before life returned to somewhere near normal. Now Maeve had told Grace the truth, she knew she had to shake the despondency from herself because of necessity. She had children to rear and rent to pay and she needed money to do it.

She couldn't rely on Kevin totally. Liam had advised her to see what she was entitled to and she roused herself to do so and was delighted by what she found out. Kevin called round that same evening and she was able to tell him about it.

'I get one pound six shillings widow's pension, and together with the fifteen shillings family allowance, that makes two pounds and a shilling.'

'It's still not a fortune, Mammy,' Kevin said. 'I want you to take some more money from me. The Mosses doubled my wages after they heard of my father's death.'

'Ah, that was kind of them, but I don't need any more,' Maeve said. 'My rent has been reduced. I now have to pay only four shillings instead of six and six. I tell you son, I'll be in clover.'

In clover, Kevin thought. Because she's not being starved or frozen to death she's in clover! He said nothing, but was determined to continue to supply her with some money, together with the basket Gwen Moss packed for him on Fridays, as well as ordering and paying for coal for as long as it was needed.

Kevin wanted to buy suitable clothes for them all too. He'd been paying into a clothing club since he'd begun full-time work, as he promised himself he would. The damned points system for clothes and household goods was a nuisance, especially as the allowance had been reduced since the war ended. But he didn't need new things himself; he had plenty and his points could certainly be used for the others. He was determined, by hook or by crook, he'd bring a better standard of living to all his family, and in particular his mother, and take as much worry off her as he could.

But Maeve was grateful for the widow's pension and family allowance from the Government and didn't want Kevin to beggar himself for her sake, though despite her protests, he seemed to see himself as the breadwinner in the family.

'Grace will be working next year,' Maeve told Elsie one day. 'All the weans are growing up. Mary Ann will be two years old in July and I have a good pair of hands on me. I can work for my living and Kevin doesn't have to try and do it all.'

'Let the boy help you if it pleases him,' Elsie advised Maeve. 'Nearly every time the lad comes here he has something with him for you, or one of the weans.' And Elsie was right. In Kevin's quest to see them all more decently clad, he'd bought nighties for Bridget and Mary Ann, and the first pair of new shoes Bridget could ever remember having. Then there was a scarf and balaclava for Jamie and a warm cardigan and stockings for Maeve.

No one asked where he got the stuff from. Grace knew some of it was bought legally with coupons and some was bought from the spivs that ringed St Martin's Square in the Bull Ring, or from those with suitcases packed with illicit stuff, who knocked on people's doors. They did a roaring trade. Women had been starved of pretty underclothes, and serviceable but fashionable day clothes for too long. They welcomed the men offering camiknickers and pretty brassieres and a choice of frocks, warm cardigans, and rayon or the new nylon stockings that were just sneaking in from America. It wasn't the prices the spivs charged only, though in general they were much less than those charged in the shops, but the fact that they took no coupons, or very few, for the money handed over.

But the new winter coat Kevin was buying for his mother he'd picked in a draper's shop near the Mosses' quite legally. The wool-mix coat and matching hat were in saxe blue. It was costing him seventeen and six, and the gloves the same shade as the coat another two and six, and Kevin had been paying for it every week since he'd begun work. The whole lot was to cost him seventeen coupons as well as the price, but still he was determined to present his mother with the outfit before the winter chill of 1946 began to make itself felt.

Maeve knew Kevin felt the burden of the whole family rested on his shoulders and she worried about it because, broad though they were, they were still the shoulders of a young lad.

'Oh God, Elsie,' she cried often, 'if only I could earn money of my own like I did before.'

'Aye,' Elsie remarked drily. 'It's a damned pity they've all stopped shooting each other and there's no need for you to mind children for their mothers while they make bullets and cartridge cases or assemble machine guns.'

'Don't be so stupid, Elsie. You know what I mean.'

'I know these babbies won't always be small,' Elsie said. 'In time you'll maybe be able to look after yourself. Till then take all the help you can get.'

* * *

Then one Saturday in the early autumn of 1946, Elsie came in with news of Angela Bradshaw. Maeve had seen little of her for some time, but knew Deidre's parents were having trouble looking after such a small child. And now Elsie said, 'The Welfare have been called in about her. The old woman's lost it, they say, and they've taken her away to a home and the child can't be left on her own with the old feller. They've sent for the father, Matthew Bradshaw, and he's coming home on compassionate leave. I mean,' Elsie went on, 'it isn't as if the old man is in any way grateful, and all the neighbours do for them as well. He's often downright rude. Their next-door neighbour was just telling me about it in Mountford's. She said Angela will probably have to go into an orphanage till Matthew is demobbed.'

Maeve thought long and hard after Elsie had gone home that day. She thought about Deidre and her kindness, both to her children and to Maeve herself, and the tragedy of all that had happened to them, and Matthew's devastating loss. Eventually she put on her coat and left the house, calling to Grace to mind the weans. Women, taking a breath of air in their doorways, watched Maeve and wondered where she was bound on a fine autumn afternoon without her children.

Matthew Bradshaw, who'd been home only hours himself, was very surprised to see her. He didn't know Maeve that well, but he knew Deidre had thought a lot of her.

'Hello, Mrs Hogan.'

'Can I come in, Mr Bradshaw?'

'Of course,' Matthew said, recovering his manners.

Maeve stepped into a living room very like her own in size. She looked round and noticed the thick film of dust that covered everything. Dirty plates, bowls and cups littered the stained oilcloth that covered the table, while papers and rubbish lay strewn across the floor. Every dining chair housed more rubbish, or piles of creased and grimy clothing, and the lino stuck to Maeve's feet.

And just across the room, a grubby child with green mucus trailing from each nostril, sat on a filthy rug before an ash-filled grate nursing a cloth doll. Her long dark-brown hair lay matted on her head and fell in tangles around her face, her dress was soiled and food-stained and her bare feet begrimed black.

The sour smell of neglect and squalor hung over everything. Maeve remembered how Deidre had loved and cared for her baby and thought she'd be turning in her grave to see Angela living in such conditions.

It brought tears to Maeve's eyes and she left Matthew's side and squatted beside Angela as Matthew said, 'I'm sorry it's such a mess. I only arrived today myself. I've already had a go at the old man for letting it get into such a state. He's taken to his bed now, sulking. Apparently it's not for the first time either.'

Maeve wiped the little girl's nose with a handkerchief she had up her sleeve and gently pushed her tangled locks from her face, and all the time the child sat mute and unresponsive. But her solemn brown eyes watched every move and showed Maeve her confusion and unhappiness.

'I thought the neighbours came in,' Maeve said.

'They do when he'll let them,' Matthew said bitterly. 'Apparently he's kept them out now for a week. God, he lives like a pig! '

'He's an old man,' Maeve said gently. 'He's not up to dealing with a child.'

'Well, he won't have to any longer,' Matthew said, and Maeve didn't miss the anguish in his voice. 'I must hand her over to the local authorities. They're coming to take her in the morning. They say it's the only way.'

'Do you want that?' Maeve asked with a shiver. She'd heard terrible tales of children given into care. Some, she understood, had been sent to Australia or Canada, and without the parents being aware of it at all. Other children had been taken to the authorities by frantic parents often bombed out and destitute, who asked for their help till they got on their feet. But when they did, they'd often search fruitlessly for their children and sometimes never got them back again. She didn't know if all the tales were true or not. She just knew she'd not risk it.

Maeve tried to rise to her feet, but the child clutched at her. Angela had known little kindness in her short life. She'd been passed from pillar to post, but this lady had sat beside her, talked softly and touched her hair gently, and she didn't want her to go. She was just turned two and a half, too young to understand what was happening, but old enough to pick up on the strained atmosphere.

She didn't know the man who said he was her daddy and who had had a row with her grandpa. She was afraid of her grandpa because he shouted at her and at the neighbours too, but she didn't want to go anywhere with the strange man either. She didn't want to lose sight of the kind lady, though, and she held on to her tightly.

Maeve took the small hand clutching at her coat and felt Angela's fingers tighten in her own. She'd already made a decision. She'd made it when she wiped the muck from the child's face and saw her trembling lips and the eyes sadder than any child's eyes should ever be. She knew what she was going to do, for Deidre, and Matthew too, for the child was all he had left.

'She can come home with me. I'll look after her.'

'You?'

'We haven't much, but what we have is clean and I have a wee daughter of my own just a little younger than yours. I'll love her like one of my own, which is more than can be said for any orphanage.'

Matthew knew she was right. He recalled his wife telling him that Maeve Hogan had minded children for working women in the war. She was a widow now, he understood. He'd heard the talk in the street and the consensus of it seemed to be that whatever manner of man her husband was, she was better off without him. But still he could imagine money was tight, though he doubted, even from the few minutes he'd spoken to her, that she'd offered to mind Angela for the money.

The child had taken to her, that was clear enough, for she was clinging tight to Maeve's hand as if she'd never let it go. People told you children had a sixth sense on such matters. And it wasn't as if there was a queue of people waiting to take care of Angela, anyway.

'I might be in the army for some time yet,' Matthew said. 'I'm part of the army of occupation in Berlin. Will that bother you?'

'Not in the slightest.'

'I'll pay for her keep.'

Maeve looked at the man with the same sombre brown eyes as his daughter and said, 'I wish I could say I'll look after her gladly and without payment, but I'm not in a position to do that, so I'm grateful to you. But it's not why I'm offering to do it.'

'I know that,' Matthew said shortly and added, 'will you take her now?'

Maeve was anxious to get the child out of the house and clean her up. 'No time like the present,' she said. 'If you could get her shoes and socks and coat and pack a few wee things for her, we could be back in my house in time for dinner.'

And when Matthew Bradshaw stepped into Maeve's house a little later with Maeve and Angela, the table was set for a meal. Maeve's children clustered together in the room and a young girl, who looked like a younger version of Maeve, stood at the stove.

The home, Matthew saw, was lacking in many creature comforts, but he felt the warmth of the family wash over him and he knew Maeve Hogan was a remarkable woman. He'd been in the depths of despair, not knowing what way to turn and she'd offered him a solution. He'd never forget it.

The children stared at the dirty little girl holding hands with their mother. 'This is Angela,' Maeve said briskly. 'She's going to stay with us for a wee while.' And then while her children still stood speechless she chided, 'Come away out of that. Don't be staring at the poor wee thing. Come and say hello to her. Grace, lay out another couple of plates.'

Mary Ann didn't follow the example of her brother and sister and speak to the little girl, but she smiled at her. She was just turned two years old herself and she liked the look of Angela, though she was the dirtiest little girl that she'd ever seen.

'And say hello to Mr Bradshaw,' Maeve went on. 'He's Angela's daddy, but he has to go back to the army.' The children chorused their greeting and were bursting with questions, but Maeve forestalled them until they were all sitting down to eat.

Much later, Matthew went back to his in-laws' house happier than he'd been for a long time. He'd enjoyed his time at the Hogans' table and the company of the lively chattering children.

And before he'd left, Maeve had bathed Angela in a tin bath pulled before the fire filled with pans of water heated on the gas cooker. Matthew could hardly believe the transformation. Days and days of accumulated muck had been scrubbed from Angela's body and kneaded from her scalp. She emerged pink and rosy-cheeked, and when she was dressed in an old nightie of Mary Ann's Maeve rubbed her hair till the excess water was off and then combed it through, teasing out the tangles as she went.

She looked angelic and there were tears in Matthew's eyes when he picked her up to say goodbye. But Maeve had seen the child squirm uncomfortably and realised Angela didn't know her father and hoped soon the man would be able to get to know his daughter properly.

Not everyone was pleased with Maeve's decision to look after Angela Bradshaw. Elsie said if she'd known what Maeve was about to do, she'd never have mentioned it in the first place. 'Haven't you enough on your plate already, girl?'

'Maybe I have, Elsie, but I couldn't leave her to be taken into care. It was just seeing her there, so dirty, but worse than that, so . . . oh, I don't know, so uncared for, unloved. It broke me up, Elsie.'

'So you upped and brought her home,' Elsie remarked drily.

'Yes I did,' Maeve said defiantly, 'and I don't care what you say, it was the right thing to do.'

She wrote the same in a letter to her mother. Annie was concerned that Maeve would wear herself out, bringing up another child as well as her own. Maeve wrote back and assured her that one more child made little difference and that Mary Ann was easier to manage now that she had a playmate. She added that the money Matthew Bradshaw gave for little Angela's keep was useful.

Kevin just said it was only what he would have expected from his mother, and the rest of the neighbours, according to local gossip, seemed to think she was some sort of saint, Elsie told her.

If they only knew, Maeve thought, but she just gave a wry smile to Elsie and said, 'I'm anything but a saint, Elsie. I'm just trying to get along, like anyone else.'

TWENTY-ONE

Nineteen forty-seven began with blustery winds and icy cold, but no one could have guessed that they were in for the worst winter in living memory. Postwar Britain was an austere place, teetering on the verge of bankruptcy and the rations that people had struggled with for years were tightened still further while eggs and all meat were in short supply and considered luxury items. The Government advised the nation to have two meat-free days a week.

'We're one up on them already,' Elsie said. 'We've not been eating meat on Fridays for ever.'

'I don't know that we're going to have that much choice in it either,' Maeve said. 'If the stuff's not in the shop, then you can't buy it, even if you have the money and the coupons.'

And Maeve spoke the truth: many people were wearied and depressed by further restrictions when it was almost two years since the war had ended. It showed in the unrest and disillusionment in the labour market.

Added to that, the people had been making do and mending for years. Most of their clothes were shabby and, more often than not, threadbare. Certainly the undernourished, demoralised people in their inadequate clothes were no match for temperatures that fell to –16° Fahrenheit. Factories, offices and schools were forced to close, due to the fact they had no coal to heat the places and the only light many had were from candles. To add to the general misery, most of the transport workers went on strike, making it well nigh impossible for workers to get to their place of work, even if they were so inclined.

Billowing, relentless snow fell day after day, whipped by gusting winds into drifts big enough to cover a man. By night the snow froze, making the roads and pavement surfaces like sheets of glass, which were then covered by even more snow. Anyone who ventured out was in constant danger of being swept into a drift or slipping on the icy pavements and breaking a limb.

Pipes burst all over the city, roads were impassable, and those trains that tried to run were either delayed or cancelled altogether. The foodstuffs weren't getting through to the shops, and people had to queue for hours and be in receipt of a rent book to receive even a meagre share of coal. Everyone in the slum dwellings of the city was cold. There was never enough coal to heat the draughty houses sufficiently, the wind seeped under doors and round ill-fitting window frames, and no matter how many layers of clothes people wore, most were constantly chilled to the marrow.

It was a dismal winter for paperboys and -girls at that time, and Kevin told his mother he was exhausted by the time he got back to the shop.

'It takes me hours, Mammy, the snow is so deep,' he said. 'I'm wet to the skin wading through it. Mind you, the papers are often delivered to the shop late to start with, and some days they don't come at all. And,' he added with a grin, 'it's a good job I'm not expected to turn up at school after the round. It would be the strap for me every day for lateness.'

Maeve smiled with him and tried to be grateful to Gwen Moss, who, Kevin told her, had dry clothes ready for him to change into, with a hot breakfast to set him up for the day. She tried not to resent the woman who did these tasks. What did she want, she asked herself angrily, that Kevin would stay in his wet clothes and go hungry all morning? What was the matter with her and why should she care who did these things for her son as long as they were done? Hadn't she enough already to feed and try to keep warm?

She gave herself a mental shake and firmly told herself not to wallow in self-pity. She reminded herself she could have had him home every night, for he'd offered as soon as he learnt of his father's death.

And Maeve had wanted him to return more than anything else in the world, but then she'd had a sudden flash of his bedroom at the Mosses' that she'd been taken to see one Friday when she'd gone to collect the five shillings Kevin had to hand over for Brendan every week. She'd stood stunned, and gazed round the room. Kevin's wooden bed stood against the wall and was covered with soft blankets, a quilted eiderdown and a peach-coloured candlewick bedspread, with a wooden wardrobe at the foot. Beside the bed was a small table, housing a bedside lamp enabling him to read in bed. He even had his own crystal set! His very own wireless! Luxury indeed. There was lino on the floor, but a fluffy blue carpet almost covered it. There was a chest of drawers against the other wall with a desk beside it, and a bookcase above it held a fair few books that Kevin had either bought or acquired. Perhaps from a selection Stanley had.

The furniture all matched, and Maeve knew there would be no chamber pot under her son's bed for, next to the kitchen, just along the passage, was a lavatory with a bathroom beside it. Maeve had once visited the bathroom to wash her hands and had seen the bath and washbasin, both with hot and cold taps above them. There was scented soap and thick soft towels to dry your hands on. She thought of her own stark cold tap over the sink, with a hard cake of carbolic soap and a bit of hessian they used in place of a towel.

How could she ask Kevin to leave that luxury and return to his dingy back-to-back home, sharing a bed with his wee brother and the attic with all of them? There was only an orange box for his clothes and the room was lit by a flickering candle, for there were no gas mantles in the attic. He'd once mentioned casually that he sometimes had a bath three times a week. Would he still do so if he had to first make sure everyone was in bed before pulling the bath down from the hook, and filling it with pans of hot water, and then of cold, and emptying it the same way, or go stealing through the streets in the evenings after a day at work, to the public baths, clutching a bar of soap and hard towel and risk catching pneumonia coming home?

No, Kevin was better off where he was and she'd told him so. He'd tried hard to hide his relief, but wasn't entirely successful and, at the time, Maeve had been hurt by his reaction.

Still, that was water under the bridge now, and Maeve knew Kevin's predicament would have been worse that winter if he'd had to walk back and forth to Latimer Street. She worried about him enough as it was. She was grateful that she had enough money to buy food for the weans, even if it was only bread or potatoes. It filled them up and she knew from experience you felt the cold more if you were hungry as well.

Eventually, the unrelenting cold brought on a wave of illness, first to the very young and the very old. All the children went down with flu, the same time that Alf developed severe bronchitis. Maeve helped nurse Alf, for he was very ill indeed. It was touch and go with him for a time, and Maeve and Elsie had been run off their feet. Alf took so long to recover he decided to retire from work. He'd turned sixty-five the previous year and so was of an age, but Elsie complained she didn't know how she'd cope with him under her feet all day long.

Then Angela's grandfather died, closely followed by Lily Hogan. Maeve attended both funerals and stood shivering in the piercing wind that was shrieking across the graveyard, knee deep in snow. She tried to feel some sorrow at Lily's passing, but she couldn't. They'd never got on, and she couldn't pretend now that they had, just because she was dead.

And yet she wondered if Lily had ever had a day of true happiness in the whole of her life. Married to a bullying, domineering husband, she'd reared sons who'd gone on to bully their wives, and cowed daughters frightened of their own shadow. Not much of a testament to a successful life, Maeve thought as she'd watched the coffin being lowered into the grave.

Grace turned fourteen on 9 February 1947 and she was mightily glad that her birthday would fall before the government plan to raise the school leaving age to fifteen came into effect on 1 April 1947. She was as desperate to officially leave as her two friends, Ruby Willis and

Bernadette Cleary, not that any of them had actually been able to go to school much that dreadful winter. Although sometimes Grace would have actually preferred school to being confined in that small house day after day.

For Grace's friends, leaving school spelled freedom and money in their pockets for the first time. Neither of them wanted it postponed for another year and they were forever going on about it. Grace wished they'd shut up about all the money they'd soon be earning because, although she had a job to go to, she knew she'd still have very little left in her own pocket to spend.

'I'm going to go to the cinema every night once I start work,' Ruby said one day.

'I'm not, not every night,' Bernadette put in. 'I want to go dancing too. That's where you meet the boys.'

Grace was shocked enough to reply, 'Urgh, you're disgusting, the pair of you!'

'What's up with you, Holy Hannah?' Ruby taunted. 'We're just being honest.'

'Anyroad, how're you going to spend your dosh?' Bernadette asked.

'I won't have any left to spend,' Grace snapped. 'What I earn will have to go to my mother.'

'All of it?'

'Yes, all of it.' That wasn't strictly true. She knew Maeve wouldn't take all her money but she was aware that, even now, there was little to spare in the house. She'd managed to get a job easily enough in a draper's shop where Kevin had seen the coat he'd been determined to buy for his mother. Going in to pay it off each week, he'd got talking to the girl behind the counter and when he heard that she was leaving to get married in March, he put a word in for his sister, knowing she'd be looking for a job soon.

He had said nothing until he brought the coat home, fully paid for, in November, and gave it to his mother. Grace knew her mother had been more than glad of it that winter.

She knew she would never forget the look on her mother's face, when she opened up the box that the shop had packed the coat in. She had wished she could have afforded to buy her something like that too.

However, she knew that would be a long time coming, though she went round to see the owner of the draper's shop, a Miss Overley, as soon as the weather allowed her to. The interview went well and Grace was to begin in the shop the week after she left school. Miss Overley told her that would give her two weeks with the older girl before she left – enough time for her to learn the job – but her wages would be just ten shillings and sixpence. 'Let's see how you shape up,' the prim Miss Overley said.

Grace was nervous of the woman at first. She was extremely thin, especially in the face, with the skin drawn tight across her hollowed cheeks and so wrinkled that deposits of face powder ran along the deep ridges on her face by the end of the day. Her lips were thin too, her nose slightly beaked and her black hair, liberally streaked with grey, was piled on top of her head. Her green eyes darted constantly around the shop missing nothing and, though she spoke very correctly, Grace knew she could screech at her well enough if she did anything wrong.

But then Grace reckoned a job was a job and she knew her mother preferred her there rather than see her in a factory. She seemed to think it was a step up for her, and Grace didn't mind. But, knowing her mother was losing five shillings family allowance once she was fourteen, she insisted Maeve take nine and six from her each week.

Maeve protested she'd have nothing left, but Grace told her she wanted nothing.

Eventually the last day of school came and, for once, it was a day when the girls were able to get there through the snow. They said goodbye to their teachers, thankfully turned their back on their schooldays and left arm in arm, laughing uproariously at nothing at all.

Just a couple of weeks after Grace began work, Matthew Bradshaw was demobbed. He returned home with nowhere to live, for the house had been let to someone else. He couldn't stay at Maeve's while he searched for a suitable place for himself and Angela – that would have been considered highly improper – and so for a while he lodged with a mate. All through his time serving in Berlin he'd looked forward to the day when he would take his small daughter to live with him.

He'd taken no account of the scarcity of housing in Birmingham at that time. Maeve was sympathetic towards him, but also practical. 'Even if you were able to find a suitable place,' she said, 'you'd still have to have Angela minded during the day while you're at work. Let her stay with me for a bit and you get yourself sorted out with something near at hand so you can see something of her. And,' she added, 'while you're about it, put your name down for one of those prefabs. They're going up all over the place and have two bedrooms, bathroom, and hot and cold running water. Little palaces, so I've heard, and just right for the two of you.'

'I had thought to buy,' Matthew said. 'I have the gratuity from the army and I've saved a fair bit too. Renting would be like dead money, wouldn't it?'

'Maybe,' Maeve said. 'But I think houses to buy will be just as hard to find as those to rent. At least if you get offered a prefab, it will mean you and Angela can be together and it will give you a chance to look round.'

Matthew knew what Maeve suggested made sense and, as there was no one he'd prefer to have looking after his daughter than Maeve Hogan, he let Angela stay with her, put his name down for a prefab and, for the short term, looked for accommodation for himself near to Latimer Street.

He found a room in a house just off the Balsall Heath Road – a bare and very basic room. It was scarcely adequate for him and wholly unsuitable for a small child. He doubted anyway he'd convince Angela to come and live with him there because, despite Maeve's valiant efforts to remind Angela she had a father who, when he returned she would live with, she took not the slightest notice. She regarded Maeve as her mother and even called her Mammy like the others did, ignoring Maeve's pleas to call her Auntie Maeve.

The Hogan children genuinely liked Matthew Bradshaw. They found him patient and, above all, kind. None of them had had much experience of kind men. On those cold blustery evenings, he would spend hours entertaining them playing Ludo or Snakes and Ladders. He knew card tricks too, and his many stories of army life entertained them for hours.

The light of his life though was Angela, who was then just over three years old. Despite her tender years, it didn't take the child long to see that, though her father liked the others well enough, she was the special one in his life and he would give her anything she asked for.

On fine evenings, once the weather began to improve, he'd often take the two little girls for a walk. Angela liked the company of Mary Ann – they'd become fast friends and she'd go few places without her. When he took them out at weekends, he spoilt them both outrageously. Maeve had taken him to task about it, but Elsie said it was only to be expected. 'After all,' she said to Maeve, 'when he missed so much of Angela's early childhood, isn't it natural to be like he is?'

Maeve decided not to worry any more about it. She had no wish to quarrel with Matthew, for she liked him a great deal herself and his company at the table made a welcome change to the weans' chatter. As Elsie said, 'Better that way than the other way.'

In mid-March the great thaw began and, although people had looked forward to it, in many ways it was as dangerous as the freezing ice-bound city had been. The melting snow slithered from the roofs of houses and factories alike to lie in sodden grey lumps in streets and courtyards. Eventually it dissolved to dirty, sludgy water that gurgled in gutters not fitted to take such a deluge. Roads were turned into rushing streams and many cellars and houses in that area were flooded.

Elsewhere, rivers burst their banks and homes were destroyed, some villages disappeared altogether. The springtime grain rotted in the fields and it was estimated two million sheep had drowned. Many people had lost everything and had to be rescued themselves from the roofs of their houses, or nearby treetops. Maeve tried to count her blessings – she'd got off lightly compared to some, though water had penetrated the cellar and soaked the coal.

The great mopping-up operation began as the days got warmer. Sometimes there was even a watery sun to be seen in the sky. Children began to play noisy games in the courtyards and streets again, the women watching over them as they gossiped in their doorways.

Everywhere, with the weather so much improved, people began to go out and about, though Grace still stayed in the house in the evenings. Maeve worried about her, but Grace appeared not to care that her two friends had money to go out enjoying themselves.

Whenever Grace met them in the street, or at the shops, they described their nights out at the cinema. They'd enthuse about Laurence Olivier in *Henry V,* or Trevor Howard in *Brief Encounter*, and they'd even been to see *The Jolson Story,* one of the new musicals from America.

And Bernadette Cleary got her wish too, for the dance halls were very popular with the young. 'But you don't know how to dance,' Grace protested.

Bernadette shrugged. 'You soon pick it up,' she said. 'It ain't fox-trot and waltzes and that now, you know.'

'No, it's jitterbugging,' Ruby put in.

Jitterbugging had been introduced from America, and at first had shocked the regular dancers and those who owned the dance halls. So disturbed were they that some dance halls tried to ban the craze, but those that did soon found their ballrooms half empty. Jitterbugging was what the young wanted, and that's what they got, dancing to the music of Tommy Dorsey and Duke Ellington. Music that made you tap your feet.

'You should come with us, Grace. Have a laugh,' Bernadette said, though they'd almost given up asking her, for she'd always refused.

Grace would have loved to go dancing, but it cost money and she hadn't much to spare. She didn't want her friends to feel sorry for her, so she said she didn't want to go. In one way she didn't. She felt that both she and her mother

354

should pay for what they did to Brendan, not be out enjoying themselves as if it didn't matter.

She wasn't desperately unhappy, but she was lonely. She had Monday and Wednesday afternoons off and Kevin was also free on Wednesday afternoons. Seeing Grace's despondency, though not understanding the reason for it, and urged by his mother, Kevin had invited her to town with him and they'd mooched around the Bull Ring together. Grace had enjoyed it, but it had been a strain.

She'd been used to telling Kevin most things and confiding in him if she was worried or anxious. It was a habit she'd fallen into in Ireland, but now there was so much she couldn't say and it had caused a barrier between them. Kevin was aware of it, and felt saddened that he no longer knew or understood his sister.

Maeve thought she was probably as excited about Bridget's First Communion in June as the child was herself because she'd missed both Kevin's and Grace's and she was determined to enjoy every bit of Bridget's special day.

Her mother had sent over the dress and veil she'd made for Grace. Bridget had squealed with delight when she'd opened the box and peeled the tissue paper away to reveal the dress. Maeve shook it out, and put it on the hanger she had ready as she watched Bridget's mouth drop open.

She'd seldom seen, and never worn, anything so lovely. It was shimmering white satin, with a scalloped neckline and puff sleeves and the skirt was full from the waist and held that way with stiff lace underskirts. The top layer of satin was caught up at intervals and secured with bows of satin ribbon, and the veil attached to a coronet decorated with white roses.

'Oh, Mammy!' said Bridget.

Maeve felt tears in her eyes as she saw the dress. She had a photograph of Grace wearing it of course, but the photograph hadn't really done it justice. Maeve knew that with the rationing and shortages in England, Bridget's dress would be one of the nicest in the church.

'I'll wear that one day,' Mary Ann said to Angela.

'And me.'

'No, not you,' Mary Ann told her. 'You're not a Catholic. Only Catholic girls get to wear dresses as nice as that.'

'Why?' Angela demanded.

Mary Ann didn't know, but wasn't going to admit that. Sometimes she was a bit annoyed with Angela. She had a daddy all of her own and she shared Mary Ann's mammy. Mary Ann thought she did enough sharing already with Kevin, Grace, Bridget and Jamie and it felt good to get one over on her little friend. 'It just is,' she said firmly.

And it was a wonderful day. It answered all Maeve's prayers and Elsie took photographs of Grace in her finery and then of the whole family. This time, it was Maeve's turn to send photographs to her mother, rather than the other way round.

It was in late autumn when Grace, who'd never spoken of her days at work, unlike Kevin, who often made the weans laugh as he mimicked the customers, came home with some news about her employer. Despite her initial enthusiasm for Grace to work in the draper's shop, Maeve had often felt sorry for her daughter, because she'd been none too keen on Miss Overley on the few occasions they'd met. But Grace said she didn't mind her and always maintained that she was kinder than she looked.

'Anyway, she's even better at the moment,' Grace said as she looked around the table, checking that she had everybody's attention before dropping her bombshell. 'It's probably because her son has come to find her after all these years.'

Maeve stopped with her fork halfway to her mouth. Everyone stared at Grace, though the younger ones hadn't realised the significance of her words.

'But the woman's never married, has she?'

'No, Mammy, she hasn't.'

Maeve thought of the prim and proper woman with the stiff manner and she said, 'Grace, are you sure?'

'Oh aye, Mammy, it's all come out now,' Grace assured her. 'Miss Overley says she doesn't care about people knowing. She gave him up for adoption. It was a long time ago and he's oldish, about forty or so I'd say. His name is Richard Prendagast,' she said. 'He didn't know he wasn't the Prendagasts' son, till his mother, I mean Mrs Prendagast, was dying. Then she confessed it all. Ever since he's been looking for his real mother.'

'Ah, Miss Overley must have been frantic, so she must, to have given him away like that,' Maeve said sympathetically. Since the war, the stigma of having a child out of wedlock had changed somewhat because, after it, more and more girls found themselves in that position. But forty years ago . . .

As far as Maeve understood, the workhouse was usually the only course open to 'fallen women'. Small wonder her manner was sometimes sharp. Poor woman. How she must have suffered. Maeve shivered. 'She must have been desperate altogether,' she said.

'She said she was,' Grace told them. 'And she'd always regretted it after. But she's like a different person now, Mammy, softer somehow. Her son's a nice man, he doesn't blame her or anything. He said he had a good upbringing and he was very fond of his adoptive parents. He feels Miss Overley was brave to have given him up.'

'Is he married, her son?'

'He was,' Grace said. 'His wife and baby were both killed in an air raid in nineteen forty.'

'Oh, what a tragedy!' Maeve cried. 'This terrible war!'

'Aye,' Grace said. 'I think Mr Prendagast has suffered as much as any, but he's so kind and thoughtful. He's got money too. His adoptive parents were quite wealthy and they left him everything, including a large house, which he's just sold.'

'And what are his plans now, then?' Maeve asked.

'He wants to invest in his mother's business.' Grace gave a shrug and went on, 'She might take some notice of him because at the moment she's not selling enough to keep the place going. I've tried to tell her that she needs to concentrate more on modern stuff, but she'll never listen. Now the war's over clothes are bound to be off ration soon and then, unless we stock things people want, they will pass us by and take a tram or a bus into town and buy their clothes from the chain stores, and you can't blame them.

'She goes on about how she learnt her trade as a dressmaker's apprentice, and then started out selling dresses and accessories in a high-class department store,' Grace said. 'And how she saved every penny piece to buy her own place. She doesn't seem to understand that the war has changed how people think and the old-fashioned quality clothing shop will soon be a thing of the past. I've told her that people are starved for bright and cheerful clothes, along with pretty and modern underclothes; people even want stylish baby clothes these days.'

'So how do you know so much?' Maeve asked, impressed.

'Because it's what the people tell me time and again,' Grace said. 'I'm the one in the shop, remember. At the moment everyone has only so many points and because of it, clothes have to be multi-functional and style is of less importance. Things are bound to change, and soon. We need to be ready for it, or we'll miss out. I know how much money Miss Overley takes in that shop in a week. Sometimes I think she's hard-pressed to pay my wages, let alone buy in new stock.

'Anyway, Richard Prendagast was a textile designer before the war, shades of his mother, I suppose, so he knows a bit about it and he also knows I'm talking sense. Miss Overley will probably give in to him, for the last thing she wants is for him to go off somewhere else. I mean, she's only just found him, hasn't she?'

Maeve tried to imagine just how the old lady must have felt, for she'd felt bad enough when she'd been separated from Kevin and Grace for six long years, and then she'd always known where they were. She'd had letters from them and photographs to show her how they were growing. She didn't know that she'd have been able to cope if she'd given them away like that. But in those days the poor woman probably had no alternative and she found herself with great respect for Miss Overley and intrigued by her son.

Soon after Grace had dropped her bombshell about her employer, the whole country seemed absorbed with the marriage of Princess Elizabeth to Philip Mountbatten. There was great play made of the fact that Princess Elizabeth – like everyone else – was subject to clothes rationing. Few believed it, but when the marriage took place with great ceremony on 20 November, the skirts of the trousseau the princess had chosen were calf-length only. It showed, said the papers, true patriotism and that the people were not alone in their suffering.

And they were suffering, juggling worries over their allotment with decisions over whether it was best to buy much-needed underclothes or essential outer clothes. Maeve fervently hoped that Grace was right and clothes rationing would be finished with soon, for like almost every woman in the land, she was heartily sick of it.

Kevin came round for his dinner the following day. He'd been busy in the shop and the family hadn't seen much of him for a few days, so he hadn't heard Grace's news about her employer. But he had some of his own news concerning the same woman.

Amy Overley went into Moss's shop at least once a week, and everyone knew Kevin had always found her starchy and unapproachable. But he said he'd been astounded when she'd come into the shop just a couple of days before. Her hair was no longer scraped back so severely, but fluffed a bit at the sides, and her face had lost its pinched grey appearance and seemed fuller, and she certainly looked happier. Kevin said she'd actually smiled at him and he could never remember her doing such a thing before. He could even smell perfume as she leant over the counter.

She'd remarked on the pleasantness of the day while her order had been attended to, something else she'd never done before, and both Kevin and Syd had been flabbergasted when she first enquired after Gwen and then after Kevin's family. They'd both watched her walk out of the shop with a bounce in her step.

'Well, what did you make of that?' Syd asked. 'If I didn't know better, I'd say she'd been on the bottle.'

'I'd say it's amazing the great tonic happiness and contentment is,' Maeve said and told her son the story Grace had come home with.

'If you're right, Mammy, it's a great shame happiness can't be bottled,' Kevin said. 'Because you'd hardly believe Miss Overley to be the same woman as the one I've been serving for months.'

Maeve said nothing, but felt immense sympathy for the woman harbouring such a secret over the years and fearing she'd never see her son again.

TWENTY-TWO

All in all, Maeve was glad to see the back of 1947, but as the winter again began to bite she was nervous, like many more, that they'd suffer in the same way as they had the previous year. While not as harsh as the winter before, it was severe enough and, as Maeve looked out of the window one bleak Friday afternoon in mid-February, she thought it was hard not to be depressed with the freezing, short winter days that meant the gas lamps had to be lit in mid-afternoon.

She gave herself a mental shake and told herself to stop wallowing in self-pity, surely a luxury she couldn't allow herself. She decided to make herself a reviving cup of tea. Elsie had collected Angela and Mary Ann about half an hour before to 'help' her bake and it was a luxury for Maeve to have time on her hands. If she hadn't, Maeve felt she might have pulverised the pair of them, for the weather had kept them cooped up far too long and they'd both become fractious and bad-tempered.

Maeve was glad of the break. Much as she loved her children, she was looking forward to the girls starting school the following year. Then she'd be able to get a job of some sort and take some of the responsibility from

362

Kevin. She'd barely poured the tea when the door opened and Grace stepped into the room followed by a man Maeve had never seen before.

But though the man was a stranger, Maeve knew immediately who he was. In one glance she'd taken in the clothes that spoke of quality: the thick woollen overcoat and scarf, the tailored trousers and good leather shoes. He removed his trilby hat as the girl began explaining that Richard, Mr Prendagast, had brought her home early and insisted she stay there for a few days because of her bad cold.

Maeve knew all about Grace's cold and the cough that kept them all awake in the attic. She'd dosed her with linctus – still scarce even now – but when she'd suggested Grace have the day off she'd refused. Maeve knew why. Their finances were still very finely balanced and Grace had a horror of missing time and perhaps losing money through it, or incurring large doctor's bills.

Maeve ushered them both towards the warmth of the fire, insisting that Richard remove his coat so that he'd see the benefit of it later. In taking it from him, she noticed that, despite his large mouth and decisive chin, he was a very handsome man, with deep chocolate-brown eyes set in a friendly, open face.

Maeve smiled at him and when he returned the smile, his whole face lit up and suddenly Maeve felt weak at the knees. Maeve felt desire course through her that she hadn't experienced since the early days of her courtship with Brendan. She saw by Richard's eyes that he'd felt the same pull and it had shaken him too. Maeve turned away and busied herself pouring more tea from the pot for the two of them, while over on the chair by the fire, totally unaware of anything untoward happening between her mother and her boss, Grace went on protesting that she was fine.

'I told him I was all right, Mammy,' she croaked, although it was obvious she wasn't: her voice was husky with a bad throat made sore from coughing, her face flushed, eyes red and her nose blocked.

'You're far from all right,' Richard said firmly. 'To battle your way through this every day is madness. Anyway, if you don't want to think of yourself, think of me. I don't want your germs.'

'Mammy, tell him. I'm fine.'

'I'll do no such thing,' Maeve said. 'I told you not to go in today.'

'Well, how will you manage in the shop without me?'

'Don't worry,' Richard told her. 'I can go behind the counter you know.'

Grace's laughter pealed out and she cried. 'Richard you can't. We sell corsets and underclothes. I can just see women buying from you.'

As Maeve handed him the tea he was grinning at the picture Grace had conjured up and it was as he took the cup from Maeve their eyes met again. Richard had been stunned by the strength of his feelings meeting Grace's mother for the first time. He recalled Grace saying she took after her mother and she did, but Grace's beauty was, as yet, immature. Her mother, on the other hand, was lovely and not just for her beauty alone. It was everything about her. He couldn't remember ever feeling the way he did that moment and he had no idea how to deal with it.

But Maeve gave him no time to analyse his feelings. She was already silently castigating herself. Brendan had been dead less than two years and might still be alive if she hadn't taken a hand in it. What was she doing having any sort of feelings for another man? Men would have no place in her life. She was not free. She was bound by guilt.

She turned her back on Richard deliberately and sternly told herself to stop behaving like a lovesick teenager. But when as he handed her the empty cup he caught her eye yet again, she had the same heart-stopping reaction and this time she couldn't prevent the crimson flush of embarrassment that reddened her whole face. Grace continued talking to Richard about the shop and Maeve was thankful that she'd noticed nothing amiss. She was glad to let her daughter continue the conversation because her own mouth felt too dry, and she doubted that she could have uttered a word.

Much, much later, when Maeve lay sleepless in bed, she kept remembering Richard's face. She wasn't totally surprised that she dreamt about him, but what did throw her completely was not only how erotic the dream was but, more importantly, how she'd responded. In the cold light of day, it made her face flame to think of it.

She was angry with herself. The first half-decent man she'd looked at for years and she went all doe-eyed about him. It was ridiculous! But what of him a little voice said? Didn't he feel the same? Well, if he did, Maeve told herself briskly, he'd have to get over it. She was unavailable and he'd have to realise that. She had a grand family altogether, her elder children in work and the others fine and healthy; money wasn't plentiful, but it was at least adequate and she had a good friend and neighbour in Elsie. What more did she want?

But Maeve knew what she wanted, the feel of loving arms around her, longing lips upon her own, the feeling that she was special to someone. But it could never be, and she faced that. She would treat Richard Prendagast with politeness and nothing more. In time, she assured herself he would get the message.

But when Richard did arrive the next morning, to enquire after Grace, but really to see Maeve again, he was a different person, and that was because he was confronted by two little girls.

Mary Ann had turned three and a half and her fair hair had darkened as she grew. Her eyes were a hazel colour, like Bridget's, but Angela, who had just turned four in January, had the dark-brown eyes of her father and brown curly hair. They were both pretty little things, used to plenty of attention from adults, so they watched the visitor come into the house with interest.

Grace had told them all about Richard Prendagast. She, who'd once said little around the tea table, had spoken more since the day she'd told everyone the strange tale about the man and his mother. They might not have understood the significance of it all, but they knew all about Richard Prendagast. Even their Kevin said the fellow was a grand man and told of how the first time he'd come into the shop, he'd shaken hands with Kevin and said he was delighted to meet a brother of Grace's.

These things, as far as the younger children were concerned, marked him down as a nice man. Then at the table the previous evening, their mother said that Richard Prendagast had brought Grace home because she had a cold. Jamie had remarked gloomily that he didn't think any of the teachers at St Catherine's would bother to take any of them home even if they fell over in a dead faint, and they'd all laughed. All this the little girls remembered as the man was ushered in by Maeve and they both smiled at him.

And Richard recoiled. He'd forgotten about the little brother and sisters Grace had told him about. He'd had nothing to do with children since he'd had the letter telling him of the death of his wife and child. He couldn't handle being around them. Their shrill voices and uninhibited laughter seemed to mock him.

And now two little children were smiling up at him. He felt his loss as keenly as if it had just happened, and it twisted inside him like a hot knife so that he wanted to cry out against it. Instead, he put on a mask of indifference, the barrier he'd hidden behind for years, and he saw the little girls' smiles fade and their eyes fill with confusion. He hated himself, but knew that was the only way he had of dealing with his grief.

Maeve saw the aloof look on his face as he glanced about the room and didn't connect it with the children; though she thought it odd he'd made them no greeting. She thought he was looking down his nose on where she lived, looking down on all of them, showing plainly that Maeve and her family were not good enough for him. Whatever he might have felt for Maeve was well and truly gone, she realised, and she knew she should have felt relieved. Instead, she was angered by his arrogance. She hated snobs above all other people, but the man before her was Grace's employer, so she still made him a cup of tea but silently this time, without any pleasant chit-chat and taking care not to look at him, annoyed that he could talk as easily and pleasantly to Grace as he had the previous day. But then she reminded herself Grace was just his employee, and in his eyes of little account, and most of what he said to her daughter, she thought of as patronising and smug.

Maybe, thought Maeve, he imagined I had designs on him yesterday? Her cheeks felt hot at the very thought. Well he needn't bother. I don't want anything to do with him and I'll soon let him know it.

Richard knew nothing of Maeve's thoughts, but he knew Grace was worrying about forfeiting her wages if she were to stay away from work and that was the reason she was badgering him to let her go back before she was better. As his eyes had raked the room earlier, he'd seen the poverty of the place, though not dire poverty such as he'd glimpsed at other places. The children and Maeve and Grace were respectably and decently dressed, obviously adequately nourished, and a fire burned merrily in the grate. But the furnishings were shabby, though the room was clean, and he guessed there was no spare money in the Hogan household.

So, it was to relieve Grace's anxiety as much as her mother's that when he eventually rose to his feet to leave he said to Maeve, 'I'll see you're all right for money, don't worry. You'll not lose out because Grace is off sick.'

Maeve bristled immediately. He could patronise her daughter, she thought, but it wasn't going to work on her. 'I beg your pardon?' she snapped.

Richard was surprised at her curt tone, but continued. 'I know Grace's wages must be important to you. I understand you're a widow?'

'We manage fine, Mr Prendagast,' Maeve said sharply. 'We might not have the fine clothes and car that you have, but we still have our pride, thank God. We have no need of hand-outs or charity either, and I'll thank you to remember that.'

Richard wasn't the only one startled. The little girls looked up from their play and saw Maeve with two high spots of colour on her cheeks. They knew that spelt trouble and when directed at them it was usually followed by a smacked backside. They wondered what the man had done to annoy their mammy so much.

Grace's head was bent and tears of shame trickled from her eyes. She was mortified. She couldn't really believe what she'd heard. For her mammy to speak like that to Richard and him only offering to see them all right!

Richard recovered first. 'I assure you I'm not offering handouts or charity.' His words were deliberately condescending and he went on stiffly, 'This will be in the nature of sick pay and only what Grace is entitled to. My mother tells me Grace has not had one day off sick since she began at the shop. I just wanted to reassure you. However,' he continued, 'I'm obviously taking up too much of your valuable time, so I'll bid you good day.'

Maeve opened her mouth, but she knew there was nothing she could say to retrieve the situation so she was silent, and Richard strode across the room and wrenched the door open.

Grace only waited till it had slammed shut so hard it shuddered before turning anguished tear-filled eyes on her mother. Maeve's own face was burning with embarrassment and her eyes smarted with tears of anger. Just like people of that type, she thought angrily. Put me down right and proper. Made it look like I was the one at fault.

She was in no mood for her daughter's reproach. 'Oh Mammy.'

'Don't "Oh Mammy" me, Grace,' she snapped. 'The man thinks too much of himself and less than nothing about us. That much is evident.'

'Mammy, he didn't mean that, you don't know him, he's good and kind.'

'Well, you keep your opinions Grace, you have to work with the man, but I'll keep mine and you'll not change them,' Maeve said firmly and Grace said nothing more.

369

So when later Elsie asked Maeve what she thought of Amy Overley's son, Maeve was quick to tell her. 'Thinks himself above the likes of us,' she said. 'An arrogant sod altogether. You'd not like him at all.'

'Grace seems to like him well enough.'

'Well I don't,' Maeve said flatly, but Elsie knew there was more to it than she was letting on.

Richard never came again and Grace wasn't surprised. Part of Maeve was thankful but, perversely, the other half of her longed to see him again.

'What's the matter with me?' she asked herself one day. 'Haven't I enough to satisfy any living body?' And when the answer was a 'No', she refused to listen to it, climbed the stairs to her bed alone and told herself she was happy to be that way.

Grace was soon back at work, at first quite embarrassed to meet Richard again, but with her he was his normal cheerful self and she was glad that he didn't hold her responsible for the way her mother had spoken to him.

Richard, in fact, thought he'd had a lucky escape and he thanked God Maeve had shown her true colours before he lost his head altogether, because he couldn't deny that she'd rekindled emotions in him that he'd thought were buried for ever. It meant nothing. That just meant he was a normal red-blooded male. That was all. Anyway he knew that there could have been no future for him with any woman with young children. He could never have borne it, so perhaps it was better this way.

Everywhere spring was in the air, everyone was looking forward, and yet Maeve was feeling very despondent and achingly lonely. What she would have done without

370

Matthew she didn't know. He didn't know the true reason for Maeve's lethargy and lack of interest in everything around her, Maeve hardly knew herself, but he was unfailingly patient. He said it was small wonder she felt as she did. Hadn't she already gone through six years of a bloody and often terrifying war? Then there was the loss of her husband, followed by the worst winter in living memory, and now they'd just gone through another severe winter. Little wonder, he said, that the reaction to all the stress had left her tired and out of sorts.

Maeve told herself Matthew was probably right. Wasn't that a more likely explanation than being depressed over a man that surely could mean nothing to her, even if he was seldom out of her thoughts?

Grace, sensing her mother's malaise, tried to cheer her up by telling her of the happenings at the shop. Every time Grace mentioned Richard's name, Maeve's heart gave a flip yet she forced herself to listen. She heard of the large extension Richard had planned by knocking down two storerooms that were little used. 'It's so that we'll be ready to stock the cheaper chain-store clothes once rationing is over,' Grace said. 'At last someone has listened to me.'

Maeve was pleased her daughter enjoyed her job and that Richard didn't take any antagonism he might have felt towards her out on her daughter. Then, just two days after Grace had told her about the alterations taking place, she'd come into the house panting and red-faced, having run all the way home. Maeve turned astonished from the stove and Grace threw her arms round her. 'Mammy, I've had a rise,' she cried, her voice high with excitement. 'From next week I'll be earning seventeen and six. Kevin won't be the only one able to buy you things.'

'We have enough,' Maeve said. 'I'm always telling Kevin the same. He'll be pleased for you though. Now perhaps you'll be able to go out a time or two with your friends.'

And when Kevin came round later for his tea, he said he was glad his sister was at last being appreciated. He'd had a rise of his own just a fortnight before bringing his wage to three pounds and ten shillings. It had been his second rise since the death of his father. The first had been to compensate him for the loss of his paper-round money, as he gave up the round, urged by both his mother and Syd, who said he needed his help in the shop, after the dreadful winter of 1947.

Maeve remembered how excited Kevin had been with his second rise and with reason, for it was quite a phenomenal amount of money for a boy of his age to earn, but like Grace, Kevin saw it only in terms of how much more he could help his mother.

'I have no need of it, son,' she'd told him.

'Well some day you may have,' Kevin had said. 'Put it away.'

And Maeve did that. After Brendan's death, the cash box in Elsie's house was redundant. Any money Maeve had spare now was deposited in the Post Office account she'd opened up.

'Well now,' Maeve told her two older children round the table that evening, 'you do plenty for me and I'm grateful, but I'll not take all your wages. Soon, Angela and Mary Ann will be at school and then I'll look for a wee job for myself.' And maybe that will lift me out of the doldrums, she thought to herself.

Maeve insisted Grace keep five shillings of her wages for herself, which meant for the first time she had money to go to the pictures, or jitterbugging – now often called jiving – with her friends Bernadette and Ruby. Maeve encouraged her to go, reminding her that she'd only be young the once.

Jiving was still frowned on by most of the older generation but the young people didn't care. Maeve had no problem with Grace going. She liked to see the young people enjoying themselves. She remembered the restlessness of her own teenage years that had sparked the flight to Birmingham, and she helped Grace find new clothes to wear and adapted those she had already.

Nylons were the hardest thing to find and very expensive, but Grace was undaunted that she hadn't got a pair. Instead she would rub gravy browning over her legs and Maeve would draw the line down the back for her with an eyebrow pencil. She would watch her go out, proud of her beautiful daughter, glad she'd managed to put that dreadful night behind her and behave like a normal teenager.

But Grace was still very interested in her job and once the alterations were completed, she wanted Maeve to come and see how the place had changed. Maeve had never wanted anything less, but Grace was so enthusiastic and insistent that she found herself agreeing to go.

Almost as soon as Maeve entered the shop, she felt the man's eyes boring into her and her face grew hot with embarrassment. She tried to forget he was there, as she looked the place over and, almost in spite of herself, she was full of admiration at the transformation of it. She listened to Grace and Miss Overley enthusing over it, and discussing the alterations and the new stock they'd now be able to order.

But all the time, Maeve was aware of Richard and, though she was uncomfortable, she wondered whether she should apologise to the man for snapping at him that time because she knew he hadn't deserved it. He'd been more than generous to Grace after all and it wasn't totally his fault that he thought her home a slum. He couldn't help the way he'd been brought up any more than she could.

But then she wondered if this wouldn't be just as embarrassing in a way and, anyway, how could she do it without his mother hearing and requiring some sort of explanation? Perhaps, she decided, it would be better to ignore the whole incident and just try to act naturally and be pleasant to the man.

Richard meanwhile was in a similar dilemma. He still didn't know what he'd done to offend Grace's mother, but it didn't seem that important any more. He had no wish to be on bad terms with her and if that meant apologising, then so be it. It was no big deal to say sorry. He crossed the room towards her and she turned and gave him a smile that quite dazzled him and he just stood there, transfixed for a moment.

Afterwards, when Maeve analysed it, she could recall nothing of importance that had been said between them that day. But the atmosphere had been charged with emotion; so much so, that Maeve was surprised it hadn't been apparent to Richard's mother and her own daughter.

However, Amy had been aware of something. She'd seen that certain look pass between Maeve Hogan and her son. She wasn't totally displeased. She'd been worried about Richard's loneliness for some time. He was a handsome man still, she thought, even allowing for a little bias, and yet he'd shown no interest in any of the opposite sex. What had happened to him had of course been a terrible tragedy, but she knew more than anyone that life had to go on.

So she'd been delighted at the easy way he was talking to Grace's mother. Maybe now, she thought, he'll be able to put the past behind him and find someone with whom to share his life. And with the pride of a mother, she also thought that whoever he chose would be a very lucky girl.

Grace was just glad that her mammy had got over whatever it was that had made her snap at Richard and maybe now she could mention his name in the house without her mother going all peculiar.

In fact, Grace was to find that after that day, her mother suddenly became very interested in Richard Prendagast. Grace was unable to tell her much about his background, though, apart from snippets, because Richard seldom talked about himself. Grace could have told her mother that he was always asking about her too, but she didn't in case her mother wouldn't like it. Maeve had a thing sometimes about discussing their business with strangers.

Maeve herself was annoyed that she thought so much about Richard. She told herself she needed a change – it was the sameness of every day that was getting to her and putting too much importance on things, blowing them up out of all proportion. Her restlessness had been noticed and commented on by Elsie, but Maeve had brushed her concerns to one side and told her that she was fine.

Then one Friday evening towards the end of May, Maeve was alone in the house. Grace had gone dancing, the children were in bed and Kevin was never round on Fridays, because the shop stayed open till late. Elsie had been in, but had gone back home. Maeve had never made a habit of calling into Elsie's of an evening when Alf would be at home, but since his retirement she'd done it less and less, though she admitted to herself that she would have welcomed company that night.

She could always busy herself through the day, but when the jobs were done and the children in bed or about their own pursuits the time hung heavy on Maeve's hands. She enjoyed Matthew's company and wished she had the nerve to ask him to stay on, but she had her name to think of, if not for herself, then for the children. But all too soon it was the children's bedtime and not long after that, time for Matthew to return to his comfortless room and then the evening stretched endlessly ahead.

She took up the paper Matthew had left that evening and skimmed through the headlines. Until the outbreak of war Maeve had never bothered herself about world affairs, but then it began to matter to know what was going on and where the places were that had cost so many young lives. She used to like discussing things with Matthew, for he was a well-read and intelligent man and could explain things to her in a way that she understood.

Once, in common with many, Maeve had had a naïve and idealistic view of what would happen after the war. After all, they'd not only fought a world war, but won it too and now that it was over, the men would come home and everything would go back to normal. But, of course, it couldn't be like that with the turmoil the whole world was in.

Europe, in particular, was in total disarray, and full of dispossessed and homeless people, unable or unwilling to return to the places they'd originally come from. Matthew had told her that it would take some time for everywhere to settle down again.

She was startled from her reverie by a knock at the door. Most people didn't knock so Maeve opened the door cautiously. 'Mr . . . Mr Prendagast,' she stammered. Recovering herself, she went on, 'I'm afraid Grace isn't in.'

'I know. She told me she was going out tonight. I came to see you.'

Even his voice lent a weakness to Maeve's limbs, but she felt something else too, the ache of loneliness gaping wide inside him, recognising it so clearly because she felt it too. She couldn't ask him in – it would be worse than allowing Matthew to stay on – and yet she opened the door wide and he walked into the room.

They didn't touch in any way – Maeve knew she'd be lost if they did. She tried not to meet his eyes and they sat together and talked and drank the tea Maeve made. They talked of the shop and how it was progressing and of Grace, whom Richard was quick to praise. He asked after Kevin and the Mosses and herself, though not the younger children, Maeve noticed in surprise.

When Richard eventually got to his feet and thanked Maeve for the lovely evening, she had to fight the urge to put her arms round his neck and kiss the sadness from his eyes and beg him to stay longer. She told herself sternly not to be so silly. He'd come to see her and now he was going and that was that.

When he'd reached the door, he turned and said simply, 'Thank you, Maeve. Can I come again?'

Maeve knew what she should have said, an emphatic 'No', but instead she found herself saying, 'Yes, I'd like that.'

And she did like it over the next weeks when Richard came, usually twice a week, and always when Grace was out. Maeve didn't tell anyone of Richard's visits and he never brought the car, but of course there were few secrets in the courtyards.

The women complained to Elsie about it. 'They're both free agents,' she said. 'What's the harm?'

'She'll get her name up, that's what. It's hardly decent with children asleep above her head.'

'Aye. You must see it, Elsie. Christ, some evenings one man had scarcely left the place till another enters it.'

'Tell her, Elsie. You're her friend. It's for her own good we're saying.'

'She knows him well,' Elsie protested. 'There's no funny business going on. He's Grace's employer for heaven's sake.'

'And what d'you think his sort take up with the likes of us except for funny business?' one asked. 'Don't talk daft. You weren't born yesterday.'

But Elsie said nothing to Maeve. She couldn't bear to take the light away from her eyes or the spring from her step that hadn't been there this long while.

Richard and Maeve had relaxed enough after his first few visits to discuss the world situation and in particular the new National Health Service due to start up very soon. Sometimes they would laugh over some absurdity, or Richard would recount a tale, or tell Maeve a joke, and she'd think, I'll tell Matthew about that. But she never did.

She knew this wonderful happiness that seemed to bubble away inside her wouldn't last. He'd make new and more suitable friends and then no longer need her and she must face that. He wasn't looking for permanency and neither was she. As long as no one knew about it she told herself she could cope.

Amy Overley knew something was up with her son. She didn't know where Richard went and would never quiz him, but she knew he was seeing a woman. Amy had no idea who the woman was, but she was making him very happy and she asked Grace if he'd confided in her. He hadn't and it wasn't a question Grace could ask him, but she told her mother that night that Amy thought Richard was in love. She had no idea how many times a week Richard met his woman, but Amy seemed to think it was some big romance and so she told Maeve he was meeting this new love of his almost every night of the week.

She'd expected her mother to be pleased and was surprised when the blood suddenly drained from her mother's face and the hand dishing out the potatoes shook so much that she missed the plate entirely and deposited them on the tablecloth. 'Mammy,' cried Grace alarmed at her mother's pallor. 'Are you all right?'

'Yes,' Maeve said, rising to her feet. 'I've a bit of an upset stomach that's all. Dish up the dinner, will you, Grace. I'm away to the lavvy.'

She knew she had to be by herself. Grace's words had upset her so much, she staggered like a drunk down the yard and then sat on the toilet seat gripping her trembling hands tight between her knees. What the bloody hell had I expected? she asked herself angrily. He comes to see me twice a week, no more, and all he gets is chat. Did I expect him to live like a bloody monk the rest of the time? The man is attractive and has no ties and is at liberty to see who he likes. He's made no promise or commitment to me and I hope he never does. It would spoil things between us, because I'm not free to accept any sort of proposal.

She covered her face with her hands and gave a moan of sadness. Tears trickled through her fingers, and over the back of her hands, but she made no effort to wipe them away. She thanked God everyone else would be at their tea and not witnessing the fact that Maeve Hogan was breaking her heart in the lavvy and God alone knew what it was all about.

Eventually, when she became calmer, she wiped her wet eyes, cheeks and hands with her apron, and faced facts. Richard had never touched her, or muttered endearments, or shown in any way that she was more to him than a friend, serving a need at that moment. She had no need to feel betrayed or let down, nor any right either. God, she felt a fool, and she vowed not only would she not question Richard, but also she wouldn't behave any differently to him.

She tried, she really tried, but Richard sensed the slight distance she put between them the first few times he visited after that. He worried about it, wondering if he was making life difficult for Maeve by visiting her so openly. He'd tried to be discreet but with the close proximity of the houses, he knew many would be aware he called and he also knew no one would believe how innocently they spent their evenings together.

He wanted to broach the subject with Maeve but he could never bring himself to, afraid she would say it would be better if he didn't come round so often. So he said nothing and tried not to think of the future.

The long-awaited National Health Service came into operation at midnight on 5 July 1948, giving everyone free access to proper regulated healthcare. Maeve knew what security that represented for the poor, who now could call out, or visit the doctor with their families, without having to hide from the rent man the following week. Richard couldn't really appreciate that level of poverty when Maeve tried to explain it. It seemed to emphasise the difference between them.

In one way she was pleased when the schools closed for the summer holidays two weeks later. She told Richard it would be difficult to see him then as the children's bedtimes were much more relaxed and children played out in the summer evening till much later than normal. Maeve thought she was releasing him to visit his new lady more often, but Richard was devastated by Maeve's decision. He knew she was right, though, for he couldn't have borne to knock her door under the scrutiny of playing children and the women standing in the doorways looking him up and down. And then in Maeve's house to come face to face with her own children. That would be a form of torture to him.

At first, Maeve was too busy to miss Richard much, for with the children going to bed later, Matthew could legitimately stay later too and this Maeve urged him to do. He began taking the children, any who wanted to go, to Calthorpe Park on nice evenings and often to the Lickey Hills at the weekends. Sometimes Maeve went with them and other times she'd wait at home preparing meals for their return. Matthew himself seemed happier and more settled and less intent on pleasing Angela all the time. Maeve thought the situation could only improve after Christmas, when Angela would begin school, and was glad she'd said nothing about it to Matthew. The times she allowed herself to think of the relationship she'd enjoyed with Richard, she thought the friendship had run its course and died a natural death as she'd always expected it to do eventually, while the women of the court presumed Elsie had made the woman see sense at last.

But as the days passed, full though they were with the children at home, a form of desolate lethargy seemed to seep into Maeve, until it was filling her days and it was an effort to rouse herself to do anything, or take an interest in anything either. She faced the fact that she ached to see Richard again and also faced the fact that she couldn't.

Richard had moved on, as she knew he would one day, and she must do the same. He had a new woman in his life and she must try to fill the aching void in her own and not wallow in misery. And she tried to snap out of it and pull herself together for the children's sake and Matthew's. They all knew something was wrong, but whenever they asked her she said she was fine. She was far from it and at times the sadness almost overwhelmed her and she had the urge to curl in a corner and howl out her distress. But, of course, she could do no such thing and soldiered on, yet as the holidays drew to a close she felt as if a large block of lead had been attached to her heart and she knew there was damn all she, or anyone else, could do about it.

TWENTY-THREE

The children had returned to school and the September nights were drawing in when Grace came home from the pictures one night and told Maeve Chris Cleary, the brother of her friend Bernadette, had asked her for a date. She'd told him she'd have to check with her mother before she gave him an answer and did she have any objection?

Grace was only fifteen, but sensible, and she also knew right from wrong and Maeve had only to look at her shining face to know she more than liked the lad. Added to that he was a decent, steady boy, apprenticed to a toolmaker from a family Maeve knew well, and she gave her blessing.

She wasn't prone to self-pity normally but was shaken by a bout of it one evening just a few days later. She'd waited up for Grace, who'd gone dancing with Chris, and when the pair burst through the door just after eleven, their faces were flushed with the sheer exhilaration of youth. Maeve was suddenly struck with a pang of nostalgia and even jealousy towards her own daughter.

She wondered how her life might have gone if she'd married a different man from Brendan. She felt she had nothing to look forward to. One by one, her children would all leave her and she, who'd struggled to bring up her family, would be left without one belonging to her.

She would never resort to what some women did in such circumstances. Frightened of a lonely old age, they feigned frailty to hang on to one of their children, usually the youngest. The child would grow middle-aged and then old, tied to his or her mother by a sense of duty, till all chances of a life of their own passed them by. Never would she do that to a child of hers, and yet growing older and lonelier was not a prospect she looked forward to with any pleasure.

She sat in the chair before the fire she'd decided to light, for the evenings could become chill, and she stared at the orange flames licking round the sticks and tried to count her blessings. But it did no good and she still felt miserable and sorry for herself.

When the knock came at the door, she stiffened. She knew who it was, although he hadn't called for months, because he was the only one who ever knocked, but such was her mood she didn't want to see Richard Prendagast, didn't want to see anyone. She'd not answer the door. But, she told herself, he'd know she was in. He'd know she was not the type of woman to go out and leave her children in bed. What if he opened the door himself? He could – it wasn't locked – and then he would see her sitting there. Well, he wouldn't, she decided. It was her house and she'd decide who she'd have in it. She'd tell Mr Prendagast he wasn't welcome.

She leapt to her feet and swung open the door, but before she was able to say anything, Richard, seeing the sadness evident in Maeve's face, had taken a step forward into the room.

'What's happened?' he asked gently.

Maeve shook her head. The sympathy in Richard's voice had caused her eyes to smart. She had to keep control of herself and tell the man to go. 'It's just . . . it's just . . .'

The tears came then in torrents as Maeve cried out her fear of loneliness and Richard couldn't bear it. Despite his resolve, he swept her into his arms and began kissing the tears from her eyes and cheeks. It was what Maeve had longed for and for a long time, and she held Richard tight as if she never intended to let him go. Still clasped together they moved towards the fire.

Their lips met and the passion of that kiss surprised them both. Maeve felt as if she was drowning in it. Never, ever, not even in the early days with Brendan, had a kiss made her feel like this. Richard's tongue gently teased her partly open lips, and she seemed to melt against him while desire filled her being.

Richard's hands snaked up Maeve's back under her blouse to unhook her brassiere. In the recess of Maeve's mind, she knew she should stop this madness. She was behaving like a wanton, and with her children above her asleep in the attic.

Richard had her blouse unbuttoned and Maeve wriggled free of it and her brassiere, which she dropped on to the floor. Her breasts lay in the palms of his hands. He lowered his mouth to them and he and Maeve sank down to the rug on the floor. She felt her nipples rise into peaks and she gasped and moaned with pleasure such as she'd never ever felt before.

She felt his hardness against her and knew what Richard wanted and knew she would let him have it, because she wanted it too. In her courtship with Brendan she'd often wanted the culmination of their lovemaking, but when it actually happened after marriage, it had never lived up to the promise of what she'd expected and needed. It had always been over in minutes and she'd been left uneasy and frustrated, not understanding why she felt that way.

At first, she'd responded eagerly to Brendan's embraces. There had been no one she could ask about such a thing, but she had wondered if it was something that needed practice.

Once Brendan had known of her pregnancy, he'd given up any attempt to make it enjoyable for her. He seemed to neither know nor care how she felt, but would just take her as and when he wanted until any desire within her had shut down totally. But this man, Richard Prendagast, had opened it up for her again.

But unlike Brendan, Richard seemed in no hurry. He was kissing her neck, throat and lips, muttering endearments while he unfastened her skirt, which she wriggled out of; the stockings and suspender belt she swiftly pulled off. Despite her years of marriage, no man had ever seen Maeve Hogan naked, nor had any man trailed down her belly with his lips as Richard was doing, causing her to give little whimpers of pleasure.

She could hardly bear the excitement which was mounting in her, and as Richard slipped his hand between her legs, she gasped aloud and then, amazed at her own daring, undid Richard's trousers. He shook his underpants off and gazed at the woman he'd loved for months.

'Oh God, Maeve, you're beautiful!'

What Richard was doing to Maeve was taking the breath from her body and she gasped out, 'Go on, please go on.'

But Richard stilled her voice with his lips and as his tongue probed her mouth and her excitement mounted to fever pitch, she felt him, at last, enter her. She heard herself giving little shouts and yelps as waves and waves of sheer rapturous pleasure swept over her again and again.

Richard gave one sudden exultant cry and it was over. As they lay entwined in blissful contentment, Maeve realised that she was almost thirty-seven years old, and she'd been loved, truly loved for the very first time in her life. The experience had been wonderful – glorious – and she'd shown plainly how she'd felt. Oh God, how she'd enjoyed it. She felt bad about that, for she knew that few women truly enjoyed sex, judging from the remarks they made about it, and she wondered what Richard had felt about her total abandonment.

But Richard had guessed almost straight away that despite her marriage Maeve had little experience of true lovemaking. There was an unworldliness about her. Knowing that, once he'd known she was as keen for it as he was, for he'd never have forced her, he was determined to make the experience an unforgettable one.

Despite not loving his wife, Valerie, he'd been extremely fond of her and they'd had an active and very satisfactory love life even before marriage. But with Maeve, lovemaking had a new dimension for him. He was also aware that in her eyes the fact that she'd shown such pleasure would probably make the whole thing even more sinful. And he was right, it did. Suddenly shame, deep shame, filled every part of her being.

Richard felt bad too; angry for letting himself get so carried away. God, he could offer this woman nothing. Much as he loved her, her children would stand as a barrier between them both, destroying any form of happiness they might have had. But he should say something; he couldn't just leave her like that. He watched her guiltily getting into her clothes, carefully avoiding his eyes, and knew the depths of her shame. The Catholic Church had done their work well and their teachings went deep. There was no need for her to feel that at all, the fault was his, but Richard knew she'd never believe that.

But he had to try. He wasn't given the chance, though, because Maeve forestalled him. 'I don't know what came over me,' she said in an apologetic voice that was little more than a whisper. 'I've never done that, not in the whole of my life.

'Maeve, Maeve . . .'

And suddenly Maeve couldn't take any more. She didn't want the man anywhere near her, let alone in her house. Dear God, it was hard enough to live with the degradation heaping itself upon her without having him witness to it all. 'Just go! Get out! Go!' she cried, her voice rising to a shriek bordering on hysteria.

Richard knew then the best thing he could do was leave. 'I just wanted to say I was sorry,' he said gently.

'Being sorry will change nothing,' Maeve snapped. 'Now please just go. I can't take any more and, for God's sake, never come back.'

Richard looked at her, longing to comfort her and knowing he couldn't. He couldn't risk it for himself and he doubted Maeve would let him anywhere near her again, and he turned regretfully away. He was bitterly upset that he'd allowed his feelings for Maeve to over-whelm him in that way and so cause pain to the woman he knew now he loved deeply. And Maeve was right, no way could they risk seeing each other again. Because of his actions they could no longer be friends and as he walked away, Richard thought the future looked very bleak.

Maeve barely waited till the door closed behind him before bolting and locking it and then, having filled every pan and kettle she had, she pulled the bath from the hook at the back of the door.

Later, in bed, her skin tingling still from the scrubbing she'd given it, she analysed what had happened that night. She recognised that she'd not repulsed the move Richard had made towards her, but welcomed it – returned it. He'd forced her to do nothing against her will. He had in fact transported her to paradise. It was shameful, she was shameful, and it was blatantly obvious she could never see the man again.

She was unable to sleep and lay waiting for the sky to lighten sufficiently for her to get up and face the day, although she did so with little enthusiasm.

Elsie, of course, had noticed that Maeve wasn't right. She'd also noted Richard's absence all summer and had thought the affair, such as it was, had burnt itself out. She was glad she'd said nothing to Maeve about it. She'd missed Richard's last visit and so didn't connect him with the air of gloomy sadness that Maeve was steeped in most days.

When Maeve, in an attempt to allay any suspicions her friend might have, said she was concerned about a letter she'd received from her mother, Elsie believed her, knowing how Maeve felt about her family. And Maeve was anxious about the letter her mother had sent.

It had arrived two days after she'd sent Richard packing and it helped take her mind off what had happened between them, the thought of which had been getting between her and her sleep until she feared she'd go mad.

The letter had put her problems in perspective somewhat. The first part of it had been puzzling enough.

Nuala should have taken final vows by now, but she always says she's not ready. I never thought she was nun material myself, nor your father either, as you know. He told her, and more than once, nuns were unnatural. I sometimes wonder if she'd have made such a stand if he'd not gone on about it so much. You know full well how he can be.

Maeve did know. She remembered how he'd gone on and on about her leaving home and going to live in England in the first place. His arguments and moodiness had just strengthened her resolve, and indeed that was one of the reasons she'd not fled back home at the first sign of trouble – not wanting to admit he was right. She thought her mother probably had a point. But then the letter went on, more worrying than ever.

Still, I don't say anything to him about it, for he's gone very old-looking lately. I think the farm is getting too much for him, not of course that he'd ever admit it, but it's wearing him out.

Maeve didn't really know what to do about the letter, but in the end she knew she'd have to let Kevin see it. He knew what his grandmother was really saying. They needed him back on the farm and he couldn't go, even if it meant giving up his inheritance; he couldn't leave his mother to cope on her own.

Maeve hadn't a worry now about having money enough for the coal in the winter, or for the gas meter for the lamps and the stove and that was how Kevin wanted it. He'd bought two paraffin lamps for the attic, as he didn't like the idea of a candle stuck to a cracked saucer with a dab of wax, and he bought the paraffin for those too. He also made sure the children and his mother were dressed decently and he still brought a basket of food around every Friday afternoon.

Maeve had been especially grateful for this when the dock workers had gone on strike in June, and food had lain rotting on the quayside until the troops had been called in to shift it. The rations were slashed immediately because of it. Kevin was very good then about getting them a wee bit extra. He knew his mother was more comfortable than she'd been for years, but he couldn't just leave her to get on with it again. He wrote and told his grandmother how the situation was.

Grace also knew her mother was worried about the letter and it helped explain the times Maeve snapped at them all or seemed in a dream and even lethargic some days. But there was nothing she could find to account for Richard's temper and the brusque manner he'd developed seemingly overnight. He was in the shop before her every morning and she left him there at night, and every day he looked worse – hollow-eyed and pale. Grace thought he might be ill, but neither she nor Amy would risk incurring his wrath by asking him if he was all right.

'I think the love affair has ended,' Amy confided to Grace one day, by way of explanation of Richard's mood.

'I thought you said that was all over in the summer.'

'I thought it was,' Amy admitted. 'He hardly went across the step the whole time and he was certainly edgy, but nothing to the way he is at the moment.'

Grace felt sorry for him, and wished he could find someone special in his life, but for the time being they all had to live with it.

And with Maeve, who seemed to be writing or receiving letters from Ireland almost on a daily basis.

'What the hell's up with Mammy?' Kevin asked Grace one day in early November.

'It's this business with Nuala and being so worried about her da and all,' Grace told him.

'Is that all it is?' Kevin said. 'She looks as if she has the weight of the world on her shoulders. She hardly ever smiles, even when the weans do something funny, and I try my damnedest sometimes to cheer her up and she just sits there. I can't remember the last time I heard her laugh. She didn't even comment when I brought the paper home with the pictures of the new baby prince in it.'

Grace knew exactly what her brother meant. Young Princess Elizabeth had given birth to a son, Charles, on 14 November, and his photograph was all over the newspapers. Even Matthew had said the birth of the child was a good omen, a child of peace, but Maeve didn't seem interested.

In fact Maeve was interested in very little because she was intensely unhappy. She couldn't ever remember feeling as sad, not even when she was going through hell with Brendan. She'd lost the only man she'd ever loved and it was only right. She shouldn't, couldn't, go unpunished for what she'd done, but she had no idea having to reject him would hurt so much. It was like a physical pain. Matthew was like a tower of strength to her. He was much quieter than Maeve by nature anyway, and thought it only natural that she didn't go about laughing and carrying on when she was worried about her family.

'Leave your mammy be,' he advised the children. 'She has a lot on her mind just now. She'll be all right when things are more settled.'

But soon there was something else to worry Maeve because National Service for young men over eighteen was increased to a year and a half in December. There was still much unrest in the world and Maeve was frightened. Kevin would be eighteen the following year, and would be called up with the rest and she had no desire for him to die in some foreign field somewhere, or any other damned place either.

'Hasn't there been enough killing already?' she demanded.

Matthew knew what was bothering Maeve. 'It's all the resettling after the war,' he assured her. 'It will have been sorted out well before your son is in the firing range. Don't worry.'

She tried not to. Matthew had a calming influence on her and she was very fond of him, and invited him to go with her to Elsie's house on 31 December, where, along with many neighbours and friends, they welcomed in 1949.

'Four years since the war ended and still rationing goes on,' Maeve complained to Elsie one day in early spring.

'Aye, we've tried the lot now,' Elsie agreed, 'horsemeat and whale meat. We'll be reduced to eating snoek yet.'

'Not on your life,' Maeve said. The blue fish in cans had been introduced in 1948, but hadn't proved popular. Maeve couldn't bring herself to try it. Whale meat had been bad enough, though horsemeat was slightly better if you could forget where it came from.

'What's the use in talking about it?' Elsie said. 'It just makes you bloody depressed.'

'Aye, you're right,' Maeve agreed. 'And I've a lot to be thankful for. At least the children are fine and healthy.'

'And how's Matthew these days?'

'Oh, you know Matthew, he'll never change,' Maeve said.

'Are you blind, girl,' Elsie replied. 'He has changed this last month or two. He has a fancy for you. Don't you see it?'

Maeve looked at Elsie steadily and Elsie realised that Maeve really hadn't known. 'You're imagining things.'

'No I'm not!' Elsie stated emphatically. 'Stares you in the face, it does. Surprised you haven't seen it yourself. D'you think he stays on every evening because your hearth is cosier than his own?'

'No,' Maeve could have said. 'He stays because I want him to.'

After seeing the New Year in together, Maeve thought it daft to be sending Matthew home early each night as though they were schoolchildren. She was in control of her own life and if she wanted Matthew to stay then she would ask him. At least, she thought it might stop her thinking of bloody Richard Prendagast. And he'd been pleased to be asked. Being Matthew, though, the only thing that had bothered him was Maeve's reputation and only when she assured him it would be fine did he agree to stay, but not very long and not every evening either. He knew, he said, how rumours could spread. Maeve, not knowing how she'd been viewed by the women in the court when Richard used to visit, told him not to be so silly.

In a way, the women didn't mind Matthew so much. After all, they said, at least he had a legitimate reason for being there, and then again he was one of their own. 'Wonder if she's told him about her fancy man,' Trudy Gaskins from up the entry said one day and added spitefully, 'Maybe he needs to know.'

'Not from you, or anyone else either,' Elsie said firmly. 'You keep your gob shut, or you'll have me to reckon with. And that goes for all of you and all,' she snapped, glaring round the gossiping group. 'Maeve has had it hard long enough. If you ask me Matthew's sweet on her and if you spoil it for her and besmirch her name into the bargain, by God you'll be sorry.'

'I didn't say I was going to say owt anyroad,' Trudy said with an offended sniff.

'Well, make sure you don't,' Elsie warned.

Most of the woman thought much the same as Elsie, because many knew Maeve had gone through the mill one way and another, and yet she wasn't one for loading her problems on anyone else. Added to that, despite everything, she'd brought her kids up decent. And then look at the way she took in little Angela Bradshaw to stop her being put in an orphanage when she had already plenty on her plate. It was time the woman had a break.

Meanwhile, Maeve, unaware that she was the subject of gossip, wondered if Elsie was right and Matthew did have a fancy for her. Surely he would have said something about it? Maybe she was too close. She saw him as a friend only and maybe he realised this and so was nervous of broaching the subject, yet Matthew was a man like any other. Perhaps they needed to talk about it. Matthew had to understand his future could not lie with her because she wasn't free to marry any man.

She knew things were coming to a head, and when Matthew asked her to go for a walk with him one evening in May, she agreed. She knew the complexion he'd put on her acquiescence but she saw it as her chance to put him right. She had to convince him she saw him only as a friend, thereby setting him free to find someone special to share his life – someone far more deserving than she.

'I can't be out too long,' Maeve said, for though Angela and Mary Ann were in bed, she'd left Bridget and Jamie listening to the wireless and Grace immersed in a book.

It had rained that afternoon and washed the dusty pavements clean, and even the sooty air smelt slightly fresher, Maeve thought as she stepped outside. The heat hadn't yet gone from the day, but there was a slight breeze blowing, a very pleasant night for a walk, even in the narrow streets. Side by side they strolled all the way down Latimer Street and Grant Street, talking easily as they'd done for the past months. It was just as they turned into Bell Barn Road that Matthew reached for Maeve's hand. She pulled it away as if she'd been stung.

'Oh no, Matthew,' she cried.

Matthew looked at her with slight reproach. 'I thought you knew how I felt about you, Maeve,' he said. 'I care for you and I know you care for me.' He pulled her gently round to face him and covered her hands with his own.

'I . . . Yes. I do care for you, Matthew, but . . .'

'Maeve, we're neither of us in the first flush of youth,' Matthew went on. 'And I won't lie to you: I loved my first wife dearly. She was so happy when she was carrying Angela. Now I owe it to her to provide a proper home for our daughter.'

'Is all this just for Angela's sake?'

'No,' Matthew protested. 'I am deeply fond of you. You must know that. My wife is dead and I've mourned her for years. Now it's time to live again.' He looked into her eyes as he said, 'I know your marriage was not happy,' and when Maeve made a movement of protest he went on, 'Now I'm not speaking out of turn. It's a well-known fact, and I can understand that you're not keen to try marriage again. That is why I've waited. I'm nothing like

Brendan Hogan, Maeve. I've a good job, and I'm a steady sort of chap.' Maeve knew that was true, for almost as soon as Matthew had returned home, he'd got his old job back as a welder at the Midland Radiator Company in Aston Road. 'Maeve,' he said, 'I like my own fireside, and that's the truth.'

Maeve looked at Matthew. She knew him well and what she liked most about him was his kindliness. It was the first thing she'd noticed when she'd arrived on his doorstep, offering to take care of his daughter. She couldn't remember ever taking much notice of him before that but she'd been struck that day by his brown eyes, still kind and gentle despite the horrors of war they'd witnessed, and his own devastating tragedy.

Matthew could be described as wholesome, maybe not the most exciting of men, but dependable, good and honest, and that was why she couldn't marry him. She'd never imagined getting another proposal of marriage. Matthew had said they were not in the first flush of youth, and they weren't, but Maeve no longer felt young. Maybe she had years of life still left to her and maybe not. Either way, she'd never considered sharing those years with another man.

She just wanted to live in peace. She wondered how Matthew would react if she ever told him what she'd done to Brendan. She felt certain he'd want nothing more to do with her. Not that she'd ever do it, of course – she'd never put them all at risk that way. She wished that Matthew hadn't spoken because now he'd moved their relationship to another plane. When she rejected his offer, she doubted they'd ever be able to return to the easy, companionable friendship they'd enjoyed previously, which had sustained Maeve in so many ways.

For that reason she spoke gently and with sincere regret. 'Matthew, I can't marry you. It's not that I don't like you – far from it – but . . .'

'I understand your hesitation,' Matthew said. 'And, believe me, I have no desire to rush you. Think carefully, though, of what I have to offer you and your children.'

Maeve tried to pull her hands away, but Matthew held on to one and they walked on together. Maeve knew whatever Matthew said she must refuse him. Richard Prendagast had never mentioned marriage to her yet she'd given herself to him and gladly. She'd been absolutely shameless, but she almost welcomed the pain of losing him, which was still with her, as just punishment.

Matthew was a much more honourable man and she wondered why he didn't stir her senses like Richard did. But she couldn't marry him either, and in time she'd make him see that. And if because of it she lost his friendship, then so be it.

Matthew, aware of the silence between them, suddenly said, 'I expect you're wondering why I've spoken to you now.' Without waiting for a reply he went on, 'It's been on my mind for some time – a year, maybe longer – but I sensed you weren't ready. Now I've been told I'm in line for a prefab, but a two-bedroom place would be no good for all of us if you and I decide to marry. I have my army gratuity, which I've added to over the years, and as I earn a decent wage I could probably afford to buy a house big enough for all of us.'

A place of her own. It was a dream that Maeve had never allowed to surface. A place with a proper kitchen, a bathroom that had running water, hot as well as cold, a lavatory that wasn't situated down the yard, electric lights and a garden that was safe for the little ones to play in.

Suddenly into Maeve's mind came a picture of their home in Latimer Street and the court and the deprivations of both, and she asked herself if she had the right to condemn her family to spend their childhoods in such a place because of some high moral stance, when someone was able to offer something better.

She'd killed Brendan and nothing on God's earth would change that, but should she allow the children to suffer for her crime too? Should she tie Kevin to her for life, to provide for her and look after her and compromise his own life in the process?

'Maeve, can I ask you to please think about my proposal and what it could mean for your family?' Matthew asked her, suddenly breaking in on her thoughts.

That at least Maeve could promise to do. 'Give me a week,' she asked, 'to think things over.'

But before the week was up, Maeve received a letter from her mother. Nuala had finally decided a nun's life was not for her and left the convent, but was being given a hard time by some of the people in the town. Maeve could imagine that. It would be seen as a disgrace by some to have started any sort of religious life and then to come out of it. Her mother wrote:

> She has a great desire to leave, for a wee while at least. Could she come and stay with you just until she decides what to do with herself?

Maeve was delighted and excited. Her little sister was coming to stay with her – though Nuala was not little now, of course. She'd be twenty-three, and, Maeve imagined, a little lost and unhappy.

Well if she was, she'd soon change that, Maeve decided. She wondered whether her sister coming to stay would mean she should decide to turn down Matthew's proposal. She sought advice from Elsie. Elsie hadn't been a bit surprised by Maeve's news of Matthew's proposal of marriage and thought Maeve should be over the moon.

'Isn't that what you want, to lift the burden of responsibilities from the shoulders of your two older children?' she asked, and added, 'You know Matthew well enough. God, he's been nearly living in your house anyway since he was demobbed. You know he'll give you and the children a decent life and lift you all out of this muck hole.' She shook her head in disbelief. 'I can't believe you said you'd think about it. You need your bleeding head examining, you do really. As for your sister coming over, what difference will it make?'

'I don't know how she'll take to the news,' Maeve said, 'or any of them, really. He's not a Catholic, Elsie.'

'I know that, but he's not the bloody devil incarnate either. Are you waiting for love's young dream, is that it?'

'No, not really,' Maeve said. 'Anyway, I do love Matthew, but I'm not in love *with* him if you know what I mean.'

'Oh, I know what you mean all right, but how are you so sure that you don't feel that way for Matthew?'

Because I know what it feels to be in love with someone so that you ache to be with him, Maeve might have said. It's not a comfortable way to live, but you just can't help yourself. You long for your lover to touch you all over in places you'd usually be too embarrassed even to talk about. That's being in love and that's what I don't deserve, but though I still feel guilty about thinking of marrying someone as good and kind as Matthew, who I know will be good to me, if I do, everyone will benefit.

But none of this could Maeve tell Elsie. She'd probably not have listened anyway, because at that moment she was so mad with Maeve for maybe passing up a better life for herself and her children that she wanted to shake her.

'Tell you what, girl,' Elsie snapped, concern for her friend making her irritable. 'Would you fall on his neck with gratitude if he told you he was going to keep you short of cash each week, come home drunk every night and beat you senseless now and again to keep you in line, like?'

'Elsie, don't be daft,' Maeve said, but a tentative smile played around her lips. 'I take it, then, you think I should say yes?'

'I don't know why you even said you'd have to think about it.'

And Maeve knew Elsie was right. She'd been wrong to hesitate. She'd tell Matthew as soon as possible that she'd be pleased to marry him.

TWENTY-FOUR

Maeve went to meet her nervous, apprehensive sister at New Street station just three days later. Nuala fervently hoped that Maeve wouldn't ask for explanations of why she'd left the convent, for she had none. She'd been sure at the time she entered that she had a vocation. Certainly that was what had given her the strength to hold out against her father's ravings and her mother's quiet resignation and become a postulant.

She didn't know what had caused dissatisfaction to creep in. She'd prayed devoutly for her vocation to return as fervently as it had been before and eventually asked for an appointment with the Reverend Mother. The older nun didn't know what ailed Nuala either, but she felt that nothing would be gained by keeping her there when she was full of doubt that she could devote her entire life to God.

'Go home for a wee while,' she suggested. 'Wait on the Lord. He will speak to you, if you open your heart to listen.'

And God might have tried, but Nuala was unable to hear anything. All she heard and felt was the condemnation of the townspeople. 'Thought herself above us.'

'Vocation my foot!' 'Sent home in disgrace, she was.' Nuala didn't have to hear their words to know what people thought. She saw it in the whispered conversations and the nudges in her direction, and the disdainful looks they cast her way. She saw it in the set of people's heads, or the way their lips pursed, and in those that ignored her altogether.

Annie hadn't wanted her daughter to enter the convent in the first place, but was nevertheless confused by her decision to leave.

'What went wrong, pet?' she'd asked, and Nuala had shaken her head helplessly.

'I don't know, Mammy.'

'Will you leave the cutie alone?' Thomas had burst out. He, for one, was glad his daughter had left that unnatural shower up at the convent. 'She's seen sense at last, and come home, and that's all there is to it,' he'd roared at them all.

No one had argued with him, not then and certainly not two days later when he'd come in from the fields with a grey face, complaining of a tightening in his chest and tingling in his left arm.

Nuala couldn't help feeling she was partly to blame for the heart attack. The doctor had told her it was nothing to do with her.

'Done too much,' he'd said. 'Told him about it, but he's a stubborn old fool.' He'd told Thomas to see it as a warning and packed him off to the hospital for a few days, and it had pained Nuala to see him there so wan, and his brown, mottled and misshapen hands looking so odd against the white bedspread.

'Don't you worry about any of it,' he'd told Nuala. 'I'll soon be back in harness.'

But both Nuala and her mother knew he wouldn't be.

This was the tale Nuala related to Maeve and her family that first night of her stay. Matthew had left early, sensing the family needed to be alone together. Mary Ann and Angela had been dispatched reluctantly to bed, but as it was an occasion, Jamie and Bridget were allowed to stay up. Kevin had come over to see his aunt, and hear the news, though it was not at all good.

'He wasn't even ill. That's why it was such a shock,' Nuala said. 'Two of the men working for Tom are seeing to the place and Tom says they can stay till Daddy's more himself and then decide what's to be done.'

Kevin felt torn in two. He knew what Nuala was saying as clearly as if she'd spelt it out in letters six foot high. He needed to go back and claim his inheritance and take the heavier work from his grandfather's shoulders. He knew his grandfather would never sell. Instead he would soldier on for as long as he could, but the next heart attack could kill him. But what of his mother? How could she cope without him and his money? And how could he just desert the Mosses after all they'd done for him? But he couldn't do anything.

He swallowed hard and said, 'Mammy, I must go over there and see for myself.'

'No!' Jamie cried. He'd hated the idea of Kevin moving out of the house to live above the shop and still missed him greatly, but the North of Ireland seemed like the end of the world.

'I've got to,' Kevin said, ignoring his young brother. 'The farm will be mine one day.'

'Yours?' Maeve cried.

'Aye. Grandda is willing it to me.'

Maeve's eyes opened wider. Kevin had never said. He'd never let a whisper of it pass his lips for fear his father

404

should get wind of it. Maeve knew he wanted to go back, but had assumed it was only because he enjoyed the life.

'Did you know this?' she asked Nuala.

'Oh, aye. Everyone knows it,' Nuala said. 'Daddy always said Kevin was the only one, apart from Tom, with a feel for the place.'

Grace said nothing. Besides Nuala, she was the only one there who had known all the time about Kevin's inheritance and she was jealous of it, jealous of the life he would have because of it.

'What about Mammy?' she burst out, her voice high and troubled. 'You can't just up and leave Mammy.'

But Maeve knew, however hard it was, she had to let Kevin go, for if she didn't, and anything happened to her father, she'd never forgive herself. God in heaven, then there would be two men's deaths laid at her door.

She wished Matthew was beside her as she said to her two older children, 'Don't worry about me, either of you. Kevin, you have my blessing to go back to Ireland. The only regret I have is that I'll not be with you. We'll manage fine without the money you've given me over the years. The need for it is almost at an end anyway, because I'm getting married to Matthew.'

The children gazed at her open-mouthed. Only Nuala, strangely, was not totally surprised, because she'd seen Matthew and Maeve together before he'd left that evening. She'd sensed their closeness and seen the looks that passed between them and she'd felt happy for her sister.

'Mammy, you can't,' Grace said in an agonised whisper.

Maeve glanced at Grace and wished with all her heart she'd taken her to one side and told her about her and Matthew quietly, for she saw the girl was shocked. She'd agreed with Matthew to leave the announcement of their wedding plans till Nuala was over and settled in, but she realised she should have given a thought to how Grace would react.

Grace was shocked, dreadfully shocked. She'd never thought for a moment her mother would marry again and, after all, she was old. Matthew was too. There had been no clue; she'd never seen them even holding hands, never mind kissing. If she had she'd have told her mother straight out that it wasn't right. She must see that.

But she wasn't able to say anything, not now and in front of everyone. Anyway, the younger children, though they'd been surprised by the news at first, began firing questions at their mother.

'Not now,' Maeve said, cutting off their chatter. 'There'll be plenty of time for that later. We haven't set a date yet, but when we are married, we'll be moving from here. Matthew has enough saved and earns enough to probably enable us to buy a wee house of our own. So, you see, it's good news for us all.'

'Can we tell Mary Ann and Angie?' Bridget asked.

'Not yet awhile,' Maeve said. 'Keep it to yourselves. There's no secret about it, but I shouldn't have said anything really without Matthew being here. I just did it to put Kevin's mind at rest. Matthew might want to prepare Angela. And,' she added, 'it's really time you were both in bed.'

But before Jamie obeyed his mother he turned to Kevin. 'Are you going to live back in Ireland, then?'

Kevin shrugged. 'I don't know,' he said, and he really didn't. He saw his little brother's eyes swim with tears and he felt for him. He drew Jamie towards him and promised, 'If I stay there, Jamie, then next year you can all come and visit and stay for the whole of the summer.'

To Jamie, the following summer was aeons away, but he didn't bother protesting further. He knew there was no point once grown-ups decided things, and he turned away so that no one should see the tears that trickled down his cheeks, and made for the stairs after his sister.

'I don't know what to do about the Mosses, Mammy,' Kevin said as his brother and sister disappeared up the stairs. 'They've been good to me, good to us all. It's like slapping them in the face to leave them now.'

'You gave them no indication you might?'

'No, Mammy,' Kevin said. 'I didn't think I would have to – well, not for years – I mean I never thought of you getting married, and with the others all so little I thought I was set here for years.'

'Mammy can't marry,' Grace insisted. 'She knows she can't.' Kevin looked at his sister. Didn't the little fool realise that her mother's marriage was her passport to freedom? Kevin liked Matthew – it would be hard not to like him. But even if he'd hated his guts, he'd have tried to be pleased for his mother. He believed that Matthew would treat his mother properly and he couldn't understand how Grace could be so selfish.

Kevin got to his feet. He'd like to give his sister a piece of his mind, but not now, not on Nuala's first night here. But if he didn't get off now, he'd say something sharp to her, for her whole attitude was annoying him. His movement drew his mother and Nuala's eyes from Grace.

'Are you away?' Maeve asked.

'Aye, Mammy. I want to get back and talk to the Mosses before it gets too late. I think the sooner they know, the better.'

'What do you think they'll do?'

Kevin shrugged. 'Get someone else, I suppose.'

And what if he gets to Ireland and finds Daddy too ill and old to help him? Maeve thought. Will he stubbornly stick to it, even if it means him grubbing along to make a living – and not just for himself, but his grandparents too? Will he let the worry of it all put years on him, or will he realise if it's too much for him and come home only to join the dole queue because he's given up the job at the shop that has kept us from starving many a time?

Maeve suddenly knew what she must do.

Kevin was nearly at the door, when she said, 'Kevin, I could take on your job while you're gone. If Syd and Gwen, agree, that is.'

'You, Mammy?' Kevin's voice was high with surprise. 'Haven't you enough to do here? Anyway, what about Matthew?'

'Hear me out, son,' Maeve said. 'I'm not talking about for ever. Why don't you go over to Ireland and see how things really are? If it doesn't work out, if you feel you can't run the farm yourself with Daddy as he is, then so be it, and when you come back I'll step aside for you.'

'I don't know, Mammy,' Kevin said, shaking his head. 'It's long hours and often there's heavy lifting to be done. Anyway, there's no doubt about the farm. It's mine, or will be mine. I will work it with Grandda or without him.'

'Kevin, it's not that easy. Whatever your grandda wanted, his illness might have changed all that,' Maeve said. 'The place may have to be sold so that they can buy somewhere more suitable for themselves, d'you see?'

Kevin's mouth was set, his lip stuck out, and he almost looked the image of his despised father. But though there was no savagery behind his eyes, there was determination and Maeve knew he had no intention of selling the farm if he had any say in the matter.

She said, 'Go for a month first, son. I'll hold the fort here. I know what I'd be taking on. Didn't I work in Mountford's before the war? Then, if after a month, you decide to stay in Donegal, I'll stay on at the Mosses while they look round for someone to take the job on permanently.'

Nuala had been listening to her sister and knew her advice to Kevin had been sound. He'd written and told the family how much he enjoyed the work in the shop. She thought it would be stupid of him to burn his boats totally until he was sure what he wanted out of life and here was Maeve holding out a lifeline to him. 'Your mother's right, Kevin,' she said. 'I'll be here to see to things for a while at home, if she takes over your job.'

'And what will Matthew say?'

'He'll see the good sense of it,' Maeve said confidently. 'And it won't affect him, will it? I'm sure Nuala will cook him a meal the same as I do and neither of us is wanting to rush into marriage.'

There it was again, Grace thought, that reference to marriage. Surely her mother could see it was wrong? How could she go on as if nothing had happened when Brendan died and plan to marry someone else, anybody else?

She heard her brother promising he'd put the idea of Maeve taking his job to the Mosses that evening. Grace didn't say goodbye. She was glad to see him go because she knew she had to speak to her mother about the night her father was killed, and Kevin mustn't ever know the truth about that.

The door had scarcely closed after Kevin when Nuala turned to Grace and demanded, 'What in God's name is the matter with you? Don't you like this Matthew?'

Grace's eyes met her mother's. 'Don't,' Maeve said. 'Don't burden someone else.' But Grace had to speak out. It couldn't wait. She turned to Nuala and said, 'Mammy can't marry anyone, not just Matthew, and she knows it.'

'Grace,' Nuala said gently, feeling sure she knew what was bothering the girl, 'your father has been dead some years.'

She saw the shudder run through the young girl and her eyes darkened and seemed to sink into her face as she said almost in a whisper, 'I know how long Daddy's been dead, Nuala, because I helped to kill him.'

Nuala jumped back from her niece as if she'd been shot. She didn't believe her. She'd heard this kind of thing before. Grace had done something to disappoint, worry or anger her father and thought her action had precipitated his death just as Nuala had blamed herself for her father's heart attack.

'Stop there,' Nuala said gently. 'You're not at fault.'

'But I am!' Grace cried, and it was only the thought of the children in the attic that stopped her screaming the news at her aunt. 'I hit him with a poker and knocked him out.'

Maeve sighed. 'Aye, you did, but I finished him off.' And then, turning to her sister, knowing that now she'd have to tell it all, she went on, 'I put a cushion over his head and held it there until he was dead, and the most shocking thing of all is that neither of us is a bit sorry about it.'

Nuala stared at them both, the older sister she'd always looked up to and her young niece who'd shared her home like a sister for six years. She thought she knew them and loved them, but their words chilled her to the marrow.

'D'you know what the two of you are saying?' she cried.

'Aye we know,' Maeve said with a sigh. 'And this isn't much of a welcome for you either. I'd rather you'd not been a party to it, but then maybe there were things to be said.'

'Maeve, have you no conscience about what you've done? Have you no shame, no guilt?'

Suddenly Grace was furious with her young aunt, who'd seldom even had a cross word spoken to her in the whole of her life. 'You know damn all about it,' she snapped at her. 'My father believed clouting and punching his wife when he just had the notion in his head to do it was his right. Mammy caught it mostly, and Kevin. It was to protect Kevin as much as herself that she took us to Ireland and then she came back to face it on her own. My father also thought it was his right to spend every penny he wanted on beer, cigarettes and betting on the horses. He didn't give a tinker's cuss that the rest of us might freeze or starve to death because of it. You should have seen the state that the little ones were in when we came back here to live. They were just skin and bone and dressed in rags.' She faced her aunt defiantly and said, 'They'd had a bloody awful life and when Kevin tried to stand up to him my father really showed how brutal he could be. You can think what you like, but we're a damned sight better off without him.'

Nuala was stunned both by Grace's assault on her and also by what she'd said. 'I didn't know,' she said. 'I mean, I knew how it had been, but I thought it was better.'

'Well it wasn't,' Grace said bitterly. 'Even Kevin doesn't know the half of it. He hated Daddy so much, if he'd known some of the things that he did to Mammy, he would have sought him out and murdered him himself.'

'Dear God, this is awful,' Nuala said. 'And this is why you said your mother shouldn't marry?'

Before Grace could reply Maeve put in, 'Believe me, Grace, I once felt the same, but the guilt is mine alone. I

411

can't let the lot of you suffer because of it. When I'm married to Matthew, your lives will be better and he'll not regret it. I'll spend the rest of my life making him happy.'

Grace knew her mother was right: the little ones could not be made to suffer for any of it. Her mother was reaching out for a better life for all of them. In everything and in every way Maeve put her family before herself. Grace had no right, either, to condemn her brother and sisters to live in a back-to-back house with all its deprivations and lack of amenities when there was an alternative. And Matthew was lovely and would be good to them all.

Maeve turned to her sister and said, 'Are you disgusted by us, Nuala?'

'No, not at all,' Nuala answered. 'I admit I was shocked at first, amazed in fact. God, it's terrible, so it is, what you had to put up with. What did Brendan beat you for? Did he give you a reason?'

'He could give me a punch or clout for anything,' Maeve said. 'Because I looked at him wrong, or because he'd had a bad day, or someone had annoyed him at the pub. But the real beatings he always imagined he had a reason for. The last time, the night he died, he took his belt off to me because he'd found out about the family allowance. I'd been claiming it since the end of the war and he felt I'd cheated him. I'd not told him because he would have reduced my money and it was hard enough to manage as it was. Well, it would have been impossible, really, without Kevin's money.'

'He didn't just hit her,' Grace put in. 'He flayed her. By the time I came in he'd almost whipped the clothes from her back.'

'Dear God.' Nuala felt angrier on her sister's behalf than she could ever remember feeling about anything before, and she reached out for the two of them and held their hands. 'I think the pair of you did the world a service,' she said. 'People like Brendan Hogan deserve all they get. And neither of you has to worry that I'll ever tell anyone this, because I shan't. Both of you should forget it happened and get on with the life the Good Lord gave you. Don't let Brendan blight your life, or he will have won.'

It was just what Maeve and Grace wanted to hear, and both of them were reduced to tears. Nuala put her arms around them and the three women cried together.

The first week at the shop, Maeve had been so tired, it had been an effort to drag herself home at the end of the day. Nuala saw this and worried that her sister would wear herself out, so did everything she could to lighten the load. Maeve was thankful she was there.

Maeve had been working less than a week when Syd, who'd disappeared that day out on business of his own, suddenly burst through the door in a fever of excitement, urging both Maeve and Gwen to 'come and see what I've bought.'

Intrigued, they followed him out of the shop to gaze in wonder at the green and yellow van parked in the road directly opposite the shop. Gwen was as surprised as Maeve, for Syd had told her nothing about it either, and she stared at it open-mouthed.

'What have you done, Syd?' she exclaimed.

'What's it look like?' Syd cried. 'Bought a van, ain't I? I can deliver the groceries to the big houses in this, and in no time too. They can phone the orders through, like. It will be a new service we offer.' And he nodded at Maeve and went on, 'I'll teach young Kevin to drive when he comes back.'

'Don't be daft, you can't drive yourself,' Gwen said fearfully.

'The bloke I bought it off took me round and showed me the ropes,' Syd said. 'Nowt to it. Young Kevin will pick it up in no time.' He looked across at Gwen and went on, 'Don't start worrying now. I always intended buying summat like this. Would have done it years ago if it hadn't been for the petrol rationing, but now the ration has been increased I reckon we'll be all right.

'Come on, old girl,' he chivvied Gwen, who still looked apprehensive. 'Give us a smile. Van will look a treat painted up with our name on the side, and if we save a bit of petrol we can take a bit of a run out of a Sunday.'

Maeve wrote and told Kevin about Syd's van and how Gwen treated it like an unexploded bomb, but Kevin's answer, although he said he was glad for Syd and could understand how Gwen felt, for she hated all mechanical things, made Maeve doubt he'd ever come home.

I've never worked so hard. Grandda must have been bad for some time as the place is very run down. Uncle Tom said I can keep the two farm hands as long as it takes to get the place straight. Grandda can do little at the moment and he tires easily.

Maeve knew how much hard work the farm was in the spring and summer seasons, and remembered she'd seen little of her father or even her brothers then, as they were out during all the hours of daylight.

Three weeks after Kevin had gone to Ireland the letter came that Maeve had been semi-expecting.

I can't leave Grandda, Mammy, and I don't want to. This is my place and where I want to be. Tell Mr

Moss I'm sorry – I'll write to them myself too, for I owe them a great deal. I'll be home to see you all and get the rest of my things once the hay is collected in.

Maeve felt as though she'd lost Kevin all over again. She decided to speak to Matthew about going to Donegal for a wee holiday in the summer the following year. It would do them all good and she longed to see her parents again. And it was right that they should meet Matthew. She was sure they'd love him as much as her children did.

By the time she got to the shop to tell Syd the only vehicle Kevin was likely to drive in the near future was a tractor, it was to find they already knew. Kevin had written to them as promised. They were disappointed, but could see that Kevin had responsibilities to his grandfather and the family farm. Maeve felt sorry for them, for she knew how much they'd thought of her son.

But Gwen preferred Maeve to Kevin working in the shop because she was company for her. She'd never had a woman friend before and had never felt the lack of one until recently. She'd been Syd's wife and helpmate, and Stanley's mother, and it had been enough. But with Stanley's death and her slide into the depression that isolated her from the shop she was lonely. She hadn't realised how lonely till the arrival of Maeve. Gwen soon began looking forward to her company during the day and especially at mealtimes.

From Maeve's early days in the shop, it had been apparent to Gwen that she was seemingly unafraid of entering turbulent water and avoiding any mention of Stanley Moss's death in case it should upset Gwen. She didn't appear to see her as a poor creature who needed special consideration as others, including Syd, had thought of her, but only as a mother who'd tragically lost her only son.

In her first week at the shop they'd all been talking about Kevin one day over dinner, and how much Maeve would miss him.

'When he and Grace were away before,' Maeve had said, 'my mammy took photographs of them to show me how they were growing up. Sometimes I was upset to see them doing things I couldn't share in, but in another way they were a great comfort. It also helped the others remember their older brother and sister. Even now, that album is one of their favourite books.'

Then Maeve, with a look at Gwen, had added, 'When I used to come and take the money from Kevin on Fridays, I saw all the photographs you have of your son. He was a fine-looking boy.'

It was said so naturally. Syd held his breath and Gwen stared at Maeve speechless. They never spoke of Stanley, fearful of upsetting each other. But their son had been twenty-five when he died, with twenty-five years of the laughter, tears and worry that the rearing of any child brought about. Gwen realised suddenly that it was unnatural never to talk about him at all. Maybe if they had, they'd have been able to offer each other some comfort. It had been as if his life were something to be ashamed of, or as if he hadn't existed, and yet he'd been the light of their lives.

She knew that not a day would go by that she'd not think with regret that his young life had been snatched from him and yet she knew he'd always felt the war to be justified – he'd told her that often. She'd loved him and been proud of him and it was about time she said so.

'Yes,' she'd said to Maeve, and though her eyes had shone with unshed tears, her voice had been firm. 'Stanley was a fine boy and I was and am very proud of him. I was his mother for twenty-five years and I only wish it had been longer.'

Syd had felt the breath leave his body in a huge sigh. He'd wished he could put his arms round his wife, for he knew what the declaration had cost her, but he'd been embarrassed to show affection in front of Maeve.

Maeve had no such reserve and she'd grasped Gwen's trembling hands and felt the raw emotion running through her body. 'And so do I wish you'd had him longer,' she'd said. 'We owe a debt to all those who gave us our freedom and I for one will never forget it.'

Syd had watched them with tears in his own eyes. He knew the healing process for Gwen, which had been chipped away by Kevin, had been split asunder by his mother. The bond between Maeve and Gwen Moss had begun at that moment and it grew deeper as the days slid by.

Gwen looked forward to Maeve coming in each day, enjoying both their easy chats together, the confidences they shared and the support they were to one another. She found talking about Stanley easier and easier the more she did it and Maeve was able to build up a complete picture of the boy, his adolescence and early manhood, which had been snuffed out far too soon.

In return, Maeve told Gwen about her other children, her family in Ireland and her youngest sister living with her. Gwen knew of Maeve's violent, unhappy marriage, and she thought that Brendan was no great loss to mankind. She remembered he'd tried to strangle her Syd and, to her chagrin, neither Syd nor Kevin had wished to

417

press charges. The man had got away with it and she'd been glad when she'd heard of his death.

Kevin had been much happier too, though he'd been worried over how his mother would cope financially, and Gwen told Syd to double the boy's wages. She'd not actually met Maeve at that time, though she'd appeared at the shop every Friday for the money for Kevin's father, until his death, but of course that had been some years before.

The shambling apologetic creature Gwen had sometimes glimpsed at that time had been an object of pity and bore no resemblance to the confident woman that stood before Gwen later and offered to take her son's place in the shop. It was the fear that had once surrounded Maeve that had given her such a defeated look.

Gwen didn't want to lose Maeve; she'd shaped up better than she'd ever have thought. She knew she was getting married, but she seemed in no hurry. There wasn't even the date fixed yet, so why shouldn't she work there till the deed was done? Maeve had told her now all the children were at school she'd intended looking for a job.

Because the hours were long for a woman with a family to see to, Gwen put it to Syd that they should offer the job to Maeve with reduced hours. In fact, so anxious was Gwen to keep Maeve, she said she would serve in the shop the hours Maeve couldn't do. The shop held no terrors for her now, and more and more she'd been standing in while Maeve or Syd took a break. Syd was glad to see his Gwen so recovered, yet he didn't want her to work full time either as she'd once done. It was time for her to put her feet up a bit. This arrangement with Maeve might be the answer for them both.

The new arrangement meant Maeve could leave at half four on Tuesdays and Thursdays, while retaining her half-days on Wednesdays, and the Mosses suggested another half-day on Monday. Only on Saturdays would she work to six and Friday she wouldn't be home until about half-past nine because it was the shop's late night.

Maeve discussed the matter with Matthew. 'Do you want to do it?' he asked dubiously.

'Yes, yes, I do,' she said. 'I always intended taking a job when Angela and Mary Ann began school. I didn't want full time, though, but I could manage this, and I like the work and the customers.'

'Yes, but your idea of taking a job was surely before we decided to marry,' Matthew said, and Maeve saw the set of his mouth and knew he was displeased. 'You'll have no need to work outside of the home then,' he went on, 'nor little time either. You'll have plenty to do and I don't want Angela to become a latchkey child.'

Always Angela, Maeve thought, but she bit back her irritation. She was, despite Matthew's disapproval, loath to give up the semi-independence she was enjoying and the satisfaction of receiving a wage she'd earned. Maybe she'd feel differently when the ring was on her finger and Matthew was able to provide for his family.

But until then Maeve knew she'd have to proceed with care. She knew Matthew wasn't that keen on her working because she was sometimes too tired to go for a walk with him in the evenings and really it was the only time they could be alone.

She knew she must try harder and not rely on Nuala to keep him company. Not that she seemed to mind. She'd fitted into the family so well it was almost as though she'd lived there all her life.

Mary Ann too was delighted with Nuala's company and became very fond of her. 'She's *my* aunt really,' she told Angela rather smugly, 'but you can share her if you like.'

'She will be Angela's aunt too when her daddy marries Mammy,' Bridget pointed out. 'And you two will be sisters.'

Mary Ann and Angela regarded one anther gravely. Such a thought had not occurred to them.

'And Mammy Maeve will be my real mammy then,' Angela said triumphantly.

Maeve was the only mother she had ever known and she loved her dearly. But she liked Nuala too, and so did her daddy, and she was more than willing to go out with them, especially on Saturdays when Maeve was working all day.

And that was really what Matthew was complaining about. 'I never get to see you,' he moaned.

'Let me work for just a little longer,' Maeve pleaded with him. 'You must admit the money will be useful.'

Matthew couldn't argue with Maeve, for once she'd agreed to marry him, he'd immediately started looking at the price of houses in the areas they'd discussed living in. Not only were houses in short supply and snapped up almost as soon as they were empty, the scarcity of them had made the prices shoot up and Matthew knew his gratuity and savings would barely scrape up the minimum deposit.

'How long is a little longer?' he asked Maeve eventually.

'Just another six months or so, till after Christmas,' Maeve said. 'Then we can get married in the spring.'

Matthew reluctantly agreed and sealed the bargain with a kiss. Maeve submitted eagerly to his embraces and kisses too, knowing they needed time alone. He never pressed her to go further than she wanted to – he was that type of man.

Sometimes, in his arms, she remembered the lovemaking of Richard with a pang of regret. Matthew did not disturb her senses in the same way at all, but she allowed him to go a little further as the weeks passed, feeling sure that was what he wanted. After being away for years and having no wife to offer him any sort of relief or comfort when he came back, she'd been worried that once she'd agreed to marrying him, he'd take his lovemaking further, especially as she'd already been married. But he seemed in no hurry, and seemed happy to go at Maeve's pace, and she loved the man for his consideration and understanding.

Anyway, she'd had enough of Brendan groping and pawing at her just to satisfy himself to last her a lifetime, and until Richard came into her life, she'd lost all interest in sex. She imagined Matthew would be a gentle lover and was determined to please him when they were married. She owed much to him and she'd never forget it, or make him regret marrying her. Anyway, making love with Matthew would help banish the thoughts of her and Richard cavorting together, which she still thought of guiltily and far too often.

She was determined to make this Christmas, the first since she agreed to marry Matthew, a wonderful one for the whole family, with presents for everyone – provided of course that the things were in the shops. She'd already saved a tidy sum in the Post Office, and by Christmas there would be more. She was as excited as the weans and could hardly wait for Christmas morning.

TWENTY-FIVE

Gwen loved nothing more than a wedding and was very excited about Maeve's, which was to be undertaken in a registry office with the reception held in a room off The Bell public house in Bell Barn Road.

'D'you mind it not being done properly?' she asked Maeve one day. 'You know, in a church and everything?'

'It doesn't worry me in the slightest,' Maeve said. 'The way I see it, I was married to Brendan in a church by a priest. We made vows about honouring and obeying, for richer for poorer, for better and for worse. Those words haunted me for years. I want my marriage to Matthew Bradshaw to be totally different.'

The clergy, however, had different ideas. Eventually, the news of Maeve's marriage filtered through to Father Trelawney. He quizzed Bridget about the hours her mother worked and presented himself at her doorway one Wednesday afternoon in late September.

Maeve used the Monday afternoons to do her washing and Wednesday afternoon to do the ironing. Often Elsie would come in and talk to her while she ironed, help her to fold the sheets and make them both fortifying cups of tea.

That afternoon Elsie was just about to go next door when she spotted the priest coming down the entry and decided to stay where she was. She knew fine where he was heading for and why. So did Maeve when she saw the man's shadow darken the window.

She gave a sigh of exasperation, and put the crumpled clothes back in the basket, removed the flat iron from the bars of the fire, and made the tea she'd intended for Elsie before she answered the priest's imperious rap on the door.

'Well, hello, Maeve,' he said, making his way into the room. Maeve helped him off with his hat and coat, which she placed over the back of the chair in which he sat. 'We haven't seen you for this long while.'

'I do go to Mass, Father,' Maeve put in quickly, handing Father Trelawney a cup of tea. 'But I go to the early one.'

'And why not at nine o'clock with your children?'

Maeve shrugged. 'I have a lot to do on Sunday, Father. Matthew, my . . .' she glanced at the priest and went on, 'my fiancé likes to see something of me. We often go out for the day.' But there was another reason, one this priest could never know. Since the confession Maeve had made at St Chad's, when she'd admitted to killing her husband, she'd never gone to confession again.

There was no point, for she couldn't truthfully say she was sorry for killing Brendan, or indeed that she wouldn't have done the selfsame thing again. No priest could therefore absolve her sins, and sometimes she felt her soul must be as black as pitch. She couldn't add to that the mortal sin of missing Mass but she wasn't in a state of grace and therefore could not go to the rails and receive Communion. The old priest who took the early Mass was doddery now, nearly blind, and not aware totally of what was going on. He wouldn't notice whether Maeve took Communion or not.

423

Not so Father Trelawney. He'd be down badgering about the bad example she was showing her children until in exasperation she might just hurl the truth at his sanctimonious face.

The priest watched Maeve's face working. He doubted that she was being totally truthful and guessed she'd deliberately chosen to go to the one Mass he didn't preside over. But there was no point in tackling her about that – she'd only deny it. There was a far more pressing problem that he had to address.

'Matthew Bradshaw,' he said. 'Is he the man you intend to marry?'

'I don't merely intend to, it's a fact. As I said, he is my fiancé and we are to be married in March next year.'

'Maeve, the man is not of our faith,' the priest reminded her gently.

'I know that. What of it?'

'Maeve, surely you realise the significance of this? Will he turn?'

'No, Father, he won't.'

'Have you asked him?'

'No, and I won't either,' Maeve snapped. 'I married a man of my own faith and look where that got me. Matthew will make me a good husband and my children a good father. To be honest, I don't give a damn what religion he is, or even if he has any religious leanings at all.'

The priest was affronted, Maeve could see, and he was also aware Maeve didn't seem bothered about it. He shook his head sorrowfully and said, 'You realise you won't be able to marry in church.'

'I know that. We are to be married in the registry office, like many before us.'

'So, you'll not be married in the sight of God, then. You understand that?'

Maeve gave a grim laugh and said, 'D'you know, Father, I don't think that God is as small-minded as you would have us believe.'

'God will not be mocked, Maeve!' the priest cried, shocked.

'Will you listen to me, Father?' Maeve said grimly. 'It's not God I'm mocking.'

'Maeve, whatever you say, you will be committing adultery every time you sleep with this man Matthew Bradshaw. Any children born from the union will be illegitimate – bastards!'

Bitterness rose like bile in Maeve's throat and her eyes sparked with anger. She turned to the priest and pressed her face close to his. 'Who are you to call names of me and mine?' she demanded. 'I bring my children up to be decent human beings and good Catholics and I will continue to do so, and for their sake and no one else's. As for any children I might have had with Matthew, I'm afraid that will never happen. I thought you knew that Brendan fixed that for me with one of his beatings. As well as him killing my unborn child, he damaged my insides so badly I can never carry another.'

Maeve saw the look of shock on the priest's face and knew he hadn't known, but Maeve had no sympathy for him. 'Never again will you have a hand in controlling my life,' she spat out. 'I shall live it as I see fit.'

There was nothing further Father Trelawney could do. Maeve had made her position very clear and the priest was clearly offended. He got to his feet, put his cup and saucer on the table and accepted the hat and coat Maeve gave him without a word. She left him struggling into it, crossed the room and opened the door wide.

'Good day, Maeve.'

'Father,' Maeve said, inclining her head slightly. As she watched him walk across the cobbled yard, reaction set in. Her legs began to shake and she sat down at her table, sank her head in her hands, and wept.

And that was how Elsie found Maeve a little later. She put one arm round Maeve's shoulder and pulled her hands from her face with the other hand.

'Come on,' she said. 'Don't let the old bugger upset you. You've wept enough tears in your life already to float a battleship. Don't let that prating bloody hypocrite break you up.'

'He said . . . he said—' Maeve began through her gasping sobs, but Elsie cut across her.

'Who gives a damn what he said? He said plenty to you before and none of it a blasted bit of use.'

Maeve knew Elsie was right, and she was the only one Maeve could talk to. She couldn't load her confrontation with Father Trelawney on the children and neither Matthew nor Gwen Moss could begin to understand the power the priests had.

She asked for Nuala's advice and opinion that night in bed, for her sister had come to know Matthew very well, especially as they now also worked in the same place. When Maeve's hours had been reduced, Nuala had said she'd look for a job herself, not wishing to be a drain on Maeve indefinitely, and Matthew had got her set on at his place almost immediately.

So Maeve, valuing her opinion, said, 'You know Matthew's not of our faith, Nuala? Does it bother you, my marrying him?'

Nuala hoped Maeve hadn't heard her gasp of surprise and dismay. She didn't want to discuss Matthew. She'd managed to keep her own feelings for him in check so far and she swallowed hard and willed her voice not to break.

'No. Not if you truly love him and he you,' she said, and asked, 'You do love him, don't you?'

Maeve was nothing if not honest. 'I care for him a great deal. I do love things about him, but not as I once thought I loved Brendan.' And Richard, she might have added.

'Maybe you did love him at the time.'

'But then why didn't it last?' Maeve cried. 'Is all love like that? Will it always shrivel up and die? If it does you can keep it! True deep friendship and caring for one another like Matthew and I do seems more enduring than a grand passion, don't you think?'

'I'm the last one to ask, aren't I?' Nuala said, hoping to close the conversation. Her heart was thudding against her ribs and the roof of her mouth was dry. She loved Matthew with all her being, but she thought he was unaware of it and Maeve must never, never know. She lay quiet for a minute and then went on, 'After Christmas I'll be moving out. You'll want to start married life without me hanging on to your coat-tails.'

Maeve made a sound of protest, but Nuala knew she had to go; to stay and watch Matthew and Maeve together would be torture, and too dangerous for all of them. She went on, 'No, listen, Maeve. There's a girl I work with, and at home there's just her and her mother and they have a lodger to help pay the rent. The one they have now is leaving to get married after Christmas. I've asked her to give me first refusal on the room.'

'I thought you'd be moving with us.'

'Now, why would I?' Nuala said, and added, 'You'll need all the space and some time alone.'

Maeve knew Nuala was right, but she also knew she'd miss her about the place and hoped her sister wouldn't find her new life too strange.

Maeve looked at Brian Hogan, the father of her late husband, as he lolled against her front door, obviously awaiting her return from her job at the shop. It was the Monday following the priest's visit, and she had a mountain of washing awaiting her attention, but knew first she'd have to deal with the man she'd always detested.

She made him no greeting, and just managed to avoid wrinkling her nose at the fetid stink coming off him as she approached.

'Come on,' Brian growled. 'I thought you finished at that place at one o'clock. My feet are stuck to the floor in this perishing cold.'

'I do finish at one,' Maeve said testily. 'But I have to walk home, you know.'

She smelt the man's sour breath, a mixture of stale beer and cigarettes and the decaying stumps of teeth going rotten in his mouth, and wondered, as she fumbled to open the door, how he'd known she was working in the shop. She surmised it must have been Father Trelawney that had told him.

Brian Hogan followed her in and looked about him, and Maeve was pleased that he could see the room looking so comfortable. There was a fire laid in the grate ready to set a match to, with a full scuttle of coal beside it inside the gleaming brass fender. She saw Brian's eyes swivel to the wireless and accumulator one side of the chimney breast, the mantelshelf full of ornaments and knick-knacks, and the table covered with a blue-and-white-checked cloth, and was annoyed with herself for caring one jot about his opinion.

She noticed the man was stooped and now looked very old. She knew he no longer worked; he'd retired the previous year and now existed on the old-age pension. It wasn't much, and Maeve hoped he wasn't on the scrounge, for not a penny piece would he get out of her.

'Any tea then, girl?' Brian snapped out. 'God, my tongue's hanging out.'

Why didn't she tell him to go to hell? Maeve thought. To get out of her life and leave her alone and get tea in his own house. Instead, she filled the kettle and lit the gas. She felt sorry for Carmel, the wife of Brendan's youngest brother, who had the care of the crabbed old man.

Maeve remembered how at Lily's funeral it was suggested she take on the care of her father-in-law, as she no longer had a husband to care for. She soon told the Hogan family what they could do with that notion, and in no uncertain terms. She'd made clear she'd not even cross the street for a man as vindictive and cruel as her Brendan had been and she knew his father was the same.

Still, it was apparent that there was little being done for Brian Hogan by anyone. He'd obviously not shaved for days, and while stubble covered one half of his face, grimy wrinkled skin covered the other, with sagging pouches beneath the bloodshot eyes and the hair matted on his head. He was fatter than Maeve remembered, with his distended belly straining at the buttons of his donkey jacket. The state of his filthy hands, with black-encrusted nails, that reached out for the cup of tea Maeve handed over turned her stomach.

She knew he'd slurp the tea, and was relieved that at least he drank from the cup and had not tipped it into the saucer as she'd seen him do before now. She wondered what he wanted, and how soon she could get rid of him, and decided to ask.

'Why have you come?'

Brian swallowed another mouthful of tea, though it was scalding, wiped his mouth on the greasy sleeve of his jacket and said, 'What's this about our Kevin going to Ireland? Why did no one tell us?'

'Why should we tell you?' Maeve said. 'Kevin's well old enough to decide what to do with his life. If you were concerned about your grandchildren you'd have been down before this to see them. No one ever came from your house except Lily, and then not often.'

'You could have come up to our house.'

'The time or two I did, I wasn't made welcome,' Maeve said. 'Anyway, Kevin's gone. Is that all you've come to ask?'

'People say he's run away to avoid the draft.'

'Well, they're wrong.'

'Funny thing to do, though, isn't it? To just take up and leave like that?'

'It's not any of your business, but I'll tell you anyway,' Maeve said, facing Brian Hogan squarely. 'Kevin went back to the farm because my father, who was running it virtually single-handed, had a heart attack. The farm will be Kevin's after his death, so he obviously wanted to go back and help him.'

At her words, she saw the light of speculation leap into Brian's eyes. 'What d'you mean? Your old man will leave Kevin the farm?' he blustered. 'What does a lad of that age know? Best thing you can do when it does fall into his hands is sell it. Get a bit of money for yourself.'

'I have no intention of doing that,' Maeve said stiffly, knowing that it was the possibility of money that was interesting Brian. One sniff of it and the whole Hogan clan would descend on her like a pack of wolves. 'Kevin will keep the farm,' she said. 'It's been in our family for generations and my parents think he's a born farmer. I have no need of money.'

'Ah yes,' Brain said with a sneer. 'I heard that you were getting married, and to a Prod as well.' He licked his lips and said, 'It's disgusting, that is. Father Trelawney told me. And you only able to marry in the registry office. That's not a proper marriage, not in the eyes of God it isn't. You'll be living in sin. I wonder what Brendan would make of it all?'

'What Brendan would make of it?' Maeve repeated with a screech. Fury almost consumed her. 'Why should he make anything of it? The man's been dead over three and a half years. And I'll tell you something else: I'm free to marry anyone I like, and in any way I choose. I don't give a damn for you, your family or your opinions.'

She crossed to the door and flung it wide open. 'Go on, get out. You've had your say and much good it's done you. I'm finished with the lot of you.'

Brian took his time draining his cup of tea and then got to his feet slowly. 'Brendan should have beaten that bad temper out of you while he had the chance,' he said with a sneer.

'Get out!' Maeve screamed, beside herself with rage. 'Get out before I brain you with a bloody saucepan.'

And she knew she was capable of it. She forced herself to stand by the door as Brian shambled out. She wanted to launch herself on him and scratch his eyes and rake her nails down his face. She longed to knock him to the floor and bang his head over and over on the cobbles and kick his body as Brendan had often done to her.

She slammed the door shut when Brian was barely through it, shaking with temper. She refused to give way to tears.

Brendan had made her cry time and enough and she'd not allow his father to let her weaken that way. She gathered up the washing in a frenzy. They'd seldom had such a good maiding as they had that day and after it Maeve found the bad humour had been worked out of her – and she saw the funny side of it. She wondered that she'd let a dirty shabby old man bother her and she remembered the look on his face when she'd bawled at him. She chuckled to herself and knew that she and Elsie would laugh about it later.

Kevin came home for a week in November, just after his eighteenth birthday. Maeve and the whole family were delighted to have him back. Maeve's heart swelled with pride as she held him close. He'd shed the last of his boyhood whilst he'd been away, she realised, and knew her son had become a man. Jamie was like a dog with two tails, and sat at Kevin's feet listening to him speaking about the farm that he himself had never seen and of the grandparents he'd never met.

Grace felt a wave of homesickness wash over her as Kevin spoke, and she plied him with questions. Kevin, glad his sister was totally better of whatever had ailed her about their mammy's engagement, answered her readily. He'd noticed the difference in his sister immediately. She certainly wasn't the same girl who acted so strange the night Nuala had arrived, when she'd moaned on about their mother not marrying a man who'd been her friend for years. Instead of congratulating her, she'd acted so oddly and he'd been determined to take her to task about it at the first opportunity.

But she'd seemed to have got over it on her own. Maybe, he'd reflected, it was something girls went through. There had been a mate of his at school in Ireland who'd known

432

all about girls, having a bevy of older sisters and an inquisitive nature. It was all to do with hormones, he'd said. In the quiet corners of the school yard, he'd whispered about things that had happened to girls that the other boys could scarcely credit. Kevin had watched Grace overtly for weeks afterwards, dying to ask her questions, but knowing she'd never discuss such things with him.

Still, whatever it had all been about, he was glad she'd got her hormones sorted out at last. It would be one person fewer to worry about. In fact he found Grace amazingly good company and allowed himself to be bullied into going dancing with her and her friends. He protested every step of the way that he'd never be able to do it, and then when he got there, took to it so well that he seldom sat down all night.

Grace had often asked Nuala along with them too, but she never would go, though Grace didn't think it much of a life for her aunt, staying by the fireside night after night. Maeve told Grace Nuala had probably got out of the habit of socialising after all the years of being in the convent. The only places Nuala ever went were to work and sometimes for a walk in the summer evenings, usually accompanied by Matthew, Angela and Mary Ann. Now, in the dark winter evenings, she was inside every night, and if it hadn't been for the outings she enjoyed on Saturday, when she and Matthew would take the little girls out while Maeve worked, she'd never have gone across the threshold at all.

Grace was right: it was no life for a young woman, and she mentioned it to Elsie one evening. But Elsie's reply puzzled Maeve for she said, 'You might be worried about her, Maeve, but I'd be more worried about the time she spends with Matthew.'

Maeve stared at her. 'Elsie, Matthew's only being kind.'

'I'm not saying he isn't,' Elsie said. 'But your sister sees him more than you do.'

'Of course she does, they work in the same place,' Maeve burst out. 'Surely you're not suggesting—'

'I'm suggesting nothing,' Elsie insisted. 'But in my opinion, I'd keep an eye on it.'

But Maeve told herself Elsie was being ridiculous and she did nothing. Certainly she wasn't going to tell her sister what Elsie had insinuated. She told herself Matthew was twenty years Nuala's senior and probably looked on her as a daughter, as in fact she could well be. If she said anything to either of them it would either be seen as ludicrous, or else might cause bad feeling. Nuala might be upset at her suspicions and Matthew would almost certainly be angry. It would, at any rate, spoil the friendship between the two of them. Then Nuala would be truly lonely and Maeve would feel incredibly guilty about that.

'It isn't as if you're always gadding about yourself,' Elsie said. 'You go nowhere either.'

'I'm a married woman, Elsie. It's different.'

'You *were* a married woman,' Elsie said. 'But you're no longer married. You're courting a fellow. You should spend more time alone with him. Why doesn't he take you to the pictures a time or two?'

Easier said than done, Maeve thought. With the constraints of the family and her job, it was hard to find time to blow her nose, never mind opportunity to go out with Matthew. He didn't seem to mind much. He never moaned, anyway. 'For God's sake, we're mature people, not lovesick youngsters,' she cried to Elsie.

But in the end Maeve did say something to Matthew. He seemed evasive and reluctant to talk, but eventually she pinned him down one evening about a week after Kevin had returned to Donegal. Kevin had explained to his tearful young brother that farms didn't run themselves and a week's holiday was all he could spare, but he reassured Jamie and his sisters again that they were all welcome to stay the following summer. That suited Maeve's plans, for she'd love to go over herself for a wee holiday then and introduce her children, Angela and Matthew to her parents.

And that is the subject Maeve brought up with Matthew as they walked through the dark chilly streets in late November.

'Let's wait and see how the money pans out first,' Matthew said.

'But, Matthew, I am dying to see them all again.'

'I understand that,' Matthew said, 'really I do. But houses, even terraced houses, are very expensive. I mean, the housing shortage is such, people can ask what they like.'

'I could keep on the job at Moss's to help out,' Maeve suggested tentatively.

'No, Maeve. Bringing up the children and looking after the home will be your job when we're married. I didn't expect Deidre to work outside the home and I shan't expect you to.'

Maeve bristled. Were her wishes to be of no account? She was not to take a job, even if that job meant she could take herself and the children away on a wee holiday to the parents she longed to see again. But she bit back her annoyance, knowing that Matthew hadn't seen it that way. He'd seen it as a way of looking after her. For someone to want to look after and care about her would be a novel experience – totally different from Brendan's bullying dominance. It gave her a feeling of safety and security, and she decided not to argue with Matthew about it. Maybe they could discuss it again once they were married.

It was as Maeve was kissing Matthew good night that she noticed his reluctance, his drawing away from her slightly, and a niggle of doubt began in her mind. She pulled away from his embrace a little, so that she could see his face in the light of the streetlamp.

'What is it?'

'Nothing. What do you mean?'

'It's just that you seem odd, different.'

'Oh, Maeve, I have a lot in my head at the moment,' Matthew protested. 'I'm sorry.'

'It's not me?'

'No, of course not.'

'You haven't gone off me?'

'No, don't be silly.'

'Matthew, I'm not being silly,' Maeve said. She didn't say Elsie had expressed disquiet over their association. She had the impression Matthew wouldn't like the idea of her discussing him with a neighbour, but she had to know how he felt about her. 'Just tell me if your feelings towards me have changed,' she said.

'No,' Matthew said, and he pulled her close to him, although Maeve could still see his face. And he spoke the truth when he said, 'I care deeply for you, I always have.'

He'd never said he loved her and Maeve didn't expect him to, so what he said satisfied her.

'Maybe we should go out a time or two?' she suggested. 'To the pictures perhaps, or for a meal? We need more time alone.'

'We have to watch the pennies, Maeve,' Matthew said, and then, seeing her face fall, went on, 'Well, maybe it wouldn't hurt now and again. In fact it will do us both good. We'll see to it in the New Year maybe, all right?'

'That would be grand, Matthew,' Maeve said, and in gratitude she reached up and kissed him gently on the lips. Matthew grasped her to him and kissed her hard, parting her lips with his tongue for the first time.

Maeve yearned to be loved and even desired, and she responded eagerly, wanting to please him. Matthew gave a sigh. He ran his hands over her body and opened her coat and pressed her against him. She closed her eyes and imagined it was Richard fondling and feeling her body. She did not push Matthew away or tell him to stop, and when she felt his hands caressing her breasts she gasped, remembering Richard's lips upon them. But Matthew suddenly pulled back from her.

'I'm sorry, Maeve. I forgot myself,' he said.

Maeve reached up and kissed him. 'It's all right,' she said. 'Don't worry about it.' She knew that she'd probably never feel truly passionate about sex with Matthew but she could pretend. She cared about him too much ever to want to hurt him. She only wanted his happiness. Surely that was enough.

The following Monday morning at the shop Maeve noticed Gwen looked harassed and tired, and grey bags sat beneath her eyes.

'Are you not well?' she asked.

'I'm well enough,' Gwen answered. 'But tired out.'

'The neighbours again?'

Gwen nodded.

'Something should be done about it,' Maeve said. 'Have you told the police?'

Gwen shook her head. 'Syd wants them out,' she said, 'but it's hard this close to Christmas.'

Maeve knew it was hard, but she thought that the Mosses had suffered enough. There were two families living in the flat adjoining theirs, both rough and both, to Maeve's shame, Irish. They'd clamoured for the place when they'd heard the previous tenants had been rehoused and Syd and Gwen had felt sorry for them, especially as they had children in tow. But since their arrival, the Mosses had begun to regret their generosity. The neighbours gave Maeve little enough bother, except for the occasional noise loud enough to be heard in the grocery store, but they made enough row to disturb the Mosses' sleep most nights and the real trouble came on Friday and Saturday nights when the families, usually well oiled, came home from the pub and started arguing.

'It's nothing like your situation, Maeve,' Gwen was quick to assure her. 'God alone knows, your position was terrible, but with these families . . . Well, the women are as bad, or worse, than the men.'

Maeve could only take Gwen's word for it, never having witnessed the rowing herself. However, she believed her employers, not least because their haggard expressions bore testimony to the nights they claimed were broken with the raucous noises from the flat: thumps, crashes and screams, interspersed with Irish tunes played on the gramophone and usually accompanied by tuneless – but very loud – voices that went on into the early hours of the following morning. Then there were the fights in the yard that Syd, risking life and limb, had had to try to stop many a time to prevent murder being done, although Maeve doubted the wisdom of such action.

'What are we to do?' Gwen asked Maeve in despair that Monday morning. 'I dread going into the bedroom to sleep and that's the truth. When it gets to around half eleven or twelve, my stomach gets knotted up inside. I never know what sort of night we're going to have.'

Maeve thought they'd be better telling the people to quit – Christmas or no Christmas. She knew there was a certain class of people it was impossible to help. Whatever you gave them, they took more. Consideration was interpreted as weakness and taken advantage of, and a good example of this was the rent Syd asked for the flat, which was a mere five shillings, which Gwen had let slip hadn't been paid for months.

It wasn't Maeve's place to tell her employers how to run their affairs. She could only utter comforting noises and make Gwen a soothing cup of tea, smooth Syd's ruffled feathers and get on with the job at hand.

It was mid-December before the matter came to a head. Christmas was in the air, coloured lights framed the festive windows, trade was better than ever before with the slackening on rationing, and Maeve and Syd were rushed off their feet.

Maeve was working her last month's notice and saddened about it. Gwen and Syd had done all they could to make her stay on, but she knew Matthew would be against it and, after all, she owed him something.

Then, early one Sunday morning, Maeve and the rest of the house were roused from their bed by a persistent knock on the door.

Gwen, dishevelled and distraught, stood on the doorstep. From her garbled account, Maeve understood that Syd and two of the male members of the flat were in hospital. Gwen was beside herself. Maeve had almost expected something like this to happen and had fastened up the buttons on her coat before Gwen had finished speaking.

When they eventually reached the hospital both Gwen and Maeve were relieved to find Syd was not as bad as they'd first feared. The doctor was quick to say he thought that the milk bottle hurled from an upstairs window might have done untold damage, but fortunately all Syd was suffering from was concussion.

The two opposing families had started their disagreement in the pub, continued it on the journey home and decided to settle matters in the yard. The screams, screeches and general disturbance had been investigated by Syd. By then the women, having reached the flat and for once in agreement, had declared war against their menfolk. This had involved tipping anything heavy on to the heads of those below. Syd, who'd gone out to try to settle the confrontation amicably, had been hit in the mêlée and rendered unconscious and Gwen had thought that he'd been killed.

'Those awful people must go,' Gwen said to Maeve. 'Help me see to it, Maeve.'

And Maeve saw to it. She ignored the pleas of the family that they had no place else and the strident cries of the children, though she found that harder. She just had two weeks more at the Mosses' shop, for she was leaving on Christmas Eve and wanted the eviction all settled by then, and with Gwen's permission gave the tenants a fortnight's notice. She wasn't proud of herself for doing it – she knew how difficult accommodation was to find – but she did feel immensely sorry for the Mosses. They had tried to help the homeless families and had been kicked in the teeth for their effort.

'Never mind,' Maeve said to Gwen on Christmas Eve as they watched the two families load their meagre possessions on to a cart. 'You win some and you lose some.'

And Gwen turned her tearful face to Maeve and said, 'As long as we never lose you, Maeve, we will be content.'

'You won't lose me, don't worry,' Maeve promised. 'I'll be popping along to see you.'

But Gwen and Syd knew it wouldn't be the same. They'd interviewed people to take her place, though Maeve knew no one had been engaged. 'How will you manage?' Maeve asked for the umpteenth time as she got ready to leave on Christmas Eve, because although Syd was now officially recovered and back in the shop, he still looked far from well in her opinion.

'The way we did before,' Gwen said. 'I'll help for now.' She saw Maeve's worried eyes as she glanced at Syd and went on, 'I'll not let him do too much; don't fret. Eventually someone suitable will come along.'

Maeve knew plenty of capable women had already come forward, but Gwen had found fault with all of them. Maybe now that I've actually left, Gwen will be able to get someone else in my place, Maeve thought, as she made her way home that night.

But she resolved to push the Mosses' problems to one side. It was nearly Christmas and she had packages for the children hidden in the wardrobe in her bedroom. She had more food in the cupboards than she'd ever had before and a further basket of goodies that Gwen had given her that very evening. She gave a sigh of contentment. Now that rationing on clothes had finally ended, she looked forward to getting the children some warm winter clothes in the New Year and something decent for each of them to wear at the wedding. Life was good, she decided, very, very good, and from now on was going to get even better.

TWENTY-SIX

Because the Mosses' tenants had not vacated the flat till Christmas Eve, when Syd and Gwen had been rushed off their feet in the shop, neither of them had had time to inspect it, and when Gwen did, just after Christmas, she nearly fainted with shock at the state of it. She knew she'd never be able to clean it herself and, anyway, Syd could never manage in the shop on his own. But something had to be done about the flat and she wondered if Maeve would help her out.

Maeve was finding time hanging heavy on her hands. Christmas Day had been just wonderful and so had Boxing Day, when Matthew had treated them all to a pantomime. It had been a first for everyone, but they'd soon got into the swing of it, booing and cheering with the rest of the audience. It had been *Cinderella,* and the children had been entranced by the dazzling costumes and the sheer beauty of the whole spectacle. They'd gone home happier than they could ever remember being, and Maeve had again felt overwhelmed by Matthew's generosity.

But then Grace, Nuala and Matthew returned to work, and the children went about their own pursuits.

'I don't think I'm cut out to be a housewife,' Maeve complained to Elsie. 'Yet when I marry Matthew that's what he will expect.'

'When you get a house of your own, bigger than the dump you have now, you'll have plenty to do.'

'Maybe,' Maeve said, a doubtful expression still on her face.

'God, girl, will you look at yourself?' Elsie cried out. 'Aren't you the very devil to please? You've not got a thing to worry about, a fine man, a family to be proud of, a wedding to plan, a future secured and you're as miserable as sin.'

Maeve had to laugh, and agreed with Elsie that everything now was plain sailing for her. She knew if she was upset about anything she only had to discuss it with Matthew. The bad times were over for her.

But still she was glad, though surprised, to see Gwen, and readily agreed to help her clean the flat as long as Matthew had no objection. Matthew indeed had any number of objections. He wanted Maeve at home, where she belonged, but he didn't voice his thoughts. He knew Maeve felt a sense of loyalty towards the Mosses, and with reason, and it wasn't as if she was taking up a proper job with them again. This would be a one-off and would only take her a few days, so he gave her his blessing.

When Maeve surveyed the flat the following day she felt her heart sink. Never had she seen such filth. It made the house in Bell Barn Road, from which she'd rescued Angela years before, look clean in comparison, and the smell was indescribable.

Gwen, coming up behind Maeve, said, 'Awful, isn't it?'

'I can't believe people live like this,' Maeve said. 'And they had children too.'

Despite the coldness of the day she strode across to the windows and threw them open. All that day and the next she boiled kettles and scrubbed and bleached at the dirt-encrusted surfaces and the filthy floors. The third day she began washing down the walls and doors, and by the fourth day, the place was once again habitable. She brought Syd up for a look. Most of the lino had had to be ripped up and many of the walls, although clean, looked dingy, but most places then were looking decidedly shabby. There had been little incentive for years and no materials to renovate property. Now people were becoming bored with their dull homes and beginning to decorate again.

Syd said, 'That's grand, Maeve. I'll give the whole place a lick of paint now, put a bit of nice wallpaper on the living room and fresh lino on the floor. This time, though, we'll choose our tenants with care, make sure we get someone decent.'

'I should,' Maeve said. She gave a sudden shiver and a fit of coughing shook her frame. Syd looked at her and saw her eyes were red-rimmed and her cheeks had an unhealthy glow.

'You all right?'

'Bit of a cold,' Maeve said. 'Can't wonder at it: the weather's been bitter.'

'Aye, and you've been working in this icebox now for nigh on four days. I should get yourself away home and into your bed,' Syd advised.

'No, I'm fine,' Maeve protested. 'I'll just give the gas cooker a good clean.'

'The gas cooker will keep,' Syd said. 'Get yourself away.'

Maeve did feel groggy. She'd been light-headed since she'd got up, but thought she'd work it off. And she could have stayed in bed too. It was a Saturday and everyone had something to do. Jamie was going with a friend and his dad to see the Blues play, and Nuala and Matthew were taking the girls to the Bull Ring. Maeve knew they wouldn't be back for a good while yet. It was only just after dinner.

Syd was so concerned about her, he took her home in the van, and she was glad he had because her legs felt decidedly weak. At home it was bliss to lie back under the covers, even in the freezing bedroom, and in a few minutes she'd fallen asleep, still fully clothed except for her shoes.

When she woke up, dusk had fallen and she felt an urgent need to use the lavatory. She always spurned the bucket in the corner, unless it was in the dead of night, and so she staggered down the stairs, took her coat from the peg and, pushing her feet into her boots, she clattered her way across the yard.

She hadn't been in the lavatory very long when she became aware of low voices outside the door and she recognised one as Nuala's. They must all be back, Maeve thought, and hoped Nuala didn't need the lavatory, but then she asked herself why else would she be in that dark and secluded part of the yard?

She was just about to call out that she was in there when she heard Nuala say, 'It can't go on, Matthew. It's wrong, so terribly wrong.' Her voice sounded urgent and upset.

Maeve sat frozen on the lavatory seat. Matthew? And it was Matthew – her Matthew – that answered. 'I know and I'm as sorry as you are. I have every reason to be grateful to Maeve, I know that, and anyway I do care for her. I couldn't live with myself if I reneged on her now.'

'I wouldn't let you do that even if you'd been willing,' Nuala said.

'But, Nuala, I love you so dearly.'

'Hush, you mustn't say such words to me,' Nuala said. 'We must keep away from one another. I'm lodging with the mother of a friend at work from next week, as you know, and that will help. I'll look for another job as soon as I'm settled.'

Matthew groaned. 'I can hardly bear not to see you now and again as we've been doing. It's kept me sane these past weeks – the only good thing to come out of the whole bloody mess I've made of everything.'

'We can't go on this way and you know it,' Nuala said. 'You know full well what could happen. Our feelings for one another are such that they could easily overwhelm us. Even when we're out with the children I have to fight the urge to touch you and I have no right to you at all. You belong to Maeve.'

'I long for you too,' Matthew admitted. 'I dream about that one kiss we shared.'

'That should never have happened,' Nuala said sharply. 'I love my sister, Matthew, and I will not betray her.'

'I know.' There was a resigned tone in Matthew's voice. 'Then it's goodbye for us?'

'Yes,' Nuala said, and added sadly, 'There will be no more walks together. This is the only way we can deal with this madness.'

'Can I kiss you one last time?'

'No,' Nuala said, but her voice was husky and Maeve, listening behind the door, heard the longing in it.

'A goodbye kiss?' Matthew said. 'To remember through the bad times ahead?'

Even through the wooden door Maeve heard the sigh and then the rustle of their clothes, as they drew together. She leant against the door, devastated by what she'd heard.

446

She was deeply, deeply hurt that Matthew should talk about Nuala keeping him sane and asking for a kiss to ease him through the bad times ahead! And Nuala – what right had she to entice her man away and her not five minutes away from a life of celibacy? And if she decided marriage and a family was what she wanted, why had she to latch on to Matthew? Wasn't Birmingham chock-full of available men that belonged to no one?

And then Maeve was angry. She felt the anger running through her veins till she was almost consumed by it. She burnt with more than a fever. She threw open the door violently, startling the two people clasped together. They sprang apart and stared at Maeve as if they couldn't believe their eyes. They had no idea she'd be back so soon.

'How long has this been going on?' Maeve demanded.

Nuala couldn't speak. Her mouth dropped open, but no sound came out. She was filled with shame. The only thing she'd shared with Matthew was a kiss and it had shown their feelings for each other better than words would have done. If Nuala had been honest she would have liked it to have gone further and that in itself was a mortal sin. She knew Matthew felt the same and though the age gap between them was great, he was the man she loved and she recognised that not long after she'd arrived in Birmingham. She also knew he was the one man she couldn't have.

Matthew saw that Nuala was unable to speak, and guessed at the thoughts tormenting her very soul. From her he looked to Maeve – lovely, generous, kind-hearted Maeve – and he too was filled with shame. He heard the angry words she'd spat at them both and saw her eyes flashing even in the dim light of the yard, and knew he'd dealt her a deep hurtful injury. It was no use lying to her as well.

'I'm so sorry, Maeve,' he said earnestly. 'Nuala and I have discovered we love one another. It wasn't planned or anything like that. It just seemed to creep up on us.'

'It just crept up on you?' Maeve repeated. She was glad for the support of the door jamb, for her legs were shaking and, despite the cold, she'd felt sweat globules break out on her forehead. She wished she felt more in control, more able to cope with this. 'Were you going on to marry me and tell me nothing about the feelings you had for my sister?' Maeve asked Matthew, and he nodded miserably.

'I would have given Nuala up. I would never have cheated on you,' he said. 'We were agreed you would never know.'

'And now?'

'Now that is up to you.'

Maeve saw her dreams for the future shatter before her eyes. She'd wanted to be a respectable married woman, living with a man that she cared for in a decent neighbourhood. She wanted a father for her children and to be part of a proper family once more. She wanted a neat little house with front and back gardens where the children could play in safety. Now she knew it would never be and she remembered Elsie warning her about Matthew's friendship with Nuala. How wise she'd been. Maeve knew suddenly she'd not want to see Matthew and Nuala again.

'You think I'd marry you knowing your heart is with another?' she spat at Matthew. Turning to her sister she said, 'I want you to pack up your things and move out of my house now, tonight.'

Matthew saw Nuala stagger against the wall in shock 'Ah, will you have some pity?' Matthew cried. 'Where is she to go?'

'Pity?' Rage filled Maeve's being and she said through gritted teeth, 'Why the hell should I have pity for her?

She's behaved like a harlot under my very roof and I don't give a tuppenny damn where she'll go, as long as it's away from my house. You can both go to the devil for all I care. Now, Matthew,' she snapped, turning to the red-faced man before her, 'you go up to the house this minute and say goodbye to Angela. I'll look after the child until you can make other arrangements.'

'Maeve—' Nuala began, but Maeve hissed, 'Be silent! Don't even try to say you're sorry again. I'm away to the house now and then to my bed, for I was sent home sick from the shop today. I will leave it to you to tell the children what you will.'

And so saying Maeve pushed herself away from the wall and stood for a moment while the courtyard stopped swaying in front of her. A spasm of coughing doubled her over and Matthew realised she was really ill. Had he been able to see her face properly he'd have noticed sooner. He put his hand on her arm. 'Let me help you,' he pleaded. 'You're in no fit state.'

'Remove your hand!' Maeve said in clipped icy tones Matthew had never heard her use before.

He let his arm fall to his side and stood with Nuala, watching Maeve's shambling and erratic progress up the yard.

Maeve kept her head lowered and concentrated on putting one foot before the other, and although the cobbles of the courtyard swam before her eyes, she willed herself not to collapse. She couldn't have borne it if Matthew and Nuala had come to her aid.

She made it, though she almost fell in through the door, and Bridget turned from where she was filling hot-water bottles for their beds. 'Mammy!' she cried, and then, looking at her more closely, said, 'Are you ill, Mammy?'

'Yes, pet,' Maeve said. The short journey from the lavatory had tired her out and she sat gasping and coughing in the chair. 'Get me a cup of tea, Bridget love?' she asked between coughing bouts.

'You should be in bed, Mammy,' Bridget said worriedly. 'I'll put the bottles in your bed instead of the weans, to warm it up for you.'

'I'll go up in a minute when I've had a cup of tea and got my breath back,' Maeve promised.

Nuala and Matthew came in after her and Maeve averted her eyes, but it went unnoticed. Nuala walked past them all and went straight to the stairs and, after making a cup of tea for her mother, Bridget followed Nuala with the hot-water bottles. She watched with astonishment her aunt pushing her clothes into her case.

'What are you doing?'

'I'm leaving,' Nuala said, and Bridget knew by the catch in her voice that she'd been crying.

'I thought that was next weekend.'

'Aye, well, plans have changed.'

'Are you all right, Aunt Nuala?'

'No, child, I'm not,' Nuala said sadly. 'I've hurt your mother and hurt her badly and I don't know that she'll ever recover from it, and now I must leave here tonight.'

'What have you done?' Bridget asked, her eyes wide with astonishment.

'You won't properly understand this, Bridget,' Nuala said, 'but Matthew and I have found that we love each other.'

'You can't love Uncle Matthew!' Bridget cried. 'He's marrying Mammy.'

'No, Bridget, he's not.'

Bridget sprang away from her aunt, her eyes wide and disbelieving. Nuala wasn't interested in men. She'd been a nun! 'How could you do that to Mammy?' she cried. 'You're disgusting. Matthew was marrying Mammy. What have you done?' Nuala could only shake her head helplessly, and Bridget said, 'Well, I'm glad you're leaving. I never want to see you again.'

Downstairs, Matthew was having just as hard a time as he tried to explain everything to Jamie, Angela and Mary Ann, and also Grace, who'd stepped through the door from work just as he'd begun. All the children, including Angela, seemed to think it was a crying shame and their sympathies were all with Maeve, who lay fighting for breath in the chair.

Even Angela was ashamed of her father. Much as she loved him and Nuala too, any mothering she'd got had been from Maeve and she faced her father and said, 'I'm not going to live with you if you don't marry Mammy Maeve, and I don't want to leave here.'

'You must come with me, Angela. You're my daughter,' Matthew said gently.

Angela stamped her foot. 'I'll not,' she cried.

'You can't impose on Maeve for ever.'

Angela didn't know what impose meant, but it didn't sound a good thing to do, so she said, 'I'm not.' She put her little hand on Maeve's shaking shoulders and said, 'Tell him I haven't to go, Mammy.'

'It's up to your father,' Maeve said between her gulps for air, though her heart ached for the confused child.

Angela knew she had to make a stand. Maeve was too sick to help her and she faced Matthew angrily. 'You make me go,' she said threateningly, 'and I'll hate you for ever and ever.'

Matthew looked at his daughter's fierce and malevolent little face and knew she meant every word she'd said. For love of Nuala, he would have to give up his daughter. He knew that if he forced her away from the Hogan family, he would lose any love or respect she might have for him. On the other hand, if he gave in to her now, he might in time be able to build some sort of relationship with her later.

He gave a sorrowful sigh. 'If Maeve agrees,' he said, 'then you can stay a wee while longer.'

Maeve didn't really want a reminder of Matthew Bradshaw in her life. But then she looked at the pleading eyes of Angela, full of fear and confusion, and felt the child's hand tighten in her own, and knew she couldn't punish the child because of her father's actions. She loved Angela as much as her natural children and she smiled at the child, though it seemed to take all her reserves of strength. 'If you wish to stay, Angela, then you shall stay,' she said, and Angela gave a whoop of joy and threw herself on Maeve with such gusto that she felt waves of dizziness as Angela squeezed her tightly.

'Leave her, Angela,' Grace admonished, pulling the child back. 'Come on, Mammy, away to bed with you. I'll bring you up a wee bit of supper later.'

Maeve allowed herself to be led from the room. Bridget and Nuala had come down and stood in stony silence and Matthew, knowing nothing could be salvaged by staying, took Nuala's case from her.

'Well, we'll be off then,' he said.

No one answered and as the door closed behind them there was a collective sigh of relief. Grace came back into the room and said, 'Mammy is going to have a wee sleep and I'll see if she'll eat something later, so don't you dare wake her up when you go up to bed. She's put up with enough already tonight.'

And all the children agreed she had. Saturday was bath night for them all usually, for there was Mass in the morning, but Grace didn't feel like tackling that on her own. The heart seemed to have been sucked out of her by the events of the evening.

She was shocked by Nuala's actions. They'd been close to one another and yet Grace had noticed nothing and Nuala hadn't said. Well, Grace thought, it was over between them now. She'd never feel the same about her aunt again. She was a snake; anyone who would do that was a snake. Yet Grace felt a sense of loss, for she'd once loved Nuala like a sister and knew that no friend, and not even her mother, would be able to take her place.

But she knew her mother's sense of loss and hurt would be greater than her own. Now Grace knew she'd be trapped in the little back-to-back house all her days. The others would all leave in time, but her mammy would languish there on her own. She gave a sigh, knowing nothing she could say or do would make things better for her mother at the moment. She decided to make a cup of tea for herself and have an early night.

She usually went out with her friends on Saturday evenings, but she wouldn't leave her mother when it was obvious she wasn't at all well. Anyway, she had an idea she'd have a lot of work to do in the morning, because she couldn't see her mother being one bit better.

Grace was right, Maeve was quite ill indeed. Dr Fleming, who had to be called eventually, said she had bad bronchitis and must keep to her bed for at least a week and possibly much longer. By then, the whole neighbourhood knew of the sister who'd once wanted to be a nun, who had taken the intended husband of the other. And besides that, the man's own child was left with the woman he threw over. It was an absolute disgrace.

Elsie was a tower of strength to Maeve. Maeve knew she'd been disgusted by Nuala and Matthew's actions, but she didn't keep on about it. She just said that feelings were funny things and there was no telling where they might light, but that didn't mean you had to give in to them.

Maeve let them all talk round her as she lay in bed, a luxury she hadn't enjoyed for years, deeply hurt by Matthew's and Nuala's betrayal. She remembered the plans she and Matthew had made for the future, the way they'd talk in the long evenings by the fireside, and the joy they'd shared in the children. She wondered how and why it had all gone wrong for them. She thought she knew Matthew inside out. Well, that's it, she decided, she was finished with men. They brought nothing but trouble.

Elsie, who looked after Maeve most during the day, was worried about her because she didn't seem to be getting any better, didn't seem to want to get better either. Even Dr Fleming was concerned. He'd heard on the grapevine what had happened between her and Matthew, and thought Maeve's lethargy and uninterest stemmed from being let down like that – and small wonder when the woman had been through so much already. He told Elsie he'd been surprised to hear what Matthew had done; he'd always thought the man to be upright and decent, but Elsie didn't comment.

Gwen Moss came to see Maeve as soon as she heard she was ill and was shocked by Maeve's appearance, her eyes, which seemed to stand out in her pale face, and her general listlessness. She brought tasty morsels to tempt Maeve's appetite and little bunches of flowers to brighten the room. 'Don't worry about a thing now,' she said. 'You just get well.'

'And why wouldn't I?' Maeve said wearily, but with a ghost of a smile. 'Aren't I being ruined altogether?'

'And about time,' Gwen said emphatically. 'I was sorry to hear about your disappointment,' she went on, and blushed at the memory of the conversation she'd had with Syd just a little while before.

'I'm sorry for Maeve,' he'd said. 'And I'd not have you think otherwise, but her loss could be our gain.' Gwen had been bemused and he'd gone on, 'Wasn't it her man who was against her working?'

'Oh, Syd . . .'

'Don't "Oh, Syd" me like that,' Syd had burst out. 'I am as sorry for Maeve as you are, but now she's been jilted, as it were, she'll have to have some form of employment and she likes it here. Put it to her, Gwen. I bet she'll jump at it.'

But Gwen didn't put it to her, knowing Maeve was far from well and certainly not up to deciding such things. The week in bed stretched to a fortnight and even after that she was so lacking in energy she was content just to sit in the chair and watch others bustling around after her children and taking care of her home. She knew that soon she'd have to decide how she was going to provide for them all but she pushed her worries aside, for they wearied her.

Father Trelawney came to see Maeve as soon as Bridget told him she was in bed ill and Maeve knew, just by looking at his face, that the priest was aware of her broken love affair.

'I'm sorry to see you like this, Maeve,' he said, and as usual Maeve was irritated by his manner.

'Like what, Father?' she asked. 'Jilted, do you mean, or sick?'

Father Trelawney hid his annoyance. It was hard to continue to feel sorry for her, but he tried. 'Both, of course,' he said. 'I am sorry to see you so ill. I know the children have been very concerned. As for the business with Matthew Bradshaw . . . Well, let's say I was shocked to hear what your sister had done.'

'Why?' Maeve demanded. 'Because she's run off with my man, or because he's the wrong religion?'

'Now, now, Maeve, stop this,' the priest said. 'I will say only that I was surprised by her actions.'

'You didn't think it served me right for daring to intend to marry a Protestant?'

Father Trelawney had had thoughts so similar to those Maeve expressed that he reddened. He knew also that Maeve was making fun of him. He had been shocked to the core to know that Nuala Brannigan, whom he'd seen as a sensible, demure sort of girl, had taken up with the very same and totally unsuitable man her sister had been enamoured with.

'Elsie says people have little control over their feelings,' Maeve went on. 'Isn't that right, Elsie?' she asked the older woman, who'd come into the bedroom with a cup of tea for the priest. Elsie pressed her lips together to prevent herself smiling at Father Trelawney's obvious discomfort.

'I didn't say that exactly,' Elsie said.

'You did,' Maeve retorted. 'You said there was no knowing where feelings might light. We could all be in danger of it. Even you, Father – you could be next.'

'Maeve,' the priest admonished but quietly, because it was obvious Maeve was far from well, 'I understand you're upset and ill so I'll make allowances.'

'Oh, don't trouble yourself to make any allowances at all,' Maeve said. 'Put me down as a hopeless case.'

Afterwards Elsie gently took her to task over it.

'Oh, Elsie, he deserves it. He's a patronising hypocrite and so very easy to tease,' Maeve said.

Another Maeve described as a patronising hypocrite was her Uncle Michael, who also came to visit the invalid. He'd not been near her for months, not since he'd first got wind of her involvement with Matthew. He'd tackled her about it after Mass one day and been told to 'go to hell'. His subsequent absence and silence on the subject had signified his disapproval.

But now Maeve had been betrayed and therefore she was welcomed back into the fold of the family, and Nuala was now the black sheep.

'I wrote and told Annie all about it,' Michael said pompously when he came that bitter winter's day when Maeve was eventually allowed out of bed, but just to sit in a chair near the fire.

Maeve had also written to her mother, telling her of the latest developments. Her parents had known, of course, about Matthew, and knew he was a non-Catholic long before she'd told them of his marriage proposal, and yet they'd never criticised. They'd both just expressed their pleasure that Maeve had found someone good for her, and said it was time she had some happiness in her life.

Maeve knew her uncle, in his letter to Annie and Thomas, would have stressed the fact of Matthew's religion and given his own opinion of Nuala into the bargain, worrying them all in Ireland who could do nothing about it.

'I wish you hadn't written, Uncle,' she said. 'It can't have achieved anything and you'll probably have worried the life out of Kevin. He'll be wondering how I'm going to manage now.'

'They have a right to know.'

457

'Maybe, but it was my right to tell them, not yours.'

'And did you?'

'Yes I did, and in my own way.'

'Well,' Michael said, 'I'm glad you at least saw sense and got rid of the man.'

'It wasn't quite like that.'

'I heard you sent them both packing.'

'Not quite,' Maeve said. She didn't elaborate; it still hurt too much to discuss it.

She still missed both Nuala and Matthew very much. Just two days after she'd been taken ill a letter had arrived from Nuala. Grace discussed with Elsie whether she should give it to Maeve or not, but neither thought her strong enough to deal with it.

Even when she'd been given the letter, Maeve wasn't sure she wanted to even read the damned thing. Bitterness rose in her whenever she thought of the way that Matthew and Nuala had behaved.

True, she hadn't been in love with Matthew, but she had cared for him deeply, had valued his support and friendship over the years and had cared for his daughter when he'd not known which way to turn. Surely he owed her something?

As for her sister, Nuala had known from her first night in Birmingham how things were between herself and Matthew. If she'd felt herself attracted to him, why hadn't she fought it? Why had she gone out for walks with him and agreed to spend their Saturdays together? Why had she taken a job at the same factory and taken advantage of Maeve's preoccupation with the shop to steal Matthew away? Her betrayal still hurt like hell.

Nuala's letter expressed regret and said she was bitterly ashamed of her part in the whole thing, and Matthew, she said, was distraught. Maeve felt no sympathy for Matthew's shame, nor for any distress her sister was feeling, and she thrust the letter angrily into the fire.

But none of this did she say to her uncle, who seemed to sit in judgement on them all.

'I can't understand the man just dumping his child on you either,' Michael said, breaking the silence in the room.

'He didn't "dump her" on me, as you put it,' Maeve said. 'It was the child's own decision to stay.'

'But surely—'

'Uncle Michael, I'm the only mother Angela has ever known,' Maeve said. 'How could I turn my back on her and how could Matthew take her to the little bare room he rents and who would care for her while he goes to work?'

'That's hardly your concern.'

'Legally, perhaps not,' Maeve said. 'But she's part of our family now and she didn't want to leave us all.'

Her uncle's only response was a 'Hmph' and Maeve remembered Angela creeping up to her bedroom one day, just a few days after she'd been taken ill. She'd looked at Maeve closely and slipped her little hand into hers and said anxiously, 'Are you going to die, Mammy?'

Maeve had heard the desperation in the voice and said as reassuringly as she could, 'No, Angela, I'm just a little sick. The doctor will make me well, don't worry.'

She'd heard the small sigh of relief, and then Angela had said, 'My daddy isn't going to marry you now, is he?'

'No, pet, he isn't.'

'Will he marry Nuala?'

'I don't know,' Maeve had said and added for the child's sake, 'You like Nuala, don't you?'

Angela had loved Nuala once and enjoyed their days together, but she loved Maeve more. Angela couldn't understand why her father had hurt her so much and she hated him and Nuala because of it.

'I used to like her,' she'd told Maeve, 'but not any more.'

'Ah, Angela, don't say that. Your daddy and Nuala both love you. And if they marry she will be your stepmother,' Maeve had said.

Angela had shaken her head. 'You're my mother,' she'd said. 'I don't want either of them. I don't even want to see them.'

Maeve hoped Angela would eventually get over her antagonism for she sensed her hurt. But no way could she abandon Matthew's daughter and she said so to her uncle.

'Well, I said at the time you were silly to take her on,' Michael said. 'Everyone was talking about it. I felt you had enough on your plate already and your Aunt Agnes agreed with me.'

'Aunt Agnes!' Maeve cried. 'God, I'm surprised she remembers who I am!'

'Really, Maeve!'

'Come on, Uncle Michael,' Maeve cried. 'If she'd been a different sort of woman I might have confided in her about the dreadful state of my marriage, which you chose to believe was a bloody bed of roses. But let's leave that aside. Even after Brendan died, did she ever visit to see if we were managing? Did she ever offer a hand with the weans at all?'

'You were hand-in-glove with the woman next door,' Michael complained. 'Brendan was always going on about it.'

'Aye,' Maeve cried. 'And it was a good job I was. God knows, I'd be in a poor state if I'd had only the pair of you to rely on.'

She knew she'd upset him and when she recounted it to Elsie – leaving out the reference to her – she'd laughed as Elsie replied, 'If you're well enough to argue, girl, you must be improving.'

'Aye, all we need now is Brendan's family here to gloat over my scuppered wedding plans.'

But none of the Hogans came. Instead it was Gwen Moss who bustled in a few days after her uncle's visit, glad to see the unhealthy glow had faded from Maeve's cheeks.

'How are you, Maeve?'

'Oh, Elsie thinks I'm on the mend,' Maeve said. 'Some day soon I'll have to think about a job.'

'Don't rush yourself,' Gwen said.

'Ah, Gwen, sure the weans only have me now.'

'I know that,' Gwen said. 'Have you anything in mind?' and then went on without waiting for a reply, 'You wouldn't consider the shop again?'

Maeve's eyes widened. 'Haven't you got someone else in my place?'

Gwen shook her head. 'Never seemed to get round to it,' she said with a grin.

'Oh, Gwen . . .' Maeve was overcome. She'd love to work back in the shop, but worried about loading so much work on the shoulders of Grace and Bridget. In particular Bridget, who would have the care of the children all day Saturday without the support of Nuala or Matthew. What if something was to happen to the little ones? A factory job where she had her weekends free might be better.

Gwen saw her face working and, being a mother herself, guessed at some of the thoughts crowding her head.

Eventually Maeve said, 'Thanks, Gwen, and it's not that I don't appreciate it, but it's the hours, you see. I hate to heap it all on Bridget.'

461

'And what if you lived on the premises?' Gwen said, thinking of the plans she'd made with Syd while he'd decorated the flat next door to look like a little palace and she'd searched the shops for things to give a homely touch that she knew Maeve would like.

'On the premises?'

'In the other flat,' Gwen said triumphantly.

'Oh, Gwen, I couldn't afford it.'

'It would be part of your wages, a perk of the job,' Gwen said.

'Oh no. You were thinking of letting that flat for a goodly sum.'

'God, girl, do you think we need the money?' Gwen cried. 'We let the place for nothing all through the war and then for peanuts to the last lot we had up there, and when we finally got rid of them they owed us about three months in rent arrears.' She took Maeve's hand and said, 'It would really please Syd and myself if you'd consider it, Maeve. It would be nice to have decent people living next door to us, and the shop's not been the same without you. This way you can see to the children too, and free this house for some other family.'

Oh, it was tempting. No garden, perhaps, but a yard to play in and a place with a proper kitchen and bathroom and an inside lavatory. The long attic room would do for the girls and the other bedroom beside hers for Jamie. Grace would be near her place of work, and though the children would be further from school, that would do them no harm. As for her – well, she'd be doing a job she enjoyed and getting a wage for it.

She smiled at Gwen and squeezed the hand holding hers. 'Yes,' she said. 'I'll take it, and thank you from the bottom of my heart.'

462

TWENTY-SEVEN

Despite being tremendously grateful to Gwen, Maeve was a bit nervous of moving so close to the draper's shop above which Richard Prendagast still lived with his mother. While she'd been engaged to Matthew, she'd felt she was safe from him; now she felt vulnerable again. However, she wasn't going to pass up the chance of a decent place for the family to live in, together with doing a job she enjoyed. After all, the man was nothing to her, and especially after what had happened. She supposed he'd be just as embarrassed and as unwilling to meet as she was.

Elsie helped her friend pack up her things, knowing she'd miss her desperately. But still she was happy for the whole family and not at all resentful. It wasn't as if Maeve would be a million miles away.

On 23 February Maeve moved into the flat. She stood and surveyed it with a sigh of satisfaction. For the first few days she almost had to pinch herself to believe it was true when she woke up in her comfortable bedroom and made breakfast for her children in a bright and functional kitchen.

The Mosses had worked hard to make the flat a welcoming place and it was hardly recognisable from the dingy bare rooms Maeve had cleaned just weeks before. It had all been freshly painted and the living room and bedrooms wallpapered, beautiful curtains hung at the windows and there was now lino on the floor. And Maeve, in her turn, cleaned and polished the place with loving care, worked like a Trojan in the shop, was always punctual and never minded working overtime, and Syd declared he'd never had such an assistant.

Maeve wrote to her parents and Kevin, and told them all about the move to the flat and her job, to stop them worrying about her and particularly to put Kevin's mind at rest. She soon realised that she'd worried unduly about her close proximity to Richard, for she never saw him. Syd remarked that he used to come in now and again for razor blades, cigarettes or newspapers, but from the minute Maeve moved in, he never showed his face. Now Grace took him down a paper and sometimes cigarettes when she left in the mornings, and razor blades and matches, sweets and other sundry items for her son were added to Amy's shopping list.

For the first time, Grace began to wonder if Richard's reluctance to enter Moss's had anything to do with her mother working there, and if so, she couldn't understand it. She thought they'd got over that time when Maeve had snapped the head off Richard at their old house and for no good reason that she could see. But then Richard had changed since the early autumn, for though he was not so bad-tempered and generally grouchy any more, he seldom laughed or smiled and never told the bad jokes he had seemed to have a stock of.

Grace, of course, would not have known it but Richard was aching with loneliness and almost despair. He wished he could overcome his aversion to children and knock boldly at Maeve's door, sweep her into his arms, tell her of his undying love and ask her to marry him. He bitterly regretted not doing just that that day in September when she'd given herself to him totally.

But always when he contemplated confronting Maeve this way the image of the two little girls gazing at him solemnly would rise up before his eyes – alive and well, as his daughter, Nina, would never be – and he couldn't do it. However, in recognising that fact, he felt cast adrift. His life seemed to have little purpose and yet he knew his mother loved and needed him and for her sake he tried to hide his heartache, though not very successfully.

He worked tirelessly, both in the shop and out of it, searching for new lines, visiting fashion houses and nego-tiating with clothing manufacturers because he was now the main buyer, a role he'd taken over from Amy at her suggestion. It gave him little satisfaction, except to see that he had pleased his mother. He was only glad that hard work and long hours might enable him to fall into an exhausted sleep at night, but despite his tiredness, he still spent far too many nights restlessly pacing the floor of his bedroom.

When Grace had told him that Maeve had become engaged and, she said, to a man they had all known and liked for years whom, due to her reticence about personal matters, she'd never mentioned before, Richard had felt a pain so sharp and deep grip his stomach that it had made him catch his breath. Desire for Maeve had not diminished, and he'd felt raw base jealousy flood over him that he knew he had no right to feel.

He'd tried to get to grips with his feelings. Maeve was still a beautiful woman, he'd acknowledged that, and she had enjoyed their lovemaking as much as he had. Perhaps, in a way, he had awakened desire that had lain dormant inside her for years. But then he'd left her and never tried to see her again. So, what the hell had he expected her to do – go into bloody decline? Grace had said the man Matthew Bradshaw was good and kind and if he'd been a better person Richard would have felt happy for Maeve, but instead resentment, like a canker, had spread through him.

When Grace had told him a little later that Maeve was getting married in the spring, he'd been devastated. He went out and got roaring drunk and almost frightened his mother to death when he came home, cursing all women in the universe in a voice loud enough to rouse the neighbourhood. He'd never done it again, though there had been times when he'd badly wanted to. Even in his befuddled state, he remembered the look of terror on his mother's face and had been disgusted with himself for putting it there.

But Maeve hadn't married Matthew Bradshaw, and people said her suitor had run off with her younger sister instead. Grace had never spoken about it and Richard felt he hadn't the right to ask.

And then Maeve and her family had come to live only yards from his own shop. He couldn't risk seeing her. He knew the only way to deal with the madness inside him was to keep right away, and he asked Grace or his mother to fetch the things he needed, claiming he didn't have time himself.

Maeve knew nothing of Richard's inner turmoil. She was just glad he never came into the shop. It was obvious from Amy's manner that she was completely unaware that Richard used to visit Maeve and she was happy to leave it that way.

She also wanted to have nothing to do with her sister or Matthew Bradshaw, and she asked her mother not to give them the family's new address. Since that first letter Nuala had written once more, and then came an impassioned plea from Matthew, who claimed Nuala was eating her heart out with shame for what she'd done to Maeve.

Maeve didn't reply to any of them, nor did she answer any of her mother's puzzled queries about what had happened. Presumably, she'd eventually found out through Nuala, but the expressions of sympathy she extended towards Maeve, she never acknowledged.

Really, she would have preferred not to think of them at all. The children never talked about them either, because unknown to Maeve, Grace had insisted they say nothing and upset their mother further and possibly make her ill again.

None of the children wanted that and especially not Angela. Her daddy had been nice to her, but Angela knew if she had to choose between him and Maeve, Maeve would win every time. She would do nothing to upset her, or even annoy her, when she then might feel inclined to give her back to her father.

So a pall of silence hung over the whole family with regard to Matthew and Nuala, and Annie worried about the unhappy situation between them. Though she deplored what Nuala had done, the child was her own flesh and blood and she wrote long letters to her, suggesting ways of healing the rift between her and her sister.

Meanwhile, Maeve and the children were invited over to Ireland for the summer. Maeve, though she had originally intended to go to introduce Matthew to the family that year, did not want to go on her own – it would emphasise her singleness to her, she imagined – so the idea was shelved.

Then out of the blue came a letter from Annie with news of the marriage of Matthew and Nuala, which was to take place in mid-July, just as the summer holidays would begin, and they were offering to take the children over to Ireland to stay with their grandparents as they were touring Ireland as part of their honeymoon. Her mother wrote to Maeve, 'Don't be thinking we haven't the space now, for Kevin and Tom together have built on an extra room at the back of the cottage and opened up the roof area.'

Annie didn't go on to tell Maeve the whole family was relieved that Matthew and Nuala would be touring the country and not staying about the farmhouse, or even the town, for very long. Nuala had been the baby of their family and the apple of her father's eye, which was why he hadn't wanted her shut behind the walls of a convent. But this latest exploit . . . He couldn't help it, he felt Nuala had let him down. He said Maeve had been dealt a bad enough fist in life as it was, without Nuala going up and taking her man from her.

Tom was inclined to agree and Rosemarie, who'd always been jealous of Nuala's relationship with her father, said she wasn't surprised, as Nuala had no idea of fair shares. She said it was only to be expected for hadn't she been given everything she'd wanted all the days of her life?

Kevin took no part in the argument. His concern was for his mother alone, but he did tell his grandma privately that he really didn't want to meet his aunt and her husband at all. 'They'd not have much of a welcome from anyone here, it seems to me,' he said. 'Then with Grace telling me how sick Mammy has been over it and how upset she was, I'd be hard pressed to even be civil to them.'

But Annie told Maeve none of this in her letter. She just urged her to let the children travel over to Ireland with Nuala and Matthew.

'Please let them come, Maeve. I'd love to set eyes on my own grandchildren and see young Grace again.'

Maeve's first reaction was to refuse. How dare Nuala marry the man promised to her and then take him on the holiday to Ireland that she herself should be having? No, it was more than flesh and blood could stand. How could her mother put her in that position? Maybe it was a ploy cooked up by them all to get back into her good books. Well if so, it wouldn't bloody well work!

And then she caught sight of the children's eyes staring at her. They knew the letter was from their grandma in Ireland – she wrote often enough for them to recognise her writing – but none of them could understand the expression on Maeve's face.

'What's the matter, Mammy?' Jamie asked.

'Nothing,' Maeve answered tersely, but Grace noticed she screwed the paper in her hand so hard her knuckles showed white. She tried to remember if she'd ever discussed going on holiday to Ireland with her sister; she knew she had with Matthew. It was as if they were sticking a knife back into the wound that still lay open and raw. It hurt like hell and Maeve bit on her bottom lip in agitation.

'Is summat up with our Kevin?' Jamie asked, seeing his mother's distress.

Maeve made an effort to pull herself together for the children's sake. Jamie's thoughts were all for his brother, while the girls, she noticed, sat mute, as if afraid to speak, but all their eyes were upon her.

She forced a tremulous smile to her lips when she turned to Jamie and said, 'No, Jamie, Kevin is fine.'

Maeve wanted to burn the letter. The children had plenty to occupy themselves with during the summer holidays, she told herself. But her conscience smote her. Had she the right to stop her children from meeting their grand-parents for the first time and being reunited with Kevin because she'd had a fallout with Matthew and her sister?

She faced the fact that it was jealousy, pure and simple, grinding away inside her that made her want to reject the whole thing. What sort of mother would she be to refuse them a couple of weeks on a farm where they could run and play at will? She knew they'd be fed good wholesome food and the fresh air would bring the colour back to their pale faces.

She sighed and said, 'Your grandmother has written and invited you all over to Ireland for a wee holiday. I can't be spared here, so . . .' Maeve stopped and swallowed the bitter gall in her mouth before she went on, 'Your Aunt Nuala and Uncle Matthew will be taking you over.'

Her eyes met the sympathetic ones of Grace and Bridget, and she knew they both realised how much it had cost her to say what she had.

Jamie, however, was concerned only with practicalities. 'How long for?' he demanded.

Maeve was uncertain. She scanned the letter again. 'I don't know. A fortnight, I imagine.'

Jamie let out a howl of protest. 'Kevin told me the whole summer,' he complained. 'He promised.'

'Jamie, don't be so silly!' Maeve admonished, her voice sharper than she intended. 'Be grateful for what you have. You'll have to come back when your aunt and uncle do, you know that.'

But even as she spoke, she was working possibilities out in her head. Maybe Gwen and Syd would agree to her taking a few days off in early September. She could fetch the children home in time for school and be able to see her parents again.

But even as she turned the possibilities over in her head, Grace said, 'Maybe I could bring them back home. Richard was only talking about me taking a holiday a few days ago. If they agree to let me go in mid-August, when Chris begins his National Service, I could have a fortnight and bring the children back with me. I'd quite like a break then. I'm bound to be a bit upset when Chris goes and I'd love to see everyone again.'

'Who will take your place?' Maeve asked.

'Well, Miss Overley comes into the shop more now than she did,' Grace said, 'but trade is picking up so well that Richard said we might soon have to get in another assistant. Anyway, he seems to think they'd cope.'

'You're still as busy, then?' Maeve said, knowing that since rationing came to an end the shop had become as popular as Grace had prophesied. Moss's had been busy enough with all the new foodstuffs flooding in. Sometimes things not seen for nearly ten years were suddenly available again.

'We're rushed off our feet,' Grace said. 'And we have some nice things too. You should come and have a look round.'

That was the last thing in the world Maeve intended to do, but she said nothing to her daughter. Instead she said, 'Well, there's a lot to do if all of you are going and the first thing is to write to Mammy.'

The children were beside themselves with excitement at the thought of going to Ireland for the whole seven weeks of the summer holidays and meeting their grandparents and seeing Kevin again. But if Matthew and Nuala had expected their offer to soften Maeve's attitude towards them, they soon found out how mistaken they'd been.

Maeve sent them both a stiff and formal letter, telling them the children would meet them on New Street station on the day of departure.

Gwen took all the squealing happy children, packed up with bags and cases and high on excitement and expectation, in a taxi. Maeve waited till they disappeared from view before returning to the shop, feeling slightly desolate without them. Elsie had offered to take the children to the station, but Maeve had refused. She knew Elsie too well. Loyal to a fault and a staunch friend, she'd think nothing of giving out to Matthew and Nuala in the station in front of everyone, if she felt so inclined, and that was the last thing Maeve wanted the children to witness. But it was Elsie Maeve went to a few days after the children's departure, unable to shake herself out of the doldrums.

'What's up?' Elsie asked. 'Missing the kids?'

'Like mad,' Maeve admitted. Her life had been full of children and now to lose them all except Grace was hard to take. She was immensely glad of her job, but once the evenings came, she was often lonely, especially as Grace was usually out making the most of Chris's last few weeks as a civilian.

Grace was terribly worried about him going anyway because of the war in Korea. It sounded serious. Taxes were raised to pay for it and the Government talked about restrictions and people making sacrifices, and most thought they'd done enough of all that already. But Grace was especially worried about Chris because although most of the UN forces deployed so far were American, she thought it was only a matter of time till Britain and therefore Chris would be in the thick of it.

So Maeve didn't blame her for her concern and certainly didn't begrudge the evenings Grace and Chris spent together.

'You want to get out more,' Elsie told Maeve. 'You don't need to bury yourself at home night after night.'

'What d'you expect me to do?' Maeve snapped. 'Drape myself over some bar stool like a prostitute? I'm all right, Elsie. I'm content.'

Elsie chuckled. 'I think contentment sits easier on old bones,' she said. 'And I'm not suggesting frequenting pubs, but surely you could go to the pictures a time or two. I bet Gwen Moss would jump at the chance of going with you.'

She was right of course. Gwen was delighted at the whole idea and they went first to see *Kind Hearts and Coronets,* and from then on it was a weekly or twice-weekly treat the two of them enjoyed.

Chris left to begin his National Service on 17 August, and Grace went to see him off. Maeve took one look at the white, tear-stained face of her daughter when she returned and was heartily glad she had the holiday to look forward to.

Maeve thanked God Kevin was well out of it in Ireland, but didn't say so, for it would hardly be helpful to Grace. A few days later she saw her off at New Street station on her way to her grandparents and she knew she was going to miss her as much as the younger ones.

As expected, British troops were sent to help the Americans on 29 August. Maeve said nothing to Grace in her letters to the children in Ireland and hoped such news wasn't seen as important enough to be broadcast on Irish wireless.

She told herself experienced troops would be sent first. Chris had been in the army less than a fortnight – hardly time enough to learn how to hold a rifle, let alone fire it.

She hoped and prayed that he would return safely, for she knew that Grace felt deeply about him; they'd even been talking of engagement when Chris finished his National Service. She prayed for a world where youngsters could grow up in safety and peace, and when she confided it all to Elsie, she said, 'You're asking for Paradise, Maeve, and I think we'll see that soon enough.'

The children returned home bronzed from the sun and full of beans. They'd obviously had a wonderful time and Maeve was glad she'd allowed them to go. They were full of what they'd done and who they'd met, and spoke of their grandparents and Kevin and their Uncle Tom and Auntie Rosemarie and numerous friends and neighbours. They never mentioned Matthew or Nuala, not that first evening home, nor in the days and weeks afterwards. They didn't even mention the trip over, though Maeve knew it must have been an adventure for them, but as Maeve couldn't bring herself to do so either, she never got to know.

Jamie had just passed his ninth birthday in November when Maeve noticed a change in him. She knew he was missing his brother and felt for the lad with no father figure in his life. Angela too, after the initial excitement of the holiday, seemed quieter and a little introverted. Maeve would often find her sitting alone and staring into space, and wondered if she missed her father. Perhaps seeing him again had made her realise that. She wouldn't speak of it, Maeve knew, because none of them would risk upsetting her, but nevertheless something was making the child unhappy.

Maeve examined her feelings towards her sister and Matthew and found that what they had done now hurt her less. Time had clouded the resentment she'd felt. Though she had no house and garden in some leafy suburb, she had now a decent place to live and a job she enjoyed.

Really, if she'd married Matthew she could not have been happier. He would not have wanted her to work and yet she would have perhaps been miles away from people she knew, and lonely at home all day. And although Matthew would have been a good father and a good provider, Maeve wasn't at all sure he would have been a totally fair one. Would he have made any difference in the way he treated Angela from the rest of the children, and would she be continually looking for discrepancies?

Eventually Maeve faced the fact that Matthew had not done her much of a disservice at all and it had been her pride that had received the biggest jolt – that and the expectation of a better life for the children that she'd seen crumble away that had made her angry and resentful. Maybe Christmas was the time to heal the breach. She felt she'd been wrong to break off all contact between Matthew and his child, and it would help Jamie as well to have a man he could perhaps visit and talk to. She decided she would send them both a letter and see how they felt.

But Jamie wasn't yearning after Matthew. He had a real-life hero on his own doorstep and that was Richard Prendagast. Ever since he'd come back from Ireland and left Kevin behind, he'd mooned after him. Grace had told him all about the medals Richard had won because of his bravery in the war. Not that he'd told her himself. In fact she'd said he'd seemed really embarrassed about them, but his mother had shown them to her one day when he was out of the shop.

Jamie wished he could do something to get himself noticed by such a brave man – wash his car perhaps, or run errands, anything. But Mr Prendagast never seemed to notice him, however long he hung about in the street outside the shop, and when he'd plucked up the courage one day to ask if he could wash his car, Mr Prendagast had looked surprised and a little annoyed. 'Not now. Why don't you run along and play somewhere else?' he'd said, just as if he was a little kid like Mary Ann or Angela.

Grace had no sympathy for him. 'Why should he be bothered about grubby little boys like you?' she'd said. 'He's a busy man. Leave him alone.' So now, Jamie just watched him in secret, dying to speak to him but too scared of making him angry to try.

Richard hardly gave the child a thought. All children he considered nuisances or worse. Grace, who'd shed her childhood and was now a young woman, he got along with well. She was bright and had some good opinions on how the shop should be managed – what would sell and what wouldn't – and didn't mind expressing them.

'This Christmas,' she'd told him in summer, 'with the new styles coming into the shops, women will want frivolous lacy underwear, nylons at any price and figure-hugging dresses and knitwear in various colours. They want to remind themselves they are feminine and they never want to hear the word utility again.'

One Saturday in November, nearly a week after Jamie's birthday, Richard set off for the warehouse in his car, armed with a list of requirements that Grace wanted, for she'd been right and most of the stock he'd bought had been severely depleted. She also wanted more of the special items brought in just for Christmas for the women to buy for their menfolk: boxed cufflinks, tiepins, hankies and silk ties with matching scarves.

It was as she was doing the final alterations to the window, decorated especially lavishly for Christmas, that she spotted her young brother lurking in the shadow of the shop, watching Richard pull away, and she guessed he hadn't wanted Richard to catch sight of him.

She went to the shop door and called, 'What are you doing?'

'Nothing,' Jamie said.

Grace sighed. Her brother looked the picture of misery. His collar was turned up against the fine icy drizzle that was falling, his hands were stuffed in his pockets and his socks concertinaed down to the tops of his scuffed boots. 'Well go and do nothing someplace else,' Grace snapped. 'In fact go home before Mammy finds you hanging around the streets after dark.'

No way was Jamie going home yet to be bossed about by Bridget and tormented by Mary Ann and Angela, or found a million and one jobs to do for his mother. It was nearly half-past four and his mother wouldn't be home till after six. Time enough to go home then.

The point was, he didn't know what to do with himself and he was suddenly furiously angry with Grace for, first of all, spotting him and then trying to tell him what to do.

'Bugger off,' he cried, 'and mind your own bloody business!'

Had Grace not been at work, she'd have chased Jamie and boxed his ears. As it was, she stood and watched her brother hurtling his way down the road, knowing the effect his words would have on her temper, and she sighed again and returned to the shop.

Really, she thought, the boy was getting impossible and though she was loath to tell on him, she really thought it was time to enlist the help of her mother before he got out of hand altogether.

Jamie hadn't a clue where he was going, so long as it was well away from Grace and her poxy shop and away from the Mosses too, and he ran along Bristol Street towards Latimer Street, where they used to live.

But as he passed Bristol Passage, the small alleyway that led from Bell Barn Road, he heard the clatter of boots and boys of various sizes burst on to the street. The first boy, Gary Pritchard, was carrying a ball.

'Hiya, Hogan,' he cried. 'Want a game?'

Jamie knew Gary – he knew them all – but Gary was in his class in St Catherine's and he stared in awe at the ball in his hands. He had a ball, a cheap rubber thing that you only had to look at wrong for it to develop a hole. But Gary's ball was of thick leather, like a proper football. He ignored the question and said instead, 'Where did you get it?' and he stroked the ball almost reverently.

'Me dad,' Gary said proudly. 'For me birthday.'

'Yeah, probably fell off a bleeding lorry,' one of the other lads said jealously.

Gary rounded on him. 'Shut your mouth, you, or I'll shut it for you,' he said, and turned back to Jamie. 'Are you in, or not?'

'Where you making for?'

'The rubble tip?'

Jamie knew where he meant. There had once been shops and houses on the corner of Bristol Street and Colmore Street that had been turned into rubble courtesy of the Luftwaffe. Just lately the heap had been levelled and the rumour was they were building something on it, but nothing had been started yet. The boys often had a kick about on it and Jamie had been expressly forbidden to do so because it was too close to the road. And now it was dark as well.

'We won't see owt,' he complained.

'Course we will. There's streetlights on Bristol Street, ain't there, and others in Colmore Street at the side? We've played there before, anyroad. It's OK.'

Maeve's face passed before Jamie's eyes and then Richard's, and his own eyes hardened. He was fed up with grown-ups telling him what to do. At that moment he hated the whole world.

'Yeah,' he said. 'I'm in.'

It was, Richard reflected, a filthy night, cold and rain-sodden, the drops dancing in front of the headlights. He'd be glad to get in and he was in a rush because he wanted to catch Grace before she left. He wanted her advice on a new line in silk camiknickers and matching slips. They were pretty enough, but pricey at twenty-five shillings and elevenpence each. He thought they'd probably sell for Christmas, but he'd value Grace's opinion because he didn't want them left on his hands at that price.

He shivered suddenly. Next time he got a car, he reflected, he would get one with a heater, and he promised himself both a bath and a whisky to warm himself up before his tea.

The traffic had increased as he turned into Bristol Street, both with workers driving home, and with buses and trams laden down with shoppers. The rain had suddenly increased too, and the swishing of the wipers was almost hypnotic. He put his foot down. The sooner he was home the better.

On the rubble tip, the boys played on, oblivious to the drizzle that had plastered their hair to their heads, seeped into the shoulders of their jackets and had turned their socks to soggy mud traps. But, suddenly the rain increased in ferocity and Gary called out, 'Better call it a day, lads. Our dad will be in any minute, anyroad.'

'Here y'are, Hogan,' the lad dribbling the ball called out. He gave it an almighty kick and it sailed through the air to Jamie. He leapt for it and felt it scrape past his fingertips. He watched in dismay as it bounced past him on to the pavement and then rolled into the road. It was caught by the wing of a passing car, which bounced it to the far side, where it lodged in the tram tracks.

Behind him he could hear Gary's frightened voice crying, 'Me dad'll kill me if anything happens to that ball.'

'I'll get it for you,' Jamie said, feeling guilty that he'd not been able to leap high enough to catch it. There was a tram rumbling up the tracks, but he knew it was far enough away for him to reach the ball first. He leapt into the road before anyone could stop him and, in the blinding rain, he didn't see the car heading straight for him until it was too late.

TWENTY-EIGHT

Richard didn't see where the dark shape came from. One minute the road was clear and the next there was a boy in front of him. For a second, he caught a glimpse of the boy's eyes, transfixed with terror, and though he slammed his brakes on hard and swung the wheel towards the pavement, he knew he hadn't a hope in hell of stopping in time. There was an unearthly scream and a sickening thud as the car slammed into the boy, lifting him into the air and throwing him down on to the road, where he lay perfectly still. The car drew to a grinding halt, the wheels crushed against the kerb.

People came running out from their houses and from the shops. Richard, dazed himself, pushed away the hands trying to help him as he struggled out of the car. He'd hit a child – he may have killed a child. That thought kept resounding in his head.

He felt nausea rise in his throat as he stood outside of the car at last, willing himself not to faint. He'd never fainted in his life, but he felt mighty odd.

He couldn't see the child – he was surrounded by people – and one turned as Richard made his way towards them. 'Are you all right, mate?'

Richard shook his head impatiently. 'Ambulance?' he said.

'Aye, someone's phoned for one. Gone for the mother, and all. Poor sod, eh?' the man said. 'Can't blame yourself, mate. He just ran in front of you. I seen it all, I did.'

Richard pushed his way through the crowd, but when he went to touch the child lying so frighteningly still, someone said, 'I wouldn't, mate. Do more harm than good. Wait for the ambulance, I would.'

But Richard didn't need to turn the boy over to know who he was. It was Jamie Hogan, Grace's young brother, the one always hanging round the shop. In the glare of the headlights he'd left on, he saw the boy's white face and the big gash on the side of his head where blood was oozing on to the road and mingling with the rainwater. 'Oh God!' Richard breathed.

He stretched out two trembling fingers and put them to the side of Jamie's neck, as he'd done to many colleagues in the war. The pulse was there, but slight. 'Oh God,' he said again.

He began to shiver so violently, his teeth chattered, and as he stood up again, he staggered. Comments and suggestions came from all sides.

'Poor sod is in shock.'

'Sit him on the kerb.'

'Put his head between his knees, he looks as if he's going to pass out.'

Someone brought a blanket from a house and put it round him. Another was laid over Jamie. Hot tears began to gush from Richard's eyes and he made no effort to wipe them away.

Maeve was cashing up in the shop when the frantic hammering came on the door. At first she ignored it; if people couldn't get their shopping in between eight in the morning and six at night, well, hard luck to them.

Her stomach grumbled and she knew she was ready for the stew she had prepared that morning. It had been simmering for two hours and Bridget had been watching it. However, when she'd popped upstairs just a few minutes before to check all was nearly ready, Bridget had said Jamie wasn't in, hadn't been in for hours. She'd have words with that young man when she saw him, Maeve thought. Being sorry for him was one thing, being soft was something else entirely, and she'd not stand for him disobeying her. She'd not have him running round in the dark streets like a hooligan. It wasn't as if he hadn't a fine and comfy home to come back to. He would get the sharp edge of Maeve's tongue that night.

The hammering on the door went on and Syd came through. 'Bloody nuisances,' he said. 'Think we haven't got lives of our own.'

'Shall I see what they want?' Maeve said.

'May as well, or we'll get no peace tonight,' Syd said morosely.

The man nearly fell through the door when Maeve shot the bolts. 'Your lad, your wee lad,' he almost yelled at her. 'He's been knocked over.'

Maeve's hand flew to her heart. 'Dear God, is he badly hurt?' she asked ripping off her overall as she flew for her coat in the lobby at the back of the shop.

The look on the man's face frightened her. 'I don't know,' the man said. 'I didn't wait to see, I just took off to fetch you.'

'Where is he?'

'Bristol Street. The ambulance is on its way.'

Maeve fled from the shop, leaving the cashing-up half done and the money in piles on the counter-top. Her only thought was to get to Jamie.

Afterwards, Maeve knew she'd always remember that moment when she saw him. Her son lay on the rain-soaked road, his lifeblood seeping away from a gaping head wound. She wanted to clasp him to her breast and hold him tight, but the policeman who'd arrived on the scene stopped her. 'He's alive, missus,' he said. 'Hold on to that.'

'Who did it? What happened?' Maeve cried, looking at the sea of faces around her. They shifted uncomfortably, but no one spoke. They all felt immensely sorry for Maeve, but it wouldn't help to know that it had been the boy's own fault. The driver had disappeared, anyway, and no one had seen him go. One minute he'd been sitting on the kerb and the next he'd just gone. The police, who'd arrived before Maeve, had wanted to know where he was as well.

One of them went to try his home – there were plenty to supply the address – but first he turned off the car's headlights and removed the keys, while the other policeman stayed to wait for the mother and the ambulance, but even he didn't give Maeve the man's name.

'They'll be interviewing the driver shortly, missus,' he said. 'Let's concentrate on getting your little lad seen to just now, shall we?'

The ambulance sirens were heard then and the crowd began to move away to make room for the vehicle. Jamie was lifted into the ambulance by stretcher and Maeve climbed in beside him. She'd never seen him so still; even in his sleep he fidgeted. She held on to one cold unresponsive hand and prayed more devoutly than she'd done for years that God would not take her son from her.

*　　*　　*

Richard had slunk home, too scared to face Maeve and admit what he'd done. Amy took one look at her tall handsome son, his hair sticking up in spikes from his running his fingers through it, the mark of tears still evident on his face, his eyes wild, and the colour drained from her face and she felt fear clutch at her.

'What is it?' she asked in a shocked voice.

Richard pushed past her, unable to answer. He dropped into an armchair, covered his face with his hands and groaned.

'What is it?' Amy asked again and when Richard continued to shake his head helplessly, she knelt before him and held him in her arms, poignantly aware that the last time she'd done that, he'd been a week old. Now her son of forty-plus was crying into her shoulder as if his heart was broken.

Eventually, Richard looked at his mother with ravaged eyes and said brokenly, 'I almost killed a child tonight.'

'Killed a child!' Amy repeated, horror-struck, but before she could ask any more there was a knock on the door.

'That will probably be the police,' Richard said calmly, and Amy went to the door as if she were in a dream and let the policeman in without a word.

When they'd first been called to the scene, the sympathies of the police had lain with the boy, ready to believe the driver had been reckless and driving too fast for the road conditions. But the many people who'd witnessed the event had hit that idea on its head. Without exception the consensus was that the driver couldn't possibly have avoided the child.

And that was what the policeman had told Richard when he asked for a statement. He could see the distress on Richard's face and it was plain he'd left the scene of the accident in panic The policeman told him to make him feel better, but Richard didn't care whose fault it was, a child was still injured or worse. Amy was glad her son had been exonerated, but still she listened horror-struck to Richard's account of his journey home from the warehouse and how the accident happened.

The policeman wrote it all down, then read back the statement and Richard signed it before asking, 'Is he badly hurt, the child?'

The policeman shrugged, 'Hard to tell,' he said. 'They were waiting for the mother and the ambulance when I left.'

Richard gave a sigh. 'It's hard,' he said. 'I knew the boy, you see.'

'I wasn't aware of that, sir,' the policeman said. 'Did you know him well?'

Richard was aware they'd been speaking in the past tense and he stiffened and then went on, 'I know the family more. My mother and I employ his sister in the business and I know his mother too.'

He wondered why he'd said that. He'd not set eyes on her nor spoken to her for months. But still he knew her; the hours and hours he'd spent talking to her, he'd come to know her. And then no one could do what they'd done together and not know someone. He could lie in bed at night and even now remember the feel of her arms holding him close, every line and curve of her beautiful body and the sweetness of her lips on his.

His mother had been startled by what he had said and had glanced over at him and caught the soft look on his face in the unguarded moment when he was remembering Maeve and was further surprised. So, she thought, that was the way of it. He's sweet on Maeve Hogan and she

486

wondered if Maeve had been the woman he'd been seeing months and months before. She wondered what had gone wrong between them.

Then hadn't Grace told her Maeve was getting married to a man she knew well and she'd seemed happy enough about it? Richard had seemed to go mad for a little while. He had quite frightened her one night but at the time, she'd not connected his drinking binge to the news of Maeve's marriage. And then it had all gone wrong. Amy never knew the details; Grace would never say. The girl was very good at evading questions she didn't want to answer. Anyway, it had coincided with her mother's illness, which Amy knew she had been very worried about at the time.

But her poor Richard still loved her, that much was evident, and now there was this distressing incident with the child.

The policeman was talking of taking Richard to hospital, going on about delayed shock, but Richard was having none of it. 'I haven't time for shock, delayed or otherwise,' he'd said. 'And I'm going to no hospital.'

He came back into the room, after seeing the policeman out, holding his car keys in his hand. 'The policeman gave them to me,' he told his mother. 'Decent of him. He turned the headlights off too. I'd never have given them a thought.'

Amy ignored what Richard said about the car; she was less worried about that than Richard himself. He still looked quite feverish to her and she wasn't at all sure the policeman hadn't been right to advise him to go to the hospital. She was so concerned that in the end he relented and to please her, he let her phone the doctor to come and give him the once-over.

Dr Fleming knew all about the accident. News of it had flown round the area and he'd made it his business to find out where the child had been taken and how badly he'd been hurt. He could see that Richard was feeling guilty about it, but from what he'd heard he could have done little to prevent it at all. He didn't share the extent of Jamie's injuries with Richard, feeling that wouldn't be helpful.

Instead he said, 'Don't be so hard on yourself. The boy is alive at least.'

'Are you sure?'

'Phoned them myself.'

'Yes, but for how long?' Richard said gloomily. 'I mean what chance has a young boy against a heap of metal driven at speed straight into him?'

'The same chance as many who've survived that and worse,' the doctor told him. 'And he's in the best place. The Children's Hospital performs mini miracles daily.'

Richard said nothing. He'd seen the child lying motionless in the road and he was not a fool. But the doctor continued, 'Let them do their work, man, and let me do mine, and my concern at the moment is you.' He pulled out a prescription pad and began writing on it. 'I'm prescribing you some mild tranquillisers for you to get in the morning. I have some in my bag to see you through tonight.'

'No,' Richard said firmly. 'No, I'm sorry, Doctor, but I want no tranquillisers. I have things to do and I want to be in control of myself and not reliant on tablets.'

'It would just be in the short term,' the doctor said. 'Give yourself a break.'

'I'm sorry, Doctor,' Richard insisted. 'I have no wish to be rude, but . . .'

'It's all right,' Dr Fleming said. 'I'd probably feel exactly the same in your shoes.'

He picked up his bag as he spoke. 'If you change your mind, or you're worried about anything, you know where to find me. No, don't trouble,' he said to Amy as she got to her feet to show him out. 'I know the way.'

When the doctor had left Amy looked at her son and said, 'Are you really all right?'

'I'm fine,' Richard said, although he was feeling bone weary, as reaction to what had happened began to set in.

'I'll make you something to eat.'

'No, Mother, thank you,' Richard said, thinking food would choke him.

'A drink then?' Amy said, turning to the sideboard where she mixed him a whisky and soda just as he liked it. Richard wanted that drink more than he'd ever wanted anything, but he shook his head. To take it would be madness. He needed to go over and see the Hogans and maybe go on to the hospital, and he needed a clear head. Anyway, it would hardly help the situation for him to arrive reeking of spirits.

'Not now,' he said. 'Maybe later. I must go and see how the Hogans are coping and see if they have any news of the child.'

Amy thought that if her son had been maimed or killed as a young boy she'd never have known a thing about it; now she didn't know how she would manage without him. Her heart contracted with sympathy for what Maeve was going through. 'You do right, Richard,' she said. 'Go and find out.'

Inside the Mosses' flat Syd had all Maeve's children with him and was, with Grace's help, attempting to feed them all at the kitchen table with the stew Maeve had left simmering. Richard had worried about Grace, and the shock she would have had, and though she was very pale she was coping. She'd followed her mother to the scene and had found out what had happened and told everyone in the flat that Richard had not been at fault.

'Gwen's gone up to see Maeve's sister Nuala,' Syd said later, when he and Richard were alone in the kitchen. 'Her and Matthew Bradshaw live in a prefab in Perry Common, by all accounts. There was a falling out with them both a while ago,' he went on, 'Anyroad, Maeve thought Christmas was the time to build bridges and she wrote to Nuala a few days ago. Gwen thought Nuala's presence might be a bit of support for Maeve, like. Bloody awful do this, isn't it? I mean, as if she hasn't enough to cope with. Young Grace said the boy was in a bad way.'

Richard nodded miserably.

'Thinks the world of those kiddies, does Maeve,' Syd said. 'Even little Angela, and she's not her child at all – not that you'd ever know it.'

He saw Richard's eyes widen and realised he'd known nothing about the upset. 'No, Angela is his child, you know – Matthew's. Her mother was killed by a doodlebug when she was visiting her sister and her family down London way in 1944. The welfare people were all ready to take the child into care when the grandparents weren't able to cope any longer, but Maeve stepped in. Then when Matthew Bradshaw eventually got married Angela wouldn't leave Maeve.'

Richard was staggered by Maeve's generosity of spirit, both in taking the child in the first place and then keeping her when her sister went off with the man she'd intended to marry. But before he could express this, there was a knock on the door and Syd opened it to find a man outside, holding a boy by the scruff of the neck. 'Mr Moss,' the man said respectfully, 'can I have word?'

Syd stood back from the door, and the man, pushing the boy before him, stepped into the kitchen. In the light Richard saw the boy's eyes were wide with terror and his dirty face was tear-streaked. 'My name is Pritchard,' the man said, unnecessarily in Syd's case, for the grocer already knew him well enough. 'And this little bugger here,' and at this he poked the child in the back, 'he's me son Gary.'

He faced Syd and Richard full in the face and went on, 'Well, I gets this boy a ball for his birthday, good one you know, leather. Cost a pretty penny. But his mother never lets him out after dark; gets up to a heap of mischief then, she says. But tonight the missus had to slip out to see her father 'cos he's been taken bad, like. And what does my brave boy do then,' Mr Pritchard demanded, 'but take the ball for a kickabout? First thing I noticed when I come in was the ball was missing. Course, he said he knew nothing about it, but I got it out of him in the end.'

He looked across at the two men and said, 'The lad who was knocked down was playing football down on the rubble tip just off Bristol Street with my lad and a few others. Someone kicked the ball across the road and he went after it. I'm heart sorry that me and mine have brought such trouble to your door.' He altered his tone then and asked, 'How is the lad?'

'No news yet,' Syd said. 'But don't be hard on the boy. It was an accident.'

'I know he didn't mean to cause it, like,' Mr Pritchard said. 'But I'm trying to bring me family up decent. Still, he's lost the ball now. It was carved up by a tram and, God knows, it will be a long time till he gets another.'

The boy was still crying, but his father seemed to have little sympathy for him. 'Come on, you,' he said scornfully. 'We've wasted enough time here already.'

491

Richard and Syd watched in silence as the man hauled the boy from the room. They heard the clatter of their boots on the stairs and Richard thought of Maeve sitting alone at the hospital, waiting on news of her son.

'I'm going down to the hospital to see Maeve,' he told Syd.

'I don't blame you,' Syd said. 'I doubt if the children will be able to sleep tonight until we know more. Come and tell us when you can.'

Richard nodded, anxious to be gone.

His car was still where he'd left it in Bristol Street and he had the keys in his pocket. He looked at it with distaste. He had no desire to get into any vehicle again, but he had the feeling that if he didn't drive the car now, he'd never drive it again, like people advised getting straight back on a horse when you'd fallen off. He took a deep breath, opened the door and slid in behind the wheel.

He saw her sitting motionless and still in the stark grey hospital corridor and was smitten with pity for her, but remembering how they'd parted, he wondered if he should have brought Grace with him, or the neighbour that Grace had said Maeve was so fond of. Still, it was too late to think of that now, he thought, and he took a seat on the bench beside her. 'Any news?' he asked.

Maeve was filled with a sense of helplessness and the eyes she turned on Richard were sorrow-laden. She could have told him that the doctors said Jamie had a fractured skull and various internal injuries and a broken arm and leg and that he was down in theatre now. But she couldn't have spoken without breaking down. Then Richard might feel obliged to try to comfort her and that she couldn't have borne, so she shook her head, but said nothing.

She didn't know why he'd come here. He must have known he was the last person on earth she'd want to see. She didn't want his sympathy or pity. She'd never felt so desolate and alone in all of her life, but Richard's presence did not make her feel any better and she wished he'd go away.

Richard felt admiration for her composure, but he knew she could do with some support herself, though he was aware he wasn't the one she wanted. He thought over what Syd Moss had told him about her sister and he hoped whatever had happened between them could be resolved, because Maeve badly needed someone beside her. He had to admit, though, if the man had been first engaged to her, as Grace had told him, and left her to marry her sister, small wonder that there had been a fallout over it. He wondered too why Maeve had kept Matthew Bradshaw's child with her when the man left. It wasn't as if she hadn't a houseful of her own.

He wondered too what manner of man Maeve's first husband had been. Grace had always been reticent about personal things and particularly about her father. Richard wondered if Maeve had loved him and grieved over him still, but then he told himself she couldn't. After all, she was going to marry again, so she'd obviously overcome any sadness she might have felt at his death. A tragic accident his mother had told him, and yet Grace had never breathed a word except to say it had happened over three years before.

Richard could understand anyone being attracted to Maeve, because even now, beside her in this cheerless place, his heart was thudding against his ribs and the roof of his mouth was dry, and all because he was sitting near to her.

What he would have given to be able to turn the clock back to that one wonderful night when he'd loved her. If he'd declared his love then, as he should have done, Jamie might not be lying in this hospital. Or, if he was, at the very least Richard would be able to put his arms round Maeve now and offer her some comfort instead of sitting beside her like a dummy with his hands hanging uselessly by his side.

He glanced at her and saw that her eyes were closed and her lips were moving. He thought she was praying. Maeve wasn't praying, though, she was bargaining with God. Once she'd asked God to show her if there was any way she could make amends for what she'd done to Brendan. What if God's answer was to take her son from her? She'd not be able to stand it. Brendan had been a sadistic, violent brute, while Jamie was an innocent child. Surely that wasn't a fair exchange?

Richard had no idea how long they'd been sitting there – it had seemed like hours – when he saw the young doctor approach them.

'Mrs Hogan?'

Maeve's eyes flew open and she jumped at his voice. 'How . . . how is he?' she asked, her voice tremulous, uncertain and very fearful.

'He's a very sick boy,' the doctor said, 'but thankfully the skull fracture was not as bad as we first thought. He's come through the operation well and the initial signs for his recovery are good.'

'Oh, thank God!' It was a fervent prayer, and then Richard saw Maeve's face crumple in relief as the tears gushed from her eyes and gasping sobs shook her body. It was no controlled weeping but a paroxysm of grief, and she reached blindly for a hand – any hand – to feel the touch and comfort of another human being. And while the doctor looked on helplessly, Richard took Maeve's trembling hands in his own. As the crying continued, he gathered her in his arms and held her tight and she wept on to his shoulder.

'If she would like to see the child later,' the doctor told Richard, embarrassed by such an open show of grief, 'just have a word with Matron.'

Richard nodded.

Much later they stood side by side at the bed of the unconscious child, whom they could barely see for the bandages, plaster casts and tubes trailing across his body. Richard felt a wave of tenderness for the boy lying there, a feeling he thought he'd never feel again for a child. Jamie looked as vulnerable and defenceless as Nina had when he'd held her in his arms, and to think he was the cause of the young boy lying there injured! God, that was hard for him to come to terms with.

He was the lad who'd always been hanging round the shop, wanting to do things for him. It wouldn't have hurt him, Richard told himself, if he'd found the odd thing for the boy to do, or even tossed him the odd kind word, instead of ignoring him.

He wondered, and not for the first time, about his avoidance of all children since Nina's death. It showed a coldness in his nature and yet all his life he'd craved warmth – the warmth of a good woman, the warmth of a family. In a way it was the warmth of Maeve's personality that had drawn him to her in the first place. He looked back down to the boy in the bed and was staggered by the strong feeling of love, tinged with protectiveness, that swept over him, taking him completely by surprise.

Maeve, looking down on her son, felt the room suddenly begin to tip and she staggered against the bed. Richard put out a hand to steady her, but she shook him off impatiently. She'd been embarrassed, when her crying had eased somewhat, that she'd allowed herself to be held in that intimate way. Even more disquieting was the fact that she found herself enjoying it so much and that's why the man was so dangerous: she seemed to have no defence against him. Despite her son lying injured in a hospital bed only yards from her, she wished she could have stayed in his arms a little longer. She'd pulled herself away reluctantly and dabbed at her eyes with a tiny lace handkerchief, cross that Richard had used the fact that she'd been so upset, and not really in control of herself, to hold her in his arms. Now here he was again, taking an opportunity to touch her – taking advantage of her weakness. She'd not stand it!

'I have the car outside,' Richard told her.

'The car?' Maeve repeated. 'I don't need your car. I'm staying here.'

'There's really no point in that, Mrs Hogan,' the nurse said. 'Jamie is heavily sedated. He won't know you're here.'

'Even so . . .'

'Believe me, he'll need you later,' the nurse said. 'I should try and get a good night's sleep, if you can, and come back tomorrow.'

Maeve stood undecided. 'Let me give you a lift home,' Richard urged. 'Your children will be anxious about both you and Jamie. I called to see them before I came here and I promised to go back when there was some news.'

'Well, go. I'm not stopping you.'

'Maeve, let me help you,' Richard pleaded. 'There's no point in staying here any longer.'

'I can get home on my own,' she said sharply.

'Maeve, please! The car is parked just outside. The night is bitter cold and there will be few buses running at this late hour.'

'I don't know why you're doing this,' Maeve snapped back at Richard. 'Unless it's to make yourself feel less guilty. I do know that it was you who ran Jamie over. That it's your fault he's here at all.'

A policeman had been to see her and said the man who'd knocked her son down, a Mr Richard Prendagast, had no case to answer. It appeared that Jamie had run straight out in front of the car. But why would he do such a thing? Maeve had chosen not to believe it. She had to find something about the man to despise to prevent any feeling of tenderness welling up inside her.

Richard made no response to her accusation and, feeling too incredibly weary to argue further, Maeve allowed herself to be led down the corridor and into the car park. The cold caught in her throat and the icy rain spears stabbed at her face and soaked her coat. She felt suddenly light-headed coming out into the cold night air after the muggy heat of the hospital; the ground spun before her eyes and she leant her hands on the bonnet of Richard's car to steady herself. This time she was glad of his support – though she was damned if she was going to say so. He helped her into the car and she lay back on the seat with a sigh of relief that she tried hard to suppress. Richard got in beside her and he looked so strong, so very masculine, she had the desire to lay her head on his shoulder and let him take care of everything, for she'd never felt so hopeless and helpless in all her life.

To stop her stupid fantasy, she sat bolt upright in the car and Richard, noticing the movement, asked, 'You all right? Maybe you need something to eat?'

Maeve shook her head, though her stomach was grumbling with hunger. She knew she wouldn't be able to eat.

They travelled on in silence – an uncomfortable silence. Richard couldn't think how to break it and Maeve's mind was too preoccupied with Jamie to welcome small talk. Richard was filled with admiration for the woman beside him. Apart from the tears in the hospital, she seemed to be in full control of her emotions, but even if she hadn't been, she'd made it obvious she wanted nothing from him and he could hardly blame her.

As the car drew to a halt at the back of the shop, Maeve clambered out quickly before Richard could help her. She didn't want him to have any opportunity to get out of the car and possibly put her under an obligation to ask him up to the flat. He seemed to know this, for he made no move to leave the car, but called to her instead, 'If you're going up tomorrow remember the car is at your disposal any time, Maeve. You just have to ask.'

'Thank you,' Maeve said, feeling it would be churlish not to thank the man, but added, 'The hospital have probably got pretty strict rules about visiting and I don't know what I'll do about tomorrow yet.'

These were the words she repeated minutes later to everyone assembled in the Mosses' flat. Maeve had expected that the younger children would have been in bed, for it was very late, but they were all waiting for her.

Nuala, despite Maeve's letter of forgiveness, was nervous meeting Maeve again for the first time since that dreadful night when she'd discovered that she and Matthew loved one another. Maybe, Nuala thought, Maeve would be annoyed to see her ensconced in the Mosses' flat with a drowsy Mary Ann on her lap. Maeve could see her

498

agitation clearly and noticed that Matthew too, nursing Angela, looked uncomfortable.

But neither of them had to worry. Their relationship didn't matter any more to Maeve. It no longer hurt to see them together; in fact it did her heart good to see Angela snuggled against her father once more.

Everyone wanted to hear how Jamie was, and was relieved to know that the operation had been successful so far. Maeve said she would go up the following day and might know more.

'Is Richard taking you?' Grace asked.

'He's offered,' Maeve said. 'But I haven't accepted.'

'Let him take you, Mammy,' Grace urged. 'He feels real bad about the accident. It will make him feel better if he can do something to help.'

It was on the tip of Maeve's tongue to say she didn't give a tinker's cuss about making Richard Prendagast feel better when Syd put in, 'He ran into the road after a ball, did young Jamie. He was playing football – a gang of them were there by all accounts, playing football on the rubble tip. It was young Gary Pritchard's ball. The father hauled him round here earlier on to tell us.'

Maeve drew in a deep breath. Jamie had deliberately disobeyed her, for she'd forbidden him to play on that tip and he'd almost lost his life because of it. The policeman had been right all along: it hadn't been Richard's fault. It wasn't right to make the man feel worse than he did already and she decided she'd go round in the morning and tell him she'd be pleased to accept his offer of a lift.

TWENTY-NINE

Jamie Hogan was kept heavily sedated for almost five days, and Maeve visited him every day, courtesy of Richard, who accompanied her. She wasn't really sure when the antagonism she'd felt towards him began to slip.

Like the first fraught evening, when he couldn't seem to do right for doing wrong, they spoke little in the car on the journeys to and from the hospital, but when they did speak Maeve was civil enough. Richard knew she had more than enough to think about anyway, as for the first twenty-four hours Jamie's life hung in the balance. Even when he was pronounced out of danger, there was the risk of brain damage, as with any head injury and operation. All Maeve could do was sit by his bedside and pray. With worries like that filling her head, Richard thought it highly unlikely she'd enjoy inane chatter.

But on Thursday evening Jamie eventually opened his eyes and spoke, and though the words were slurred and indistinct, Maeve's heart seemed to skip a beat. A doctor was hurriedly summoned. He examined Jamie and later was able to give Maeve the good news that from brief tests carried out, the outlook was good. Jamie in actual fact should make a complete recovery.

Maeve was almost hysterical with joy, though she knew Jamie had a long haul in front of him. She wanted to kiss someone, but there was only the stern-faced doctor, the starchy nurse and Richard and none of them would do.

Richard, she saw, was almost as delighted as she was, and when she sank into the car with a sigh, she said, 'I was so scared that Jamie wouldn't make it. I thought that was what God was demanding from me – my son's life.'

As soon as the words left Maeve's lips she regretted them. She should have kept quiet. Richard would think she was mad. He glanced at her as he eased the car into Broad Street and asked in genuine puzzlement. 'Why did you think that?'

'Oh, it's nothing. Something I did years ago,' Maeve said, and then to turn the conversation, went on, 'When my sister went off with my fiancé, I thought that was punishment enough. Did you know I was engaged to Matthew Bradshaw?'

Richard nodded. 'Grace told me,' he said, inwardly hurt that Maeve should mention this so casually. It was as if their one evening of passion had meant nothing to her, but then why should it? She'd obviously put it behind her and gone on with her life. It wasn't her fault if he couldn't do the same.

'I was raging at the time,' Maeve went on. 'I put Nuala out of the house that very night. I felt hurt and betrayed. I didn't love Matthew, but I cared deeply for him. I wanted security, respectability and the chance of a decent house and neighbourhood to bring the children up in. Matthew, on the other hand, wanted to get out of the dismal rooms he was in to be a proper father for Angela. We'd been friends, true friends, for years and I'd have trusted him

501

with my life. I never thought he'd do what he did and with my own sister.'

'Yet when he left, you kept the child?'

Maeve shrugged. 'It wasn't Angela's fault and she had no wish to go.'

Richard thought of all the times he'd resented children just for the fact they were alive and he felt ashamed. But he was still confused by Maeve's thinking Matthew's deception was engineered by God. 'Why didn't you just confess what you did that was so wrong?' he asked. 'Then you'd get penance and that would be that.'

Not in this case, Maeve could have said. But instead she said, 'You seem to know a lot about it.'

'I was brought up to it, that's why,' Richard said. 'The Prendagasts were staunch Catholics, but after the blood bath I was involved in, I'm not even sure I believe in God any more.'

'Did you blame Him for taking your wife and child from you?' Maeve asked gently.

Richard hesitated. He'd never spoken of it, ever. Few knew anything about Prendagast's private life and fewer still of his loss. He knew if any had tried to offer him sympathy he would have rejected it. He'd kept his grief all locked away inside himself.

When the war drew to a close, his adoptive mother was just glad to have him home safe, though hardly sound – he was too disillusioned and bitter, but she understood that. She was of the generation of the stiff upper lip and deplored any show of emotion. She advised Richard to put everything, the war and the tragedy he'd suffered, out of his mind and get on with his life. Richard had tried to do that with alcohol and while it blurred the edges, the pain was still there.

And now for the first time somebody was asking him something about his loss, and asking as if she cared about the answer. Richard was glad of the dimness of the car's interior, as he burst out, 'Blame God? Maeve, I blamed the whole goddamned world. I blamed Valerie for not using the proper shelters, but taking cover under the stairs, and her parents for encouraging it. And yes, I cursed God for allowing it to happen.' There was a small silence and then Richard went on, 'I married Valerie in June nineteen thirty-nine. I didn't love her, but I liked her well enough after courting her for two years. Thanks to the generosity of my adoptive father, I was able to buy a house. I would have preferred a nicer area than Aston, but my wife wanted to be near her family and they all lived in the roads round and about. I gave in, partly because I liked her family very much, and knew they'd be a great help and support to Valerie while I was away, especially when I knew she was expecting. She was ridiculously proud of the house, which had a separate parlour and didn't open on to the street, but had a little paved area in front with a gate and our own yard at the back.

'The war that everyone knew was coming began, and I enlisted in the Royal Warwickshires and sailed to France in November nineteen thirty-nine as a member of the Expeditionary Force. The whole world knows how premature that invasion was, and how men were trapped on the beach at Dunkirk. We knew our only hope of being rescued was to reach the little pleasure boats, bobbing about on the choppy grey sea as if they were at some sort of regatta.

'They couldn't come very far in without getting stranded, so we began building pier-heads with abandoned equipment. All the time we were being machine-gunned and bombed. You'd throw yourself flat and see craters open up to the sides and front of you with men buried in them. With me were three good friends I'd had since childhood. We joined up in a fit of patriotic zeal and we'd been through a lot together. We were man-handling giant tyres down to the pier, when we heard the drone of many planes heading our way. There was no cover and we flung ourselves down, trying to burrow into the sand a little, and the bombs came whistling down. There were screams and cries and I lifted my head. Two of my friends were just yards from me and they too looked up, and our eyes met. The next minute, a blast knocked me out of the hollow I was in, and my face and mudcaked uniform and the beach were splattered with bits of skin, bone, blood and internal organs – all that remained of my two friends.'

Beside Richard, Maeve gasped, but he was hardly aware of it and Maeve knew he was back there in the hell of Dunkirk.

'There was just the two of us left, Charlie and me,' he went on. 'Shocked as we were, there was no time to grieve and neither of us could speak of it, so we just got back to the job in hand. Charlie was mown down by the Stukas. I couldn't believe it – I wouldn't believe it. I began dragging his lifeless body towards the pier-head. I knew in my head it was bloody useless, but I couldn't seem to let go. Someone had to near knock me out to get me away. I was riddled with shrapnel myself. I didn't care whether I lived or died.

'After I was patched up, I went home for a bit and held my daughter in my arms for the first time. I knew the Battle of Britain raging in the skies was all that was keeping invasion at bay, and I tried to persuade Valerie to move into my mother's home in Four Oaks. I remember Valerie laughed at me and reminded me she was two hundred miles inland. A lot of people in Birmingham thought that fact ensured their safety. But' – Richard shrugged – 'I think her decision had a lot to do with my mother's attitude. Not that she disliked Valerie any more than she would any girl who was important to me. Valerie was still feeling her way as a mother and thought my mother would probably have made her feel inadequate. She didn't say this, but then she didn't have to.

'I gave in. What could I do? I had a war to fight, but this time I was friendless and wanted to stay that way. Not only my special mates, but other men I'd become fond of had been left behind on the beaches of Dunkirk. I knew I'd not let myself get close to anyone any more. After that I became known as a loner and it suited me to be that way and, to be honest, that's how I've stayed.

'I lived for letters from Valerie. My mother wrote stiff little missives, but Valerie's letters cheered me up, telling me little snippets about her family and things the baby did. I spent hours at night dreaming about her and Nina and making plans for after the war. I wanted more children so Nina would not be lonely, and I wanted to be able to show my children the affection denied me, though Valerie and her family had gone some way to tease the stiffness out of me. I know my parents loved me, but neither could show it. I never remember my mother putting her arms tight round me, and the only contact I remember having with my father was a firm handshake the day I began school. I promised myself my own children would have more than that.

'There was little time for dreaming in the day, as we pushed on through North Africa and we encountered heavy fighting in our bid to wrest Libya from the Italians. Maeve, I saw men semi-conscious, with limbs severed or blown off completely, and others with skulls caved in, or gaping wounds, who lay bleeding to death, or had their innards blown out of their bodies entirely. Some, like my friends, had been blown into thousands of pieces and you walked over the remains of what had once been men. Some screamed in agony, or sobbed helplessly, while others called for their mothers, wives or girlfriends, and some took days to die. And over it all was the smell of death and decay and the pungent smell of blood mixed with cordite and the acrid stink of explosives.

'I'd cut myself off. I'd become desensitised to death and suffering. I had to, or I couldn't have gone on. And into this carnage came the news that Valerie and her entire family, including our baby, had been killed. I was numbed by it. I found I couldn't cry, or howl like I thought I should be doing. It was like they were nothing to me. Just more casualties of war. It wasn't that I didn't care. I was bloody heartbroken, but I never grieved for them, not really, and that has always made me feel as guilty as hell.

'I suppose,' Richard added, 'that's why I tried to blame Valerie – to help me cope with the guilt. The point is, when I did eventually get home, I realised it wouldn't have mattered where the bloody hell she'd gone that night. The brick-built shelter was a blackened shell, and the few people with gardens big enough to house an Anderson shelter and who had taken cover in them were either crushed to death or blown to pieces. The whole area was flattened.

'There was only God left to blame then and, of course, other families left intact.' He gave a grim laugh and said, 'In my rational moments, I knew this to be a stupid way to think, but most times then I wasn't rational. Even now . . . Well, until recently I've found being around children an uncomfortable experience. But, Maeve,' he said earnestly, 'I was trying to deal with the fact that my world had been blown apart. I couldn't believe I'd survived the war, when others, far more cautious and with more to live for than me, didn't make it.'

The car had drawn to a stop outside Moss's yard, but Maeve made no move to get out. She felt stunned by Richard's account of his war.

Eventually, he gave a long shuddering sigh and said, 'I'd like you to know, Maeve, that I've never ever opened my heart like that to another living soul.'

Maeve felt immense sympathy for the man she'd always felt to be deeply lonely. No wonder, she thought, he'd searched so hard and so diligently for his real mother. She could see his anguished face more clearly in the streetlamp by Moss's yard. She put her hand over one of his still gripping the wheel, and he turned to look at her. His tentative smile caused butterflies in Maeve's stomach and Richard held her hand for a moment and said, 'I'd like to think we are friends at least.'

Maeve was confused. The last thing she intended, and the last thing Richard needed, was to be misled. Whatever Maeve's feelings, she mustn't let him know. 'I'm grateful for all you've done for us,' she said carefully. 'True friendship takes time to develop, but I like you more now than I ever did. Maybe that's a start.'

It wasn't really what Richard wanted and he tried again. 'My feelings for you go deeper than just liking.'

Maeve shook her head. 'There's no point going down that road,' she said.

'There was something between us,' Richard cried. 'You can't deny it. Bloody hell, Maeve, I've dreamt often of that last evening we had together.'

And me, Maeve might have said. Instead she tried to reason with him. 'Look, Richard, it's not you. It's nothing personal. I'm scared of relationships. I loved my husband dearly and I truly thought he loved me. I don't know what it was that soured him, but I do know any love between us shrivelled up and when the endearments ceased, the violence began. But I don't know why, d'you see? I don't know whether it was something I did, or just something that happens.'

Richard was silent. He would have liked to ask Maeve what she meant by violence; he'd like to hear what her marriage was like, but somehow knew she wouldn't talk about it.

Maeve had her hand on the handle of the door, but she paused to say, 'My mammy used to say: you never know a man until the ring is on your finger. And she's right, I know she's right. I mean, wouldn't you think I'd know Matthew inside out? We were engaged and yet he must have been carrying on with my sister behind my back. It doesn't hurt any more, but it did destroy my trust in all men. That's why I'll never marry ever again.'

Well, that was final enough, Richard thought, as he watched Maeve climb from the car and walk across the yard. She couldn't have made it any clearer, and he went home dejected.

Despite Maeve's words, after that night any hostility she may have had left towards Richard melted away. She imagined few men returned from war unscarred mentally and it would be rather a hard-hearted man who hadn't been affected in some way by the things he had witnessed, besides his own more personal tragedy.

Richard steeled himself to meet Maeve's children when he picked her up to take her to the hospital, and despite his telling Maeve of the uneasiness he had always felt around children, he got on well with them. In fact his appearance in their life came at an opportune time, for Angela had finally agreed to go to stay at her father's new prefab until after Christmas, so that she could see how she liked it. It was a wrench for them all to lose her, especially for Maeve and Mary Ann, yet Maeve knew it was the right thing for the family to be together and she guessed Angela would never come back to live permanently with them.

'I must go, d'you see?' Maeve overheard Angela explaining to a tearful Mary Ann. 'Because I'm soon going to have a new brother or sister and Nuala needs me to look after her.'

But, despite her initial enthusiasm to live at her daddy's new house, on the day of departure she wept bitterly, and so did everyone else. That night Richard's presence with his stock of jokes and funny tales cheered everyone up.

There had been distrust of him at first, for Bridget particularly remembered how they'd welcomed Matthew and he'd become part of their lives and then he'd betrayed them all. But eventually even she'd been won over, and that was partly because Richard was aware that Bridget was only a year older than his own daughter would have been. He talked to her as if she was grown up and listened to her opinions, and Bridget, who was slightly resentful of her brother getting all the attention, and ashamed of herself because of it, revelled in Richard's interest in her. Bridget told Mary Ann it wasn't as if he were a complete stranger either, for Grace had been going on about him for months and everything she'd said had been good.

So Richard was accepted within the family. As Jamie began to recover, other people wanted to visit him, and

Maeve didn't go so often. But, with the new sympathy she had for Richard, she knew he'd miss driving her back and forth to the hospital. It wasn't as if the man knew many people in the area, so Maeve decided to ask him to dinner on a Sunday, or the occasional Wednesday evening when she had the time to prepare something, and soon she began to look forward to seeing him.

She always took great care with her appearance then, wearing one of her prettier blouses and best skirts, and high-heeled shoes and nylon stockings. She began experimenting with cosmetics, using a little lipstick, rouge to heighten her cheekbones, and perfume dabbed behind each ear.

She never asked herself why she took such pains and would deny she did to anyone else, but Grace was aware of it and she thought probably Richard was too. She'd seen his eyes light up in approval when he looked at her.

Syd and Gwen Moss and Elsie were aware of the shift in the relationship between Maeve and Richard. Through their concern for Jamie, and with Syd being good about running Elsie up to the hospital with him and Gwen in the van to visit the boy, the three of them had become friendly. United in their love and concern for Maeve, they watched the developments between her and Richard that Maeve described as a friendship with interest.

'A friendship my Aunt Fanny,' Elsie exclaimed one day to Gwen as they made their way home from the hospital together, it being a Friday and the van needed for deliveries. 'Called to see her the other Wednesday afternoon and she was dressed up like a dog's dinner. Said Richard was eating with them. I'm positive sure she was wearing cosmetics and scent.'

'Why don't you have a word?'

510

'What, and get my bloody head bitten off?' Elsie cried. 'Not flippin' likely. Anyroad, I tipped her the wink with Matthew and look what happened there. This time I'll let nature take its course.'

'Sometimes nature needs a kick up the backside,' Gwen remarked. 'And that business between Maeve and Matthew didn't turn out too bad, all told. D'you think she really cares for Richard?'

'More than she's letting on,' Elsie declared. 'And he's dotty about her. Can't keep his blinking eyes off her if she's in the room, you know. She'd be a fool not to take him. He's got money and she could take life easier. She's had a bloody hard haul all her life, and it would do her good to have a bit of a rest.'

Gwen pondered on Elsie's words and as soon as she was alone with Syd she put her proposal to him. They'd already discussed the possibility of leaving the shop to Maeve in their will, but now Gwen wanted to make her a partner in the business. 'But why?' Syd asked. 'She gets a good whack now and I'll raise it more if you like.'

'It's because of something Elsie said,' Gwen explained. 'You know Maeve was marrying Matthew just to have some form of security and a decent place to live? I don't want her to marry Richard for the same reason.'

'Has he asked her?'

'Not yet, but he will. I want to make sure if she agrees to marry him it's because she loves him.'

Syd shook his head. He'd never understand women, but still he had no real objection to making Maeve a partner. She'd become like one of the family, and the children had given a new lease of life to Syd and Gwen. Besides, with Stanley gone, there was no one else to leave the place to.

Maeve, however, was stunned by their generosity.

'The place will be totally yours when Gwen and I pop our clogs, like,' Syd said. 'The thing is, Maeve, where there's a funeral, there's often relatives come out the bloody woodwork, and some of them you've never clapped eyes on in your life, nor would want to neither. I couldn't stand for some third cousin twice removed or some such to inherit what we worked damned hard for and tip you into the street. I'd not rest in my grave.'

For Maeve the revelation that she owned half the shop made a difference to her, and she made plans in her head for Bridget and Mary Ann. She didn't think she'd have Jamie with her for long after he'd grown up. He loved the land as much as Kevin. Kevin had written to Maeve and told her he had a mind to offer Jamie half of his inheritance if he wanted it once he was sixteen. Maeve knew Jamie would take it and she also knew she had no right to stop him.

Now, though, Maeve owned half the shop and one day it would be all hers. They were set for life. Bridget, who loved serving in the shop, could have a proper job there if she wanted when she left school, and Mary Ann too. Maybe Syd would teach them both to drive the van. In fact, she thought suddenly, maybe he could teach her too. She wasn't in her dotage yet.

But first there was Christmas to face and Kevin was coming to share it with them and to see Jamie, which Maeve knew would be a boost to the young boy's recovery.

On Sundays Richard came to dinner, which they had in the evening, and every time she thought of it a little frisson of excitement now leapt inside Maeve but she refused to recognise it.

That evening Richard thought Maeve had never looked lovelier. The satin blouse was the same shade as her eyes

512

and set off her beautiful hair. As usual Richard had bought flowers and a bottle of wine as his contribution to the meal, and he smelt Maeve's perfume as she bent forward to take them from him. He wanted to take her in his arms and hold her tight and kiss her till she was dizzy. But instead, he gave her a chaste kiss on the cheek.

He recalled the conversation he'd had with his mother just the previous evening. He hadn't been aware that Grace and his mother were only too conscious of his slide into despondency as the days passed and he got no further in his relationship with Maeve.

Eventually Amy Overley thought it was time to take action. They'd been halfway through dinner when she'd said, 'Richard, you've never asked and I've never spoken about your father, but I think it's time to talk about him. I'd hate you to think he was just some fly-by-night.

'The point was,' she'd continued, 'my family didn't think he was good enough for me, and my father was wealthy and influential enough to put such pressure on him, he had to leave the area as soon as they were aware we were seeing one another. He'd begged and begged many times for me to go away from the place with him, but I'd always refused. I'd been too scared. As soon as the romance was discovered I was locked in my room until it was certain my lover had gone, and I'd "come to my senses", as my father was fond of saying.

'Just weeks after your father left, I discovered I was pregnant. I was frantic and scared, but pregnancy is one thing you can't hide and as soon as my father found out, he was more worried about the shame of it all than how I'd survive and he threw me into the street.

'I tried to find your father, but he'd disappeared without trace and, distraught and penniless, I had no option but the workhouse. I gave birth to you there. You were just a week old when the nuns came. They said they had a couple in their parish who'd been married years with no sign of a family, who wanted a healthy male child to bring up as their own. I wanted to keep you, but knew that would have been almost impossible on my own, and these people could probably give you every opportunity.

'I didn't have any choice anyway in the end. I was reminded that I and the child I'd had out of wedlock were dependent on the parish for our very survival. They said I should think myself lucky that decent people should want to adopt a workhouse bastard. For years and years I bitterly regretted the fact that I didn't defy my family and go off with your father when I'd had the opportunity. He was a hard-working man, he loved me and would have loved you very much. Any trials we might have suffered we would have faced together and I'd have had the joy of bringing you up.'

Richard had felt so sorry for his mother. He'd heard the catch in her voice and seen the gleam of tears in her eyes. He'd got up, put his arms round her shoulders, and given her a hug while he kissed her cheek. It was the first time he'd ever done such a thing and Amy had flushed with pleasure.

But when he would have pulled away she held on to his hands and her eyes held his, as she said, 'What I'm saying, Richard, is sometimes life doesn't give you a second chance. If you care for someone then go for it.'

Richard had known then his mother was well aware who he was pining for. Had he been asked, he would have said Amy would probably not be pleased with Maeve as a prospective bride, despite employing her daughter in the shop. But Amy had no claims on Richard. She'd given

514

them away and she only desired his happiness. He recognised that.

By Sunday evening he'd decided to confront Maeve and find out her true feelings for him once and for all. He waited till the younger girls had gone to bed and Grace had taken herself off to her friend Bernadette's for the night, and he and Maeve were sitting with a cup of coffee before the fire. Normally he would drain his cup and leave shortly afterwards, but that night he didn't intend to.

He finished his coffee and put the cup down on the table. He'd been sitting in an armchair while Maeve was on the settee, but now he moved across and sat beside her. Maeve's insides were churning at Richard's nearness and her mouth was dry, so dry that when she tried to ask him what he was doing, she was unable to. Richard picked up one of Maeve's slender hands and she began to tremble.

'Maeve,' he said, 'I must tell you how I feel about you. I know you say you feel nothing but friendship for me, but I love you with all my heart and soul. Maeve, I want to marry you.'

'Richard, please . . .'

Richard knew that Maeve felt something deeper than mere friendship for him. Her whole body was quivering and he waited for Maeve's response, his heart hammering so hard against his ribs, he was sure that Maeve would be able to hear it.

But Maeve remembered Brendan and his sweet promises before marriage, and Matthew's kindness and consideration, which hadn't prevented him carrying on with another. And then she remembered the night she'd smothered Brendan to death. She knew God would demand some payment for that. She didn't deserve happiness, she didn't deserve to be loved, or desired. A life alone was to be her penance, her sacrifice that she'd offer to God and hope he would be somewhat appeased by it.

She hardened her heart against Richard, when really she wanted to melt against him and feel his arms round her once more and his lips on hers. Wanton that she was, if she allowed any weakness she'd let him do anything he liked to her.

'Leave me alone, Richard,' she said wearily, pulling her hands away with an extreme effort of will. 'Please just leave me alone.'

'Maeve, I thought you cared for me,' Richard said, hurt beyond measure, but also puzzled.

The pain in Richard's voice cut Maeve to the quick, and she knew she had to get the man out of her flat before she threw her arms round him, covered him with kisses and thoroughly disgraced herself again. She forced a hard laugh to escape the lips that would have preferred to murmur endearments as she said, 'I do care for you, Richard, but then I care for lots of people – my own family, my children, Gwen and Syd Moss, Elsie and Alf Phillips. You are just one in a long line.'

'I see,' Richard said stiffly. He wondered how he was still able to speak, to function at all, when he was dying inside. He wanted to fall on his knees and beg and plead, but she'd told him plainly what her feelings were and his pride was the only thing he had left. 'I'm sorry that I've misread the situation totally,' he said in a voice drained of emotion. 'I think it would be better if I left now.'

Maeve wanted to hold on to his arm, tell him she was sorry, she hadn't meant a word of it, tell him he was the light of her life and that she couldn't go on if he walked out of it. But she did none of those things. Instead she said in a hoarse whisper, 'Perhaps that would be best.'

When he left the room she stayed sitting where she was. She felt numb.

She heard the crash of the door and Richard's feet on the stairs, and a low animal howl escaped from her. She felt as though all feeling was leaking out of her, leaving just a shell. She had to pull herself together, she told herself, but when she stood up to make her way to the kitchen, she staggered like a drunk. She told herself she'd lived without Richard in her life before and would do so again. She'd make a cup of tea, that's what she'd do; it would make her feel better.

But once in the kitchen she hadn't the energy. She sank on to a chair and, burying her head in the crook of her arm that she'd laid on the table, she wept.

THIRTY

When Grace came home, some time later, she found her mother at the kitchen table, her head resting on her arms, and when Grace saw the red, puffy eyes, she knew she'd been crying for some time, though her cheeks were dry. She put the kettle on and made them both a drink and sat opposite her mother, almost frightened by the deadened look in her eyes.

'Mammy, what is it?'

Maeve shrugged and Grace sighed. 'Has Richard gone? Did you quarrel?'

Maeve nodded her head mutely, and Grace guessed the quarrel had been a serious one. 'What was it over?' she asked.

'I told him to go.'

'But why? Did he offend you, upset you in some way?'

'He wanted to get too involved,' Maeve said at last. 'He said he loves me and wants to marry me.'

That knowledge did not surprise Grace in the least. 'Well, what of it?'

'I don't want a husband. I was married once, that was enough.'

'Mammy, your life isn't finished because you had a bad marriage,' Grace cried, exasperated. 'God knows, you suffered enough then. Have you told him about Daddy?'

'Not at all. Why would I?'

'I told Chris. I told him everything.'

'Grace! God, girl, you had no right.'

'I had no right not to,' Grace cried. 'You know Chris wants to get engaged when he's demobbed? I couldn't marry him and not tell him. You say you killed Daddy, Mammy, but I'm not stupid. I know someone your size couldn't have smothered Daddy unless I'd already half killed him with the poker.'

'That may be so. But still, to tell Chris . . .' Maeve said. 'You were always the one who said we must keep it a secret.'

'Mammy, Chris and I love one another,' Grace replied. 'And that involves trusting. You can't keep something like this from the man you love.' She faced her mother squarely and said, 'Do you love Richard?'

Maeve moved her head impatiently. She didn't wish to discuss it.

'Mammy,' Grace said, 'why do you deny yourself a life of your own? You've put us first in everything for years. Think, Mammy, in a few years I'll be married. Not long after Jamie will, I imagine, be going to live in Ireland with Kevin.'

I'll still have Bridget and Mary Ann. Maeve didn't say it, but the thought passed across her mind. But wasn't that the one thing she'd always been determined not to do – to bind her children to her by a sense of duty? Doubt niggled in her mind. Was that the reason she'd offer both the girls jobs in the shop, to bind them to her?

'What will you do when we're all gone?' Grace asked.

'I'll manage,' Maeve said stiffly. 'Like I always have.'

'Mammy, I don't want you to *manage*,' Grace cried. 'I want you to be happy. I think you've given up Richard because you don't feel worthy to be loved by anyone for what you were forced to do to Daddy. And you were forced, Mammy. If you hadn't, he would have killed us both and you know it.'

Maeve knew her daughter was right. She did feel unworthy to be loved. God, she'd never been loved but that once. She'd been possessed, owned by Brendan, but not loved, and Matthew had never pretended deep sensual love would be an important ingredient in their marriage. True, Maeve would never have to look for a man to provide for her now, but she knew the shop wouldn't keep her warm in bed.

Oh, dear God, the thought of bed brought to her mind what she and Richard had shared one evening months and months before. And they had shared it and she remembered Richard had sought her pleasure before his own. She faced the sudden realisation that she did love the man, loved him more than life itself and she'd lost him. She blamed no one but herself and she put her face in her hands and groaned.

'Go after him, Mammy,' Grace urged. 'Tell him truthfully how you feel and then tell him about Daddy. If you don't he will have won, don't you see? He persecuted you while he was alive and you're still letting him destroy your life now he's dead. Tell Richard everything, Mammy.'

Maeve gazed at her daughter, and knew what she was asking her to do. She'd not said a word to Matthew and would never have done, but then she hadn't loved him. But if there was true deep love between herself and Richard, she couldn't keep such a thing to herself. It would always stand between them, and might, in time, blight their feelings for one another. Without another word to Grace, she went into the bedroom to fetch her coat.

'I thought he was with you,' Amy Overley said, puzzled. 'Didn't he come round?'

'Yes, yes, but he left. I . . . I thought he might be here. I need to see him.'

Amy Overley knew by Maeve's manner that she was upset, distracted in some way. Maybe they'd quarrelled. She wondered if the words of advice she'd given her son about his father and her regret at not going with him when he'd asked her to had anything to do with it, and hoped not.

'Would you like to wait for him?'

'If you don't mind.'

'Not at all,' Amy said, knowing that if a woman pursues a man after a disagreement, it's usually to try to resolve it in some way.

But it was hard for Maeve to sit there trying to make small talk with Amy Overley, hearing the clock ticking away, and wondering if Richard was ever going to come home that night, and how he was spending the intervening time.

She felt she'd exhausted every topic of conversation and would drown in tea when he did eventually arrive. He wasn't drunk, but not truly sober either, and Maeve's heart sank. Amy, with one look at the glance that passed between the two of them, took herself off to bed.

The door had barely closed behind his mother, when Richard said, 'Come to pour more scorn on my head, Maeve Hogan?'

'I've come to apologise.'

'Apologise,' Richard said, and gave a grim laugh. 'For what? Letting me make a fool of myself and then

521

kicking the balls off me? God, you're priceless, d'you know that?'

Maeve said nothing at first. Richard was bitterly hurt. She could feel it coming out of him as though it was seeping out the pores of his skin and it gave her the courage to say, 'I've come to apologise for everything, Richard. I'm sorry for every hurtful word I've said to you. And I want to try to explain why.'

Richard stared at her. What game was she playing now? She sounded sincere, but he was still cautious. God, he'd thought she was encouraging him before and then look what she'd done! 'Explain away,' he said, his tone still harsh.

'Not here,' Maeve said. It wasn't just the fact of Amy overhearing anything she might say, or Richard's reaction to it, it was just that Maeve needed the cover of darkness to tell him what she must.

'Then where?'

'Will you come for a walk with me?'

A walk in a bitterly cold bleak night in December was madness, a jog would be more like it, and yet Richard found himself agreeing.

And so they walked side by side, Richard still bristling with anger and Maeve doubting the wisdom of what she was about to do. Not only was she putting her neck on the line, but Grace's and Dr Fleming's too.

She sneaked a look at Richard's profile as they passed under a streetlamp. He looked stern and unforgiving, and her heart sank. But he must have felt her eyes on him because he turned and said, 'Well?'

Maeve swallowed. She had to trust him and believe he loved her too much to betray her, or all was lost. 'I'd like to tell you,' she said, her voice little more than a whisper, 'what my life was like when I was married to my husband,' and she felt for Richard's hand to help her to go on.

He held it hesitantly at first, but as Maeve spoke she felt the pressure of it increase for he listened to her tale of a life of such poverty and deprivation, when even the most basic necessities were denied them. When Maeve described the beatings Brendan had administered to her and Kevin he felt white-hot rage build up inside him. Eventually he pulled Maeve to a stop, because he could hardly bear to hear what she'd suffered. He held both her hands and said, 'Maeve, I can hardly stand listening to this. For a man to so abuse you in this way . . . It's almost unbelievable! Wasn't there anyone to stand up to the brute?'

'My family in Ireland didn't know,' Maeve said. 'I did go to them once, but I was forced back by overzealous priests, reminding me of my marriage vows, and gossipy sanctimonious townspeople. But I left Kevin and Grace there, using the war as an excuse. After that, there was little point in worrying them, because they could do nothing about it. Brendan promised to change if I went back, but I knew he wouldn't.'

'What of his people?'

'They've been brought up that way,' Maeve said. 'His mother often showed the marks of her husband's fists. They'd have thought nothing of it. I have an uncle living close by, but he thought my husband a grand man like the bloody priest, Father Trelawney. I used to think they were all in it together. If it wasn't for Elsie Phillips's help and support for us all, I don't know what I'd have done.'

'I tell you, Maeve, it's lucky your husband is already dead, for I'd feel like ripping him apart for what I've heard tonight.'

Maeve gave a sudden shiver, Richard pulled her close and she buried her head in his shoulder. 'Do you want to go on?' Richard asked, and Maeve nodded her head dumbly. She had to go on, or she'd never have the courage again.

'Let's walk, then, or we'll stick to the ground,' Richard said, and as they cuddled together Maeve told him of the babies she'd lost through near-starvation and violence, and the last one, almost full term, when Brendan had beaten her so severely that he'd killed the child while it was still inside her.

She felt Richard's hand on her shoulder tighten. 'I can't have children now, Richard,' Maeve said bleakly. 'You should know that. Brendan damaged something inside me. I can never give you a child of your own if we . . . if we should marry.'

Richard's heart plummeted, though Maeve was unaware just how upset he was. He'd yearned for a child of his own – not to replace Nina, for no one could do that – but a child he'd have the pleasure of watching grow up. Now that could never be and he felt the disappointment keenly. He asked himself if it mattered. Of course it bloody mattered. But then he faced the realisation that he'd rather have Maeve on any terms, than anyone else in the world.

'It's you I love, Maeve,' he said. 'You I want to share my life with.'

Maeve hadn't been aware that she'd been holding her breath until she let it out in a huge sigh of relief at Richard's words. She went on. 'You said you felt guilty being unable to grieve for your wife and child. The last baby I lost, I lay in a hospital bed and couldn't feel truly sorry that the child had died. It was one less mouth to feed, you see, and I was consumed with guilt that I felt such little grief for the tiny baby girl who'd done no one any harm. When they said I'd be unlikely to have any more children, inside myself I rejoiced. I thought Brendan could paw and maul all he liked, and I'd be safe.'

She caught hold of Richard's other hand and swung him round to face her. 'That's how I thought of his attempts in bed, you see, pawing and mauling. It was nothing like the rapturous thing I shared with you that one night. I never knew sex could be like that; even from the earliest days of our marriage, I'd felt little. I never knew what was wrong and why I felt as I did, though I'd always been eager enough at the start, at least before I became pregnant with Kevin. That's when Brendan decided that I deserved no consideration at all, either in the bed or out of it. But when you made love to me that night, I suddenly realised that it couldn't have been me at fault, or I couldn't have responded so eagerly to you, nor enjoyed it so much, could I?' she asked urgently.

Richard knew exactly what manner of man Brendan had been. 'No, darling,' he replied. 'There are many men like your husband, who think only of themselves and nothing for their partners. It's a form of selfishness. You are a sensual woman, Maeve, and there is nothing sinful in that, or about enjoying it either. When we are married, Maeve, I will show you often how much I love you.'

He wasn't surprised that Maeve left frustrated night after night and didn't seem to know why. He wouldn't expect and decent woman would know about such things. But far more important in his opinion was the vicious and sadistic nature of the bully that she had married.

He tightened his arm round Maeve, pulling her closer to him, and she snuggled against him, feeling safe and protected. This man she knew she could trust with any secret under the sun and she began to tell him how Brendan had met his end. She made him see the horror of it, the beating so ferocious that it had almost stripped the clothes from her back. Her screams, she said, had brought her terrified daughter from her bed, and her puny efforts to stop her father had only enraged him further until Grace had picked up the poker and brained him with it.

'Oh, the relief when he fell lifeless to the floor,' Maeve said. 'Oh, Richard, you've no idea. Of course, I was frightened for Grace and I knew we'd have to make it look like an accident, but we were safe. I sent Grace to change from her blood-stained nightie to her ordinary clothes, for I knew she'd have to fetch the doctor. I leant across for the poker to clean it and Brendan opened his eyes and looked straight into mine.

'I saw hatred deep within him. I thought if he lived my life wouldn't be worth tuppence; if he recovered he would surely beat me to death and Grace would be led a dog's life. As for Kevin, Brendan had something really nasty planned for him. He kept hinting at it to keep me like a frightened wreck and I knew he couldn't be allowed to live. He was evil – I could almost smell it in the room – so I picked up a cushion from the settee and smothered him.'

'And this was why you thought God would take your son from you?'

Maeve nodded. 'I prayed about it, you know,' she said. 'And I sort of made a bargain. I said if there was any way to make amends He had to show me. After all, I did kill the man. That's why I thought He was demanding Jamie's life.'

She pulled away from Richard, looked straight into his eyes and said, 'Tell me honestly, are you shocked at what I did?'

'I'll say I'm shocked, shocked to the very core of me!' Richard cried. 'Shocked at the life you led and how you stood it, and I'm appalled at the clergy who offered no support and the society we live in which condones such behaviour.' He pulled Maeve to him again and said, 'Maeve, now answer me honestly, do you love me?'

'I've loved you for ages,' Maeve said. 'I wouldn't let myself believe it. Grace said she thought it was because I felt too unworthy to be loved, that what I did to Brendan was weighing on my conscience. She told me to tell you everything.'

'Wise Grace,' Richard put in.

'But doesn't it matter to you what I did?' Maeve asked anxiously.

'Not a jot,' Richard assured her. 'To my mind, the man deserved that and more.'

'Do you truly mean that?'

'I do indeed,' Richard said. 'And after living with such a man you deserve a life of happiness.' He squeezed her tight and said, 'I love you so much, darling. I want to protect you from harm. Nothing will ever hurt you again, I promise.'

Maeve nestled against him and Richard said, 'Maeve, did you ever confess what you did to a priest?'

'Aye, but to one at St Chad's,' Maeve admitted. 'I never asked for absolution.'

'And did you tell him what Brendan did to bring the tragedy about?'

Maeve puckered her brow in thought. 'I can't remember,' she said. 'What difference would it make?'

'Tomorrow we pay a visit to Father Trelawney,' Richard said. Absolution and the confines of the Church mattered little to Richard but he knew Maeve wouldn't be able to bear the thought of hell's flames burning her up for all eternity.

'Oh God, no, not Father Trelawney!' Maeve cried.

'Maeve, we'll have to have him read the banns,' Richard said. 'You are going to marry me, aren't you?'

'Ah, Richard, yes, yes, yes.'

'Then we must see the priest,' Richard said. 'Afterwards we will ask him for a special confession and this time, my dear, I will be beside you. No one can hurt you any more, I promise you that. Will you trust me?'

Maeve did trust Richard, it was the priest she didn't trust, but she said nothing, and submitted and returned his kisses of tenderness and understanding. Then they made their way home hand in hand.

It was two evenings later that Father Trelawney listened to the fantastic tale Maeve told him.

He knew some of it, of course, but if he'd been perfectly honest he would have to accept that for years he'd listened and believed only Brendan Hogan's version of events. And if he was honest, if Maeve had gone on her own he might not have believed her this time either, and that was scandalous. But now she had Richard Prendagast with her, and the man was no fool, and he obviously believed Maeve totally.

So the priest listened as Maeve told him of her life. Father Trelawney remembered the time she'd thrown the facts at him years before in hospital and how he'd taken Brendan to task about it afterwards. But had he ever checked with Maeve that things had changed? No, he hadn't, and he faced the fact now that he hadn't wanted to know. Brendan had told the priest he'd been sorry for what he'd done that one time, and said he'd tell

Maeve the same if the hospital would only let him in to see her.

Over the years he'd often said the priest didn't know the half of what he had to put up with and complained of the nag Maeve had become. Father Trelawney had chosen to believe it. It was easier for him that way, especially as Maeve had often been difficult with him too. But as he listened to the simple tale of the life she'd led under Brendan Hogan's tyranny, he knew with sudden clarity that she was telling the whole and terrible truth and that he had let her down.

For the first time he realised he'd done her a severe disservice encouraging her – forcing her – to return to Brendan before the war. He'd had no qualms at the time: marriage was a sacrament, ordained by God, where two people were joined in sickness and in health, for better or worse until death parted them. That, as far as he was concerned, was that – until now, that is. Now the doubts over the wisdom of his actions that he'd never previously allowed to surface crowded his mind and made him feel utterly ashamed of his weakness in believing Brendan because it had been easier.

But when Maeve came to the last night of Brendan's life, he was shocked to the core. Maeve wouldn't meet his eyes and her voice was a mere whisper and yet he doubted not a word.

And Maeve held Richard's hand so tight, she felt the bones crunch together and he put his other hand over hers and she looked at him gratefully. It gave her the courage to go on. The priest learned how Maeve had felt forced to do this terrible thing to save not only herself, but also Grace and Kevin. Dear, dear, it was dreadful – not only what Maeve had done, but why she'd done it. If what she said was true, she'd truly suffered and in so many ways for years and years. But still he saw it was this last act, the murder of Brendan, that was tearing Maeve apart. The poor woman, she must have been desperate and he was partly to blame.

He wondered if it could be considered that Maeve had acted in self-defence – not in the legal sense; oh no, he knew that – but in the eyes of God, perhaps? He didn't know. Once he would have said murder was murder, but what about extenuating circumstances?

'Maeve, are you sorry for killing your husband?' he asked her gently.

'No, Father. I had to do it and we've all been happier since,' Maeve said. 'But I'm sorry I felt drawn to do such a thing.'

Father Trelawney deliberated with himself, his head bowed. The silence stretched between them until it became uncomfortable and yet neither Richard nor Maeve felt they could break it.

Eventually, Father Trelawney said, 'Many must take responsibility for the position you were in, Maeve, me most of all. because I was told many times and ignored your plight. I am bitterly ashamed for the part I played in it and I will have to answer to God, no doubt, for I didn't come to your aid when I should have done. I'm very, very sorry. I see now how much I added to your misery and I hope you will forgive me. As far as your action went, although it was wrong and I cannot as a priest condone it, I absolve you, for it was done to protect not only yourself, but also your children and therefore could be seen as an act of self-defence.'

Richard felt Maeve's breath leave her body in a big sigh and knew he'd been right to insist she tell the priest. It would never have rested easy on her conscience if she hadn't.

'Make a good act of contrition,' the priest advised, 'as I will for my part in your sufferings.'

'A penance, Father?'

'None,' the priest said. 'You've paid the price already, I think.'

And Richard could only agree with him.

'How are you feeling?' Elsie asked.

'Terrified,' Maeve admitted, and Elsie smiled.

'You'll do fine.'

She'd come to Moss's that morning to help get the bridesmaids ready. There were Maeve's three daughters as well as Angela, who'd spent the night in Maeve's flat, and the two young ones had been so excited they'd been fizzing with it. They looked angelic, dressed in the lilac dresses in shiny satin that fell to the floor in layers, but Maeve knew what mischief Mary Ann and Angela could cook up together and she'd been glad to accept Elsie's offer of help.

She'd been a tower of strength and Maeve was gratified to see how well she'd got on with her mother Annie, who'd come across with Kevin to see her married. She was lodging just next door at the Mosses' with Maeve's youngest brother, Colin. Maeve had been surprised but delighted that most of the family had come over for the wedding, but Annie had said firmly that she was not letting Maeve marry a man she herself had not seen, not again. She'd been down that road once and that was enough. Kevin, though he'd wanted to come, had been hesitant to leave his granddad because it was mid-February and a busy time at the farm, but Thomas had insisted.

'You'll go and support your mother, boy,' he'd said. 'Would you have her walk down the aisle on the arm of a neighbour? You know she'd not ask her Uncle Michael; she had little time for him. Anyway, your grandmother can't go on her own. Don't worry about me. Tom will be giving me a hand.' Thomas had given a wheezy laugh then, and went on, 'The two of you would have me wrapped up in cotton wool.'

So Kevin had travelled to England with his grandmother and now shared a bedroom once more with his little brother, Jamie, much to the child's delight.

Maeve had been dumbfounded, proud and pleased as punch to have most of the family round her for her special day, and even her Uncle Michael had come up trumps for once and offered accommodation not only to Kate, but to Liam, his wife, Moira, and their two young children. It was lovely to think of them all there waiting for her in the church. She had much to thank God for, Maeve thought, for Jamie was now fully recovered and would be standing by the side of his grandmother in a navy-blue suit very like his brother's with proper grown-up long trousers. It was lovely to have him back home. Almost immediately, though, Maeve noticed how well behaved Jamie was for Richard. He only had to say a thing for Jamie to rush to do it. It was still a novelty for Maeve to see that.

Really, she thought, people were so kind. The Mosses had even closed the shop for the wedding and were now on the way to the church. It was as different from the slightly hole-in-the-corner job of her other wedding as it could be. She'd known few people then to invite – only her uncle and his family. Now she knew so many and Elsie said they were near lining the streets to wish her the best, because she'd seen them when she'd been helping the girls into the car.

And now it was time for Elsie to leave. Her long-suffering husband was waiting for her in the kitchen and suddenly Maeve realised she had to tell the dumpy little woman what she thought of her. She put her arms round Elsie and pulled her close, and Elsie, pleased but embarrassed, cried out, 'Give over, you'll have your dress all crushed. And if you cry you'll have me blarting my eyes out too, and what will that do to our make-up, eh?'

'Shut up, Elsie,' Maeve said gently. 'I just want to say how much I love you.'

The lump in Elsie's throat threatened to choke her and she muttered thickly, 'And I love you, girl, and more than I can ever tell you.' They drew apart as they heard Kevin's footsteps approaching the bedroom, and Elsie, dabbing at her damp eyes, said, 'I'll be away then, bab.'

Then Kevin was at the door, so smart and tall that Maeve's eyes shone with pride. And Kevin thought he'd never seen his mother look so lovely, in the dress of cream satin – not a traditional dress, but beautiful all the same with folds of material that fell halfway down her calves, clad in nylon stockings, and with shoes, hat, bag and gloves in contrasting navy. Richard's mother had done them proud, he thought, because she'd insisted on making all the dresses herself as her present. Richard told Jamie the sewing machine went on so fast and for so long there were nearly sparks coming off it and Kevin could almost believe it, looking at what the woman had achieved for his sisters and his mother.

Maeve looked wonderful and radiant, and he fervently hoped she'd be happy with Richard. She deserved happiness.

'Are you ready, Mammy?' he asked. 'The man will think you're not coming and the car's waiting outside.'

Maeve smiled. Richard wouldn't be worried about her not turning up. She gave a last look at her bedroom, for from that night it would be just hers no longer. They'd agreed to stay in the Mosses' flat as it was easier for both of them.

'I'm ready, son,' she said, and she held her son's arm and they walked out together.

If you liked this book,
why not dip into another one
of Anne Bennett's fantastic stories?

'The beauty of Anne's books is that they are about normal people
and are sewn through with human emotions which affect us all'
Birmingham Post